Blood Return

S. D. Sampley

Secrets never stay hidden.

Blood Return

S. D. Sampley

Copyright © 2023 S. D. Sampley

All rights reserved. No part of this publication may be reproduced, distributed, or transmitted in any form or by any means, including photocopying, recording, or other electronic or mechanical methods, without the prior written permission of the publisher, except in the case of brief quotations embodied in critical reviews and certain other noncommercial uses permitted by copyright law. For permission requests, email the publisher, addressed "Attention: Permission Coordinator" at the email address below.

ISBN: 979-8-9864826-3-7 (Paperback)
ISBN: 979-8-9864826-4-4 (Hardback)
ISBN: 979-8-9864826-5-1 (eBook)

Any references to historical events, real people, or real places are used fictitiously. Names, characters, and places are products of the author's imagination.

Cover art by Milcah Lagumbay
Editing by Maryssa Gordon

dwsebb@gmail.com

…
Blood Return

S. D. Sampley

Content Warning

Blood Return is the second book of a New Adult Fiction series: Moonlight Howls. While this book is mainly a fantasy, action-adventure, there are depictions of things that can—and do—happen in real life. I didn't include a content warning in the first book but upon further reflection, I realize this series needs it for the content it displays. This warning will include the previous novel as well.

This book features scenes and topics that may be troubling for some readers.

Please be mindful of these and other possible triggers and seek assistance if needed.

Blood Return

S. D. Sampley

Table of Contents

Content Warning 5
Table of Contents 7
Prologue 10
Chapter One 13
Chapter Two 22
Chapter Three 36
Chapter Four 50
Chapter Five 65
Chapter Six 75
Chapter Seven 87
Chapter Eight 97
Chapter Nine 105
Chapter Ten 112
Chapter Eleven 123
Chapter Twelve 134
Chapter Thirteen 143
Chapter Fourteen 152
Chapter Fifteen 164
Chapter Sixteen 169
Chapter Seventeen 185
Chapter Eighteen 199
Chapter Nineteen 211

Chapter Twenty 221
Chapter Twenty-One 233
Chapter Twenty-Two 244
Chapter Twenty-Three 254
Chapter Twenty-Four 265
Chapter Twenty-Five 282
Chapter Twenty-Six 291
Chapter Twenty-Seven 304
Chapter Twenty-Eight 317
Epilogue 332

S. D. Sampley

Prologue

Darkness filled my dreams, swallowing every sensation. There is nothing. I am nothing.

Floating in a viscous mixture, my entire self faded from memory. I had no idea who I was or what I was. An eternity passes, and I become nothing more than the gel I was solidified in.

Images flash in my mind's eye. A man with gray eyes smiling down at me, holding a crystal necklace. He offers it to me and places it around my neck. Two people joined him. They smile at me. Then blinding lights replace them. Screeching fills my head. I see them dead on the ground, blood spewing from open wounds. The gray-eyed man stands over them without a scratch on him. He's saying something, but I can't make it out.

After what feels like a lifetime floating in the goo, I begin to feel something: Cold. I was so cold. Over the numbness that had settled on my skin, I was aware of a prickling sensation…and something far worse.

My lungs were on fire. They burned and ached with a fierceness I had never known. I tried to draw in a breath but couldn't. My body was frozen solid. My quickening heart sounded in my ears, thudding to an incomplete rhythm.

The fire swelled in my chest to an unbearable point. I needed to breathe. I had to draw air. But my body refused to listen. I struggled and pulled, trying to tear my body free of whatever held it. Nothing moved. I couldn't even twitch a finger.

Right as I was sure the fire would consume every fiber of my being, my mouth unlocked itself. I opened wide, sucking in as fast as I could, needing the sweet relief, but was met with more fire.

I was drowning. Water flooded my mouth, down my throat, and into my lungs. But it didn't quench the fire that raged within me. It bit and chewed away at my flesh. If it was possible for the darkness to deepen, it did.

The pain settled in my gut, melting my insides. It would never go away. I would be in pain for the rest of eternity. What had I done to deserve this? If I could recall anything, I would. If I could make up for whatever I did, I would.

Something touched my shoulder. It was only a light pressure, but I felt it through the agony. The pressure moved under my arms, and then I was being towed through the liquid.

Cold wind stung my cheeks, sending a stiff shiver down my spine. A pushing sensation started in my chest, pumping at an even tempo. My body responded to this pressure by vomiting up whatever I'd inhaled.

I choked, sputtered, and coughed. My breath came in ragged gasps, my body trying desperately to replace the oxygen it'd lost. Every breath of fresh air felt like knives carving my throat, but I savored the relief in my lungs.

The world was bright, far too bright. Squinting, I tried to make out my surroundings. I was in the woods. Tall pine trees littered my field of view, and I was lying in a pile of pine straw. It poked my arms and shifted under my shivering body.

My eyes dragged the ground, coming to rest on a pair of brown shoes. At least, I think they were brown. I pulled my hand to my brow, trying to shield my vision. My hand was no help. It shook so violently there was no way it could shield the light. I was able to catch a glimpse of eyes, although I'm positive I must've been dreaming because they were purple.

I blinked slowly, exhaustion settling over me. As hard as I tried to stave off blacking out, it took me. My eyes closed and wouldn't reopen. I was left only with the lingering image of those indigo eyes.

In my dream, I was back with the gray-eyed man. We were in a house, in a cave. He was still trying to tell me something to no avail. Two wolves stood beside us, staring at me with intensity. Then a different man stood before me, one with a raging fire for eyes. His presence calmed me in a way I didn't know needed calming.

A warm feeling settled over my body, and the sounds of a crackling fire soothed my nerves. I began to notice my throat didn't hurt anymore.

Chapter One

My eyes opened, resting on a small fire in a hearth across from me. I was now in a bed with a hanging silk canopy. The blankets wrapped around me were soft as down and as warm as the fire.

The entire room was decorated in shades of purple, the covers matching. A painting of a broad castle was mounted above the fireplace, the only other color in this space.

I rolled over slowly, my body stiff from immobilization. A small window sat adjacent to the bed, eggplant-colored curtains shifting in the night breeze. Underneath it sat a tiny wooden table, a vase of flowers resting on its surface.

When I made to sit upright, I winced. My neck definitely had a crick in it. My hand cupped the side of it, rubbing small circles where it was tender. Looking down, I saw I'd been dressed in a nightgown the same shade as the canopy. It clung to my body in places I didn't realize there were things to cling to.

My nipples peaked against the sudden draft, and I covered them with my arm. Pushing the covers back, I twisted to set my feet on the floor. They touched a fuzzy surface, and I jerked them back up in fright. Glancing over the edge of the mattress, I saw it was just a wool rug. Also purple.

Placing my feet back down, I stood. My back popped in several places as I stretched, releasing some tension. A large sigh escaped my lips. I could breathe again.

My nightgown draped across my legs, resting just above my knees. It was a soft fabric, almost as soft as the bed itself, but it still clung to parts of me I didn't like.

I walked around the room, checking in the cabinets in the corner. They were empty. A frown settled on my lips. As nice as this room was, I don't know where I am, and I don't like it. I also don't like feeling so naked in this gown.

Wrapping my arms across my chest, I turned back to face the bed. Where I finally noticed a pair of clothes folded neatly at the foot. I reached out to feel them, relief flooding me when I realized they weren't the same material as what I wore.

I pulled the white long sleeve over my head, glad it was baggy enough to hide my breasts. The jeans that followed were snug, but the sweater was long enough to cover my rear.

Reaching up to touch my hair, I felt the braid it'd been put into. I was about to untangle it when a knock came.

I jumped, staggering backward and collapsing on the bed. A woman with long blonde hair, styled in loose waves, and deep blue, hooded eyes peaked her head around the door—her square jaw set in an annoyed fashion.

She eyed me carefully before planting a fake smile upon her red-stained lips. "Oh, good. You're up. He will be pleased to hear that. I was hoping to get to you before you put on the clothes, but no problem. Come, let's get you a bath." Her hand reached for me, the manicured fingers glinting in the firelight.

I recoiled, rolling further onto the bed. "Don't touch me."

She paused, a light brow raising. "Is something wrong?"

I sucked in a deep breath, steadying my heart. "I don't know who you are, and I don't know where I am. I'm not going anywhere with you."

Her head tilted back in realization, and she stepped further into the room, closing the door. She wore a long evening gown the same shade of red as her lips. Her feet were bare.

"You've been through a lot, so I'll let the attitude slide." She bared her teeth in a smile. "I'm Avalon. Right now you're in my master's home in the countryside. He will tell you more." Her hand reached for me again. "But first, let's get you a bath."

I jerked away again, climbing off the bed and backing to the fireplace.

Her hand dropped, and she growled, "Please don't make this more difficult than it has to be."

"Get away from me."

The door opened behind her, a voice coming from the entryway. "What's going on in here?" It was a man's voice. I couldn't see him, though, as the door itself blocked my view of him.

Avalon ground her teeth together and cooed, "Oh, nothing. I'm just trying to convince our guest to take a well-needed bath."

A foot stepped around the door, followed by the man. He had wavy black hair parted in the middle and storm gray eyes—recognition flashing in them as they met mine. But I didn't know him. Not really. I only knew him from my dreams. The gray-eyed man who stood over the dead bodies.

"Leave her alone, Avalon. It's clear she doesn't want you to touch her," he said with contempt. He wore a green buttoned shirt paired with black slacks, of which his hands were shoved into the pockets.

Avalon straightened, flipping her hair over her shoulder. "She's just confused."

The man's gaze flitted to my position against the hearth, taking in my defensive posture. "Do you want her touching you?"

I fumbled for words, unsure of what to even say. When no words surfaced, I settled for a slight shake of my head.

He nodded in satisfaction and snapped his fingers. "You can leave now."

Avalon gave one final sneer in my direction before spinning on her heels to leave. She brushed her hand along the man's chest as she passed by him, letting her fingers linger on his arm. He paid her no attention, his focus remaining on me. I felt uncomfortable under his gaze.

A lump formed in my throat, making it hard to swallow. Why was he staring at me like that?

He cleared his throat and motioned toward the door. "You don't have to take a bath if you don't want to, but I do think you might feel better taking a look around this place." When I didn't move, he took a few steps toward me. I couldn't back up any further. I wanted my clothes to catch fire.

"I won't touch you," he assured me. "But I will offer you support." He jutted his elbow out in front of me.

I looked down at it and back up. My voice shook as I asked, "What's your name?"

"Jae," he responded plainly, though a sadness crept into his eyes—the gray deepening. Or was I imagining that? His elbow still rested in the air in front of me.

"Are you her master?"

The laugh that escaped his lips was neither humorous nor kind.

"Not in the slightest. I am her superior, though."

Cautiously, I reached out my senses to feel his intentions. Nothing struck me as violently as Avalon's had, so I clasped his outstretched appendage. His smile eased some of the worry in my gut, a small scar on his bottom lip catching my attention.

"Don't mind Avalon. She's always had a stick up her ass." He chuckled as he led me from the room.

The hallway was a cream color with dark wood trim, a stark contrast to the purple of my room. More paintings lined the walls, this time of differing animals. Deer, mice, horses, and wolves all stared at me. There were no mirrors or windows along this corridor, just more doors. All of which were closed.

Men clad in leather armor stood patiently at the end of the hall. Jae greeted them with a curt nod as we turned right down another passageway.

"Where are we?" I asked as I glanced through an open door, seeing a man with icy blond hair sitting on a bunk bed.

Jae was silent for a moment before he said, "We're in my father's home, tucked away in the Appalachian mountains."

I didn't know where those were, so I just nodded like I understood. "Where is the man who saved me?"

Jae stiffened, coming to a halt before two black wooden doors. "Who?"

I swallowed. "The man with the…"

He stared at me for a moment, too long to be comfortable.

"Nevermind." I really must have dreamed it, and now I sound like a lunatic. Maybe I am. I don't remember much of anything, and the last thing I do remember was a figment of my imagination.

His lips pressed into a thin line as he opened the double doors, leading me through. This room was a dining room of sorts, the only furniture being a long black table with four chairs on either side. A painting larger than me was fixed behind the head of the table, depicting a large white wolf with stunning green eyes. They followed my every move, causing me to remove my gaze from them. Even though my skin prickled as I felt the creature still watching me.

We crossed the room, and Jae opened another door, this time to a study. Tall bookshelves lined every wall, the books covered in dust. At the back of the room sat a small desk where a man sat, hunched over something.

He turned to look at us as we approached, slipping his glasses down his nose. "Ah, Jae. I see you've awoken our guest." He slammed a book shut, lurching from his position.

His figure loomed over us, as he was considerably taller than Jae and me—the perfect height to reach these bookshelves. His hair, as golden as the sun, was parted in the middle like Jae's. Except this man's hair was a lot shorter, which drew attention to his anvil-shaped jaw. His eyes were an emerald green and as deep as a pool.

He stretched his arms upward, the muscles in his body flexing under his tight brown shirt. It was distracting, to say the least.

The glasses that perched on his face drifted down, causing him to jerk to catch them. He pulled them off and tucked them into the pocket of his vest, which was black with an intricate green pattern.

"How are you feeling this evening?" His question caught me off guard. My eyes went wide, and I looked to Jae for help. He didn't look at me, though, only the ground, and dropped my arm.

"Um. Okay, I guess," I mumbled, voice still hoarse from lack of use.

The man looked at me with a curious gaze. The corner of his mouth tilted up as he cocked his head. "What do you remember?"

Again, my brain jerked and pulled to come up with an answer. Something other than the purple-eyed man. But I had nothing.

He nodded at my silence and asked, "Do you remember how you got here at least?"

When I still didn't respond, he laughed so hard he had to rest his hands on his knees. "My God." At my wide-eyed expression, he quickly rushed out, "All will be explained in due time. Would you like something to drink?"

I put a hand to my throat, noticing how dry it was.

The man took this as my answer and motioned to Jae with a flip of his hand. "Go get her something. I'm sure she's quite parched after her adventure."

Jae bowed his head slightly before retreating out of the room, and I was left alone with this stranger.

My leg started to bounce with nerves. I wasn't sure how to feel about all of this, all of these new people. This new place. Coming off the vivid dream and subsequent nightmare of drowning, everything felt surreal.

The man looked me up and down with a puzzling stare. "You really don't remember anything?"

I shook my head, a feeling of self-consciousness sweeping over me.

His expression softened, and he stepped away to pull a chair out. "Have a seat."

I got the impression he was used to people following his orders without a second thought, so I did. He rested on the edge of his desk, clutching a wine glass in his hand.

He sipped from it, brows knitting together. "We found you at the edge of the lake, soaking wet and unconscious. Jae is the one who brought you back."

Heat flushed my cheeks as I remembered what I'd been wearing earlier. Had I been wearing that? Or had he changed me into that? Either way was embarrassing.

The man noticed my blush and chuckled, seeming to read my mind. "Don't worry. Avalon changed you into dry clothes."

That still didn't make me feel better, but I guess it was better than Jae having seen me naked.

Speaking of, Jae reappeared at the door. A small white mug being carried in his left hand, a biscuit in his right. Both were still steaming.

I took the items with a thank you, cherishing the warm cup in my palm. The liquid was dark, but taking a small sniff reassured me it was okay. It smelled fruity, almost like—

"It's blackberry tea," the man interrupted my thoughts. "I'm sure Jae added in some honey to soothe your throat."

Jae nodded, still not looking me in the eye. The man dismissed him, telling him to go find a man named Jarred and begin rotations.

I wasted no time biting into the biscuit, chewing delicately on the buttery texture.

"How do you like my home?" The man gestured widely with the glass.

"It's uh...cozy."

The man smiled, a genuine curve of his lips. "I built it myself."

The biscuit went dry in my mouth, and I had to sip the tea to keep from choking. "All by yourself?" Regardless of how grand this place was, I was sure building something like this was a feat of its own.

"All by myself," he confirmed.

If he built this place, does that mean he's Jae's father? He looked too young, maybe only a few years older than Jae.

We sat in silence for a moment longer as he waited for me to eat more. His eyes watched my every move, my every chew. I'd feel even more self-conscious if I wasn't so hungry.

"Can you try and remember your name for me?"

I looked up at him and swallowed the food.

He glanced around the room at my silence. "Ah, there it is," he exclaimed as he strolled to the opposite corner. Something sat on the floor, covered in a white sheet. He picked it up and brought it over, removing the cloth to expose an old mirror.

It was framed in intricate black vines carved from some kind of rock. The mirror was dusty but still usable. He tilted it down to me and said, "Maybe seeing yourself will help."

I steadied myself and looked in. My eyes were the first thing I noticed. They were doe-like in feature and could be misinterpreted as brown in the dark but were actually golden.

So gold, in fact, it could rival his hair. My own hair, which had been braided out of my face, was a deep red color.

My fingers brushed lightly across the thick braid, trailing up to my plump cupid's bow lips.

I did remember my name. It was the only thing I remembered. The only thing I knew to be true.

"Rosetta."

He raised a golden brow. "Just Rosetta? No last name?"

I lowered my gaze, shaking my head.

The man sighed and removed the mirror from my sight. "Well, Rose, thank you for trying. I really appreciate it." He turned the mirror so it faced the wall, draping the cloth back over it. "We can work on more later; it does take a toll on someone to try and remember what can't be remembered. Finish eating, and I'll take you on a stroll outside."

I nodded and took another bite. He excused himself, but I grabbed his arm. A shockwave of anger jolted through my body at his touch. My hand released, and I bit the inside of my cheek in shock.

His face distorted into something violent but quickly faded away to the calm demeanor from before. Maybe I imagined that as well.

"I was just going to ask your name," I muttered through the bread.

Another smile caressed his lips as he bent down to clasp my hand. I braced myself for the impact of his touch, but I only felt kindness and peace this time.

"Of course. And you have every right to ask that." His thumb stroked the back of my wrist, soothing circles. "My name is Grantwell Servanus. But you can call me Grant."

Chapter Two

When I finished eating, Grant escorted me down another hallway. It was the same cream color as the others and still lined with various paintings. These, however, were of landscapes rather than animals.

One a large wheat field, another a canyon, and one of an abandoned town. They all had so much fine detail they could've been pictures rather than brush strokes.

Grant saw me admiring them, and he stopped us in front of one that overlooked a vast open space. In the distance, triangle-shaped objects could be seen, smoke drifting from a fire.

"This one is my favorite," he said softly. "It's of a small Indian village from back when they still roamed these lands. Before the settlers took over."

The look in his eyes made something turn in my stomach. "Why is it your favorite?" I asked.

He looked down at me, green eyes flashing. "I once knew someone who was married to one. They lived in a small village just like that." He turned back to the painting, sighing loudly.

"What happened to them?"

He started to walk us away from it, waving a hand as if the question didn't matter. "It burned down, and everyone died."

I choked on something. "That's awful."

He didn't respond. I wasn't sure if it was out of grief or something else.

"Did you paint all of these?"

He nodded, opening another door to yet another hallway. "Some of them, yes. Others I bought over the years at various art galleries or yard sales. I was never really that skilled with a paintbrush."

All the paintings I'd seen were of the same caliber skill-wise. If he wasn't that good, you couldn't tell.

We continued our journey through the house, Grant showing me a library, a movie projection room, and an indoor pool. With each new room, this place seemed more and more like a castle than a house.

Passing a lot of closed doors, I noted more rooms were shut off than were open. When I asked Grant about this, he said that those were rooms for the other guests of the house. And some were dormitory-style rooms for the guards.

Why they would even need guards, I couldn't begin to fathom. I guess if this was indeed a castle, it would make sense to have guards, but I hadn't seen that many Not enough to justify this many rooms.

Down one more hall, and we halted in front of a set of lightly colored double doors. Gold plating framed the wood, perfectly matching the golden handles.

He reached out, twisted the knob and pulled the door to us. The first rays of sunlight began to stream in as the doors perfectly faced the sunrise.

A gasp left me as I took in my surroundings. We sat atop a low hill in between two mountains, the sun peeking through the valley in front of us. Tall trees lined the path, and wildflowers bloomed in every open spot. A low swaying oak stood to the right of the yard, a wooden swing hanging from one of its branches. A warm breeze kissed my cheeks, bringing with it the smell of a summer's rain.

Blood Return

Any tension still lingering in my body evaporated. I took a cautious step forward, looking back to Grant for courage.

The sun lit his eyes into a multitude of different greens, all shifting, and blending. A bemused smile planted on his lips as he gave me a nod of approval.

Stepping further into the yard, I was too preoccupied to notice a man stabbing a spear in my direction. I yelped, jumping back and slamming into Grant. His body was so rock hard I felt like I'd smacked my head on a brick wall.

I thought I heard a deep growl come from Grant, but that was impossible. It was too inhuman of a sound to come from him. But his face morphed, turning into something terrifying as he stepped around me.

He knocked the spear away so hard that the tip broke completely off, smashing into the corner of the house.

"What do you think you're doing?" His voice became deep and guttural, taking on an animalistic tone.

The man holding the other end of the spear—dressed in dark leathers with a helmet—shook uncontrollably. He stuttered out some kind of response unintelligible to me, but it seemed to satisfy Grant.

He huffed and shoved the man backward, barking out, "Go make a round of the grounds and get out of my sight."

The man looked ready to pass out as he nodded and sprinted away to the side of the house. Another guard—dressed in a similar fashion but with a sword—soon replaced him.

Grant took a deep calming breath, smoothing out his shirt. His smile returned, and he turned to me with a wide gesture. "Sorry about that. He takes his job a little too seriously. It won't happen again."

My brows pulled together as I tried to process what had just happened. I didn't get long, though, before Grant was taking me by the hand and leading me further into the yard.

Getting a better look at the outside of the place, it definitely seemed way too small to have as many rooms as it did. It was a little off-putting and made me question everything I'd seen. To me, it looked like a small cottage you'd see an elderly retired couple buy.

Grant noticed my cautious eyeing of the quaint house and chuckled. "I bet you're wondering how we could have so many rooms, and yet the outside looks so small."

My eyes flew wide as I stared at him in wonder. "How'd you know that?"

He patted my hand reassuringly. "It's what everyone thinks when they first come here."

"Oh." I turned my gaze to the vast landscape around us, drinking in the summer breeze. The sun had risen slightly higher into the sky, illuminating a large lake about a mile down the embankment just hidden in the shadow of the mountain.

Grant cleared his throat and said, "That's where we found you."

Again my brows knitted together. What was I doing way out here in the mountains? And why couldn't I remember? As hard as I tried and pushed for a memory to come forward, the only thing I could remember were those purple eyes. And as far as I could see, no one here possessed that striking eye color aside from Jae and Grant—whose eyes were no impressive shade, just vibrant.

"Rose?"

It took a second for my brain to process he'd spoken my name. "Yes?"

He wet his lower lip in thought and opened his mouth to say something before another voice interrupted.

"Sir? There's been a sighting."

His eyes flicked to where the voice came from, any light leaving them. His jaw set, and he nodded. "We'll be right in."

When his attention returned to me, the once bright emerald eyes were now cold and distant. The sun was positioned perfectly behind him, casting a radiant beam of morning glow behind his blond hair.

It was so stunning, so beautiful. If I could paint as well as he could, I'd paint this sight. I don't think I've ever seen something as breathtaking as him backlit by the rising sun.

"Come. There will be a meeting taking place, and you will get to meet more of my entourage." He gestured behind me, allowing me to take the lead back inside.

A guard waited for us in the hallway, shield strapped to his back. A crescent moon emblem with two slashes through the middle decorated its front. A spark flickered at the back of my memory. I knew that symbol. But where?

Grant gave one curt nod to the man, who then motioned for us to follow him. We went down another series of hallways before entering a small stairwell hidden behind a corner. There were no windows, the only source of light coming from torches on the wall.

The bottom opened up into a large sitting room, maps and blueprints lined the brick wall. A brown couch stood before a similarly colored coffee table, both planted on a red wool rug. On the couch was the silver-haired man I'd seen briefly before and the woman I'd first encountered: Avalon.

She lay draped across the man's lap, fingers twirling in his hair. The man looked irritated, his lips drawn tight and eyes focused on the wall. At the back of the room stood Jae, hands shoved in his pockets, chatting lazily with a short, brown-haired woman.

Everyone's attention zeroed in on us as we made our entrance. Avalon bolted upright on the couch, red hazing her cheeks. They were all dressed in casual attire except for her, who sported a black pantsuit.

Grant let go of my hand after directing me to the couch and stood in front of the room. A fire blazed to life in the cold hearth behind him. His back straightened, and he seemed to grow a foot taller. He commanded the attention of the entire room without even saying a word.

"What's the sighting?" he demanded, brushing some invisible lint from his shirt.

Avalon sat back on the couch, trying to seem relaxed. Though, the very noticeable lines on her forehead said otherwise.

She pursed her red-stained lips and said, "It's not really a sighting so much as Trinity just caught wind of her scent."

Grant's eyes narrowed at the back of the room. "And why is Avalon telling me this while you're here?"

Soft footsteps peddled toward us, coming to rest just behind me. An equally soft voice responded, "The trail led nowhere, anyway. So it doesn't matter."

Looking up, I saw the brown-haired woman. She had deep hazel eyes and a scar across the bridge of her nose. She was rather rugged looking, but I couldn't help but feel her face was familiar to me.

She glanced down at me, a crooked smile growing on her lips. "Who's this doll?"

"Don't change the subject, Trinity." Grant held up a warning finger to her.

Huffing, she crossed her arms defensively. "The trail went cold about a mile north of the pinewoods."

"How many?"

"Just the Beta and the Human."

He processed this for a moment before turning to the man opposite me on the couch. "Take Sebastian and head for the pinewoods. Make sure to scrub the entire place. I want to find them."

The man opened his mouth to protest, but his teeth clacked shut. He nodded and stood, stretching his arms in front of him. "What about her?" He jabbed his thumb toward Avalon.

Grant smirked, something twisted behind it. "She already has something to do. A punishment to atone for."

The man turned to grin at her. "See what you get when you go killing off people you shouldn't?"

My blood chilled. Did he say kill people? Glancing out of the corner of my eye, I noticed the hard lines of muscle beneath everyone's clothing. Something I'd neglected upon the first encounter.

Avalon hissed, "Bite me, dog."

"Enough." Grant's voice boomed throughout the room. "Leave. Both of you. Trinity—" he pointed to the woman behind me, "—go with them. Make sure they do the job right."

"Yes, sir." Her footsteps were almost imperceptible as she walked out from behind me. I could now see the silver knife she had attached to her leg.

"Jae. Go help Avalon."

I could almost hear the hesitation coming from behind me. But with one stern look from Grant, his footsteps approached. He didn't say a word nor glance in my direction even once as he stalked up the stairs. Avalon followed him with a giddy prance to her step.

Then Grant and I were alone, save for the guard at the entryway. He seemed to glare at something behind me for a moment before shaking his head. "I'm sorry, I forgot to introduce you to everyone."

"It's okay. I already knew two of them."

He strolled over to take a seat next to me. "The other guy, his name is Jarred. He's one of my generals. Best one I've met so far. The woman, I'm sure you heard, is Trinity. Fun fact, she's actually a twin. Her sister used to work for me."

"What happened?"

His eyes went distant, and his jaw clenched tight. "She was murdered. Our home base was infiltrated, and they killed her as she tried to defend it."

My heart skipped a beat, sinking into my gut. "That's awful. I'm so sorry."

He sucked in a deep breath, returning his focus to the present. A thin worry line still bore on his brow. "It happens when you're in a war like this. You lose a lot of good people. But we got revenge."

"Is that what Jarred mentioned to Avalon?" I paled, waiting on the response.

Grant loosed a breath, then nodded.

"What was her name? If I may ask."

"Akāla."

"What even is this room?" There were so many maps, too many to be coincidental, and some that looked genuinely fake. I could've sworn I saw one labeled, 'Fairy Kingdom – Mercury.' That definitely couldn't be real.

He looked where I was and coughed up a laugh. "This is just the room I have for meetings with my entourage. My niece drew some of those maps when she was young for her imaginary friends."

"You have a niece?" That's nice of him to keep his niece's drawings.

"And a nephew. Though, the nephew is estranged."

"She must feel very special since you hung up all her drawings."

He chuckled bitterly. "She thinks too highly of herself sometimes. But that comes with the territory. She is a queen."

"A queen?"

Grant suddenly stood up, reaching a hand down for me. "Come, I'm sure they've already prepared breakfast. That single biscuit won't hold you all day."

Smiling, I took note of his sudden change in topic and avoidance of answering and grabbed his hand as he escorted me back upstairs.

Learning the layout of this house would be my most daunting task. I wasn't sure how he could remember every shortcut and turn. But within a minute of us arriving up top, we landed in the dining room I crossed earlier.

The wolf painting stared me down, drawing an uncomfortable squirm from me. The black wooden table was bare aside from a bouquet of white daisies, not so much breakfast.

Grant took up a seat at the head of the table, placing me to his left. Once I was seated, he snapped his fingers, and a trail of wait staff shuffled into the room, all carrying a silver dish-covered platter. The food may have been disguised, but the smell that permeated the air was mouthwatering.

One by one, they all stepped forward, placed their trays down, and removed the lid. Underneath were stacks of pancakes, waffles, bacon, biscuits, toast, eggs every which way, and fruit. I had to consciously keep from letting my mouth hang open.

Another snap of his fingers and empty glasses appeared before us. "What's your poison? Lemon water? Orange Juice? A mimosa, perhaps?" He smiled with that last question, of which I had no idea what that was.

I gulped, glancing between Grant and my empty glass. "Would it be possible for me to get the tea I had earlier?"

A brow raised in amusement on his face. "I'm sure we could manage that." He nodded to a male servant carrying a pitcher of water, and the guy disappeared into another room. Moments later, he returned with a steaming black mug. He glided across the space to me and gingerly sat the cup to my right.

"Thank you," I said sheepishly, my cheeks glowing with warmth. I didn't want them to go to special effort to get that for me; I would've taken the orange juice.

Grant wasted no time and greedily stacked his plate with a mound of food. I followed suit and dove into the fruit and waffles.

We didn't speak as we ate, and the silence was oddly comforting. It sat in between us like a blanket, warm and unmoving. I had the feeling there would be many more silences in his presence, as he didn't seem the babbling type. He gave off the impression that he only spoke when necessary. It didn't bother me, as I was still trying to figure out who I was and what had happened to me.

Once we finished eating, the wait staff gathered our plates and the remaining food. I kept them from taking my mug, as I wanted to keep sipping on it.

Grant noticed my refusal to hand over the cup and leaned back in his chair, grinning. "You know I can arrange for a pot to be left in your room."

"Oh, no, that's okay. I don't want any special treatment. I just wanted to finish these last few sips," I said as I chugged the last remaining bit.

He studied me for a moment, head cocked to the side. Even after I handed the mug off, he watched me. The silence became constricting, deafening. I felt like a lab rat under his gaze.

"What now?" I asked after the quiet had grown too unbearable.

Grant shrugged, finally removing his eyes from me. "Whatever you want. I don't have anything to do until this afternoon."

I bit my lower lip in thought, a question burning on the tip of my tongue. Should I ask him? Would he even answer? Was it any of my business anyway? No, it wasn't. But if I was going to continue staying here, I needed to know for my own sanity. "What did Jarred mean when he told Avalon she shouldn't have killed Akāla's killer off?"

A muscle feathered in his jaw, and I could tell he did not want to talk about this. I really wanted to know why Avalon shouldn't have killed that person, considering he mentioned it being revenge, but I didn't want to make him uncomfortable.

Before he could decide how to answer, I changed subjects. "Could I see more of the outside?"

Seeming to not mind the change, he kicked back from his chair. "Of course." His face softened as he reached a hand for me. Our fingers intertwined, heat blooming my face. His palms were smooth, and his long fingers completely encased mine.

Once we were outside, I gulped down the breeze. The sun was slightly higher in the sky, still perched between the two mountains. It warmed my cheeks and filled me with joy. I knew deep down I much preferred the company of the sun to that of the moon, but I had no memories to back it up.

Grant watched me as I strolled to the swing under the oak and plopped down on the wooden seat. Kicking the dirt underneath, I leaned my head back and closed my eyes. The smell of flowers danced around me, filling me whole. Listening to the birds chirp in their nests, I could've fallen asleep.

I was so preoccupied with nature that I didn't even notice Grant had walked up behind me and was now gently pushing the back of the swing.

My eyes flew open as I grappled for balance, not prepared for the motion. He instantly caught the back of the chair and halted its movement, clearly suppressing a smile.

"That's not fair. I wasn't ready!"

"You sat on a swing. How could you not be ready?"

I crossed my arms in protest, and he relented, letting go of the swing. "Come. There's more to see."

I hopped down, following where he walked to the side of the house. Around the corner, I was greeted with the sight of a massive greenhouse. Workers buzzed around, carrying flowers and vegetables in their arms.

"We grow our own food here," Grant said with delight. "Most of what you ate this morning was picked right from this greenhouse."

My face must've relayed my awe as Grant offered to take me inside. I tried to calm my enthusiasm but felt like a bobblehead as I nodded.

He shook his head with a smirk and took my arm, leading me through the door. Everyone we passed was hard at work tending to the plants, but they all took a moment to nod to us as we passed.

Beautiful flowers hung suspended from the ceiling in giant clay pots, with the edibles on the ground in a long conveyor belt-style row. To the left were a few rows of shrubs and vines, with baskets scattered underneath.

"Blackberries," Grant noted as he studied the direction of my gaze. "What we make your tea with."

"There's so many," I observed, noting there were more of them than any other edible plant.

"It's sort of our specialty," he explained as he walked me further into the greenhouse. Toward the back, he stopped in front of a tub of flowers. The petals were dark purple in the center, with white-tipped ends. They were long and curled backward, displaying their freckled inner core. It was stunning.

He spoke another language to the gardener tending to them, pointing mildly to the bucket. The gardener nodded with eagerness and rummaged around the flowers for a few seconds before brandishing one. It had larger petals and seemed more vibrant in color.

Grant said something else and took the flower, turning around to hand it to me. I blinked in shock and hesitated to take it, not wanting to ruin its perfect composure. But eventually, I reached out and plucked it from his hand. He watched me with warmth as I bent my head down to smell it.

"It's beautiful," was all I could muster to say. And it was, in every sense of the word.

"Netty's Pride."

"What?"

The corner of his mouth quirked. "The lily. It's called Netty's Pride. It's an Asiatic hybrid."

"Oh." I didn't know what any of those words meant, so I nodded like I understood.

He guided me out the backdoor of the greenhouse and further around the corner, where we reached the backyard. I almost dropped the flower at the sight before me.

Despite the house sitting atop this hill, the backyard was completely flat and seemed to span straight into the distant trees. A pond with small, brightly colored fish sat in the middle with a willow tree dangling over it. Rocking chairs adorned a small porch, with a picnic table placed neatly outside of it.

Apple and Peach trees lay scattered across the small field, with deer nibbling the fruit.

They didn't shy away at our approach, and I was able to stand right next to a small buck. He tilted his head quizzically at me and began nosing my pockets.

I looked to Grant for reassurance. However, he only stared at me with newfound wonder.

"What's wrong?" My cheeks flushed again.

"No one has ever been able to approach the deer out here."

My throat tightened as I looked back to the deer nuzzling my arm. Grant had to be exaggerating, as this animal almost seemed like a pet.

Slowly, I raised a hand to the top of the deer's head. Holding my breath, I reached my fingertips out. The buck studied my outstretched hand for a second, sniffing it. Then his ears pricked forward, and he dashed for the woods, tail standing high.

I whipped my head back to Grant and saw he was speaking with Jarred. Jarred's hazel eyes lingered on me as his words dropped. Cold pricked my skin where his gaze had been. Grant peered over his shoulder to see what Jarred was staring at and became visibly upset when he noticed it was me.

He said something in a hushed tone I couldn't understand. Jarred nodded, turning his gaze to the ground. He remained still as Grant turned back to me and shoved his hands in his pockets.

"I'm afraid I must cut our adventure short. Something has come up that needs my attention. Jarred will escort you back to your room." He reached a hand out and brushed away a lock of hair that had fallen across my cheek. "I promise to make it up to you later," he said with a quick pinch to my chin.

I clutched the flower closer to my chest and nodded, watching the back of his broad shoulders as he stalked away. Jarred appeared to my right, catching me off guard. I hadn't heard him move at all.

"This way, Rose." His voice was deep and had a nasal quality to it. I noticed his chin was oddly pointed, drawing the rest of the features forward on his face. He refused to make eye contact with me, and I had a sinking feeling whatever Grant said to him had something to do with it. However, it didn't bother me too much, as his gaze sent icy chills through me.

He walked me back inside the cottage and stayed silent the rest of the way to my room. He stopped just short of the black wooden door and placed his hands behind his back. "If you need anything, there's a phone in your room that connects to the staff room." His eyes connected with mine then, and they grew in size. Cat eyes stared back at me, all predator. His breath hitched as he cleared his throat, nodding for me to go in.

I thanked him for walking me and turned the knob, entering my room. When I shut the door, a nagging voice in the back of my head told me to lock it. At first, I shook my head and ignored it. Why would I do that? They've given me no reason to believe they'd harm me. But after a few seconds, I could still see Jarred's shadow through the crack under the door, and I felt wary enough to turn the latch.

Moments after I'd locked my door, his footsteps padded down the hallway and out of earshot. Relief flooded through me for an unknown reason.

I turned to place the flower on my nightstand, where I was greeted with the sight of a small glass vase half filled with water. I shook my head with a smile and plopped the stem into it.

Sitting on the edge of the bed, I glanced across the room to where the dresser sat, and on top of it was a steaming silver pot. I stalked toward it carefully, unsure of its contents, until I got close enough to smell it.

Then I feverishly grabbed the cup that had been coincidentally left beside it and poured. A dark liquid filled the glass smoothly and piping hot. I raised it to my lips and smiled once again.

Blackberry tea.

Blood Return

Chapter Three

My dreams left me tossing and turning. I woke in a cold sweat, restless and scared. A fire blazed next to the bed, but it shared none of its warmth. Swinging my legs out from under the blanket, I strolled across the room to the now-cold pot on the dresser. There was still another cup worth of tea in there, and in all honesty, I didn't mind drinking it cold.

I emptied its contents and crawled in front of the hearth, trying desperately to chase away that nightmare. I couldn't remember what happened exactly. I just knew it utterly terrified me. Some kind of monster had been after me. I guess I should be thankful I can't recall what it looked like.

I was definitely thankful I'd closed my window before I went to sleep. It was darker than usual as a storm raged on. Thunder rumbled outside, shaking the walls.

For a brief second, I entertained the idea of walking around the house to clear my head. But then I got nervous thinking about the maze of hallways I hadn't yet learned.

Grant never returned that evening, and I didn't feel brave enough to call down for dinner. So I'd gone to bed hungry, nursing the leftover tea. I hadn't left my room since coming back here that morning, and I was starting to get antsy. I needed an out, a distraction, and food.

Gathering up whatever courage I could muster, I searched around my room for something to light my way. After several minutes of painstaking digging, I came away empty-handed. There wasn't even a candle in here.

My resolve wavered. I didn't want to be wandering this house at night in the middle of a storm. But I knew if I didn't, I'd go mad cooped up in here. There was nothing to do but stare at the ceiling and out the window. Quite frankly, I wanted nothing to do with that window. I should've drawn the curtains shut, so I didn't have to look out.

To steady myself, I decided that's just what I would do. I would go shut the curtains so I could relax a little.

I rose from my seat on the carpet, walking slowly toward the single window. The rain pelted the glass with a new fury, and lightning struck, briefly illuminating the outside. I cast my eyes to the ground, not wanting to stare out into the black and possibly see something I didn't want to see.

I'm not sure why I was so terrified to look outside at night, but something screamed inside of me not to look. To shut the curtains and get away from the glass as quickly as possible.

Reaching for the purple drapery, I went to pull it shut when it snagged on something. I pulled again, trying to loosen it without looking. But whatever had its grip on the fabric was not letting go. I had to look.

Gradually, I peeled my eyes from the floor and up to where the curtain was stuck. A nail jutted out of the side paneling, keeping the curtain from fully closing.

Thunder rumbled.

With a shaky hand, I picked the material off the nail and began closing it when lightning struck again. And my eyes saw it.

There, not twenty feet from my window was a dark figure. The light couldn't penetrate whatever it was but instead made it stick out from everything else.

My body screamed, and my heart pounded away inside my chest, but my feet were rooted to the spot. I couldn't move.

Fear was a wild animal inside of me, clawing its way out and bounding across the walls. Lightning struck again, and the figure was closer. It was too dark for me to see it without the light, and even with the light, I couldn't tell who it was. Or what it was.

The rational side of me wanted to think it was just a guardsman and he was posted there for the evening. But the other side of me knew that wasn't correct. What guardsmen would be standing like that? Would it be so dark I couldn't even tell who he was? No. It wasn't even dark. It was void of all light and features. It was just a shadow.

Lightning struck once more, this time close by as thunder crashed into the house. And the figure was running for me.

I screamed and fell backward, finally able to move my feet. Scrambling up, I didn't look a second time to see if it was still there. I bolted for the door, yanking and pulling until I remembered I had locked it earlier.

My fingers fumbled with the lock, and I silently cursed them. Sweat beaded my brow, and my breath came in heavy gasps. The next lightning bolt cast a shadow in front of me, and I saw a humanoid figure in it. Oh my God, it was at the window, and I couldn't tell if that was thunder or if it was banging on my window.

I was crying now, trying desperately to get out of this cage I'd trapped myself in. Then freedom. The door swung open, and I fell face-first into the hallway, sliding my knee across the carpet. But I couldn't linger on that burning pain. I was up in a flash and sprinting through the halls.

It was dark. Only a few candles lit my way. My tears disrupted any vision I had left, anyway. Every few feet, I would trip and stumble or run into a corner. I knew I would bruise after a particularly nasty bump into a hallway table.

After a minute of blind running, I stopped, resting my hands on my knees and gasping for breath. I had been screaming, but it seemed as if the house was completely empty.

There were no guards, no staff, nothing. Granted, I couldn't see much through my blurry tears, but someone would've stopped me if they had seen me. Where was everyone?

Thunder rumbled again, causing me to flinch instinctively. I dared a peak around the corner I'd shrugged around and saw nothing but the empty hallway. A sigh filled my lungs as I leaned against the wall. It hadn't followed me.

Suddenly, all my aches and pains hit me. My left knee very clearly had gotten rug burn and a nasty case of it. It was red and angry, with a few droplets of blood streaming down my leg. There was a small cut on my upper right thigh, probably from where I'd rammed into that table, and my sides hurt from slamming into corners.

Looking around, I felt slight despair, as I had no idea where I was. There were no paintings here and barely any doors. A staircase lay at the end of the hall from where I stood, reaching up into this jungle of a house.

I pried a candle from its hold on the wall and began walking cautiously ahead, testing a few of the doors. They were all locked, of course. My only options were to go up the stairs or turn back and go a different way.

Dread filled me at the thought of turning around, just in case I ran into whatever it was at my window. So up the stairs, it was.

They were metal and dug into the soles of my bare feet. What's another scratch to add to the list? They wound in a spiral up into an even darker part of the house. What maniac doesn't put lights everywhere?

Carefully making sure each step I took was correct, I made my way up. The candle helped a little, but this place seemed to soak up any light, causing it to be hard to see two feet in front of me. That made me anxious, more anxious than I'd like to admit. I just hoped whatever had been at my window stayed at my window. If I ran into it on these stairs, I'd go tumbling before I let it grab me.

At the top of the stairs, I felt a little better as some paintings had been hung in this hallway. I knew it didn't mean much in the grand scheme of things, but their familiarity made me feel more comfortable.

Thunder rumbled again, vibrating the floors. I could hear the wind howling outside. Whatever storm this was, it wasn't going away any time soon.

As I made my way down this hallway, I continued testing doors. They continued to be locked. It wasn't long before I came up on a dead end, facing a large window. My feet inched forward to take a look out, but I forced myself to back away. I didn't want to know if it was out there. If it had somehow managed to find me here after I'd run so blindly, well...I didn't want to think about that.

I rolled my shoulders and turned around, marching back down the hall, when something stopped me dead in my tracks. A tapping sounded. Rhythmic, intentional. And it was coming from behind me at the window.

My heart began pounding once more as I listened. When I didn't turn around, the tapping got louder and more intense.

I couldn't resist, and I slowly turned around. At first, I saw nothing, but then lightning flashed. And I saw it.

It was perched outside the window, tapping with its fist. A dark figure.

I ran. The candle blew out almost instantly from the force, and I tossed it over my shoulder. I started screaming again, for help, for someone, anyone. I rounded a corner, full-on sprinting and screaming when I tripped. I hadn't seen this other set of stairs, and I was about to go crashing down them.

Instinctively, my arms rose to protect my face as I waited for the blow. But it never came. Something had grabbed the back of my nightgown and was towing me backward.

I screamed and kicked, thinking it was the shadow creature. But after I was thrown into a lit bedroom, I noticed it wasn't. It was Jae.

He cupped my face with both hands and was screaming at me, frantically asking what was going on.

I was hyperventilating too bad to be able to talk. My body shook, and everything hurt. I just threw my arms around his shoulders and sobbed. Finally, someone had found me.

He froze as soon as my arms locked behind his neck. But after a second, he wrapped his around me and rubbed my back. I sobbed uncontrollably into his shoulder, only noticing then he wasn't wearing a shirt, and I was crying directly into his skin. Whatever, I didn't care.

He rocked me slowly back and forth on the floor, talking in a calming voice and rubbing my back. After a few minutes, I stopped crying as hard, and instead, hiccups filled their place.

I broke away and rubbed the wet mess off my face and his shoulder.

"I'm sorry," I whispered. But he wasn't concerned with that. Instead, he grabbed my arms and again asked me what had happened.

My mouth opened to tell him right as the door flung open. I shied away, covering my face. A booming voice not unlike the thunder outside reached my ears.

"What the hell happened?" It was Grant.

I flung my arms down and met his agonized face. His eyes scanned over me, lingering on the cuts and rug burn. He wiped at my cheeks and turned to face Jae.

Jae was now in the doorway, shaking his head. "I have no idea. I heard screaming, and when I opened the door, I saw her running through the halls. I got her just as she was about to fall down the stairs."

Grant looked back at me, eyes blazing. "What happened, Rose?"

My hiccups were in full force now, and I still was sniffling with the after-effects of my crying. "There was someone outside my window trying to get in." Vivid flashes of the figure penetrated my eyelids; I didn't even want to blink anymore.

Both Grant and Jae went rigid. Without a word between the two, Jae bolted down the hall and started to sound an alarm. Within seconds the halls were buzzing with soldiers. Where they had been when I was screaming for my life, I didn't know.

"What did they look like?" Grant snapped, pulling my attention back to him.

I started shaking my head uncontrollably. "It was a shadow. It had no face, just empty blackness. It was up here, too. At the end of the hall." It made no sense, but it scared me nonetheless.

Something changed in Grant's eyes at my words. A switch had been flipped. Immediately he scooped me up into his arms and began carrying me through the house. Jae appeared behind us, giving me a reassuring smile.

We made our way through the house, down the stairs, and to another bedroom. This one was huge, three times the size of mine. A large canopy bed sat against the far right wall, with living room furniture decorating the other.

Grant sat me down on a plush footrest and kneeled before me. His fingers were delicate as they traced over my knee and as they slid their way up my thigh.

Heat flooded my cheeks at his touch. Luckily, he pretended not to notice.

"Go get some supplies," he barked to Jae.

Without hesitation, Jae fled the room.

It seemed like only a few seconds had passed when he returned, carrying a tub of hot water, bandages, and some kind of ointment. He placed them at my feet next to Grant, who did not so much as say thank you to him.

"Leave us," he said curtly. "And deal with that problem."

When Jae left the room, Grant took three very deep breaths. He rolled his neck and released tension in his shoulders. He didn't look at me.

"You should've called someone." His voice was thin, like he was restraining himself from yelling.

I wrapped my arms around myself and shivered, still sniffling. "I..." I trailed off, not knowing what to say. That I was too scared? I didn't have time? I didn't think about it? They all sounded like excuses, so I chose to stay silent. I mean, I had been screaming.

He turned his face up, again studying me. The green in his eyes glowed faintly in the dim firelight. After my silence continued, he chuckled and took a damp rag out of the tub.

"I suppose I can't completely fault you. You did scream loud enough to make sure someone heard you regardless." He brought the rag to my knee and began patting the blood away.

I hissed in pain at the touch to my raw wound. His jaw tightened noticeably at my yelp. As he dipped the cloth back into the water to clean it, I got to admire him.

As bulky as he was, his face was considerably softer. He had the harsh jawline and thin-bridged nose, but his cheeks looked soft. His lips glistened, and even from my point of view, I could see they were well taken care of.

He pushed the edge of my dress up, revealing the cut on my thigh. With one smooth motion, he placed the rag to it and gingerly wiped at it. This hurt, too, but not nearly as bad as my knee did.

"So what happened? Exactly, I mean." His voice was softer, with a hint of remorse in his words. He still didn't meet my eyes, but he seemed intent on listening to whatever I said. So I told him everything, starting from when I woke up.

As I spoke, he continued to clean my wounds. Occasionally, he would make a passing remark of "Huh" or "Oh," but he never interrupted me. Once I was finished recanting the awful details, he was dressing and bandaging my knee.

He sighed, shaking his head. "I'm sorry I wasn't there for you."

My brows pulled together as I watched him stick a Band-Aid on my thigh; it had sunflowers on it. "You didn't know."

Then his eyes met mine, and a wave of emotions crashed through me from that gaze. Something tethered between us in that small space. It was like nothing I could explain. He pinched my chin with his thumb and forefinger and tilted my head side to side, inspecting for other cuts to tend to. When he didn't find any, he nodded smugly to himself and began stowing away the supplies.

He said nothing further to me for the next half hour, only handing me a glass of water and speaking with different guards as they came in. I didn't understand anything they said as they spoke in hushed voices again. It's irrational for me to get upset over that, as I didn't really need to know what they were saying. But I knew it was about the figure, and I wanted to hear what they had to say about it.

Finally, Grant bid them goodnight and strolled back to where I sat. He knelt down once more in front of me and placed a hand on my good knee. "They scoured the entire property and couldn't find it."

My heart sank. Did that mean I imagined it all? The alternative was that it was real, and it got away.

"But," he continued, "they will stay up all night guarding you if you wish to go back to your room."

Without warning, my body began to shake. My breathing became labored, and my pulse stuttered. Just thinking about going back into that room alone almost sent me into an anxiety attack.

Grant noticed this immediately and rose to sit beside me. He wrapped his strong arms around me and pulled me tight. "You don't have to. It's okay. You can stay here if you want, and I'll keep watch over you."

A chuckle escaped my lips before I could stop it. "I don't think I could go back to sleep if I tried."

He gently squeezed my shoulders and pushed me back to look at him. "Whatever you want."

I breathed deeply, trying to force my body back into a calm state. "Okay." My voice was shaky, almost unrecognizable to my ears. I looked down at myself and noticed how dirty I'd become. Where he'd cleaned my wounds left an obvious patch of clean skin. Embarrassment was ripe throughout me.

Grant noticed what I had and lifted my chin once more. "I have a private bathroom right in this room if you'd like to rinse off."

"You just bandaged me up, though. The water would ruin it."

He gave me a beseeching look. "Rose. I can always redo it. If you want to rinse off, then you can. If it'll make you feel better, then I have to insist."

A smile crept on my lips, and I looked away from him. "I would like to, yes."

Without hesitation, he leaped from the footrest and marched to an adjacent door. He disappeared inside, and I could vaguely hear the sound of running water. He returned shortly after, holding out a towel for me.

"Water's a little hot. It'll draw the heat out of some of your wounds."

I made my way over to him and graciously took the towel. Peering inside, I saw a bathroom the size of my bedroom, with no windows and covered in marble granite. A tub sat carved into the floor, and bubbles filled the surface of the water.

As Grant made to shut the door, I stopped him. I didn't want to be alone right now, but I also didn't want him to see me naked.

"Do you think after I get in, you could come sit with me? I still don't feel comfortable being alone." I hoped the bubbles were enough coverage, but looking at the mountain he had created, I was almost sure they would be.

Now it was his cheeks that flushed red. He looked at the floor and cleared his throat. "I don't think that would be appropriate, Rose."

"Oh." Another shockwave of embarrassment rolled through me. "Okay." I started to close the door when he wedged his toe in it.

"Call for me when you're in."

A grin spread across my face, causing my cheeks to swell. I nodded and hastily shut the door. Placing the towel next to the tub, I practically ripped my tattered nightgown off.

The water was hot. Extremely hot. I stifled a squeal as I lowered myself down into the cascade of bubbles.

Once I was sure my body was thoroughly covered, I called for Grant. The door opened, and I immediately started laughing.

Grant walked in with a small desk chair, completely blindfolded. He tested the floor with his feet, searching for a sturdy place for the chair. He seemed satisfied with a particular spot and took up residence there.

"That's a bit overkill, isn't it?" I called to him while rubbing some bubbles down my arm.

He shook his head and folded his arms. "I think it's perfectly reasonable. I'm not at risk of seeing you naked, and you have me for company. It's a win-win."

"I think it's overkill."

"I can go back out, then?"

"No!" I giggled. "No, it's perfectly reasonable."

As I took the rest of my bath, being careful not to disturb my bandages too much, he talked to me as much as I wanted. About anything. I didn't have much to say on my end, but I convinced him to tell me a story from his childhood.

He told me a story about him and his brother breaking their mom's most expensive vase and then trying to make a replacement. It was rather light-hearted, but I could hear distant sadness in his voice.

When I was getting ready to get out, I paused. "Um. I don't have anything else to wear."

His face blanked at the realization. "Give me a moment." He disappeared back out into the room, and I heard him shuffling through drawers. He came back carrying a purple button-down silk shirt with matching pants.

I couldn't keep the amusement from my voice as I said, "You really like purple, huh?"

His mouth twitched, and he tossed the clothes onto his empty chair. "It's a very flattering color. Get dressed before I take it back."

My smile never faltered as I slipped on the new clothes, which were surprisingly warm, considering the thin fabric. I walked back out into the room, toweling off my wet hair. Grant was resting on the couch, reading a book. He shut it promptly as I approached and took in the sight before him.

"Do I need to rebandage?" he asked with a sharp look at my legs.

I frowned and raised one pant leg to show him the now-soaked bandage on my knee.

The right side of his mouth quirked as he sat up, beckoning me over. I plopped down beside him, stretching my legs into his lap, and he began unraveling the bandages. As his fingers began brushing my bare leg again, I couldn't stop the fluttering that began in my chest.

When he finished, he rolled my pants legs back down and patted my ankle reassuringly. "All better?"

"Thank you." I nodded, noticing he didn't immediately remove his hands from me.

His eyes bore right through me, straight into my soul. "I still think you should try and get some rest."

Cold filled my chest at the thought of returning to my room and falling asleep. I think I'd rather jump out a three-story window than return.

My head tilted down with shame as my lower lip quivered. "I can't go back there right now."

"Who said you had to go back?"

I raised my eyes to his, catching his smug grin. "And where would I go?"

Without hesitation, Grant pointed to the bed across the room. He didn't say anything, but I could assume that bed was his. I could tell even without the hints. It was huge and covered in green sheets with a blackout canopy curtain surrounding it. I wanted to ask what he needed the curtain for but felt I might become even more embarrassed with the answer.

"I don't want to take your bed; I can just sleep on the couch—"

Before I could even finish my sentence, Grant scooped me up in his arms and was halfway across the room. I blinked, wondering how he'd gotten over here so fast, and started to worry if I'd sustained another head injury.

He practically threw me onto the bed, then loomed over me. Looking up at him from this position, my face turned beet red, and I instinctively shut my legs. He looked down at my obvious nervousness with a raised brow and a shake of his head. Leaning down to where our noses almost touched, my breathing stopped. His eyes traced a path down my nose, to my chin, and back up again before he said, "Move."

My eyes went wide as his voice halted me in place. I knew it was the exact opposite of what he'd said, but I couldn't comply. When I didn't move, his jaw clenched in annoyance, and he grabbed my waist with both hands.

Panic raced through me at the thought of what might be happening. My throat began to restrict, making it hard to breathe. Then he slid me over and pulled the blankets down.

"Overreact much?" he asked with a smile.

He knew what he was doing. I was sure of it. Why else would he be smiling like that unless he knew exactly what was happening? Stunned, I looked to the spot he'd opened up for me, unable to speak once more.

Then he raised up off of me and bid me goodnight, shutting the curtains. I almost gasped for air once he was out of sight. Confusion and heat blasted through my veins, cluttering my mind and ramming my heart. My gut twisted in all the wrong ways, and I flipped over, worried about potential vomiting.

When nothing came up, I silently crawled under the blankets and pulled them over my head. For the next hour, I lay in silence and anxiety that he might return when I fell asleep. Somewhere in the back of my mind, I knew it was ridiculous; he'd done nothing to me. He'd helped me. And yet my body revolted at the thought of having intimacy with him if that's even what happened.

Thinking back on it, his bed is rather too large for him to reach standing at the edge. He would've had to crawl up here just to pull the covers down for me—like he'd done. And where he'd laid me originally, I was in the way. He was right. I am overreacting.

I turned and crushed my head with a pillow, feeling embarrassed all over again. No doubt this would have some kind of impact on how he acted around me further.

Thunder rumbled once more, and I was acutely aware that I had blocked out the storm the entire time I was around him. Not even the rain reached my ears. That confused me even further.

Eventually, I forced myself to quit thinking about it and try to sleep. If it was a problem tomorrow, then I would handle it tomorrow. He must understand a little since I couldn't even remember who I was.

That needed to be my first priority if he was still willing to help me. I needed to figure out what had happened to me and who the purple-eyed man that saved me was.

I needed to go back to the lake.

S. D. Sampley

Chapter Four

The next morning I awoke to a tray of food on the opposite pillow. A mug of steaming tea sat on top of another flower stem. I could tell by the shape of the petals it was the same type of flower he'd given me yesterday. However, the colors on this were slightly different. It was still dark purple in the center—almost black—but the edges were a fluorescent orange.

As I bit into my melon slice, I wondered what the name of this lily was. It had to be something ridiculous and yet utterly charming for no reason.

Opening the curtains, I noticed I was completely alone in the room. Over on the couch were haphazardly spread blankets and pillows, indicating someone had slept there. The bathroom door stood ajar with no light on. Where that person was now, I had no idea.

I carefully climbed down from the bed and tiptoed over to the main door, pressing my ear against the cold wood. When I didn't hear any sounds, I cracked it open. A guard stood mere inches from my face, clad in armor from head to toe adorned with the same moon symbol I'd seen before.

He hadn't noticed me, so I shut the door, running a hand through my hair. My fingers got caught in a few tangles, and I sighed in frustration. That's what I get for going to bed with wet hair.

How I knew that information, I had no idea.

As I struggled to unknot the strands of my hair, voices reached me from beyond the door.

"Any news?" That sounded like Jarred.

"No, sir. The grounds were completely clean during every sweep. Whoever it was, is long gone."

Jarred let out a hard sigh. "They'll be back. The girl?"

"Still asleep."

"Well, wake her up. Grant is expecting her downstairs."

Suddenly the door swung wide open, exposing me behind it, my fingers still tangled on my head.

I stared wide-eyed at them before waving with my free hand. Jarred stood before me, carrying a garment bag, with a less than amused face.

"Get dressed," he said sharply, tossing the bag at my face. I nearly avoided having my eye taken out by the hanger as the material wrapped around my head.

"Where is Grant?" My voice came muffled from behind the wad of fabric. When I managed to drop the bag into my arms, I noticed Jarred staring at me. Except his eyes were rather low on my body.

Uncomfortable, I said, "Nevermind." And slammed the door shut. This was the second time I'd caught him staring, and it got worse each time. I wondered how long I could put up with it before I finally said something.

I didn't move from my spot by the door as I unzipped the black bag and considered the outfit inside. It wasn't really an outfit, more so a dress. A long, purple dress. I scoffed at yet another item colored this way and pulled it out.

Golden lace was stitched into the bottom skirt, trailing up to the bodice in a liquified state. It had sleeves that were also stitched in gold lace.

The fabric itself felt lightweight, and it stretched nicely. It was way too nice of a garment for me to wear, especially if I was going to go to the lake and recover my memories. But it was the only thing I had at the moment, aside from these pajamas. So I begrudgingly slipped it on.

I left my hair the way it was, not having a brush or a hair tie to keep it back. When I opened the door, Jarred still stood there. His eyes raked over every inch of me with a gaze I didn't like.

"Ready?" he purred.

I nodded, keeping my eyes low as he walked me through the house. He led me down a set of stairs to a room I had never been to before.

Bookshelves reached the ceiling, lining every inch of wall in this area. There wasn't a window in sight, and the only light came from a low-hanging chandelier. It was reminiscent of the study I'd first met Grant in. In the middle sat some reclining chairs and a coffee table, of which Grant sat on the edge, nose buried in a map. Trinity hovered over his left shoulder, pointing at something I couldn't see.

Grant looked up as we entered, a snarl plastered on his face.

Jarred halted in the doorway, clearing his throat. "Any other orders, sir?"

"Find Avalon and go over the details of last night. I want a full report by this evening."

With a curt nod, Jarred disappeared back into the house. Leaving me to stand awkwardly where he'd left me.

From his position on the table, Grant studied me once again over the rim of his glasses. Without looking at Trinity, he asked, "They always take the survivors?"

"If there are any."

He turned his attention back to the map and neatly folded it into a square before handing it to her. "Make note of that. We can use it later."

She nodded, tucking the paper into her belt of weapons before strutting out of the room—giving me a wink as she passed.

After a moment of silence, Grant nodded to himself in approval. "It suits you."

I knew he meant the dress, but his compliment didn't make me feel any less self-conscious. But I managed to squeak out a "Thank you," anyway.

"Did you like the flower?" he asked as he shut his book, folding in his bookmark.

"It was beautiful," I said quietly, staring at my feet. "What's it called?"

"Forever Susan."

I couldn't help it. My mouth turned up in a smile. It was just as weird as I expected it to be.

"Who comes up with these names?" As I looked up with a raised brow, I almost fell back in terror. Grant was now standing directly in front of me, glasses in his pocket. I hadn't heard him move at all, let alone stride over a yard to stand in front of me.

He shrugged his broad shoulders in a non-committal motion. "I don't ask."

Trying to slow my beating heart, I changed the subject. "This is a nice library."

His eyes narrowed as he inevitably caught what I was doing. "It's my favorite spot in the whole house to be alone in."

"I can see why." One could find themselves utterly cut off from the world here, with its lack of windows and secluded nature.

Grant continued to stare down at me, looking down the bridge of his nose. I felt more scrutinized than I ever had. It seemed to grow each day, and I wasn't sure how to handle it. "What do you want to do today?"

I gulped. This was it. The moment to ask to go back to the lake. I didn't see a reason why he wouldn't take me, especially if it could help me. So why did I feel so cautious? "I want to go back to where you found me."

His eyes narrowed even further, barely slitted now. "Why?"

"To see if it could jog my memory. Fix it."

"That's a three-mile hike, Rose."

My head lowered in defeat. "Oh." Honestly, I didn't care how far of a hike. Even in this extravagant gown, I'd run there if need be. I was itching to rediscover myself, and what happened to me. I needed to know. Most importantly I needed to figure out who the purple-eyed man was, and why he saved me. I'd probably also ask him where he'd been this entire time, as well. Why did he abandon me at the lake after he'd saved me?

When I said nothing else, Grant grabbed me by the elbow and steered me into the hallway. I struggled to keep pace with him as he nearly dragged me through the house.

We finally reached the end of a hallway, where a lone white door stood. Grant knocked three times, then twice. A pattern I could only guess meant some kind of secret code to whoever was listening.

After a few seconds, the door swung wide, and Jae appeared looking like he'd just rolled out of bed. His eyes went wide at the sight of Grant, and he tried quickly to fix his appearance.

"So sorry to wake you." Grant's words were laced with venom as he practically spat them at Jae.

Jae gave up trying to make himself presentable and nodded. "My alarm didn't go off."

Grant held up a hand to silence Jae. "We'll deal with it later. I have a task for you."

Straightening his shoulders, a worry line creased Jae's forehead. "Sir?" Then he noticed me still in Grant's grasp, and his eyes grew to that of saucer plates.

I waved with my fingers, still unsure why I had been dragged here like a sack of potatoes.

"She wants to go back to the lake," Grant explained, "to jog her memory." He dropped my arm and gently pushed me in Jae's direction.

He still stood wide-eyed, looking back and forth between us in sheer confusion. "She does?"

"Mhmm." Grant raised both eyebrows as if to drive a point home. "I want you to take her."

Jae pointed a finger to his chest, worry lines creasing his forehead as his brows deepened. "Me?"

"Yes. I have something to attend to today. You're the one who found her, and she wishes to fix the problem. So fix it." His last words were punctuated on every syllable, followed by a low grumble. Jae ducked like a submissive puppy.

Turning, Grant pinched my chin and tilted my face to his. His green eyes were dark in this light, like cheap jade. "If anything happens today, anything at all. You scream, and I'll be there." He leaned in and planted a small kiss on my forehead, lips barely brushing my skin before they were gone. Then he walked away, leaving me at Jae's doorstep.

I looked at Jae, just as confused as he appeared to be. Grant had turned abrasive and withdrawn in his actions seemingly overnight. I could almost feel the whiplash settling on my shoulders.

Jae reached out and grasped my arm, pulling me inside the room and shutting the door. "Stay here," he grumbled as he shuffled past. Snatching clothes off a lone chair in the corner of the room, he disappeared into what I could only assume was the bathroom.

The room was disheveled but in a clean way. A pile of clothes rested on the same chair, stacked as high as the wooden back would allow. The blankets lay in turmoil on the bed, flipped every which way and then more. The walls were bare, and even the window was void of any curtain or blind. The mirror residing on top of an antique white dresser was covered in a fine layer of dust.

This didn't appear to be the same room he'd taken me in last night, but to be honest, I was too afraid to really remember what that room looked like.

Quietly, I strolled over to the wooden box and jingled the knob on one of the drawers. I really shouldn't be snooping, but something bugged me about the state of his room.

The sound of running water solidified my resolve, and I peeked inside. Empty. Opening another, I was greeted with the same sight. All of these drawers were empty, which meant all of his clothes lay on that chair.

It wasn't a lot, and the fact that they all lay in a mess told me everything I needed to know. He wasn't planning on staying here.

I'm not sure why that was the thing that came to mind in this situation; he could just be a messy person. But something in the back of my mind told me he wasn't and that this definitely meant he didn't intend to be here for long.

The water abruptly shut off, and I backed to where I'd been before, acting like I hadn't moved. Jae entered shortly after, now wearing a cream button-up with a leather vest and black pants. His hair was wet, and I could still see steam rising from the top of his head. He took one look at my gown and scowled.

"You're wearing that to the lake?"

I crossed my arms over my chest in a defensive gesture. "I don't have anything else. This is what they gave me this morning."

He eyed me in a way one would a fish that had just beached itself. "Alright, then." He finished lacing up his boots and directed me to follow him.

We made our way down a flight of stairs into a tunnel made of dirt and cobwebs. I shied away from bumping into one web, only to crash into another. I shrieked and began swiping at my arm furiously. Jae appeared, brushing off the remaining bits of sticky string.

"Thanks," I mumbled, a shiver making its way down my back.

He nodded, and we continued forward. A damp breeze caressed my cheek, warm and subtle. Something musky reached my nostrils, and my brain racked itself, trying to come up with an answer. But it was only when we spilled out of the exit did I realize what it was.

We'd come out at the back end of a barn. Horses on both sides of the alleyway turned their heads to look at us. A few nickered as we passed by, hay dripping from their mouths. At the very end was a dark brown one with a small white spot on its nose. The nameplate read *Cherry Blossom*, and it was in front of her stall that we halted.

Jae reached over, a peppermint appearing in his hand. Cherry Blossom eagerly smacked her lips and scooped up the candy. He smiled and ruffled the top of her head and ears.

"I didn't know you guys had horses," I observed, glancing around with fascination.

Jae shrugged, scratching the horse's neck. "Yeah, we hardly use them but have them just in case."

"Is she yours?"

He chuckled dryly with a shake of his head. "No. But she is my favorite. Back up," he commanded the horse as he reached for the door latch.

Cherry Blossom backed away from us, bobbing her head inquisitively. When Jae opened the stall door, she did not charge the opening. She remained where she stood and watched his every move with her big brown eyes.

Jae grabbed a leather halter off a hook, and she willingly stuck her head into the hole. My eyebrows rose, impressed at the obedience this horse displayed.

"How'd you teach her that?" Somewhere in the back of my mind, I knew some horses didn't willingly put on their gear.

"Lots of treats," he said with a grin, leading her out of the stall. "She likes sweet potato the most."

I trailed behind him, trying to stay clear of the horse's hind end. "They can have that?"

He stopped at the front of the barn, tying the end of her rope to a metal rung built into the wall. "Horses can have almost anything in moderation."

Cherry Blossom let out a puff of air, side-eyeing me. *What are you wearing*, she seemed to ask.

Jae appeared beside me with two brushes, handing me one. "It's quicker if we double up."

Grabbing the stiff bristles gingerly, I began following his lead as we started to brush her. In no time, what little dirt was on her was gone, and Jae began saddling her.

The saddle was a light tan color with a dark seat and cacti stamped into the leather. It had a thick horn at the front and a square body. It definitely only sat one person.

"Uh, are we only taking her?"

"Yes."

I brushed my fingers through Cherry Blossom's silky mane and chewed on my lower lip. "How are we going to fit two people? Wouldn't that be hard on her back?"

Jae straightened and sighed. "If we were to double-ride her all the time, yes. But she is in good enough shape for this one trek." He rubbed the side of his hand down her cheek, wrapping around to the other side. His eyes turned sad as he stroked the white spot across her nose.

"Do you come down here a lot?"

"Every chance I get." He fell silent for a moment, passing another peppermint to her mouth. "Let's go."

He turned toward the double doors, horse in tow, as I struggled to keep up without spooking Cherry Blossom.

With a press of a button, the doors swung wide, revealing a wooded pathway lined with blackberry bushes.

"What's with all the blackberries?" I asked as Jae swung up into the saddle.

He shifted back and forth, seeming to readjust the saddle's placement.

"Is he your father?"

Jae gave pause at my question, cutting his eyes toward me, but he said nothing.

"He can't be. He looks your age."

"It's a long story. Come." He reached down a hand, fingers splayed.

I looked back and forth between him and his hand. He was insane if he thought he could pull me up there with one hand.

When I didn't take his outstretched palm after a few seconds, he leaned further down and grabbed my arm. Then I was flying through the air, only to moments later be straddled behind Jae. I wasn't in the saddle but rather behind it.

Immediately, I wrapped my arms around him, trying desperately to not fall off. I was completely off balance and, quite frankly, terrified. It was much higher up here than it looked from the ground.

His back shook with a chuckle at my frantic behavior. "When was the last time you rode?"

I squeezed my eyes shut and interlocked my fingers. "I don't know."

Jae went quiet again. I could almost feel his regret for asking me. He said nothing more as he clicked to the horse, and we began moving.

It was a grueling hour trying to balance myself. My arms went numb halfway, I could barely feel my toes, and my thighs hurt.

The forest was silent. Eerily so. No birds sang. No rodents chirped. Not even the breeze dared to whisper. What these woods held beyond this cut path, I don't think I'd ever want to know. My skin crawled with every crunch of earth under the horse's hooves.

Through a clearing in the trees, I could see the faint shimmer of water. As we trotted up, a groan of relief escaped me.

Jae pulled us up just short of a small tree and peered over his shoulder at me. "We're here."

But my arms were stuck, almost glued around his waist. I don't think I could move even if I wanted to. My arms tingled in an unbearable way.

"I-I d-don't think I can move," I stuttered.

He gave a half smile as he pried my paralyzed hands from him. As I dragged my hands back, my sleeve caught on something. There was a hole in his shirt on the left side, and something had snagged the fabric.

I reached with my free hand and felt his raised skin through the hole. He flinched and shoved my hand away. I didn't miss the glare he shot me. I also didn't miss what it was I'd touched.

A scar. Wicked and gnarly. I don't know where it started, but I could tell it wrapped around his waist. What could've caused a wound like that? I didn't want to imagine. The pain he must've been in.

Jae managed to swing his leg around without taking me out and slid to the ground. He reached up, grabbed me under the arms, and pulled me down.

As soon as my feet touched the ground, my knees buckled. I fell backward into Cherry Blossom's hip. She jumped slightly at the sudden movement but stood in place long enough for me to right myself.

I patted her side apologetically. Her ears had turned back toward me, and I couldn't tell if it was annoyance or pity that sat in her eyes.

Jae pulled the reins over her head and walked her to the edge of the lake, allowing her a moment to get a drink. He loosened the saddle and removed her headpiece, where she promptly strutted over to a patch of tall grass and began happily munching away.

"Aren't you afraid she'll run away?" I asked as I fixed my skirt, which had bunched up on itself on the ride.

He shook his head and slung the headstall over his shoulder. "She has great recall. She won't go anywhere."

Plopping down on the shore, he motioned for me to join him, and I did.

Looking out across the vast expanse of water, some emotion crawled up my neck. Flashes of the darkness crossed my mind, and the feeling of burning in my lungs returned.

I gulped and fiddled with the lace on my sleeves. The purple of my gown dredged up the memory of those eyes. That piercing gaze.

"So. Do you remember anything yet?" Jae's deep voice broke the silence around us. I noted there were still no animals to be found or heard.

"Just drowning." I frowned, trying to force something else to emerge but to no avail. Looking over, I noticed Jae fidgeting with something around his neck.

Upon closer inspection, I saw it was a crystal necklace with a golden spiral in the center.

"That's beautiful," I noted.

He stopped wringing his hands around it and hastily tucked it back into his shirt. "Don't change the subject. What else?"

Lines creased my forehead as I thought, but it all came up blank. "It's all blackness before I'm in the water." It was more than blackness. It was a wall. A solid wall of emptiness sat in my mind. Every time I retreated there, I hit it but knew there was nothing behind it.

He placed a soothing hand on my shoulder, turning me so I had to look at him. "That's all?"

I shrugged.

Jae didn't like that answer. I could see it in the tightening of his jaw. "You mentioned before someone saved you. What did they look like?"

My heart thudded, pulse quickening. "I think I probably imagined it." Who would even have purple eyes? That doesn't exist. I had to have been imagining it.

Closing his eyes, he took a deep calming breath. When he reopened them, they swirled a brilliant white color.

Wait. Were they that bright of a color before?

"Rose." His voice pulled me, forcing any thoughts out of my head completely. My heart slowed, and I felt my entire body relax.

"Yes?" My own voice felt far away, like I was hearing it through earplugs.

"What do you remember exactly when you were pulled from the water?"

I didn't even hesitate. "Burning. My lungs burned. I couldn't breathe. I was cold. There was someone beside me. They wore brown shoes."

"What else?"

"They had purple eyes."

Jae flinched as if I'd struck him. He blinked slowly, never removing his gaze from me but seeming to think. Something clicked behind his eyes, and he grasped me with both hands as he said, "I need you to do something for me."

"Anything," I gasped. And I would. I would do anything at that moment. His voice was so hypnotic, so enticing.

"Trust the shadows. Don't be afraid of the shadow man."

I nodded, not one ounce of fear settling in me. Why would it? He said I shouldn't be afraid of the shadow man. I can trust the shadows.

"And if Grant asks what happened here, tell him there's nothing to be found. You won't remember this conversation." He looked away then, instantly releasing me.

A headache started to form at the back of my skull, and I squinted at the too-bright sun. What just happened?

I was still at the lake, Jae beside me. Cherry Blossom was still in the grass. My chest heaved with a gulp of air, and I shut my eyes tight.

It was then I heard them. Hundreds of chirps and squawks. I peeled open one eye to see a dark mass circling the top of a tall pine.

It slowly drifted down, missing the tree entirely and settling on the ground twenty feet from me. Hundreds of tiny black birds chirped and pecked at the ground. I stared at them, wondering where they'd come from.

A few turned their heads side to side to look at me, inching closer. Suddenly the whole swarm flocked toward me. They didn't attack but rather settled next to me with curiosity. A few perched on my shoulders and one atop my head.

I giggled, looking over to Jae with excitement. "Look!"

He was already looking. In fact, he stared at me with newfound wonder. "There haven't been any animals in this part of the woods for years."

"What are they?" I asked as I reached over and let one step onto my finger. I pet the top of its head, and it chirped a merry tune.

"Starlings."

"I wish I could whistle and see if they would sing it back." Sighing, I let the bird hop off my hand onto the ground.

"You can whistle."

I frowned. "How do you know?"

He went silent, only a scowl written across his face. "We need to get back." He moved to get up, and the birds took flight back to the trees.

A feeling of Deja vu swept over me from the deer incident yesterday. Jae was giving me the same look Grant had, and I didn't know what it meant. Why did the animals allow me to get so close, yet flee when anyone around me moved?

Jae hauled me to my feet and gave a low whistle. Cherry Blossom perked up and trotted over, Jae palming another peppermint into her mouth.

I groaned when it was my turn to get back on her. My body was killing me, and I wasn't sure another hour would be good on my knees.

"Jae!" A deep voice bellowed from in the tree line.

Cherry blossom snorted, ears pricked forward. Underneath me, her back tensed and buckled.

Two horses burst into the clearing: Jarred on a stocky gray and Trinity on a leggy red.

Jae lifted his chin and puffed his chest slightly. "What?"

The horses stopped a few feet in front of us, panting and sweating profusely like they ran them the whole way here.

"Grant needs you urgently."

Air rushed through Jae's nose in a snort, a muscle twitching in his jaw. "He does know I'm already doing something he asked me to do, right?"

Jarred narrowed his eyes. "Does it matter?"

"What is it about?"

"The queen has arrived," Trinity blurted before Jarred could even open his mouth. "Grant asked for you specifically."

Jae's back stiffened, muscles bunching and coiling. As he wheeled Cherry Blossom around to follow them, he muttered under his breath, "I'm so sick of this place."

Chapter Five

Jae left me in the barn, too caught up in what the others had said to remember I was there. A guard took the horses and got them settled back in their stalls. I wanted to help, but my head still pounded, and honestly, I would be in the way more than anything.

This dress was too hot, too itchy. I scratched at my sleeves and tugged on the bodice, trying to fan some air to my suffocating body.

I tried asking a guard how to get back into the house without going through the dirt tunnel, but no one answered me. They all stared straight ahead, unmoving, unblinking. It was unnerving.

After procrastinating around the stable, petting the other horses, I decided it was time. No way was I going into that silent forest by myself to wander around until I found the house, so the tunnel was my only option.

Sucking in a deep breath, I dove into the darkness. There were absolutely no lights in here, and with the setting sun, I had no outside source either. That meant I had to feel my way with my hands.

The spider webs, leaves, and bugs I ran into nearly sent me into a blind panic, but that would do me no good. I'd run around in full hysterics last night and had only injured myself.

Walking swiftly, I started to fear I had gone the wrong way. This place seemed much longer than it did this morning.

Just when I'd decided to turn around and go back, my fingers brushed against something different. Colder than the rest of the dirt and smooth. Metal.

Tracing the outline, I determined it to be a door. Maybe it was the door back to the house.

I scrambled around for the doorknob, only to grasp a thin handle instead. It wasn't twistable, so instead, I pushed. Then pulled. Then pushed again. But the door remained sealed.

Frustrated, I kicked it with my toe, only to instantly grab my foot at the sheer pain that stalked up my feet. That was stupid.

I tried one more time to push the door open. This time my feet slid out from under me in the slick dirt, and I clung to the handle to stay upright. It was then the door slid to the side. It was a sliding door.

A lantern hung mounted to the wall several feet in front of me, illuminating the hallway. It wasn't dirt anymore, but rather smooth stone. This wasn't where I'd come from earlier, but voices reached me from a distance.

I stepped inside and shut the door, yanking the lantern off the hanger and holding it in front of me as I crept up.

No spiderwebs here.

The hall made a sharp right turn about ten feet ahead, and beyond that were a set of cobblestone stairs. The bottom of the stairs opened up into a small circular room where a fleece blanket, pillows, and a pile of books rested on the floor. I'd inadvertently found someone's hideout.

Feeling embarrassed, I started to turn around until I heard the voices again. They were closer now, and I could almost make out exact words. One voice sounded like Grant, the other Jae. I thought I could hear a woman's voice too, but I didn't recognize it.

Whipping my head around, I searched for the source. Only to find a small vent at the top of the room where a faint light pierced through its holes.

It was just high enough that I couldn't reach it myself, but if I stood on my tiptoes on the books, I could see.

This vent led directly into the room I'd first met Trinity in, with the weird maps. If I tilted my head up, I could see their faces.

Grant was fuming, a vein popping out of his neck. Jae stood beside him, and they both stared down a slender, brown-haired woman. I couldn't tell who she was, but by the sound of her voice, it wasn't anyone I knew.

"So you find all one hundred of them, and I can't even have one?"

"I created them. I decide where they go." Grant's voice rang with an echo of finality.

"You have so many. I deserve a couple. I brought you your mortal enemy!" She stomped her feet, which were barely noticeable underneath her pecan-colored ball gown. Light blue jewels scattered along the bottom, creating a crescent moon pattern.

Grant's fists clenched, whitening his knuckles. "I wanted to handle that myself, but you decided your ego was more important."

The woman scoffed, tossing her brown hair over her shoulder in one graceful move. "You should be grateful. Now that she's out of the way, you can carry on with your plan without worry."

"That wasn't your decision to make, Ketura," Jae snapped, shoving his hands in his pocket.

"Oh, don't start with me, Hazelton. You're the one who volunteered to do it yourself. Also, it's Queen Ketura to you." She sneered at him, hands on her hips.

Jae flinched at her words, which made Grant even angrier. "His name is Hyeon SeokJae, and you will refer to him as such."

Ketura shook her head. "I will do no such thing. I am a queen, and you will do well to remember that, Uncle."

Grant stepped forward, using his height and build to tower over her. "Is that a threat, Ketura?" His venom-coated string of words made me want to scramble.

She didn't back down from his intimidating stance and instead placed a golden crown atop her head. "Yes. If you've forgotten, I got rid of my second in command—the best one I've ever had—just for you. I can have this entire operation shut down within minutes if I wanted to, don't forget that, Grant. You're only able to be here because of me."

Ruffling her skirt, she sauntered past him to the corner of the room. "I want five soldiers by the end of the month, or you will regret it." She finally turned so I could see her face.

She was tanned to that of desert mountains with a petite face, full lips, and a vicious glare behind her hazel eyes. *"That is a promise."* And then she disappeared up the hidden staircase I knew to be over there.

Jae let out a huge sigh, shoulders slumping. "I really hate that wo—"

His words were cut off violently as Grant struck him across the face. I clasped my hands over my mouth to stifle the yelp that almost burst out. I couldn't give away my location now.

"Is what she said true, Jae? Did you volunteer to kill her?" Grant didn't look at him, but his tone of voice made my neck tingle.

Jae clutched his jaw, blood dripping out of his newly busted lip. "I didn't want anyone else getting in trouble for it."

"I didn't ask you that."

"They were going to do it regardless!"

Another hit across the face, and Jae collapsed onto the couch. Grant snatched Jae up by his shirt and drew him close. "What I asked only requires a yes or a no."

Jae sucked in whatever liquid pooled in his mouth and nodded. "Yes."

Grant released him and brushed his shirt down flat. "Why?"

"Because Avalon was dead set on doing it to win some kind of favor with you. And I knew if anyone else did it, it would've ended much worse for them when you found out."

"So you did it to protect them?" Grant asked with genuine concern.

"Yes."

Grant scoffed and turned to face a map on the wall. The same map I'd asked about before. "Don't ever do anything that foolish again. You may be my favorite son, but you're not exempt. I'll deal with Avalon later." He reached into his pocket and procured a handkerchief, tossing it onto Jae's lap. "Clean yourself up and send a message to Mercury. I'm going to need his help. Oh, and how did it go with Rose today?" He added in a tone that suggested they were merely chatting over lunch and not after he'd struck him twice.

Jae bitterly wiped the blood off and shrugged. "There was nothing to find."

Grant reached over and patted Jae's shoulder. "Good. Where is she?"

"I left her in the stables."

The books below me began to wobble, not tolerating my weight anymore. I made the decision to jump down, falling forward onto my knees. I became aware of the stinging in my fingertips. I'd gripped the edge of the grate so hard it left an indention in them.

That was a lot of information to process, but I didn't have time to sit and think about it. I had to get back to the stables before Grant found out I was gone.

I bolted for the door, slamming into it and sliding it aside with a fury. Grabbing my skirt in both my hands to give my legs room to move, I shot back down the dirt tunnel.

Webs glued to my face and arms, but I paid them no mind. I'd gladly take a dozen spiderwebs to the face if it meant I reached the stables before Grant did.

What if he discovered I wasn't there and hit me like that?

My lungs were screaming. I didn't have time to stop and let myself catch my breath. I had to get there before him.

Turning the corner, I skidded to a stop across the dirt floor. My lungs and throat hurt, and I couldn't draw in a deep enough breath to satisfy my body. My hands instantly went to my knees as I heaved and panted, my hair sticking to every drop of sweat on me.

My dress felt ten pounds heavier. It constricted me, not allowing me to draw in any air. I had to get it off me.

I began clawing at the back zipper, desperate to get some relief, when a pair of warm hands grabbed me. I felt a slight tug, and the dress loosened.

My breathing became ragged as I sucked in deep breaths, trying to slow my heart. It never even occurred to me to look for the hand's owner.

Grant's emerald eyes appeared before me, filled with concern. He had crouched down to look at me as I was bent over. His hands never moved from my waist.

My skin crawled at the feel of his hands until I realized he was holding my dress in place. The fabric was loose enough that without him, it would've fallen completely off me.

"Are you okay, Rose?"

I was still gulping down air, unable to speak. Looking at him, feeling his hands on me, all I could think about was him hitting Jae. The look of fear in his eyes as blood ran down his chin.

My heart rate started to slow, and my lungs finally decided to expand fully. My legs shook, and no matter how hard I tried to stay upright, I collapsed into Grant.

"Did you see the shadow again?" he asked more frantically this time, arms tight around me.

Something inside me screamed to lie. Say yes and let that be my story. He couldn't know I saw what he did.

But I was afraid my voice would betray me, give away my deceit. My mouth opened and closed several times before I resigned myself to a single nod.

Whatever it takes to keep him from knowing.

A low grumble came from his chest as his top lip curled. He looked over to a nearby guard and jerked his head toward the tunnel.

Several of them flocked toward the entrance, drawing weapons. But before I could see anything further, I was lifted into Grant's arms. He turned away from the tunnel and took me into a small room adjacent to the tack room.

A mini fridge sat in the corner under a shelf filled with black towels. He pulled a few down and splayed them across the purple rug in the center of the room, all without putting me down.

Once there was a sufficient layer of towels on the ground, he gently laid me on top and wrapped another around my shoulders.

At the release of his hands, my dress collapsed. I scrambled to grab the fabric, trying to avoid exposing my chest.

Grant ran a hand through his hair, took a deep breath, and stared at me. He seemed to grow three feet in height, or maybe I was shrinking away from him.

My cheeks flushed under the weight of his gaze. I became highly aware of all the skin left bare from my now torn dress. The zipper hung in three pieces behind me.

"What were you doing in the tunnel?" His voice was low, almost husky.

My throat tightened in a gulp. "I was trying to get back to the house," I mumbled.

A scoff burst from his lips. "Trying to get back? You were trying to get back to the house? By yourself? After what happened last night?"

"I waited a while in the barn, but nobody came for me."

He slammed a fist on the shelf, causing the wood to crack and splinter. "I can't protect you when you do that."

I flinched involuntarily. Without thinking, I blurted, "Did you want me to stay in the barn all night? Jae left me because you ordered him to, and I was stuck."

In a flash, Grant had kneeled before me, my chin in his fingers. His eyes blazed like a raging forest fire. My mind instantly went back to that image of him hitting Jae.

Was it my turn? I should've kept my mouth shut.

But he didn't strike me. A single tear streaked a path down his left cheek as he pulled me into him. His arms squeezed tightly around me in a hug I did not expect.

My body went rigid, my mind still fluttering with the scene I'd witnessed earlier. I didn't know what to make of his mood swings or his outburst of violence against his son.

He retracted, holding firm to my bare shoulders. "Don't ever feel like you're stuck here. Any of the guards would have walked you safely."

My face pinched. "They all ignored me when I tried to speak to them."

The fire returned to his eyes, and his grip began to sting. "What?" A vicious quiet settled between us.

Did I just trigger another episode? I really didn't want anyone getting hurt because of me.

"Don't hurt them. It's okay."

A golden brow raised at my words. "Why would I hurt my staff?"

My lips were sealed shut. I turned my eyes down to the gown I wore, now dirty and ripped. I really needed to get my own clothes, somehow.

His fingers locked on my chin again, gentler this time, as he tilted my face up. "Would you like to go back to the house now?"

I nodded, and once more, he scooped me up in his arms. It was probably for the best as I couldn't keep my dress up sitting still, much less moving. Plus, I don't think my legs would've actually carried me.

He didn't take the tunnels, instead choosing to take a path through the quiet forest. I tried to ignore the eerie silence, but it seeped into my core.

Luckily it only took around ten minutes for him to walk me to the back door of the cottage. He stopped in front of his door and carefully opened it. Once inside, he sat me down and quickly turned his head. I assumed it was in case my dress slipped too far down.

I felt my cheeks heat once more and glanced around for some clothes. I found the pajamas I'd discarded earlier today folded neatly on the foot of the bed.

Grant also seemed to notice the freshly washed set and handed them to me. He softly brushed my loose hair out of my eyes, his buttery voice taking on a lighter tone as he said, "I didn't mean to get upset with you earlier. I just don't want anything to happen to you."

My head nodded even though I didn't want to. I didn't trust those words, not after what I'd seen.

He studied my face for a moment too long to be comfortable. "I know I scared you, and that's something I will have to make amends for."

When I still didn't respond, his mouth twisted. "I have a meeting tomorrow out of town. I want you to come with me."

"Meeting?"

A small smile played on his lips. "Yes. It would be a great opportunity for you to get out of the house, and we can have a more thorough search for the intruder with you safe."

Now it was my turn to study his face. He seemed so genuine now. Doubt and regret flooded my brain at my reaction to him earlier. Maybe I had overreacted a tad. But it didn't change what I'd seen.

"Okay," I said meekly, looking down at the pajamas still in my arms. I wanted to get out of this gown as soon as possible.

Grant placed a kiss on my forehead and began to head for the door. He stopped right before he reached for the handle and turned to ask me, "Oh. I forgot to ask. How'd it go at the lake today?"

"There was nothing to find." I shrugged. I wasn't sure where that came from, but I felt almost compelled to say it. The more I thought about it, the more I realized it was true. I didn't find anything, and there probably wasn't anything to find anyway.

He nodded thoughtfully, glancing at the dark bathroom across the room. "Do you want me to stay again? For the shadows?"

I shook my head. "No, I think I'll be okay tonight." I wasn't afraid of it anymore anyway.

For some reason I knew they couldn't harm me. They weren't here to hurt me. And I knew I could trust them.

As I climbed into bed, I tried to think back to what changed my mind on them. A small part of my brain tried to scream I was still terrified of them, but it seemed so far away. Like an echo in a canyon. An overwhelming calm enveloped me at the thought of the shadows, chasing away any lingering doubt.

Whatever had changed my mind on them, I was glad. Maybe now I would actually get some sleep.

Chapter Six

A helicopter landed in the backyard the next morning to take us to the airstrip. It was a small, local one, with only our private plane on the runway.

My eyes must've been huge staring at the white jet because Grant wrapped an arm around my shoulders with a chuckle.

"She's something, huh?"

"She?"

His strong jaw flexed with a grin. "Caroline."

My brows wrinkled as I glanced at the plane and back. "You named the plane Caroline?" I couldn't even figure out how he could afford it.

"Why not? People name their cars all the time. Mines just…better." He gave me a reassuring squeeze and helped me up the stairs.

The interior was shockingly not purple. Red carpet lay beneath dark leather seats. A marble bar sat at the rear next to a plush couch and glass table.

"How can you afford all of this?" I asked in awe, reaching out to brush my fingertips against the blankets draped across the seats. They were made of wool and completely black in color, almost void of light.

Avalon slammed into the back of my right shoulder, sending me tumbling into one of the seats. She glanced over her shoulder and put two fingers to her lips.

"Oops. Sorry." She half rolled her eyes and continued down the aisle.

Grant glared after her. The glint in his eyes telling me he'd deal with her later. He reached down to help me, but I waved him off.

"It's fine. I'm probably just gonna sit here anyway." My voice came out breathy and dry. I wet my lips and adjusted the skirt of my dress.

He'd given me another beautiful gown to wear this morning, though this one was much easier to walk in.

It was made of a soft golden material that shifted into a deep blue in certain light. It hugged right below my belly button before cascading down my legs, stopping just short of the ground so I didn't drag it. The neckline rounded into two-inch wide straps that crossed at the back.

I was admiring the color-shifting fabric when I noticed Grant looking at me expectantly.

"I'm sorry. What?"

The corners of his mouth twitched as he leaned back in the seat across from me. "I said I came from a very wealthy family and put my money to good use. Investments and businesses. That's how I'm able to afford this."

I fidgeted with the seat buckle as I said, "You must be a very important person."

He eyed me as he took a sip of the brown liquid from a small glass that wasn't there a moment ago. "You could say that."

After the plane took off and reached altitude, Grant excused himself and walked toward the bar. I remained seated but took the time alone to look at everything else.

Avalon lay on the couch, her legs in Jarred's lap. Trinity stood at the bar, a green bottle in hand. Jae sat adjacent to me, eyes closed and head tilted against the window.

There were no guards in here, even though I'd seen two board the plane earlier. There wasn't anywhere else for them to be, as there were only two doors in here. One that led to the pilot area and the other to the bathroom.

I scanned once more before my eyes connected with Jarred, and my stomach flipped. His eyelids were half lowered as he stared at me, stroking Avalon's head. A hungry grin spread across his lips as I held his gaze.

Quickly I turned back around, trying to melt into the seat. Reaching above me, I snatched the blanket down and draped it around me. For the rest of the flight, I pressed my body as close to the window as I could. Anything to get out of his line of sight. It didn't matter how much distance or materials I put between us. I could still feel his eyes burning into my back.

When we landed, I noted the outside world was very different from the rolling mountains I'd become accustomed to. Snow covered the ground, and there were many evergreen trees packed together.

My body began to shiver as soon as the air touched me. It was a nasty, wet, cold that sank deep into my bones. I wrapped my arms around myself, wishing I'd taken the blanket from the plane.

Then the blanket magically appeared as Grant wrapped it around me. I turned my eyes up to him in surprise.

"How'd you do that?"

He tucked the edges of the blanket into my folded arms with a raised brow. "Do what?"

Warmness began to wash over me as the wool touched my bare arms. The cold melted seamlessly away. "I was just thinking about having the blanket."

He shrugged, a corner of his mouth tilting up. "Great minds think alike."

As everyone got off the plane, I noticed the two guards reappear. They'd been nowhere on the plane that I could see, yet here they were. Dressed in all black with weapons strapped to their hips—a couple guns and knives—the crescent moon emblem pinned to their collars.

My mouth twisted as I took in the severity of their presence. The fact we needed guards at all times wasn't for nothing.

Grant placed a hand on the small of my back as we made our way to the gray building ahead. My eyes had a hard time focusing on its features and dimensions as it almost blended in with the snow.

It wasn't an airport per-say, just a warehouse. Inside were three black vans with tinted windows.

Grant, Avalon, and I climbed into the last van. I couldn't see who took the other two.

As we drove, the view became more obscured by evergreens and hills. The snow had begun to come down in a flurry, causing the driver to pump the brakes a few times. My stomach flipped every time.

"Where are we?" I asked as we turned onto a dirt road.

Avalon snorted, her hand perched on Grant's knee in a possessive fashion.

"Does it matter?" she quipped.

I didn't respond, instead looking down at the blanket in my lap.

"Canada." Grant's voice was quiet, almost indistinguishable from the sounds of the road. But I caught what he said.

Canada. A completely different country. All for what?

When we pulled into a clearing, I knew. Hundreds of cars were parked haphazardly in the grass in front of a white mansion. It was three stories and had a tall fence wrapped around the backside. I could see the fence continued on, but not how far.

The vans halted in front of the double doors, where more guards appeared dressed the same as ours.

I started to reach for the door handle when Grant stopped me.

"Hold on just a second, Rose. I have something for you." He motioned to Avalon, who begrudgingly removed her hand from his knee and reached into the seat pocket. She removed a black box the size of her palm and presented it to him.

Taking a peek inside, he seemed satisfied and turned it to face me. It was a necklace, the most beautiful necklace I'd ever seen.

A giant teardrop-shaped blue stone glittered at the center of a row of diamonds. The chain was silver and had a small row of fringe diamonds near the gem at the center.

I reached a tentative hand out and lightly brushed the jewelry. It was way too nice for me.

"Here. Let me put it on you."

Turning my back to him, I folded my hair into my hands. He reached across and gently clipped the necklace into place.

It shocked me with how lightweight it was. I expected it to be a little heavy, considering the size of the stone.

Pinching the gem between my fingers, I turned to face him. "What is it?"

His eyes trailed the jewelry before they met mine. "Iolite."

"It's beautiful. Thank you."

The smile he gave me sent flutters bounding through my chest. Though the images of him hitting Jae quickly followed behind.

Avalon huffed at our exchange and reached across me to push the door open. As she climbed over me, I noted her pantsuit peeking out from under her coat, which was the same red as her lipstick. Her signature color, I guess.

Grant placed a gentle hand on my back again as I slid out of the vehicle. Immediately Trinity appeared at my side, arm outstretched.

She wore similar attire to the guards. However, she covered her weapons with a thick fur coat.

"You're coming with me for this event," she whispered in my ear as I took her hand. When I glanced back at Grant, she patted my hand and said, "Think of it like I'm your personal bodyguard until we get back on the plane."

I gulped. "Why are we so heavily guarded?"

Trinity gave me a sidelong look, having to raise her chin to look me in the eyes. "You'll see."

And see, I did. We walked through the mansion, up three flights of stairs, and came to a set of black double doors. I could see a balcony of sorts just beyond.

Grant stood at the back of the group, adjusting the sleeves of his wine-colored button-up, with Jae and Jarred positioned on either side of him. Avalon was at the head, tapping her foot impatiently.

I stole another glance at Jae, who seemed as cold and distant as the frost land outside. He didn't look at me. He didn't look at anyone. His eyes were permanently glued to the doors. I wondered if he really was planning on leaving. I could understand why if that's how Grant treated him.

A part of me wanted to bring it up to him, but then he'd know I was spying on them. And I wasn't sure if I trusted anyone enough to tell them that yet.

A sharp whistle caught my attention, my head snapping around to the source. It was Avalon. She waved her red-tipped nails above her head and began to silently count down from five.

Trinity removed her coat and passed it to me. My brows knotted as she shoved the fur into my hands. "You left the blanket in the car."

I looked down, suddenly noticing the lack of warmth around me. My cheeks heated as I slipped on her jacket. It fit me surprisingly well, considering how much shorter she was than me.

"Thank you," I mumbled.

She tucked her hair behind her ears and shrugged. "It's not your fault Grant didn't give you proper attire."

When Avalon reached one, the doors flung wide, and we were ushered forward. I stepped out into the cold air once more, feeling my breath kick from my lungs. But not from the chill.

Thousands of people stood below the balcony, spreading all the way back to the forest. As soon as they saw us, they began to roar.

Trinity guided me to the side while Grant took up front and center. The crowd went wild at the sight of him.

So many people. All screaming and cheering. It was almost deafening. My heart pounded as I scanned the mass below. Some people I could make out, but others seemed blurry. Like I was looking through murky water. My eyes hurt when I stared at them for too long. A few guardsmen along the outskirts of the crowd were the same way. A blob of dirt in the sea.

Banners flapped in the breeze, all printed with the same logo. This must be Grant's logo, or else it wouldn't be everywhere. I wonder what it stands for.

Grant soaked in the applause, his smile as wide as his arms. After a few moments, he raised a hand to silence them, and they all fell deadly quiet. It was as if he had flipped a switch.

"Before I begin, I would like to thank you all for taking time out of your day to join me here. I know some of you traveled a very long distance, and I want you to know I appreciate you. I would also like to thank the generosity of our queen for allowing me to use her home." He made a grand gesture to our right, where I noticed a woman sitting in a chair.

She was the same woman I'd seen with them yesterday. Though, looking at her close-up, she seemed younger than I thought. Maybe close in age to me, whatever that was. Her brown hair lay braided down her back, with a golden crown atop it all. Today she wore a light pink dress with flowers sewn into the bodice. A matching fur coat sat across her shoulders.

Jarred gave a slight bow in her direction, and she tilted her chin in acknowledgment. So they knew each other, then. Obviously, if she was Queen, everyone would know her. But I got the feeling it was deeper than surface level. Her eyes lingered on him far longer than I expected.

Grant said 'our' queen. But nobody had mentioned her before now. If she was my queen, I should've been informed since they know I have no memories.

Agitation began to swell within me. I swayed from left to right, rubbing my arms in a soothing motion. I had no memories and no information about what was going on around me.

I leaned down to Trinity's ear and whispered, "She's Queen?"

Trinity, unwavering in her laser focus around us, responded, "Yes. For us."

What did she mean *us*? Was I included in that? The way Trinity avoided eye contact with me I had a sneaking suspicion I wasn't. "She's not *my* queen?"

"No."

This took me aback. What was different about me? What did that mean for me anyway? Could I get away with not listening to her? Could I skip the formalities like bowing and such?

Probably not. That was more so a sign of respect than anything else. If she even acknowledged me to begin with. She always had her nose turned up whenever I was near.

"Why?" I asked after slight hesitation.

Trinity didn't respond, and maybe that was for the best as Grant had begun speaking again. I wondered if the cold was messing with me because some of his words were as blurry as those people in the crowd.

"How many of you have experienced personal harm because of the—"

The crowd roared their response.

"How many of you have had to relocate your families to keep them safe?"

Another roar.

"No more. I am taking charge against these senseless attacks against our communities. No more will you hide in the shadows while the rest of the world lives out their lives. Oblivious."

A few shouts in agreement. The crowd began to buzz with excitement.

"They have brainwashed our brothers and sisters into joining them. They have done nothing but lie, cheat, and steal their entire existence. No more! Why should we suffer for the actions of those not with our Almighty God? He who blessed us with our longevity, health, and gifts. It's all to him we give thanks."

Hundreds of people shouted 'Amen!' in response. I don't think I'd ever been more confused. Was there a war happening? Who were these people? Had they really been displaced from their homes? And what was Grant to them? A leader? Why wouldn't that be the queen?

"I would like to announce that we have the high ground against them. We are prepared, and we will defend our homes, our families, your families. My army is now ready."

The crowd absolutely erupted with cheers and shouts. They couldn't be settled.

Grant waited peacefully for them to quiet, looking around at them with a wicked grin. Once they finally realized he had more to say, they all fell silent.

"The next time they attack one of our communities, they will feel God's wrath upon them. It's time they go back to Hell from whence they came. Let the Demons take back what they created and anyone who dares defend them."

Another jolt of electricity shot through the crowd, and they cheered and rumbled. I could see a few people raising their fists in support.

"One day, we will be gone, and it will be our children and our children's children who inherit the earth from us. Let's make sure they look back with pride and reverence for what we will accomplish. May every individual realize the importance of our stance against these—. And let them know we will not tolerate any more. We will not hide. No more."

Fireworks shot overhead, exploding with all kinds of vivid colors and patterns. I'm surprised it could even be seen against the white backdrop of the landscape. Then to our right, a giant pyre lit with flames. The crowd chanted unintelligible phrases and threw things at it.

My head swam not only from the blurry people and words but the ever-growing list of questions.

I should ask him. But I couldn't. I knew it was my fear that stopped me. Watching him hit Jae like that sent me spiraling. I didn't think he'd ever hit me, but I couldn't shake the feeling.

As the speech finished, we were quickly driven straight back to the airport. I gave Trinity her coat back and settled into my chair with the blanket once more.

Grant seated across from me, water bottle in hand. "So?"

My eyes flicked to him momentarily. "So what?"

He frowned, unscrewing the lid and taking a long drink before continuing. "The speech?"

I picked at the skin on my lips absentmindedly. "Honestly, I still have no clue what it's about or why. I'm very confused."

"That's natural. You still don't have your memories, so." He studied my face, looking for any reaction.

I met his eyes. Those soft, green eyes. He looked at me like I was the only person on this plane. "So if I had my memories, I would understand?"

A muscle feathered in his jaw. He clearly wasn't expecting me to ask that. "I don't know. I would hope so."

Nodding my head, I turned back to the window. He did know. He knew a whole lot more than he was willing to let on.

"What does your symbol mean?" I asked as I eyed the emblem pinned to his collar.

He stroked his thumb across it tentatively. "The moon represents my people, and the half-filling is the evil that threatens to overtake us. The two slashes are our fight against it."

I bit the inside of my cheek and pulled the blanket tighter. "Are you in a war?"

"Yes."

"Why? You mentioned a God, but I can't understand what religion would have to do with it."

He cocked his head, studying me with a stare not unlike that of a cat watching a bird. "Tell me something, Rose. If you were to come across a set of people with no moral regard for the lives of those you cared about, who actively sought to destroy them, and then discovered they were quite literally created by Demons, what would you do?"

I blanked, skin growing hot around my neck. "Demons don't exist."

He chuckled dryly. "You shouldn't worry yourself with these things anyway."

I should if it included me. Which he made sure it did by bringing me here. But it seemed he wasn't inclined to provide any further information on that subject. In fact, it seemed to aggravate him that I was so curious.

"Who was that girl? The queen?"

Grant made a noncommittal sound. "My niece. Something else you needn't worry yourself over. She's not your queen."

So I was told. "But why not? What makes me different?"

"Lots of things," his voice rang with warning. If I continued asking questions, I wouldn't like what followed. But

I had to. I had absolutely no memory of anything. Questions were my only reprieve.

"You're not going to tell me, are you?"

"It's best if you discover for yourself. No one can tell you what you are or who you are."

That was easier said than done, especially when I was starting from ground zero. Would he even answer my questions about the army he mentioned? Were they the soldiers the queen had mentioned in that room? Were we at war? With who?

The plane began to take off, and Grant leaned his head back, closing his eyes. I would get nothing more out of him for the remainder of this trip. Why did he even bring me? All it did was cause me more anxiety and fill my head with questions.

One answer I do have is that Grant definitely isn't the man he portrays. There's a lot of secrets and hidden rage beneath his collected demeanor. And I would find out what they were.

Chapter Seven

I spent that night in my room, tossing and turning. As my eyes opened to the rising sun, I could've sworn I saw a shadow figure watching in the corner. But as I blinked the sleep away, it vanished.

A fresh gown waited for me outside my door, wrapped in a purple bow with another flower. Unfolding it, I laid it out on the bed to examine.

This dress was similar to yesterday's in the flow and feel but vastly different in appearance. It was the same color green as Grant's eyes, with crystals that shifted rainbows in the light banding across the waist. They bled down the skirt like dew drops on a foggy morning.

Mesh sleeves hung loose, draping my arms like Trinity's fur coat did. I almost didn't even feel the fabric on my skin. It was so light and soft.

The flower was yet again another lily, this time with white petals with a pink stripe down the center and freckles. It was beautiful, but the gesture felt empty now.

Luckily, I'd finally been given a hairbrush, and I spent about thirty minutes brushing through the knots and tangles that had accumulated. When I was done, I braided my hair loosely across my shoulder.

Making my way down the halls, I managed to find myself in the dining room. Jarred, Avalon, and someone I didn't recognize sat at the table conversing quietly.

Jarred looked over at me as I entered, drinking in my appearance. I consciously crossed my arms over my torso and sat as far away from him as I could get. Which ended up being next to the new person.

It was an older man, maybe early thirties, with a bald head and milky-colored eyes. He stared straight ahead as he chewed, listening intently to whatever Avalon prattled on about. His gaze never left the opposing wall.

The food in front of me wasn't as full as the days before. Only some berries and pancakes sat in front of us.

My stomach was still turning from yesterday, so I didn't grab anything. However, when a waiter approached me with a mug of tea, I gladly accepted.

"I'm Sebastian," came the man beside me. His head had turned toward me, but his eyes remained blank. He had his hand out to shake mine, and when my skin touched his, he frowned.

"I'm Rose."

"You have a lovely aura, Rose." And then, under his breath, he said, "And so the soul was tinted gold."

My eyebrows pulled together as I released the shake. "Pardon?"

"Don't listen to him," Avalon chirped. "He's blind. He can't see anything."

Sebastian swiveled his head to her. "Yet I see you pining over someone who will never love you back."

Avalon sneered at him, "Oh, I should weep into my cup." Slamming her chair back, she dragged Jarred out of the room with her.

I relaxed a little now that his hungry gaze was gone, but my skin still prickled like I was being watched.

Sebastian chuckled, popping a strawberry in his mouth.

I peered at him out of the corner of my eye. Was he really blind? That would explain the milky eyes and lack of movement. But when he looked at me a second ago, it felt like he could see me.

"What's an aura?" I asked cautiously, sipping the tea.

Sebastian leaned back in his chair, chewing thoughtfully. "It's a ring of colored light around one's body that shows a person's energy. Everyone has them, but few can see them."

My mouth skewed to the side at that information. "You can see them, though?" I didn't want to outright ask him if he was actually blind. That felt rude.

"Yes. It's one of the few things I *can* see."

"What's mine look like?"

Sebastian took another look in my direction before saying, "Like glittering gold. But there's a purple edge."

"Oh." I didn't know what that meant, and the way he was looking at me kept me from asking.

It was so weird. I could almost feel his eyes searching my brain. Goosebumps pricked my arms, and I turned my eyes away from him.

"What does that mean?"

He stood from the table and gave me a reassuring touch to the arm. "Good things, I suppose. You're kind, caring, compassionate. But there's a dark edge to you as well, just waiting to come forward. Be wary of that." Then he, too, left the room.

I sank lower in my chair, feeling as alone and confused as I had my first day here.

The next few weeks all blurred together in repetition. Wake up. Eat. Wander the house. Be avoided by everyone. Bathe. Eat. Sleep.

I grew so bored I began plucking grass from the front yard and counting how many I could pick at one time without getting the root.

Everyone seemed busy as of late, barely speaking more than a few words to me. I never saw Sebastian again, and maybe that was for the best, as he kind of creeped me out.

I started to wonder if I'd imagined him in the first place, but then remembered Grant had mentioned him the time I went to the map room.

He was an odd man for sure, and I still didn't know what the hell he meant by 'soul tinted gold.' Perhaps I wasn't meant to hear it.

One thing remained consistent, though: I always got a new flower every morning. I didn't know their names, but they were still very beautiful. On the days Grant could not see me, which was more often than not, I'd also get a heartfelt letter telling me to enjoy my day but to not leave the house.

One morning, after staring at the yellow petals of a new lily, I grew fed up with being alone and decided I was going to pin down Jae and make him talk to me. I had so many burning questions, and they needed answers.

He wasn't in his room or the map room. I checked the dining room and the study. Nowhere. Only silent guards.

I spent two hours wandering the halls before I stumbled across a new set of double doors. It actually had a nameplate beside it reading: workout center.

Not knowing where else to look, I decided to push through.

Inside was a war zone. Small fights were taking place all over the tiny space. Some of it was hard to see, like the crowd at the mansion. My eyes hurt to look at it.

Suddenly, a spear lodged itself into the wall to the right of my head. I shrieked and ducked, wrapping my arms around my head.

"Yo, what the hell is she doing in here?" A voice shouted from across the room.

Then silence filled my ears. I looked up to see the fighting had stopped, and only four people stood staring at me.

Trinity with a blue staff in her right hand, hair pulled back, and knives belted across her waist. Avalon perched high in the rafters, checking her nails. Jarred with a double-bladed ax, full armor, and a helmet. And then Jae, sweaty with no weapon and shirtless, revealed the scar I'd noticed before.

It wrapped from his belly button around his side to his back. It was gruesome, and I didn't even want to imagine what could've caused a wound like that.

"What are you doing in here?" Jarred demanded as he stalked toward me.

I stood, glancing around in utter confusion. It had been chaos only moments ago, but now it looked as if nothing had happened.

Jarred halted a few feet from me, taking in my sour expression with a grin.

Jae appeared to his left, looking more concerned than anything.

"What happened? There was just a battle going on here!" I frantically glanced between their stares, begging for some kind of answer for once.

Jarred nodded as if he finally understood something and chuckled. "Avalon, show her."

With a snap of her fingers, a giant man came barreling toward us. I screamed and cowered, waiting for impact. But Jarred stepped up, swinging his ax high. As soon as the blade touched the man, he fizzled out and disappeared.

Jarred turned back to face me with an animal grin. "It's a hologram," he explained. "It's how we practice without actually getting hurt." He flipped the ax over and used it to prop himself up.

"Hologram?"

Jae grabbed my elbow and steered me toward the door. "It's fake. You shouldn't be here."

I snatched my arm away from his grasp and seethed. "I wouldn't have to if you'd quit avoiding me."

A sharpness reached his gray eyes at my words. "Is that what you think?"

"Whoa, whoa. What's going on here?" Jarred purred.

"Nothing," Jae snapped. "Go back to your room, Rose."

"No."

Jarred squeezed behind us and blocked the exit door. "I wanna hear this. Maybe Grant will, too."

A vicious rumble bellowed from Jae, who shoved me behind him protectively. "Is that a threat?"

Jarred sniffed, wiping a bead of sweat from his brow. "Not at all."

"Then let us out."

"No."

I could almost see the anger radiating off of Jae. Maybe it was a bad idea to confront him after all.

"Jarred, let them through," Trinity called from behind us.

"Not until I hear what this is about."

In the blink of an eye, Jae was nose to nose with Jarred. "Move. Or I'll make you move."

An evil glint lit in Jarred's eyes. "Is that a threat?"

"Absolutely."

Trinity appeared, shoving her staff in between the two men, effectively separating them. "Jarred, move."

Jarred shrugged, stepping aside. "Don't worry. We'll have plenty of time to discuss this later."

Jae immediately latched onto my arm a little hard and yanked me through the door. We stumbled down the hallway until we were out of sight of the workout center. Then he spun me around, jerking me into the wall.

"Ow." I cradled the shoulder that took the impact.

Jae's eyes softened when he realized he'd hurt me, and he beckoned to see the injury.

The sleeve had torn, and the area was red where I'd hit.

He frowned, biting the inside of his cheek. "That's gonna bruise. I'm sorry."

"I don't care."

"You should."

"Why? Because of Grant?"

His demeanor flashed cold, and he stepped back from me, saying nothing. He stared down the hall, eyes going distant.

I twisted my mouth to the side and crossed my arms. "You're afraid of him."

"You know nothing."

"I know he hits you."

Jae flinched, my words taking a visible blow, but he stood his ground. "You're wrong."

"Am I? You stare at the ground every time he's around and follow his orders like a little puppy. Everyone does!"

"We have to."

"Because he'll hit you otherwise?"

"Because he's my commander."

"Did he command you all to avoid me?" I demand, stomping my foot as my temper flared.

He ran a hand through his hair, puffing his cheeks up. "You need to drop this."

"Or what? You'll hit me too?"

Hurt flashed through his gaze. "I would never. Grant is…complicated."

"Because he's your dad, right? Is that why you follow him and let him walk all over you?"

"No."

"Who is Grant anyway? I keep hearing about this war you're in, and people getting killed, and that speech he gave. But nobody will explain anything to me."

Jae propped himself on the wall, obviously in effort not to slam his fist into it. "That's because we *can't*."

"But why? Why am I made to sit in silence and suffer alone like this with no memories and no guidance? I'm going absolutely insane!"

Jae threw his hands up in exasperation. "What do you want from me, Rose?"

Folding my arms, I stared him down. "I want to go with you."

Confusion wrinkled his brow. "What are you talking about?"

"The clothes in your room. You don't put them away. You have nothing in there that suggests you live there or even stay there aside from that pile of clothes in the chair. If you're leaving, I want to go with you."

He slammed his hand over my mouth, looked both ways down the hallway, and glowered at me. "I'm not. I can't."

I shoved his hand away. "Can't? Or won't?"

His mouth opened to respond when we were suddenly interrupted by another voice.

"Who's leaving?"

I turned my eyes to look over Jae's shoulder and met the hooded lids of Jarred. He couldn't have been there long as Jae had just looked, but his face read like he'd heard everything.

Jae placed himself in front of me. "Nobody."

Jarred, still holding the ax, sized us up. His lips turned up in an empty smile. "She's not going anywhere."

My heart sank, skipping beats as it went. He stepped closer, seeming to grow in size.

"Don't touch her," Jae growled, the sound coming from deep within his chest.

"I outrank you. You don't get to tell me what to do." He stepped closer.

Jae scooted back closer to me, almost pinning me to the wall. "You know Grant would have your head if you laid a hand on her."

Jarred licked his lips excitedly. "Grant's not here." With lightning speed, he reached around Jae and snagged me around the bicep. Yanking with force, he tore me from my position, the motion causing me to stumble and fall, crying out from the pain as my shoulder joint pulled from its socket.

My fingers pried uselessly at his hand, trying desperately to get out of his grasp. The tendons and muscles in my shoulder ached as they tried to pull the joint back in but kept being pulled apart by his hold on me.

"You're coming with me." His icy eyes gleamed with satisfaction, a malice I'd yet to see in anyone. My heart raced with a newfound fear. A prey to a predator.

Then hands appeared around Jarred's face from behind, and with a quick jerk of his chin, his eyes went dark. He collapsed in front of me, a limp mass, eyes wide and unfocused.

Grant stood in his place, face flushed and panting.

I looked back and forth between the two for only a moment before realization hit. And then I screamed.

My one useful hand hovered over my face as I panicked.

Jarred was dead. Grant had snapped his neck. No. It was more than that. My eyes suddenly focused on the raw, bloody edges under his neck.

He'd ripped his head from his body.

A small stream of blood trickled from the corner of his mouth, pooling on the wood below. Still, his lifeless eyes bore into mine.

I struggled to breathe between my screams, throat burning from the effort. Unwilling tears began to fall, my body feeling hot and shaky.

It was as if I wasn't even in my body. My head turned and tumbled, my vision blurry. But I could've sworn I saw myself slumped on the floor, screaming at his body.

Grant stooped down to me and swiftly realigned my shoulder. The sickening, deep thud it made emptied my stomach. I wretched every last bit of food in me and wretched more when I saw it melding with Jarred's blood. At the end of it, I was drooling more than vomiting, even though my stomach insisted I had more to throw up.

"Get her out of here," Grant ordered.

Without hesitation, Jae hooked me under the arms and began towing me down the hall. I never stopped screaming—or was it crying? It had turned into a horrific mixture of both, just struggling to get air at the same time.

I couldn't keep track of time, it all ran together, and in an instant, I was back in my room. Jae cast me a warning look before slamming the door shut.

Tripping on the now torn skirt of my dress, I scrambled to lock the door. My screams subsided, turning into loud sobs as I struggled to push my dresser in front of it.

After a few painstaking minutes of pressing onto my still throbbing shoulder, I managed to wedge the dresser under the knob and across the doorway.

My knees gave way, and on the way down, I hit the side of my head on the corner of the barricade I'd made. It stung, and I was almost sure I saw blood where my fingers touched. But my mind was far too enveloped in what I'd just witnessed to care.

The image of his lifeless eyes followed my every move as I curled into a ball on the floor and cried myself into total darkness.

Chapter Eight

Darkness came, but I didn't sleep. No, I doubted I would ever sleep again for the rest of my life. I couldn't. How could I when the only thing I could see was Jarred? Every time I blinked, there he was, staring at me behind dead fish eyes and bleeding from the mouth? His neck was bent at an odd angle I hadn't noticed originally.

His gurgled last breath haunted the silence. Noise had to be happening at every second. I opened the window, kindled the dying fire, hummed. Anything but allow the quiet to invade, where his presence lingered.

My shoulder never stopped aching, and I couldn't tell if it was from the initial injury or the resetting of the joint. It didn't matter, in all honesty. I had more daunting things on my mind.

It had been blood on my fingers earlier when I hit my head. Luckily, it was only a small cut that clotted fairly quickly. But some blood had dried in my hair, and it too pulsed a dull thrum.

The sun rose after an ever-dragging night, bathing the room in a fresh light, but I felt no warmth from it. At some point, I'd managed to peel the dress off of my sweaty body and crawl under the covers. I couldn't remember when I'd done that. It all blurred together like a whirlwind…ending with Jarred's face.

I didn't like him, I won't lie. He made me very uncomfortable, but I didn't want him to die. Especially not in front of me. Not like that.

Not long after the sun reached its peak, a knock sounded at my door. I pulled the covers over my head, hoping if I ignored it, whoever it was would go away. But they didn't. The doorknob jiggled a few times before everything went silent. For a heartbeat, I thought they were gone until I heard the voice.

"Rose?" It was Grant. "Rose, I brought you breakfast. Can you let me in?"

I bit my lower lip to stifle the cry forming in my throat. *Go away. Go away. Please go away.* There was no way I could look at him right now, no way I could stare him in the eyes.

"You don't have to," he continued, quieter than before.

Even as kind and as remorseful as he sounded, I still was too terrified to leave the safety of my bed. He snapped so suddenly and killed someone just as fast. I hadn't even seen him before it happened. He'd materialized out of thin air and ripped someone's life away from them without a second thought. That made him very dangerous to me.

"I'll leave it out here for you. I'd like to talk if you feel up to it later." The tinkling clunk alerted me to the tray being set on the ground. Footsteps thudded down the hall until they faded from earshot. My stomach rumbled and bubbled, but I couldn't move. I wouldn't move. What if it was a trick? What if he was still out there waiting for me to pop my head out?

I wasn't hungry anyway. Thinking of eating made me want to hurl. No, I think I will stay here under the covers where it's safe.

A small part of me knew I wasn't truly safe under this thin sheet and blanket. However, if I had to face that reality right now, I would lose it.

I left a sliver of the covers open to let in the light, as I refused to remain in the darkness on purpose.

Time melted and mixed together, sending me spiraling into another fit of hysteria as I was reminded of drowning. It seemed to flow exactly as it had then: infinite, empty.

When the light began to throw a golden hue, I lowered the blanket. A warm breeze drifted through my open window, which felt like opening an oven to me after being buried all day. My body was sticky; I was red-faced and drowsy. I needed a bath but was still not willing to set foot outside this room. At least not in the house itself.

I padded to the window, pushing the table aside and ducking low enough to not be seen if anyone stood there. When peering over the sill, I was met with nothing but grass. No guard was posted. I began to lift myself up and through the window when a guard walked into view.

Releasing my hold, I practically threw myself to the floor, hoping and praying he hadn't seen me. But as I listened, his footsteps continued walking away from my window. Peeking back, I was once again met with nothing but grass.

So not stationed.

A plan began to take shape in my mind. It was fuzzy and lacked any conviction, but it was a plan, nonetheless.

Sliding down the wall until my knees were pulled into my chest, I breathed deeply. If I could figure out the time span between the guards passing by, I could make an escape. And I would escape.

A shadow crossed the edge of my vision, and I flinched momentarily before whipping my head to the location. Nothing was there. Yet, as I stared, another shadow passed where I'd once been looking.

A nerve pricked as I turned my head once more, sending shooting pain up my neck. I rubbed the spot, still seeing nothing.

"Hello?" I cautiously called out, my voice carrying barely more than a whisper.

No answer, but the shadow did reform in my peripheral. I didn't try to look at it directly this time, just studied it as I focused on a spot on the wall.

"Who are you? What do you want?" Of course, I received no response. It was a shadow, after all.

Its presence oddly calmed me. I felt no animosity from it, nothing to give me pause. It simply stayed at the edge of my vision like it waited for something.

Sighing, I buried my face in my arms. This was surely a sign I'd gone crazy.

"Rose?"

Raising my head, I thought the shadow had spoken to me. But when I heard the shifting of feet outside the door, I knew Grant had returned.

"You didn't eat," he observed, picking the tray up. "I'm sorry. I didn't mean to scare you. I'm just trying to protect you." When I still didn't respond, he added, "Even if you're upset, please eat something."

His feet stomped away, showing his hidden anger under the words.

I almost burst out into laughter at the idea of me just being 'upset.' He'd murdered someone in front of me. I think that pushed me well beyond upset.

Feeling another wave of tears well up in me, I slammed my palms to my eyes, pressing so hard I saw stars. "What am I going to do?" I whispered to the figure in the corner.

Still no answer from the shadow, but when I opened my eyes again, it had shifted closer to my actual line of sight.

The sunlight faded, drifting further and further below the horizon. The fire blazed to life in the hearth I hadn't noticed had gone dead. And the shadow remained, taking on a shape that never really settled between being strictly Human or a blob.

The soft pitter-patter outside alerted me to the incoming rain, and I reached up to shut the window. Couldn't risk the fire going out from the wind or water. It was the only thing keeping me sane.

That night was spent huddled under the window, staring into the fire, and every so often talking to my new shadow companion. I talked out my ideas for potential escape and took its shifting form to be yes or no answers.

I cried several more times, overcome with grief not only for Jarred but for myself. I didn't truly know who I was, and I would probably never know. I'm sure if Grant had his way, I'd be locked in this house for the rest of my existence, made to wear pretty clothes and eat beside him at dinner. I had no purpose, and that was the most devastating of all.

The shadow never left me, not as long as I kept from looking at it directly. It kept me from spiraling even deeper inside myself.

The morning came, and once again, I'd not slept, and my body began to feel every bit of that decision.

My head pounded, eyes were blurry, and my mouth felt cotton dry. Not only did my stomach rumble with hunger, but I was so incredibly thirsty. All the crying I'd done had wiped me out. Swallowing was hard and did nothing to wet my mouth. My lips were chapped and stuck together on top of the dried tears crinkling my cheeks.

So, when the tray of food arrived this morning, carried by Jae today, I debated heavily on opening the door.

I crawled over to it, leaned my ear against the door, and licked my lips. I heard when Jae sat the tray down and when he took up residence beside it on the floor. My heart sank as I realized I would not be getting anything to drink, not while he sat beside it.

Anxiety ripped its way through me as I thought of every possible scenario of me opening the door, and none of them ended well.

After a few minutes of silence, he began talking, not about anything in particular—in fact, he was merely describing anything his eyes landed on—but just kept the silence from being too loud.

The shadow lingered by the fire, shifting its form like crazy. It was trying to tell me something, but it moved so fast I couldn't make out an answer. In my limited interaction with it, I only understood yes and no.

A soft tap right by my head jolted me backward.

"Can you just let me know you're alive, at least?" The plea in Jae's voice, and the memory of him trying to protect me from Jarred, forced me to give two soft knocks with my knuckles.

"Thank you. I know you're probably not hungry still, but I did bring some water. You need to have something to drink soon. The body can only go three days without water."

Well, I would drink something if you left. I'm not opening the door with you out there.

And as if he had read my mind, I heard him get up and walk away. Once I was sure he was gone, I pried the dresser out from under the knob. My arms were weak and shaky, and I was lucky to scoot it a few inches. I was low on strength and resolve.

The door opened just wide enough for me to squeeze my hand through and grab the bottled water sitting on the tray. Eggs and toast covered a round plate, the smell wafting from them, turning my belly. But that nagging voice at the back of my mind told me they could be drugged. Anything to catch me off guard and get in here. The water was sealed, and I knew for sure they couldn't have tampered with it.

Shutting the door, I used my shoulders to push the dresser back—toes digging into the carpet for leverage until it was safely wedged once more.

I downed the water, forcing myself to go slow enough as to not choke. I felt instantly better and wiped the excess from my mouth.

The shadow formed near the window, and I took that as a sign to investigate.

Blood Return

When I peered over the ledge, I saw one guard walk by, inspecting everything as he went. When he left, I didn't drop down. Instead, I waited and counted the passing time. The next guard made their way past my window exactly two minutes after the previous one. That didn't allow much time for an escape.

My room was on ground level, so getting out won't be an issue. I bet getting to the tree line at the edge of the field would be my most difficult task, as it looked like more than a two-minute sprint. If I could even sprint running this low on energy.

I would have to sleep and eat before I tried to leave, as there was no way I could do it in the state I was in currently. But that meant facing the dark, where Jarred waited with the nightmares that would surely accompany him.

The shadow drifted over by the fire, and I ran my ideas past it. It didn't give me a clear answer to any of them, which frustrated me. I needed to get out of here.

That evening Jae returned, speaking to me for another hour or so about random things before taking the tray and leaving once more.

The fact he didn't bother to apologize or talk about the event made me feel better, yet worse, all at the same time.

How dare he pretend it didn't happen. How dare he pretend it didn't shatter me completely. But also, thank you for not continuing to bring it up and throw me right back into the thick of it. Thank you for not treating me like a wounded animal.

I wanted to be strong. I needed to be. That's how I would survive. That's how I would find out who I really am.

I fought off sleep the entire night, my eyelids growing heavier with each passing minute. But I couldn't let sleep take me. With each blink, I was thrust back into the hallway, staring at my vomit mingling with blood.

At some point, I must have fallen asleep because when I opened my eyes, I was facedown on the carpet. I felt like a truck had run me over. Like that nap had made it worse than if I'd just stayed up.

When dawn arrived, I was empty. Everything hurt, and I was filled with the sudden determination to escape. I had half a mind to climb through the chimney if I was sure I wouldn't get stuck.

The shadow lingered by the window, creating another idea. I opened the glass panes, waiting for the guard to pass. The silence of the forest seemed to swell with each passing second. Something wasn't right about those woods. Something was out there. I felt it deep down. Of which I would rather face than go out there in the hallway…with him.

The guard passed. Now was my chance. I didn't care how thirsty I was or how exhausted my body felt. I had to get out of here.

But before I could make my move, a knock at the door signaled Jae's arrival with breakfast. Pain pinged in my gut at the smell of the food, my mouth watering uncontrollably. I was so hungry. I contemplated eating a bite for extra strength before Jae's words sunk in.

"Grant is having a special dinner tonight. He said you are to wear the garment he brings you and come willingly, or he will break down this door and drag you there himself."

Chapter Nine

The gown I'd been instructed to wear was different from every other. The skirt draped behind me like a train exposing the satin pant legs. It was periwinkle in color but shifted hues of red and blue in different strokes of light.

It had long sleeves which started in the middle of my arm, with a straight neckline that settled under my collarbones.

There were no jewels this time. The fabric did all the work.

I wrapped my hair on top of my head, hoping to hide some if the dried blood that still cling to it.

The dark circles under my eyes had gotten worse. Not sleeping these last few days had really taken its toll on me. But that didn't matter. As soon as this dinner was over, I was getting out of there.

Trinity was the one to escort me to the dining hall, dressed in black leathers. She didn't say anything other than a greeting. Whatever small talk I tried to make only got shrugs and muffled sounds in response.

That was fine by me. I was still reeling from the events a couple days ago. I wondered if maybe she also was upset. I didn't know how close she was with Jarred or if she even cared. I'm sure losing a comrade was tough, nonetheless.

A part of me was glad he was gone so I didn't have to sit under his weighted gaze. But I wouldn't wish death on him, especially not the way it happened.

I could still see it when I closed my eyes. The memory never faded, no matter how hard I tried to shove it down. How his eyes rolled back. The crack of his neck snapping. The gurgled sound that escaped his throat. The blood and vomit.

A shiver ran down my spine as my stomach twisted. If I'd had any food in me, I definitely would've thrown it up.

The hallways were quiet. My heartbeat rang in my ears to fill the silence. Guards were at every single door now, dressed in full armor, the symbol adorned across their chest plate. As stoic and unmoving as the wall behind them. Their presence made my heart drop.

If there were this many inside, how many did he have outside? How many lurked around the corners that I couldn't see?

We finally arrived in the dining hall, and I was greeted with a solemn sight.

Guards lined the entire room, a few blurry and hard to look at. The black table was bare and nearly completely full of guests.

Jae sat on the right side near the head of the table with Avalon next to him. Sebastian was next to her, seated beside an empty chair. Nobody spoke, instead choosing to chew on their grief.

I sat in my usual spot on the left side across from Jae, with Trinity taking up the seat next to me. Nobody looked at me.

We sat in silence for a few minutes before the doors opened, and a familiar face walked in. It was the queen, with a few of her own guards.

Her eyes were puffy as if she'd just been crying, and she carried a frilly handkerchief in her left hand. Her dress was as lifeless as her face and black as night. A mourning gown.

She took up a spot at the foot of the table, fixed her brown curls, and composed herself to a scary calm.

Still, nobody said a word. But now, I couldn't tell if it was out of grief or fear.

It was another few minutes in the deafening quiet before the study doors opened, and Grant walked through.

Everyone stood when they saw him, and I followed suit. He made his way to the head of the table, nodding at everyone individually except for me. When he did look at me, I looked down at my hands.

In my peripheral, I saw him extend an arm in my direction, and I instinctively shied away. I didn't want him touching me. Not with the same hands, he murdered Jarred with.

He dropped his arm, our exchange happening in the blink of an eye, and motioned for everyone to sit. Immediately trays of food were served in front of us. Steak, potatoes, and some kind of green vegetable.

My stomach still flipped from earlier, but when I noticed Grant staring me down, I decided to try a few bites. It turned into me scooting the pieces of meat around my plate while making half-hearted attempts to actually eat it. It was rare. So rare, I was afraid the juice was blood. And then I started thinking about the blood dribbling out of Jarred's slack mouth.

Why were we even here? Jae had said this was an important dinner, but nothing was happening. We all ate in silence. I was forced out of my room for this? Forced to sit in the company of a murderer, sit next to him for this? I don't care what he said about it being to protect me, either. He didn't have to kill him. Especially not in front of me. I could've been making my escape by now.

The sounds of everyone chewing had just begun to bother me when Grant cleared his throat.

We all turned to look at him as he dabbed his mouth with a napkin.

"Ketura. I once again extend my deepest apologies for what happened."

The queen dropped her fork on her plate, not even caring when it bounced and flung juice across her arms. A new rage burned in her eyes. "Well, maybe if you could learn to control your temper."

Grant pressed his lips into a hard line. "I understand you're angry with me. But it had to be done. He was a danger to the people here."

I felt it—bile rising up in my throat. My mouth started to fill with saliva. I closed my eyes tightly, trying to will it back down. I spent the last few days trying desperately to get away from the situation, and now they were discussing it in front of me.

She dug her nails into the wood, making the worst scraping sound I've ever heard. "I don't believe you."

Grant shrugged, taking another bite of his steak. "Regardless. I'm holding this dinner to make it up to you."

She folded her arms across her chest, challenging him. "Oh? It better be the soldiers you promised me. No, better yet, I want even more now that you have taken my right-hand man from me."

"As I recall, he became my right-hand man of his own free will. The comforts of your bed no longer seemed to appeal to him."

The tension escalated. I could almost see the tethered strands connecting them pull taught.

A dark light hovered over everyone. I blinked a few times, trying to get it to go away, but it remained. The lack of sleep must be getting to me because I definitely saw a black umbrella-like cloud hovering over our heads. Almost a mist.

Ketura balled her fists, face turning red with effort. "You may be my uncle, but you forget who you speak to and what power I hold."

"Loosen your crown, my dear. I have something better for you than soldiers." He grinned, still chewing, and snapped his fingers. Two guards pulled the study doors open, and a man walked into the room.

He had dark brown hair, caramel-colored eyes, and what could only be described as a butt chin. He towered over the guards with his shoulders back and hands in his pockets.

Everyone stopped eating at the sight of him. Jae went pale, fork clanging to the ground.

Grant stood from his chair and walked over to clasp the man's hand. I could faintly see a red outline around him, more rust-colored than apple.

I rubbed my eyes, hoping my delusions would fade. But the red stayed.

"Ketura, I'd like you to meet the new head commander: Morgan Argentine."

Morgan bowed to the queen, straightening his black shirt. "Pleasure to meet you." His voice was thick with an accent I couldn't place.

She stood, circling the man with a steady eye and a finger pressed to her lips. "How did you manage it?"

Morgan smiled deadly before saying, "It's what I was designed to do."

Jae stared at his plate, eyes blinking rapidly. He was battling something in his mind. Avalon gave him a sidelong look, twirling her hair in her hands.

They all now had colors around them. Avalon with a muddy brown, and Jae a dark blue with spots of black.

Rubbing my eyes once more, they still remained. I really needed to get out of here.

"Head commander?" Ketura asks with a raised brow.

"That's correct. I will oversee the rest of the soldiers and pick those best qualified to serve you."

Ketura looked pleased, running a finger down his arm. "Do I get a say in who I want?"

"You can have whomever you like."

Trinity pushed her plate away from her, face contorted in disgust. Jae disappeared under the table, I assume to grab his fork.

Grant motioned for Morgan to have a seat, and he took up residence at the empty chair next to Sebastian. Ketura clung to his arm, drawing lines up and down his bicep.

"Yes, you will make a fine replacement," she purred.

"Are you satisfied?" Grant asked as he returned to his chair.

Ketura waved her hand, too busy staring at Morgan. But he had turned his attention to Jae, who'd reappeared from under the table.

"Are you not going to say anything to me?" He asked.

Jae finally looked at him, eyebrows raised. "What would you like me to say?"

"A hello would be nice. It's been years since we've seen each other."

"And whose fault is that?" Jae snapped, gripping his fork so hard I thought he'd break it.

Morgan studied Jae with a tilt of his head. A move Jae did not like at all. That poor fork.

"I heard you did some spy work. Sounded like you did a good job at it, too," Morgan said as he cut into his steak.

The compliment only seemed to make Jae angrier. "What's it to you?"

"Jae!" Grant chastised.

He ducked his head, setting the silverware onto his plate. I could see his jaw clenching with an unspoken response.

"You should really learn to show some respect to those with a higher rank than you." Grant's voice cut like the knives in front of us. Even I flinched at the weight of those words. It almost implied an *or I'll show you how*.

I pushed my plate away, too. Looking anywhere but at the people in here or the bloody meat on my plate.

The wolf painting stared back at me. The lights were too bright, the voices too loud. Some of the guards were blurry.

My throat began to tighten. My breathing came faster, and I wanted nothing more than to cover my ears and scream to drown everything out.

I wanted out.

I needed out.

I was so overwhelmed, but every time I closed my eyes, I saw Jarred's dead body.

"Are you okay, Rose?" Trinity's twinkle-star voice cut through the noise. It pulled me ever so slightly back to the table.

Opening my eyes, I noticed everyone was staring at me now. Heat flooded my cheeks as I gave a small nod to Trinity. But as I cast my eyes toward her, I noticed there was something off. I couldn't really place it, but something wasn't right.

Continuing to glance around the room, I began to grow confused. It all seemed too dull, too stagnant. Two dimensional.

Jae noticed my curious glancing and began slowly surveying the room himself.

Grant kept his eyes on me, softening as he took in my disheveled appearance. He'd finally noticed the bags under my eyes, my sunken cheeks, and my sickly skin.

Jae cut his eyes to me with an answer in them. One, I was on the cusp of grasping.

It was only after I looked down at myself did I realize what it was.

All the shadows were gone.

Chapter Ten

Seconds. Three seconds to be exact. That's how long it took for everything to go to hell.

The mist that hovered over us vanished, along with the colors surrounding the individuals. The table vibrated ever so slightly. If you weren't paying attention, you might not have noticed it.

But it got worse. The silverware rattled, the plates jingled. Lanterns hanging on the walls clattered to the ground.

It wasn't just the table vibrating. The walls began to shudder.

And then shadows began rising from the floor. Seeping from the walls. Humanoid shadows. They crawled through the table, peeled themselves from the paintings. Some had weapons, objects I recognized from the guards around the room.

Grant flew from his chair, screaming orders at the guards. Trinity leaped up onto the table, knives drawn. Avalon became a blur.

I ducked under the table, covering my ears. It was no use. I could still hear the slashing and dicing. The killings. Above me, a sword plunged through the table. I screamed, cowering as close to the ground as possible.

Jae appeared above me, reaching out. I reached back only to realize he wasn't grabbing me. He was after the necklace. He snatched it off my neck, breaking the chain, and urged, "Go! Run!"

I bolted from under the table, taking a glance around. That was my biggest mistake. I witnessed the most horrifying thing I have ever seen.

Avalon was surrounded by an orange light, levitating off the ground. Trinity, Grant, Sebastian, and Morgan had all disappeared.

There were a few guards fighting the shadows, but they were losing miserably. Every time they went to stab the shadow, their blade went right through it. But that wasn't the worst part.

Monsters were fighting them as well. Giant blue zombie-like creatures with open wounds, empty eye sockets, and black liquid oozing out from them. They were so tall they had to bend forward to even fit in the room. They swung wildly at the shadows, phasing completely through them.

I screeched, my hands flailing violently as I ran from the room. But there was no reprieve in the hallways. Shadows lurked there, too. Fighting the remaining guards or just staring at me.

I sprinted toward my room. I don't know what I intended to do once I got there, maybe crawl out the window, but that was the only place I wanted to go.

Careening around corners, I slammed through a shadow. Its coldness sent a shock through my body, making me stumble. My skirt was heavily dragging behind me. I reached back to fold it into my arms but couldn't get a good enough grasp on it.

I was only another corridor away from potential safety when I slammed into something real. A man.

He was about my height with black curly hair, almond-shaped eyes, and an upturned nose. He had the palm of his hand out, intending for me to stop before I ran into him.

I backpedaled, about to cry out for help, when I noticed something. His eyes were purple. A vivid indigo. The eyes from the lake.

Freezing in place, I took in his appearance more carefully. Seeing the same brown shoes from the lake as well as a matching leather jacket. He turned his palm over to face up, indicating he wanted me to take his hand.

"Who are you?" I asked, looking around for guards or…creatures.

"That's not important. What's important is that you come with me." His voice was heavy with an accent I couldn't place.

His hand never wavered in its upturned position in a lethal steadiness I'd yet to see in anyone besides Grant.

A loud bang echoed from behind me, with voices yelling in response. It wouldn't be long before someone found me and made sure I couldn't escape.

I looked at his hand again, then back to his eyes. I couldn't read them.

More yelling from behind.

Was he trying to get me out? I wanted out. I'd just been begging the universe for it. I'd made an escape plan for my room. Or was this another trap?

"Where are we going?"

"Away from here. Far away."

Footsteps thudded closer and closer. My time was running out.

"It's now or never."

My options were clear. Stay here with Grant and risk being cooped up the rest of my life with no memories. Or go with the stranger from the lake, who I have no idea if he's going to kill me or not.

I clasped his hand, and he pulled me in, wrapping his arms tightly around me. Then we were sinking. Lower and lower. Melting into the floor.

Panic started to bubble up in me until I realized we weren't melting. We were phasing. Just like the shadows. We went through the floor and into the earth, continuing to sink through the dirt.

I couldn't believe my eyes. This was impossible. Everything I'd seen in the last few minutes was impossible.

Shadows didn't move on their own. Those…things—monsters—shouldn't exist. We were phasing through solid ground.

My head spun, feeling light all of a sudden. Though I wasn't afraid of the shadows, it still didn't make sense to me.

We finally exited the ground and found ourselves in a dirt tunnel reminiscent of the one I'd been in a week ago.

He set me down gently, keeping his hands near me as I wobbled. I bent down, resting my hands on my knees to keep the vomit from coming up.

Then he was behind me, ripping off the skirt. "What are you doing?"

He didn't speak until he'd torn the entire thing off, leaving me with just the pants. "Skirt's too heavy. It'll slow us down."

Straightening, I crossed my arms. I planned to ask him who he was when he made eye contact with me. But he didn't look at me as he began marching down the tunnel. I scrambled to keep up, taking off the heels Grant had forced me to wear with this outfit.

"Wait!" I called out. "You still haven't told me who you are."

He still didn't look at me as he continued the path. He also didn't say anything.

"Hello? I'm talking to you."

With a sigh, he stopped so abruptly that I ran into him again. "Vityul."

I blinked. "Huh?"

"My name is Vityul."

I mouthed the name a few times, struggling to pronounce it properly. But he'd continued walking. He was a man of few words, much like Grant. But his seemed different.

Grant's was rooted in authority, whereas Vityul's seemed rooted in comfortable silence.

It was extremely dark in this tunnel, almost pitch black. I could just barely make out his shape in front of me, and if he got too far ahead, I lost him completely.

The smell of rainwater and earth was pungent, and roots twisted their way up from the ground. My toes caught on them several times, and each time Vityul caught me before I fell.

"Where are we going?" I asked once more, expecting more this time. But I got the same response I did in the house.

I wanted to ask him about the shadows. It was ridiculous to think he had anything to do with them because…they're shadows. But I had a feeling he knew something about it. It's no coincidence he was there to break me out exactly when the shadows attacked.

"Did you have anything to do with those shadows?"

He paused, finally turning over his shoulder to look at me. "You don't actually want to know."

"I'm asking you, aren't I?"

"Because you're tired of the silence, and curiosity is gnawing at you. But trust me when I say it's better the less you know." I couldn't see his face to read his features, but the tone of his voice told me to back off. However, I'd grown sick of being told what I do and don't want to know.

"So you're going to treat me just like Grant and never tell me anything? What next? Are you going to forbid anyone else from seeing me and murder someone in front of me?" I was almost yelling. The rage inside me reached a boiling point.

Vityul's form didn't move. I could assume he was staring at me. How he could see me in the almost nonexistent light, I didn't know.

He was quiet for so long that I thought he'd kept walking and left me alone. But then he said, "Yes."

"Yes what?" I'd asked several questions in succession.

"The shadows were me."

I reeled back, disbelief wracking my thoughts. He was the cause of those shadows? But how?

"That's impossible."

"You asked." He grabbed my arm and began towing me down the tunnel. "We need to keep moving."

"Why?" I asked.

"Because they will find you here if we stay too long," he answered, letting go of me.

"How do you do it?"

"It just happens."

"Could you always do it?"

"Are you going to talk the entire time?"

"I asked you first."

He growled, "Yes. I've always been able to do it. Now, can you be quiet?"

I had a billion more questions but decided I would appease him and stay silent. He seemed to have a lot on his mind. That's fine. It would give me more time to figure things out myself and take in the events that just happened.

We walked for what seemed like miles before the tunnel opened up into a cavern. The dirt changed to slick rock, and the sound of running water reached my ears. There was a little more light in here, still not enough to see completely, but way more than the tunnel.

"Give me your arm." The sound of his deep voice startled me after the prolonged silence.

I did as he said, and he pulled me onto him piggyback style. I was about to ask what he was doing when we were suddenly in water.

The icy liquid blistered my toes and ankles, drawing a hissing breath from my lips. Vityul shifted me, jostling me higher up. I think he was trying to get me out of the water, which I was grateful for, but it didn't work.

It was a small creek, waist-deep but incredibly powerful. With how fast the water rushed against my feet, I was surprised Vityul was able to walk so easily through it. It would've definitely knocked me over and carried me away.

We reached the other side, where he sat me down on top of the embankment. My knees knocked, thighs shaking after the long walk.

"Are you okay? We still have a ways to go before we can rest." His eyes scanned my face, looking for any signs of imminent collapse.

In the dull light, they burned plum. I could see his jaw working, making up for my silence.

"I'm fine." I take a deep breath and steady myself before my knees buckle, and he catches me before I hit the ground.

He scoffed. "Right." Then threw me back onto him.

I began to protest but relinquished, allowing my head to rest between his shoulder blades. Drowsiness hit me like a freight train. I really regretted not sleeping the past few days. Adrenaline had kept me going, but now I was crashing hard.

Yawning, I decided to ask him a few more questions to keep me awake. I didn't feel comfortable enough to fall asleep around him yet, especially when I had no clue where we were going.

"Why did you come for me?" That was the second biggest question. The first I wanted to save for the right time.

"You wanted out, didn't you?"

I could feel his voice reverberating through his chest, lulling me to sleep. I did want out, but he didn't know that. I'd just made that decision a few days prior.

"How did you know that, though? I've never spoken to you before."

I felt the crisp chuckle through his back. "The shadows told me."

"That's not funny."

"So, you'll believe I caused those shadows to attack but not that I can speak with them?" I could almost hear the smirk in his voice.

I rolled my eyes at his statement. "Shadows can't talk."

"Technically, they can't fight either."

"How did you find me?"

His shoulders stiffened. A move I took as him becoming uncomfortable. His voice was barely a whisper when he said, "I never lost you."

What did that mean? From the lake? Or before then? I wanted to ask him. Wanted to ask him why he had left me there. Why didn't he take me with him in the first place instead of leaving me in Grant's hands? But by the way his shoulders remained stiff, let me know he was done with my questions. And he wouldn't indulge me if I started up again.

He walked us further into the cave, where the walls began to curve inward, and water dribbled on me from cracks in the ceiling.

My eyelids grew heavier with each passing step. I almost nodded off a few times and caught myself just before. Yawning once more, I pinched my cheeks in hopes of waking myself up.

Vityul tilted his head, side-eyeing me. "You should rest."

I shook my head. "I'm-I'm fine."

"You haven't slept in days."

"How'd you know that?"

"The shadows."

I groaned in response and laid my forehead on the nape of his neck. "I never said I believed you made them attack, either."

He cleared his throat, hopping across stepping stone rocks. "You're taking all this rather well."

My eyebrows knitted together as I thought about everything I've witnessed and the inner turmoil it's caused me. "I wouldn't say that."

"It is a lot to take in in a short time. And there's more you don't remember."

This took me aback. My stomach fluttered, and my heart pounded. He knew something about me, something before I lost my memory.

Did that mean I already knew about all of this? Is that why Grant said I needed to do it on my own? Because if they'd told me all of this back then, I definitely would've had a mental breakdown.

We fell in silence, the sound of his shoes on the rock the only thing between us. The green light stayed the same dull shade, barely illuminating anything.

"Where is this light coming from? We're in a cave."

Vityul moved one of my ankles to his other hand, then scratched his neck with the free one before returning to hold both separately.

"Worms," he chuckled dryly.

I choked on something, not expecting that to come out of his mouth. "What?"

"Glow-worms, to be exact, on the ceiling."

My head snapped back, searching for the truth to his words. My mouth fell agape when I saw them.

Tiny green/blue dots with strings hanging from them littered the ceiling. Hundreds clustered together in sections along the path.

"Those are..." I gulped "worms?"

He laughed a fuller sound than before. "Not really worms. There's a few species that fall under the term Glow-worm, but they're actually insect larvae."

I cringed, trying to get as far away from the bugs as possible without throwing him off balance. As pretty as they were, I did not want to chance one of them touching me. It was still a bug, after all.

"These are Dismalites. Fly larvae."

"Can you please stop saying larvae?" My stomach was twisting all over again. This time I thought I'd actually puke.

But I didn't want him to stop talking altogether. This was the most he'd spoken the entire time.

"When it's night, you can't tell where the stars end and these begin. It's a nice replacement when you don't get to see the sky a lot." There was a tinge of sadness in his voice that gave me pause.

"You don't get to see the sky?"

He didn't respond. What an awful thought, to never see the sky. I didn't look at it much myself but to never even have the option to do it? I couldn't imagine and didn't want to pry any further. This seemed like a sensitive topic.

The running water, combined with his soft footsteps, began to lull me to sleep. I tried to fight it for a while, even going so far as to ask him to put me down.

"I know I must be getting heavy," I argued. "You've been carrying me for so long already."

He snorted. "It's like carrying a sheet of paper."

"I don't believe that."

"Have you felt me struggle at all?"

Come to think of it, I hadn't. Not even so much as a muscle quiver or finger twitch.

"But..."

"Go to sleep. I know that's why you're asking me. You're safe to sleep." His voice trailed off at the end like he wanted to say more.

"Am I?" I asked, brow raised to seem more confident than I was.

"What am I going to do? Kidnap you?" The hint of amusement in his voice irritated me.

"You could murder me."

"If I wanted to do that, you'd already be dead. Trust me."

"That's not the kind of thing you want to say to someone when you're trying to convince them to go to sleep while you carry them."

He let out an exasperated sigh I felt all the way through my chest. "I promise not to kill you if you shut up and go to sleep."

I opened my mouth to say more but decided it really wasn't worth it. My head pounded, and I wanted to do nothing more than exactly what he told me to do.

So I let my head drop to his shoulder, and sleep took me immediately.

Chapter Eleven

I awoke to the sound of a crackling fire. My eyes were almost glued shut with gunk, drool slid down my chin.

Wiping it away, I realized I was lying in a small sleeping bag. I sat up, feeling a knot in my neck from the way I slept.

Vityul sat by the fire, legs crossed and eyes closed. He looked to be in a trance, meditation-like state. I didn't want to disturb him, but it seems I already did.

He peeled one eye open, staring directly at me. "Sleep well?"

I worked the knot at the back of my neck, shrugging. "Nightmare." It was awful. I witnessed Jarred's death all over again and then saw his neck start cracking back into place like he was healing himself. I listened to that awful death rattle all over again. Then those monsters came for me.

"Truth be told, I'd sleep a lot better once I get out of this pantsuit-dress-whatever it is," I grumbled, scratching my ankles where the wet fabric had rubbed.

He took in a deep breath and started to get up. "We've only got about twenty miles to go, anyway. You'll be out of that soon enough."

I braided my hair absentmindedly, taking in the surroundings.

We were still in the cave system, though this one was a lot drier. Yet smaller. I could tell we'd be hunched over when standing. And Vityul solidified that thought a moment later as he craned his neck down once he stood to full height.

It would definitely make some people feel claustrophobic if they were in here too long, and I was one of them.

He walked over to me and held out his hand, helping me up. My feet hurt immensely, and I could feel the blisters that had formed over the previous day's walk.

I bent over to rub a particular spot on the ball of my foot when I noticed Vityul packing up the sleeping bag and stowing it in a small hole in a section of the rock wall. It looked to have been carved out by hand. Inside I also saw a box of matches, a bottle filled with a brightly colored liquid, and a flask.

Does he come back here regularly? Worse, does he live here? Is this what he meant by never seeing the sky? No, that's impossible. Those small items weren't enough to live on, and if we were twenty miles from our destination, he couldn't make that trip twice a day.

He saw me staring and offered the flask to me. I shook my head no until he clarified, "It's water." Then I greedily gulped it down.

I hadn't even realized how thirsty I was, how scratchy my throat had become.

"How long was I out?" I ask as I hand him the metal container.

He frowns for a moment before saying, "I'm not sure. Can't tell time down here."

I nod, unsatisfied with that answer but knowing I wasn't getting another one.

After stomping out the fire, he motioned for me to climb on again.

This time I adamantly refused. He'd carried me enough. Plus, maybe the walking would help rub out some of the aching in my feet.

It didn't.

An undetermined amount of time later, my feet were on fire. Every step was agonizing to take. I almost thought I'd rubbed all the skin off by the time we stopped for a rest break.

I tried to massage my feet but only ended up making them feel more raw. Sighing in defeat, I slumped against the tunnel wall. At least the rock offered some support for my back, even if it was rough and dug into my skin.

Vityul remained quiet the entire time, seemingly lost in his own thoughts. I decided to push my luck.

"Where are we going? For real, this time. I've already put more trust into you than I'd like from little info."

He didn't look up at me as he raised his eyebrows. "Did you now?"

Folding my arms, I tried my best to stare him down. He clearly wasn't intimidated, and a bemused grin lit his face.

"Somewhere safe," he said.

"Safe from what?"

He turned his eyes to me, and I saw the hidden anguish in them. "From..." he trailed off, furrowing his brow and looking away. "There's good people where we're going. And you'll be safe there."

"You're not staying?"

He shook his head. "I'm only here to get you out of Grant's hands and make sure you made it to the safe house. I'm leaving after that."

"Back to your cave?"

He flinched, then composed himself just as fast. If I wasn't paying attention, I would've missed it.

"That's why you said the glow-worms were a good replacement for the stars, right? Because you live in a cave like the one we came from?"

Vityul had gone quiet again. This time I wasn't sure if it was content silence or hurt silence.

"You said there's more I don't remember. Did you know me before all of this?"

He gulped audibly, wringing his hands in discomfort. "Everything will be explained to you once you reach the safe house."

"Will it? Or are you just saying that so I'll shut up?" I crossed my arms with a smirk, acting like I had caught on to his plan.

His eyes bore into mine, and even in the dull light from the insects, I thought I saw a tear run down his cheek.

"I didn't believe them when they said you looked like her. But you do."

Confusion bumbled its way through me, but before I could ask him anything, he'd changed the subject.

"So what exactly did Grant tell you?"

"About what?"

"Anything." He wrung his hands harder, moving down to his wrists.

I thought back to my time at the cottage and all the things he'd said to me. I didn't think Vityul was asking me about the types of flowers I'd received daily. No, he's probably asking about something more serious.

"He didn't outright say it," at least I don't think he did. But my mind is having trouble remembering exactly what's happened, "but I think he's in a war with someone. He invited me to one of his speeches and talked a bunch of nonsense, then wouldn't explain any of it to me."

Vityul began to stop me as soon as I'd said speeches, but I didn't notice until I finished speaking.

"He took you to a rally?" he asked incredulously.

I nodded, not understanding what the big deal was.

"What happened?" He grabbed me by the shoulders firmly, and I could feel the urgency in his grip.

"Uh…" I stumbled around my head for words. "He just spoke to a crowd of people and lit a bonfire. That's it."

Vityul peered into my eyes for a few more seconds, waiting to see if I'd add anything. When I didn't, he asked, "That's all that happened? You went back after he was done?"

"Yes," I gasped as he let go, returning to his position beside me. "Why?"

His jaw worked, muscles clenching. "He's known to do some heinous things at his rallies."

My heart sputtered in my chest. Knowing Grant was capable of hurting his son and killing someone without a second thought, what could he do there?

Vityul must've seen the worry on my face because he quickly brushed it aside. "Don't worry about it. You never have to deal with it again."

I let out a small smile, but on the inside, I knew I'd still be worrying about it.

"Come on. I'm carrying you this time. The cave expands more." He didn't give me the option to protest, either. Within seconds I was across his back again, and we were continuing our journey.

The cave did expand fairly large, really quickly. The glowing worms showed up less and less. We were almost in complete darkness again.

I shuddered, closing my eyes and burying my nose into his shoulder, where I got a whiff of his scent. It was kind of like lemon and mint. Not a combination I would've thought of, but it worked for him.

How I didn't smell this before baffled me. It was so distinct. Although I was pretty out of it before I slept, I'm not even sure what I saw was real. I could've hallucinated most of it. Those monsters definitely had to be a hallucination. Because if they were real, I would be terrified.

We kept going for a while longer until I asked for another break. My hips were beginning to hurt after straddling him for so long.

He tried to find a place to sit me that wasn't covered in spider webs, but that was a great feat as this entire place was covered.

Eventually, he just cleared out a small space with his foot and gingerly sat me there, telling me not to lean on the webs.

He didn't have to tell me twice. I regretted even asking for a break now. They were everywhere. And came out of nowhere too. There were none a few yards back.

"We can't stay here long," he warned.

I stretched my hips out and scoffed, "Yeah. I know."

But something was off with him. He shifted nervously, and I could vaguely make out his head turning back and forth. Like he was looking for something.

I took another stab at rubbing my feet when I noticed a web dancing in the wind. It bobbed and weaved in a meticulous rhythm of its own.

It was only after I glanced at another dancing web beside me did it click. We're in a cave. There's no wind down here.

I sprang to my feet, slamming into Vityul. He latched onto me, ensuring I didn't fall back down. But he wasn't looking at me. He was looking at the ceiling. Where every strand of the web vibrated.

"Vityul?" I whimpered, fisting my hands in his shirt.

His eyes turned to our left, where a section of the tunnel branched off—webs strewn across every open piece of air.

"Let's go." In the blink of an eye, I was on his back again, and he was running. It wasn't a full sprint as he kept tripping in the sticky silk.

Every time a piece touched me, it clung like duct tape. My skin stretched and pulled. This was the strongest spider web I'd ever encountered.

One particularly nasty web got stuck to my ear, and as I yanked it loose, I caught sight of something behind us. It was hard to see in the minimal light, but I saw something reflecting back at us. It grew closer, and I saw it was crawling along the webs.

It was a spider. A giant spider. Hairy, black, and with all eight eyes.

I shrieked, catching Vityul off guard, and he got trapped in a small hole filled with web. "Hold on," he said through clenched teeth as he let go of me.

My legs tightened around his waist, my arms around his neck to keep myself from falling into the web.

He'd bent over and was frantically ripping away the silk with ease. Whereas I struggled to pull one strand off.

I made the mistake of checking behind us to see where the spider was and caught sight of two more right behind it. It was about ten yards away now and closing rapidly. Its mandibles glinted with what I could only assume was venom.

"Vityul!" I cried out, smacking my hands on his chest.

He grunted with effort and yanked his leg free, running once more.

"Do the thing!" I yelled at him.

"Do what thing?"

"The shadow thing!"

He took a glance behind us and swore. "Does it look like there's enough light down here for there to even *be* shadows?"

He had a point, and I didn't like it. They were moving faster than us. They would catch us.

Up ahead, I saw another cave entrance with light pouring out from it. That must be our destination. However, I didn't think we'd make it before becoming spider food.

Suddenly, Vityul yanked me over his head, and I was soaring through the air. I landed mere feet from the entrance with a thud, my ribs barking in pain.

"Go!" He shouted to me as he turned around to face the spiders.

I leaped to my feet, terrified but determined. I wasn't going to let him get eaten, not when he'd saved me. When he'd carried me all this way. He was coming too.

I braced myself and lunged forward, pushing my way through the thick webs. The spiders had stopped before him and were clicking their mandibles hungrily.

"No!" I put out my hand, reaching for him. He couldn't go out this way. I didn't even know where to go from here.

Light sprouted from my fingertips, white-hot and angry. It beelined for the spiders, knocking them back.

I was in such shock I could only stand there when Vityul looked back at me.

Did that just happen? What was that light? Where did it come from?

There was no time to process as Vityul scooped me up in his arms and dove us through the entrance and into the light.

We sprawled out on the dirt floor, panting. I could see an opening above us, the rocks laid in a makeshift staircase. The light was too bright to make out anything beyond the opening, and I had to avert my eyes after a moment. It was like staring into the sun.

I heard the spiders jostling around the hole we'd just come from, and for a second, I didn't care if they'd make it here. I was too tired, too freaked out. But they never did, and after a few moments, they disappeared back into the darkness.

Vityul coughed, rolling onto his hands and knees. He looked over at me with a strange look in his eyes.

I knew exactly what that look was for, too. "I have no idea what just happened." The spiders, the light, the monsters. It was just all too much.

My breaths came in ragged bursts, much like my heartbeats. It wouldn't steady. I felt like it was going to beat right out of my chest. I couldn't breathe. My throat tightened, and my head became foggy.

Vityul saw this and was at my side instantly, cradling my head in his lap. "Focus. Breathe. In and out."

But I couldn't. Even my hearing was beginning to fade.

"What color is the rock?" He asked in all seriousness.

"What?" I croaked, still unable to catch a full breath.

"What color is the rock?" He said again, louder and firmer.

My eyes looked past him to the ceiling. I wasn't sure why he was asking me this, but I managed to respond, "Orange."

"What color is my shirt?"

My throat was almost completely closed now. Any air getting through felt like sucking on a straw.

"Black."

"How many fingers do you have?"

I blinked, took a deeper breath and began rubbing all my fingers together. The sensation started to bring me back.

"Ten," I said, taking one final deep breath. My lungs expanded fully, and my heart settled.

Vityul's face dropped into calmness as he rubbed my head and breathed with me for a few seconds. Once I felt better, he helped me sit up, his indigo eyes watching my every move.

"It's okay now," I reassured him. His raised brow in response told me he didn't believe me.

Footsteps reached my ears, coming from outside the entrance. My eyes went wide, and I began to scurry backward before he caught my arm.

"It's okay now." He threw my sentence back at me with a surreptitious grin.

I scowled, clamoring to my feet with a groan. My hand flew to my eyes, shielding them from the light.

A head popped out at the entrance, and at the same time, a woman's voice reached my ears.

"Y'all okay down there?"

"We're coming up," Vityul responded. "Get her some shades." He gingerly grabbed my hands and led me up the rock stairs and into the open air.

Instantly a pair of sunglasses were stuck on my head, and I could see again.

A woman with short, curly blonde hair, a round face, and wide green eyes stared at Vityul and me with angst. Beside her stood a man with deep blue eyes set high on his triangle face framed by long black hair. They both looked to be the same age as Vityul and of equal height.

"What happened?" The woman demanded, crossing her arms.

Vityul spat at his feet before saying, "Cave Crawlers." He pointedly didn't tell them what happened with me.

The man cringed, wrinkling his nose and gagging. He reached into his back pocket and brandished a white cigarette, casually lighting it and taking a puff. "We told you not to use this part of the cave system."

Vityul stared daggers at the man, who winced under his gaze.

The man raised his arms in defense. "Hey dude, I'm just the messenger."

The woman huffed and snatched the cigarette out of his mouth, stomping it into the ground. "Can't you hold off your nicotine addiction for two minutes?"

He looked sadly at his destroyed piece before pulling another one out and lighting it. "No." He smirked.

Vityul brushed the dirt off his shoulders and straightened his jacket. Then leaned over and brushed debris out of his curls before turning to me.

"This is Rhydel and Sam. They'll take you the rest of the way." He jerked his thumb toward the man and woman.

But my focus remained on Vityul. "So you're really not coming?"

Vityul shook his head. That's when Sam appeared beside us, blonde curls bouncing.

"Actually, about that. They want to see you back at headquarters."

The purple in his eyes burned hot as he turned to face her. "What for? My job is done."

She shrugged. "They figured out our secret plan and wanna talk to you about it."

Rhydel scoffed, "You mean chew him out over it."

Vityul's shoulders sagged as he pinched the bridge of his nose. "Can't you tell him to shove it?"

Sam grimaced, exchanging tortured looks with Rhydel. "It's not him. It's her."

Vityul straightened, continuing to dust off his jacket. "Then tell her to shove it."

A burst of laughter came from Rhydel, who bent over, cackling. "You're funny. You're so funny."

But Vityul wasn't laughing. He was dead serious.

"You tell her," Rhydel said as he stamped out his newest cigarette. "I don't have a death wish."

Sam patted Vityul's shoulder and grimaced. "Come on. They're waiting."

Chapter Twelve

Vityul carried me the rest of the way, much to my chagrin and complaints.

Sam asked me a bunch of questions, which helped pass the time. It also took my mind off the recent events and my throbbing feet.

She noticed the blisters and told me she had a cream that would help. I thanked her graciously. She seemed super nice.

I noticed the engagement ring almost right away. It was a small blue gem, with tiny diamonds framing it in two triangle formations.

"It's beautiful," I groaned, peeking over the top of my sunglasses at it. It still hurt to look at the world without my sunglasses, and I wasn't sure why. We weren't in the caves that long.

"Thank you." She beamed. "I proposed to my girlfriend a few months ago, and surprisingly she also had a ring for me."

She brought the ring closer to my face for me to inspect, allowing me to see that it was more than a simple blue gem. It was the color of deep ocean with flecks of red and orange that appeared in certain tilts of light.

Rhydel puffed from behind us, "Are you ever going to stop showing that ring off?"

"Are you ever going to stop being annoying?" she retorted.

He rolled his eyes, pulling his hair back with a tie. "It's in my job description."

I chuckled and rubbed my eyes, squinting at the bright light. "When can I take these off?"

Sam frowned. "It's going to take time for your eyes to adjust back. You were in the caves for three days."

My jaw hit the floor at the revelation. "Three days?" I gasped, my eyes turning to Vityul.

He stayed quiet even at my attempts to gain his attention.

"Three days?" I repeat. There's no way. It only felt like half a day at most.

Unfortunately, there's been a lot of things that happened in the last few days that seemed impossible. What just happened with those spiders, for one.

Did I imagine that? No, the spiders got thrown backward. We would've been toast if they hadn't. That light was real.

I touched my thumb to the tips of my fingers, feeling for any kind of imperfection—any difference in them. But they felt like my normal fingers.

Rhydel appeared on my left, giving me a sidelong glance.

"What?" I know I'd just spent the last three days in a cave with no bath, but I couldn't help that. My cheeks flushed under the scrutiny.

He rubbed his chin in thought. "You *do* look kinda like her. It's weird."

"Why does everyone keep saying that?" Who was the person I supposedly looked like?

"Because you do," Sam responded quietly.

Rhydel let out a harsh laugh. "Oh, don't act, Sam. You didn't even like her. You were mean to her the last time you saw her."

Sam pressed her lips into a thin line, shame radiating in her eyes. "I was angry."

"You think I wasn't? But it wasn't her fault."

"I know that now," she insisted.

"It's a little too late for that *now*."

"Where even is this person?" I wanted to find her and see if I really did look like her. And why.

"She's dead," Vityul hissed that venom-coated string of words so cold that none of us spoke again.

The sun was low in the sky by the time we arrived at a set of metal gates attached to ten-foot privacy fencing. Rhydel input a passcode, and the doors swung wide, revealing a long asphalt drive lined with palm trees.

We walked up the path, sweating profusely. Except for Vityul, who seemed comfortable in this humid weather.

The smell of saltwater permeated the air around us. A light breeze drifted, brushing against the nape of my neck and cooling me off momentarily.

This outfit was getting increasingly warm. The material was thicker than I'd originally believed, and I was dying.

We approached a botanical garden surrounded by a rock wall. A door sat carved into the wall, with guards stationed on either side.

These guards weren't like Grant's. They waved and spoke to us as we approached. They didn't wear armor like his did. In fact, they were dressed so casually no random passerby would even suspect they were guarding the place. I only knew because I'd grown familiar with the guarded stance and positions that guards took up.

This time Vityul put in the passcode after he sat me down. A strange sizzling sound reached my ears, but I couldn't find the source of it. I might be imagining again. The concrete was so hot I hopped from foot to foot impatiently. First walking blisters, and now my feet were actually burning.

Sam threw me a pitying glance before the door opened, and she shrugged inside ahead of the rest of us.

Vityul motioned for me to go first, giving me a reassuring nod.

Instantly, the air conditioning hit me like a tidal wave. I rolled my shoulders and breathed in the air, removing my sunglasses in the dim light.

Before me lay a staircase that led into the depths of the earth. I looked back at Vityul and sighed. "Down again?"

"This one's better."

"No spiders?"

"None."

Using the crook of his arm to balance myself, I made my way down the steps. It was an effort to work past the pain in my feet, which grew with every step. I didn't think it could get any worse, and yet it continued to prove me wrong.

At the bottom of the steps, we reached another door. Again a passcode was put in, and we were emptied out into a long hallway. Doors lined the path, similar in style to Grant's house. However, there weren't as many here and no guards beside them.

We went through three more doors before turning a corner, where Sam was waiting by a metal door with an intricate carving in it that swirled, caved, and branched out.
It was slightly ajar, which allowed the voices to reach my ears. It was a man and a woman. They were loudly in an argument I couldn't understand as they were arguing in an entirely different language.

Sam cleared her throat as we approached, and the voices quieted. Vityul entered first, pulling me behind him.

"Oh, look who decided to show?" the man snapped. "Thanks for coming out of the shadows." He had shoulder-length milk chocolate hair, medium olive under-toned skin, and eyes made of smoldering fire embers.

He was bulky. Even wearing the yellow long-sleeve, I could see the details in his muscles. He was also incredibly handsome, with an angular jawline, a long nose, and hooded eyes. It was so chiseled. In fact, I almost thought he had been carved straight from stone.

"Bite me," Vityul spat.

The woman—with a frame as sleek as her black hair—raised a hand to silence them both. She was striking, to say the least. With her high cheekbones, different-colored eyes, and a crescent moon-shaped scar around her right eye, she looked like a warrior Goddess. Her deep skin glowed under the candlelight.

"Enough of this," she said, her voice deep and melodic. "Where have you been?"

Vityul scoffed, stepping aside to reveal me as he said, "Doing you a favor."

Once their eyes landed on me, it was as if they'd seen a ghost. Both of their mouths fell open as they went sheet white, with the man taking a hesitant step toward me.

"Ro-Rosetta?" he whispered, eyes wide.

"How?" the woman questioned as she approached.

I took a quick look behind me, making sure they weren't talking to someone else. When I realized they were, in fact, speaking to me, I pointed a finger at my chest. "Me?" They knew me?

They both recoiled at my confusion, sharing warning looks with each other.

"You don't remember?" the woman asked, worry lines written across her brow.

I shook my head.

"What's the last thing you do remember?" the man asked with a shaky breath.

Cocking my head, I glanced at Vityul, who was as still as a statue. It's clear he didn't want them knowing about the lake. Either that, or he didn't know I remembered. And I still haven't even had the chance to confront him about it yet.

In the end, I decided to just go with the safe answer of "Nothing." Which received collective gasps from them. The man and woman looked at each other, seeming to have a conversation entirely silent.

Finally, the woman nodded and approached me with her hand out. "Well then. We better reintroduce ourselves. I'm Kenna. Leader of this operation."

I shook her hand as the man approached me next, bumping shoulders with Vityul. "Damicén." It was an odd name, but it fit his demeanor perfectly. I could just look at him and think, *yeah, he definitely seems like a Damicén*, even though I've never heard that name before. I wondered where it'd come from.

Standing awkwardly between them while they exchanged another glance, I tried to catch Vityul's gaze. But he had tuned out and gone within himself. No longer did his eyes focus on anything in front of him.

I didn't want to wave my hand in case I caught the attention of Kenna and Damicén, but my attempts at subtle eyebrow-raising and rapid blinking were doing nothing.

"Have you eaten yet?" Kenna's voice dragged me back to them.

My stomach growled in response, loud enough for everyone to hear.

She gave a small smile and motioned for Damicén to escort me. As we left, I saw her get directly in Vityul's face while ushering the waiting Sam and Rhydel into the room. The door shut behind them with finality, and as we continued walking, I wondered if they were getting in trouble. And what would be the consequences that came with it?

Jarred flashed behind my blinking lids, and my stomach rolled.

The dining room wasn't as grand as Grant's—just a few tables were placed haphazardly throughout the room. I was served a bowl of chicken noodle soup with a piece of cornbread on the side. I hungrily gulped it down like I hadn't eaten in days. Which I hadn't, but nonetheless.

Damicén watched me the entire time. His gaze didn't make me uncomfortable like the others, but it was definitely odd. He seemed to be reading everything I did and everything I thought. I was grateful for his friendly silence, though. The air between us felt much more comfortable than the silence at Grant's.

Once I finished, he escorted me to a bedroom, which was filled with two bunk beds and an old dresser.

"It's not much," he offered. "But it's all we have."

I smiled warmly and thanked him regardless. I didn't mind sharing a living space. I think I actually wanted some company after these last few days. The idea of sleeping alone with my thoughts was almost unimaginable.

"There's a bathroom to the left with a shower and some fresh clothes for you to change into. I'll be right outside. There's…a lot we need to discuss."

I nodded, sweeping inside the room and closing the door behind me. On the dresser lay a stack of newly pressed clothes. A blue shirt—a little big on me as it fell to my thighs—and a pair of black pants.

Practically ripping my sopping wet outfit off, I snatched the clothes from the dresser top and headed into the bathroom.

The fabric of both was incredibly soft compared to the itchy mess I'd had on for three days.

I ran the water as hot as it would go and rinsed off the dirt that'd accumulated. And I didn't get out until well after the water ran clear down the drain. If only it could clean my memories, too.

I groaned in relief at the freedom I felt in this new outfit. I'd grown so tired of dresses, no matter how beautiful they were.

It relaxed me to the point of needing a nap. But Damicén said he'd be waiting for me, and truth be told, I wanted to know what they knew. Because it was clear they knew more and were willing to tell me, unlike Grant.

I wondered what he was doing right now. If he'd panicked at my absence, or if he'd even noticed? Since he actively avoided me before the incident, and I avoided him after it.

But mostly, I wondered about Jae. I hoped he was okay. I hoped Grant wasn't taking out his anger on him. He didn't deserve that. He had tried to help me as much as he could. I understood now why he couldn't do more.

Suddenly the room fell into red as alarms blared in my ear. The door swung open where Damicén stood with a sour look on his face.

My hands slammed over my ears as the piercing siren pounded my eardrums. "What's happening?" I shouted over the noise.

Damicén shrugged and snagged my elbow, his other hand hovering at the small of my back. "I'm not sure."

He escorted me back down the hallway to the room we were in before. Now that I got a second look with fresh eyes, I noticed maps along the walls and bookshelves in the empty spaces. Yet another thing to compare to Grant.

Inside, Kenna and another man were scrambling around, pressing buttons and barking orders over a walkie-talkie.

Damicén shut the door behind us and called out, "Brandon, what's going on?"

"An intruder," the man responded, his blond curls bouncing as he leaped across the room. "Someone broke through the first security door."

Fear settled in my gut. Was it Grant? Had he found me anyway? Come to take me back to his prison vacation home?

My heart pounded in my ears, drowning out the sound of the alarms for a split second.

Damicén's hand tightened on my elbow in a reassuring grip. "Don't worry," he said. "They're not going to take you."

How did he know I was thinking that? It could be an obvious guess after what I'd just been through, but it still piqued my interest.

Finally, the alarms shut off, and the room returned to its normal light. We all stood in utter silence, listening for any movement. My heart galloped too loud for me to hear anything over it, so I resigned to watching their faces.

After a few gut-wrenching moments, everyone relaxed, indicating they had heard nothing.

"They must've gotten them," Brandon huffed. "Wonder who was stupid enough to try that?"

Then the door rattled. Instantly Damicén moved me behind him, Kenna joining his side.

"Friendly?" she whispered.

"I don't know. They're blocked off from me."

I didn't understand what they were talking about. All I knew was the more that doorknob jiggled, the more terror I felt.

Brandon poised behind them, palms turned toward the door as purple mist began to swirl up his arms.

I blinked rapidly, rubbing my eyes to make sure I was seeing correctly. It looked just like what Avalon had around her the night the shadows attacked. What the hell was going on?

Suddenly Vityul was beside me, gently tugging me backward so he could stand directly in front of me. I felt nuts blinking so much in succession. He hadn't been in here moments ago. Where did he come from? There's no way I missed him. This room is too small for someone to hide in.

Now four people blocked me from the door. It should've given me some comfort, knowing they had my back, but it didn't. I didn't know these people. They'd done the same thing Grant had. They'd all given me fresh clothes, food, and had been nice to me.

The mechanism on the backside of the door whirred to life as they unlocked in a series of clicks and turns.

Then the door swung open, and inside stepped a face I did not expect to see.

His gray eyes immediately connected with mine, and I burst into a smile.

Jae.

Chapter Thirteen

Jae looked awful. His hair was stuck to his forehead with sweat. His clothes were tattered and filled with holes. I thought I saw dried blood on the collar of his shirt. His eyes looked weary, and there was a cluster of mud on his cheek.

He was the last person I expected to see, and by the look on everyone else's faces, it was the same for them.

"Jesse?" Brandon's voice was barely a whisper as the purple mist faded out of view.

Jesse? Did they know him, too? But he called him Jesse, not Jae. They must be mistaken.

Brandon approached slowly, looking Jae—Jesse—up and down with a bewildered gleam in his eyes.

He clasped Jae's hand and wrapped his free arm around his neck, pulling him close.

"We thought you were dead." His voice cracked under the weight of his emotions.

Jae hugged him back, letting go of his hand and wrapping it around him. "I thought I was, too."

Brandon pushed back, taking in his appearance. "You look like shit." They both grinned at that observation, Jae shrugging his shoulders in response.

Then Damicén approached. He was wary like he still wasn't sure what he saw was real. Stopping a couple feet from Jae, he took a heavy breath and bear-hugged him.

Blood Return

Jae returned the same, eyes red-rimmed. I swear I saw Damicén's shoulders buckle in silent sobs. He leaned back and grabbed the sides of Jae's face, and said the most heartbreaking words I've ever heard.

"She's gone." Tears were flowing now from both of them. "She's fucking gone. Sacrificed herself so we could get out."

Jae nodded, giving Damicén another hug. He waved at Kenna over his shoulder, whose brown skin had paled at the sight of him.

"How?" she asked with bated breath.

Damicén gave one good pat on Jae's back before letting go and wiping the tears from his face. "Yeah, man. How did you make it out?"

Jae smeared his own tears, sniffling. "It's a long story."

"Well, tell us. You know we want to know," Brandon affirmed, wiping his nose with a white handkerchief.

"Yes. We have tons of things to go over. Like…" Kenna trailed off as she looked in my direction. However, I noticed it wasn't me she was staring at; it was Vityul.

He'd frozen in place, eyes blazing. He clearly had his hackles raised and had only grown more agitated with every word Jae spoke.

The other two noticed this as well, confusion morphing onto their faces.

"Get him out of here," Vityul demanded, voice frighteningly deep and commanding.

"Whoa, dude. He's a good guy. He's one of us," Brandon defended, stepping between the two.

Vityul scowled, shadows beginning to dance behind us. "The hell he is." But understanding settled in his gaze as he registered everyone's faces. "They don't know, do they?" he asked pointedly at Jae.

Jae's jaw clenched, but he remained silent.

"Know what?" Kenna glanced between them with suspicion.

"Don't," Jae started, "do something you're going to regret."

Damicén stepped forward in line with Brandon, eyebrows knitting together. "What is—" then his face contorted.

He went stone still, as still as Vityul had been. In fact, he stared right at Vityul, eyes widening in the silence. His breathing became labored, and after a few moments, he seemed to be released from whatever trance he'd fallen into.

He turned slowly to Jae, eyes scanning frantically until they landed on him.

"Damicén." Jae held up a hand.

"You," Damicén cocked his fist back and landed a blow directly on Jae's jaw, "son of a bitch!"

They hit the concrete below hard as Damicén continued to whale on Jae's face. Blood spurted from an unseen injury, scattering across the floor. Jae didn't fight back, letting Damicén hit him over and over again.

"We trusted you!" he yelled, a rage-induced sound barreling from his chest. "She trusted you!"

"Stop!" I screamed at the same time Brandon threw purple mist at the pair and lifted Damicén into the air with it.

"What the hell?" Brandon called to him, bewildered.

Kenna moved to be beside Jae in the blink of an eye, helping him sit up as he clutched his nose. Blood trailed in between his fingers and down his forearm.

"He's a traitor," Damicén hissed. "He's Grant's fucking son; he played us the whole time."

The look of shock that dawned on Brandon's and Kenna's faces trumped the one from earlier. They stilled, eyes going wide.

They hadn't known? It was the first thing I learned.

"What?" Kenna blinked, looking down at Jae and back to the still floating Damicén.

He was crying again, this time from anger. Pure, unfiltered anger. "He killed Talon."

I didn't think it was possible, but they seemed to grow even more shocked. It rolled over them in increments, like the stages of grief.

Brandon now shed a tear of his own as he asked, "Is that true, Jesse?" His lower lip quivered, waiting for a response. I could tell he didn't want to ask but felt compelled to.

Jae sighed, wiping the blood off his shirt. "It's true. But I can explain."

Brandon dropped Damicén and latched the mist onto Jae, freezing him in place. He didn't look like he was going to go anywhere, anyway—seeming resigned to his fate.

"There's nothing to explain," Vityul spat. "I saw the whole thing. You didn't even blink when you shot her."

Kenna stood abruptly, stomping back over to the table at the center of the room. She ran her hands through her hair and rested them on the wood. "Take him away."

"No, wait, please," Jae pleaded. "I can explain everything!"

"I'll fucking kill you." Damicén went to lay into him again, but Kenna grabbed his wrist, stopping the swing mid-air, to my surprise. She'd just been across the room, but in the blink of an eye was now the only thing standing between the two men.

"Enough," she whispered.

"But—" Damicén began to protest, then silenced himself at her steely gaze.

"Look at her," she pointed to me. "She's terrified."

I'd unknowingly latched onto Vityul's shirt in the chaos, cowering behind him. Damicén's eyes softened when he saw me shaking.

It wasn't so much from the fight as it was my memories of Jarred and those monsters. I couldn't control it. It just appeared at the forefront of my mind when I saw the blood.

"We'll deal with him later," she promised. "But for now, let Brandon take him to the chambers."

Damicén lowered his eyes in shame and let his hand fall from her grip. She nodded to Brandon, who lifted Jae off the ground with the mist and began walking him down the hallway. Jae didn't resist, his shoulders sagging in defeat.

I watched as they disappeared around the corner and listened as Damicén broke down on the floor.

Kenna placed a supportive hand on his shoulder, and he held it for comfort.

"How could he betray us like that?" he wept. A blue veil akin to the blackness seen at Grant's dinner table began to swell over their heads.

I didn't know what to do. I didn't know these people well enough to comfort them, didn't know their connection to him. All the time I've known Jae, he was just a scared kid in his own right. I saw how anxious his father made him. If he really betrayed these people, I couldn't believe it was willingly.

"Vityul, will you please take Rosetta back to her room? I don't think we will be having any further discussions this evening." Kenna motioned with her free hand out the door.

She appeared strong, but I could see the collapse behind her eyes. When we leave, she will also have her breakdown.

Vityul glanced back at me, still attached to his shirt. He raised a dark eyebrow in a silent question. I nodded, untangling my fingers and stepping ahead of him, walking toward the door.

"I'm very sorry you had to witness this," Kenna apologized as I neared her.

I was still in too much shock to respond. I wanted to tell her they had it wrong. That Jae could never do those things. But by the devastated look on their faces, I knew right now was not the time for that.

Vityul led me back to my room, anger radiating off him. Every brush of his skin against mine sent jolts up my spine, twisting my insides with the same hate burning through him. I tried not to touch him anymore.

When we arrived, he turned and walked away before I could say anything to him.

I wanted to ask what his problem was and possibly confront him about the lake. He knew something. He'd made that very obvious, and so did the others. I'd be lying if I said I wasn't a little disappointed. I wouldn't be discussing anything with them tonight. But I understood. They would grieve all over again for the loss of that woman.

Talon, I think, is what Damicén called her. What would she have done in this situation, I wondered?

Laying in one of the top bunks, I recalled all my precious conversations with Jae. And I remembered that night I looked through the vent.

Grant had struck Jae for killing someone. When I asked him about it that fateful day in the hallway, he'd clammed up. Had that been Talon the whole time? So did that mean Grant and these guys were on the same side since they were both upset at her death?

But that didn't make sense, either. Vityul wouldn't have had to stage an attack and kidnap me if they were on the same side.

The door opened, snapping me out of my thoughts. I rolled to the edge of the mattress to see Sam and Rhydel enter the room. They were sweaty and covered in grime.

Sam's eyes lit up when she saw me. "Hi, Rosetta! I didn't know they'd placed you with us." She plopped down on the bed below me with a heavy sigh.

Rhydel gave a tilt of his head in acknowledgment of me before heading directly into the bathroom.

"What happened?" I asked hesitantly.

"We got in trouble. Our punishment is to clean the cafeteria and run laps."

I tapped my finger on the railing trepidatiously. "Was it for getting me?"

Sam was quiet for a few seconds before saying, "Yes. We snuck away with Vityul to get you out of there."

I ducked my head, guilt rising in me. "I'm sorry," I whispered. I didn't want anyone to receive any more punishments because of me.

"It's fine." She waved it off. "I would do it again in a heartbeat to get you away from that man."

The water clicked off, and Rhydel emerged from possibly the quickest shower in existence. "Your turn." He nodded to Sam.

She leaped up and ran into the room, slamming the door behind her.

Rhydel climbed up to the other top bunk and laid flat on his back. He now wore knee-length shorts and a black tank top. His hair draped over the side of the bed, still dripping.

"Don't start feeling guilty. We only got in trouble because we snuck off without saying anything and scared Kenna," he mumbled, fluffing his pillow.

"Why did you do it?" My question caught him by surprise because he accidentally pushed his pillow over the edge.

His sharp blue eyes met mine as his eyebrows pushed lower on his face. He chewed on my question for a minute, but I was perfectly comfortable waiting for an answer. I might not be able to talk with the others, but maybe my roommates would tell me something.

"It has to do with stuff you can't remember," he said finally, looking down at the dropped pillow.

"Well, then tell me. Since I can't remember."

He cringed and rubbed the back of his neck. "I don't think I should. It's a lot of information to process, and truth be told, I don't know all of it. I never even met you the first time."

The first time? That meant whatever Kenna and Damicén knew was about my missing memories. I can't let them skirt it if they don't tell me tomorrow.

"Met who?" Sam asked as she returned from her shower, hair wrapped in a towel. She passed me a tube of ointment and pointed at my feet.

Rhydel motioned to me and explained, "She wants to know why we rescued her."

Sam made the same face he had when I first asked the question. "That's a better question to ask Kenna and Damicén. They were there for it all." She bent down to grab the pillow and tossed it back up to him.

I huffed and rolled onto my back. "If that even happens. They're pretty upset right now."

"Oh, they'll get over it. We made it back safely." Rhydel waved it off.

"No, Jae showed up."

"Who?" They both stared at me as if my head had turned completely around.

Crap. What did the others call him? "Jesse."

"What?" Rhydel and Sam exclaimed at the same time, with her head appearing beside me as Rhydel sat upright in his bunk.

"He's back?" He questioned. "I thought he died?"

"That's what they said," Sam affirmed over her shoulder. "Is that what the alarms were for earlier?"

I nodded.

"Why are they upset over that?" Sam dropped down, throwing her towel back into the bathroom.

Rhydel's face went blank for a moment, then his jaw dropped.

Sam's head whipped around, eyes narrowing on him. "Seriously? He did that?"

He nodded, and it was only when she slumped onto the bed below me that I realized they'd had a silent conversation similar to Kenna and Damicén.

I noted this away for later. I doubt they'd tell me right now, and honestly, I didn't know if I wanted to know. I've seen and processed a lot these past few days. Maybe waiting for Kenna and Damicén wasn't such a bad idea after all.

Small sobs could be heard below me, and when I peeked my head over, I saw Sam curled into herself, facing the wall. She had a pillow to her face, trying to mute the sound of her crying.

The lights turned off without warning, sending me into a slight panic. I reeled back from the edge, slamming my back against the wall.

"They're on a timer," Rhydel said quietly. "You'll get used to it."

"What times are they set to?"

"Seven AM and ten PM."

As I lay there rethinking everything, I knew I so badly wanted to see Jae and ask him about all of this. This time I would make him answer. He couldn't walk away. He couldn't hide what he knew any longer.

Chapter Fourteen

I dreamed I did go see Jae. He was further down into the base, where a makeshift jail cell sat. It didn't have the normal iron bars, but silver walls with a small window in the main door large enough for a face.

Jae was at the window talking to someone. I thought at first it might've been me until I turned and saw Damicén. He had his arms crossed with a pinched face.

None of them looked at me like I wasn't even there. When I waved my hand in front of their faces, neither reacted.

"I had to do it," Jae said with not an ounce of remorse.

"Bullshit," Damicén bit off.

Jae sighed, resting a palm on the door to lean on. "I had to choose someone. If it wasn't her, it would've been Rosetta. And since she was with you, that meant you were all at risk. I had no other choice. This was the only way."

Was this about me? Why was I dreaming about this?

"You could've told us." Damicén threw his hands in the air before clapping them on his thighs. "We would've found a way around it. Like we did the entire trip."

Jae shook his head, folding his lips into his teeth. "There was no way around this. And you know damn well if I'd told her, it was either her or you guys, she would've pulled the trigger herself."

"But you didn't give her that choice! You decided for her."

I saw the immediate hurt on Jae's face. He avoided Damicén's eye contact and looked at the floor. "It's different now. You think I'd risk my life leaving Grant and coming here if it wasn't?"

Damicén rolled his eyes and turned away. "You expect me to believe you after what I just saw? You can rot in there for all I care."

"I can bring her back!" Jae called desperately out to him.

Damicén paused, swiveling on his heels to face the door. He cocked an eyebrow, waiting for Jae to continue.

"That's why I chose her. I could bring her back." Jae held up the necklace I'd seen from our trip to the lake. The golden spiral reflected in the single light of the holding room, casting a glow across the floor. "She was the only one I could ensure would return."

Damicén clenched his jaw and leveled a finger at Jae. "You've lost it if you think I'm doing that whole thing again. We tried it. I know how it ends."

"No, this time is different." Jae was adamant, slamming his hand now on the door. "We can use the stone this time."

Damicén strolled smoothly to the door, almost seeming to disappear from view until he reached the window. "Did you love her?"

"What?"

"Talon. Did you love her?"

Jae went silent as he chewed on the question. Every second that passed, Damicén grew more agitated, shoulders stiffening. His fingers began to twitch along with the rapid tapping of his foot.

"I can't say."

Scoffing, Damicén began to turn away again.

"That's not fair, Damicén. I only knew her for two weeks."

He kept walking. He'd almost reached the entryway when Jae managed to say something that stopped him.

"But I can't deny the connection."

Damicén turned halfway to glare at the door. "Let me ask you something. If it really came down to it, and there wasn't an underlying plan, who would you choose between the two?"

Jae stumbled back as if the words had hit him in the gut. After a heartbeat of silence passed, he said, "I don't know."

He didn't try to stop Damicén again as he disappeared, but he did leave with him with one final thought.

"Instead of interrogating me, maybe you should take a look at your new friend."

My eyes opened as the lights flicked on in the room. I sat up and rubbed the sleep from my eyes, thinking about my dream. Why would I dream something so weird and awful?

Below me, Sam groaned in protest as she stood and stretched her arms.

"I really hate that timer," she grumbled.

Rhydel answered with an affirming noise right as a knock sounded at the door.

Waltzing over, Sam opened it to reveal Kenna on the other side.

"Good morning, sunshine," she purred. Her eyes glanced around the room before landing on me. "Ah!" She reached out of view of the door and brandished a black duffle bag. "This is for you." She held the bag out in my direction.

Before I could move to get down from the top bunk, Sam took the bag and tossed it up to me. It was an effort to not let it slam into my face.

Sliding the zipper open, I was greeted with the sight of clothes. A pair of jeans, athletic shorts, a couple tie-dyed tank tops, and a rock band T-shirt.

I looked back at Kenna, whose gaze had turned grim. "Those will fit you well enough. I'm sorry we can't go out and buy or make fancy dresses."

"Thank you," I said earnestly. I'd rather have these small outfits than be stuck waiting on a dress every day, only to have it ripped away at the end of the day.

She tilted her chin down in response and turned back to Sam. "I'll meet you three in the cafeteria in fifteen?"

Sam nodded and shut the door, turning back to me. Rhydel was up now and staring intently at the duffel bag.

My cheeks flushed as I took in their somber looks.

Rhydel noticed my embarrassment and clarified, "Those clothes belonged to Mia. One of our..." he shared a glance with Sam, "friends."

"She died last year," Sam added, chewing on her lower lip.

Taking a look back down at the clothes, I felt dirty. Who was I—a stranger to these people—to take their dead friends' clothes?

Once again, Rhydel noted my train of thought and hastily said, "Wear them. She would've wanted that instead of them gathering dust in a corner."

He jumped off the bed, landing on the carpet with a soft *thump*, and excused himself to change in the bathroom.

Sam began to change out of her pajamas and motioned for me, as well. "He'll wait until we're done before coming out."

Begrudgingly, I selected the rock band shirt and jeans. They fit me surprisingly well like she was the exact same size and body shape as me.

Once we finished getting dressed, Sam knocked on the bathroom door. Rhydel exited with freshly brushed teeth and hair, wearing clothes similar to his sleeping ones.

Sam and I entered, where she gave me my own toothbrush. It was only then did I realize they hadn't been at Grant's, and I'd gone that long without brushing my teeth.

Clasping a hand over my mouth at the realization, I started to apologize profusely. Sam just waved a hand and shrugged.

"Your teeth still look good, at least."

I smiled haphazardly into the mirror, expecting the worst. But my teeth did really still look good, considering they hadn't been brushed in almost a month. That I can remember, anyways.

We brushed our teeth and hair and made our way down the hallway. The layout was much easier to memorize than Grant's castle/cottage nightmare, considering it was just one long hallway with a single turn.

The cafeteria buzzed with people, most dressed in athletic attire, with the rest in casual clothing. Voices filled the air as they conversed and laughed with one another. It was such a stark contrast to the past month of silence.

Sam led us to a round table in the corner of the room where Kenna, Damicén, and Brandon sat.

Rhydel beelined for the buffet-style lineup of breakfast food at the center of the room while Sam waved to Brandon and gave him a squeeze with her arm. "How's Millie?"

Brandon had his mouth stuffed with what looked like pancakes, so his only response was a thumbs up. Today he wore an open button-up with a gray shirt underneath and thick black-rimmed glasses.

"When did you start wearing glasses?" Sam asked, noticing them at the same time I had.

Brandon managed to swallow his food and shrugged. "About a month ago. Who knew magic would give you bad eyesight?"

"Yeah, sure. It's the *magic's* doing and not because you stare at a computer screen all the time." Damicén sneered next to him, inviting a soft punch to the arm from Brandon. I was still hung up on that one word.

"Magic?" My voice cut through their laughter like a blade, all four of them turning to look at me.

Sam used that opportunity to dash to the food as well, leaving me behind in the awkward silence.

I sat down across from Brandon, whose face had gone beet red at my question. Of which he shoveled food into his mouth to avoid answering.

Kenna shot him a sideways smirk and reassured me, "It'll all be explained after breakfast. You should eat. You've had a rough few days and need the energy for what you're about to hear."

That made me all the more nervous. So nervous, in fact, it made me not want to eat at all. It must be pretty bad if they want me to eat before it.

Damicén must've seen the panic written across my face because he leaned over and whispered, "It's not that bad, I promise."

His words soothed me little. I forced myself to chew and swallow an apple without it coming back up.

Sam and Rhydel returned and carried on about other people. Someone named Millie and Adaim. I gathered from context clues that Millie must be Sam's girlfriend. Fiancée? It sounded like they were at a different location, one Brandon used to be at.

"Why are you guys split up?" I asked, rolling the apple core on the table.

Damicén and Kenna looked at each other before she said, "For safety."

"This place is not big enough to hold everyone," Damicén added.

I bit my lower lip in thought. "So, who is in charge of the other place?"

She smiled faintly before saying, "Adaim. My husband."

"I'm sorry." How awful she must feel to be separated from her husband and Sam from Millie.

"It's okay. Sometimes these things have to happen. I talk to him every day, anyway."

Damicén popped a biscuit into his mouth as he said, "Plus, just in case one location is…compromised, there's still some people left to fight."

My eyebrows knitted together at their words. "For the war with Grant?"

Everyone at the table stilled. As did the voices in the room.

I ducked my head at the sudden silence, cheeks flushing as I realized everyone had turned to stare at me.

"We don't really like to say his name," Kenna clarified. "Some of the people here have major trauma around the war, and his name triggers the memories."

The voices resumed, but more hushed now. Like they waited to see if I would say it again. Instead, I decided to change the subject.

"Where's Jae?" My dream from last night had him at the forefront of my mind.

Damicén's silverware clattered to the table, knuckles turning white from how hard he clenched them.

Kenna rolled her eyes and peeled a banana. "He's down in the holding cell."

"And he'll stay down there until we figure out what to do with him," Damicén bit out.

I wanted to argue. I wanted to tell them they had no right to be upset at him over that. I'd seen what Grant did to him, and I couldn't blame him for doing whatever the man said. But their grief was fresh, and nothing I said would change that.

We finished eating, and Kenna walked me to the designated room. Sam and Rhydel disappeared—probably off to do their punishments for saving me—while Damicén and Brandon fell in step behind us.

Kenna walked with such grace and dignity. You could throw her in a ball gown, slap a crown on her head, and she'd look every bit a queen. More so than Ketura. She felt like a false queen in Kenna's presence.

Standing this close to her, I could see the faintest of white at the end of her straight, black hair. Like she'd once had a layer but cut it off. Up close, the crescent moon scar was more jagged and gnarled than I'd previously believed. Something big had given her that, and I was afraid to ask what.

We reached the same room from yesterday, and Kenna motioned to the table, a few wooden chairs now placed on one side.

Brandon moved two chairs to the opposite side, holding one out for me. We slid in while the others took up residence across from us.

I tapped my fingers nervously on my thigh, fidgeting with the fabric of my jeans. Brandon picked at a muffin he'd taken from the cafeteria, glancing over at me every so often.

Damicén and Kenna were having another silent conversation, the latter making a sour face. She finally waved her hand, effectively ending the conversation, and turned to me.

She placed her hands neatly on the table, folding them together. "Before we tell you what we know. I want to know what happened after you…" she fumbled around for the correct words, "came to consciousness."

"From when you can remember is what she means," Brandon clarified, and I'm glad he did because I was a little confused by her wording.

I frowned, annoyed I would have to relive the past few days before I could find out the truth.

"Why can't you tell me first?" I asked.

Damicén swallowed, jaw working. "We're not sure how you're going to react to the information. And we don't want you shutting down before we can figure out what happened after."

"Oh." So I'm just an information dump to them. Information on Grant. Were they even going to tell me what I wanted to know after I spoke? Was it all a ruse?

I want to know how I lost my memory. If they had any idea and were going to hold it over my head to get info out of me, I think I'd rather have stayed with Grant.

Damicén sighed dramatically. "We can't tell you how you lost your memory."

My mouth dropped open. How did he know I was thinking that?

"What?" I tried to play it cool. Even though my mouth hanging open surely gave away my shock.

"We can't tell you how you lost your memory," he repeated. "Because we don't know."

I blinked. "Then what can you tell me?" And how have you spoken about what I was thinking twice now?

All three shared glances with each other before Kenna motioned for Brandon to speak.

"We rescued you about six months ago after Avalon kidnapped you."

My mouth flew open again, but I snapped it closed just as fast. That was something I could kind of believe, as Avalon hadn't been very nice to me. She looked at me as if I were a child berating her for candy. But she was with Grant. Did that mean Grant gave the order to have me kidnapped?

"Grant wasn't around then," Damicén said in a strangled voice. "You were part of a bigger plan to lure all of us to their lair."

"We got you out of their dungeons, and that's where we lost Jesse." Brandon looked down at his hands. "Or so we thought," he said the last part so quietly I almost didn't hear it.

It was still odd hearing them call Jae Jesse. And even odder knowing they knew him before this and that…he knew me.

That realization came crashing down on me. If what they were saying is true—and I'd bet money it was considering their interaction with him yesterday—then that means Jae knew me the entire time. He knew who I was and didn't tell me. He watched me struggle with my memory loss and did nothing.

Regardless of how Grant treated him, we had many moments alone where he could've said something. The lake, the barn, when he sat outside of my door those few days after Jarred's death. But he said nothing.

"We managed to get out of the tunnels through a chimney and made it all the way back to the hotel before you vanished," Brandon continued. "We're not sure how because we had multiple sets of eyes on you, but we woke up, and you were gone."

"That's why we need to know what happened. Whatever you can remember," Damicén interjected, pointing his index finger into the wood.

I rubbed my eyes, still wrestling with the idea of Jae not being Jae. Granted, I never really knew him or talked to him—he made sure of that. But I always got this impression he was there for me. There was a softness behind his eyes I didn't see in the rest.

"I woke up already in the house," I began, still choosing to leave out the lake scene. I wanted to confront Vityul about that before I told these people. If he was even still around, I'd yet to see him today. I know he mentioned leaving, and I hoped he hadn't done that already. I wanted answers.

Damicén's eyes narrowed as I spoke, leaning his chin into his palm.

"Avalon showed up, then Jae kicked her out—"

"Why do you call him Jae?" Brandon questioned. "That's not his name."

"It is his name," Damicén responded, pinching the bridge of his nose. "His *real* name."

Brandon seemed taken aback by this information. "What?"

"His birth name is Hyeon SeokJae."

I nodded, remembering when I'd heard Grant call him that in the map room.

Brandon slumped in his chair, clearly upset at this revelation.

"After what we learned yesterday, this is what upsets you the most?" Damicén asked, tongue in cheek.

"No, it's just the added lie about his name. Why does he go by Jesse to us, then?"

"I really don't care what he wants to go by."

Kenna pinched Damicén's bicep, resulting in a yelp from him. He gingerly rubbed the spot and nodded for me to continue.

So I told them everything, from the shadow creature chasing me through the house—which I could now guess was Vityul—all the way to the dinner scene.

The shock of the queen being Grant's niece was evident on their faces, along with the news of his estranged nephew.

"I thought she came into power because of her dad being on the council?" Brandon asked.

Damicén and Kenna answered in unison, "She did."

"So does this mean we can tell the council what's going on and just let them take care of it like last time?"

Kenna frowned. "It's nearly impossible to get a hearing with them. They move locations constantly to avoid—"

"Basically, you don't see them unless they want you to," Damicén finished for her. "And they don't want us to."

This silenced any further questions Brandon might've wanted to ask. He ducked his head, rubbing his thumb across a spot on his neck.

They all leaned in when I told them I'd gone to one of his speeches, itching for information. When I said a lot of the people were blurry and hard to look at, they grew confused. Then I mentioned the bonfire, and their faces turned grim. Lastly, when I revealed what I saw as I was leaving with Vityul, they all gave a knowing look.

"Forsaken." Brandon shivered at the word. "I remember my first time seeing one of those."

My eyebrows shot up, not so much at their name but at his nonchalant attitude to the creatures. "What are they?"

He cleared his throat and pointed to Damicén. "You wanna handle that?"

"I saw how she reacted to seeing it. You think she's gonna like the explanation?"

"How did you see it?" Now I was beginning to freak out. My breath started to come faster, and my heart pounded in my ears so loud I was sure they could hear it.

"Alright," Kenna sighed. "It's time we tell you what's really going on."

Chapter Fifteen

I shouldn't have eaten breakfast.

As I emptied the contents of my stomach into a nearby trash can, that's all I could think about. That apple did *not* feel good coming back up.

There's no way this was happening. There's no possible way any of this was true. Vampires and Werewolves? Witches and Warlocks?

That would explain the orange around Avalon and the purple around Brandon—if I believed in magic. If I believed in any of this at all. Which I don't. I don't believe it.

Damicén smiled widely, revealing two sharp pointed teeth…fangs.

Brandon squatted next to me, patting my back tenderly as I wretched into the bin. A small piece of me wanted to shove him off, but another part liked the comforting touch. My stomach hurt, my throat burned, and my head ached.

"If it makes you feel any better, you're handling it way better than I did," he offered with a grin. His cheeks fluffed under the weight of it, showing off his freckles.

"What did you do?"

He rubbed the back of his neck as he said, "I passed out and hit my head on a desk." He lifted his golden curls to reveal a small scar at the corner of his hairline. "Needed a couple stitches."

That brought a small giggle from me, which in turn, upset my stomach again. I turned back to the bin, but nothing came up. It was a dry heave.

Kenna loomed over him with a box of tissues and a forced smile on her face. Damicén had taken up a spot on the edge of the table, arms folded and eyebrow raised.

"Told you she couldn't handle it," he said.

Kenna reached a hand back to smack him, but he moved out of range.

Those words angered me. I'd been treated the same at Grant's, and after cowering in a dark corner there, I now wanted nothing more than to prove I could handle it. I could. I would prove to everyone I wasn't a child that needed coddling.

I pushed the trash can back and sat up, taking a deep breath. "I'm fine."

Kenna brought the tissue box closer to my face, and I graciously accepted them, using one to wipe my eyes.

Damicén scoffed, sliding off the table. "What I don't understand is how you weren't able to see it. He even managed to block out his own words."

"Magic," Brandon said like it was the obvious answer. It still felt weird that that word was now real. That I couldn't laugh it off as one big joke.

Damicén shook his head. "No spell was performed."

"That you know of," Kenna countered. But the look Damicén gave her must've meant something because she twisted her mouth and scowled.

"It's the necklace."

We all turned in unison to look who'd spoken. Vityul stood in the doorway, propped up against the frame, with a necklace dangling from his hand. My necklace. The one Jae had ripped off me under the table.

"How did you get that?" I asked at the same time Damicén blurted, "Is that Iolite?"

My head snapped around to gape at the man. "Iolite?"

Brandon stood from his crouched position near me and snatched the necklace from Vityul.

"Oh, yeah. That thing's loaded," he confirmed with a wince as he tossed it to Damicén.

He caught the jewelry with one hand. Inspecting it thoroughly, his eyebrows furrowed as he stroked the gem with his thumb. "Why Iolite?"

"Why not?" I looked between them hesitantly. What was wrong with it? And what did he mean by loaded?

Brandon cleared his throat and said, "Every crystal has certain properties they bring to the wearer. Iolite can be used to enhance clarity."

A look of realization dawned on Kenna's face as she rubbed her chin. "Sneaky."

"What?" I demanded, moving to stand.

Before I could, Vityul grabbed my elbow to help me to my feet. His hair had been pushed back with a silver headband, exposing his indigo eyes. Shadows seemed to dance in his hooded gaze.

"The necklace had a spell cast on it," he expounded. "To keep you from seeing the Supernatural or even hearing about it."

"They used a stone meant for clarity to hide it," Brandon added.

"But why try to hide it?" Damicén questioned. "It's not like she knew the difference."

Vityul shrugged and said nothing else.

"Where did you get it?" Damicén echoed my earlier question that had been ignored, a suspicious glint in his gaze.

He only answered with one word. "Jesse."

Damicén eyed him carefully, chewing on his answer. "You went to see him?"

Vityul stuffed his hands in his pockets, shrugged, and said nothing. Like he was too good to repeat himself.

Jae kept the necklace? Why would he do that? Unless he knew he'd be coming here and he could give it to them. But if he knew that, then he knew they'd be coming for me. Why didn't he warn me?

"I need to see Jae." I looked between them, silently pleading. "I have to talk to him and figure everything out."

Kenna pursed her lips and shook her head. "I'm sorry. Until we know for sure what's going on with him, we can't allow you to see him. It's too risky."

"We can't allow *anyone* to see him," Damicén emphasized with a pointed look to Vityul, who looked as bored as...well as his own shadow.

"I know you have a lot of questions for him, but so do we." She promised, "Once we get everything sorted, we'll let you see him."

That wasn't the best, considering they're still pretty pissed at him. I didn't know when it would be sorted, and I had some questions that needed answering. For my sake—and peace of mind—I could only hope they would hold true to their words. Jae had a lot to answer for.

Speaking of, now that I know he didn't leave, Vityul had some things to answer for too. Unfortunately, I had a feeling that's going to be like asking a brick wall.

"We're done here for now." Damicén cast a wary glance over us before tucking the necklace into his pocket.

I didn't wait for him to wave us away and shot out the door after Vityul—who was already halfway down the hall. "Hey, wait!"

He never slowed, seeming to glide across the concrete floor. When I caught up to him, it was a struggle to keep pace.

"Can you slow down? I need to ask you something."

He shot me a sideways look, sneering, "There's nothing you *need* to ask me."

"The hell there isn't."

"Like what?" He slammed on the brakes so suddenly I walked a few steps past him before realizing.

Scuttling back, I folded my arms across my chest and scowled. "The lake."

A muscle flexed in his jaw, the only indicator he knew what I was talking about since the rest of his face remained as blank as the wall behind him.

"What lake?"

"The lake you pulled me out of."

"I think you're confused. Grant pulled you out."

"How would you know that if you weren't there?" And anyway, Grant said Jae did it. Three people couldn't have simultaneously pulled me out, yet I only remembered one. Even then, I could feel the disdain radiating off of him every time Grant or Jae was mentioned. No way he helped them.

"How do you know it was me?"

"No one else I've met has purple eyes. Why can't you admit it?"

He remained passive-faced as he blended into the shadows, leaving me stewing in silence—coincidentally in front of my door.

I stamped my foot with an aggravated grunt and barged inside, shutting the door harder than I meant to. Grabbing the nearest pillow, I buried my face in it and screamed. Nobody was here to witness my tantrum, thankfully, so after I was done, I just crawled back into bed to cool off.

He was hiding something; I knew it. He wouldn't avoid answering my questions if he wasn't. Now I just had to figure out how to get it out of him without him disappearing.

If only I could also figure out how I kept being sucked into my dreams.

Chapter Sixteen

I didn't even realize I'd fallen asleep when I was once again see-through, hidden in the air.

Damicén stood in front of Jae's cell door, holding the necklace out to view.

Some part of me began wondering if this was real, but it couldn't be. It had to just be a very weird dream.

"What is this?" He asked Jae, who propped against the door on his shoulder.

"A necklace."

"Stop. You want us to believe you so badly but then do this bullshit. What is it?" He got closer, shoving the jewelry up to the window.

Jae sighed, straightening and squinting at it. "It's the necklace Grant gave Rosetta before his speech."

"What does it do?"

Shaking his head, Jae cringed. "As far as I know, Avalon only charmed it to encourage the wearer to…avoid Supernatural contact."

"Make them hard to see and induce headaches? Muffle words?"

He nodded.

Damicén tucked the necklace back into his pocket and crossed his arms. "Why did he pick Iolite?"

"What?" Jae seemed genuinely confused.

"Iolite." Damicén enunciated each syllable with a vicious bite to the T at the end.

Jae shrugged. "I don't even know what that is or what it does. Plus, it's not like he tells me everything. I actively avoid him when I can."

"Can you glamour her memories back?"

A shadow passed across his face. "You know it doesn't work like that."

Damicén didn't seem to buy it but let it go and moved on to another topic. "What do you know about Vityul?"

Jae shoved his hands in his pockets and slid down the opposing wall, crossing his legs. This made Damicén come closer, having to press his nose against the window to still see him. "You're getting suspicious of him, aren't you?"

"When he showed up at our doorstep unexpectedly and pledged his allegiance to the cause, I was suspicious. I'd never heard of him before, never seen him."

"I know he's not who he says he is."

Damicén scoffed with a raised brow, "And how do you know that?"

The smile that played on Jae's lips was nothing short of mischievous as he said, "I'm a tracker."

This enraged Damicén, who ran a hand through his long hair. "You're really going to play this game again?"

"You're growing suspicious of him, aren't you?" Jae countered, ignoring the question.

He stepped back, blowing a long breath out. "I can't see what's in his head—aside from what he shows me—but I saw him in Rosetta's."

Okay, this dream has definitely taken a turn into weird.

"The lake," Jae stated.

"The lake," he agreed. "She didn't tell us, but neither did he. He knows something."

"I agree, though I can honestly say I don't know what."

"I'm grateful he got her out, but he went behind our backs and took two of Kenna's pack. They could've died. In fact, they almost did."

Jae's face scrunched in confusion. "What happened?"

"Cave Crawlers."

"Gross."

"Rosetta managed to push them back with some kind of power." Damicén shook his head in what seemed like disbelief. "You think the Stone could've done that?"

Pursing his lips, Jae grimaced. "I don't know. It's possible."

Damicén nodded, looking up at the concrete ceiling. He stayed silent for a beat before he asked, "Why did you do it, man?"

Jae stood, approaching the door. "I had to pick one. Or else you all would've died."

"When did it change?" As Damicén dropped his face to stare at Jae, his eyes grew glassy and red-rimmed.

Jae pondered this for a moment before answering, "At Kenna's. I started to doubt it before that on the drive there. Talon and I had a talk," he chuckled dryly, avoiding Damicén's grief-stricken look. "But it was after the attack that I truly decided, and it grew from there. I took the first step to defect right before Orlando. You were all so different from what I'd been led to believe—from what I was raised to believe."

Damicén wiped a stray tear with the back of his hand, stare hardening. "Yet you didn't say anything. You didn't warn us."

"I thought I could do it on my own. Their plan was too far ahead for us to have changed course." Jae threw his arms wide. "Let's be real, Damicén. If I'd told you I was his son, and they'd sent me to lead you all to death, you wouldn't have listened to a word I said after that. Nor would you have believed that I was trying to change it."

Damicén smiled at that and dipped his chin. "You're right. I would've killed you. Or at least tried to."

They shared that moment together. A glimmer of something calm drifting between them. I could tell the history was there. The hurt feelings and regret said as much. But I could also tell the future lay there. Maybe, just maybe, their relationship could be rekindled.

If it was real. Why I continued to dream about this situation baffled me. I mean, it had to be a dream. Damicén knew things I didn't tell him, which meant my subconscious had to come up with them.

"You're not going to tell me who Vityul is, are you?" Damicén asked with a smirk.

Jae debated his response, tilting his head from side to side. "Truthfully, I don't know for sure he's who I think he is."

"And who do you think he is?"

My eyes fluttered open at the sound of knocking on the door. As I floundered to get off the top bunk, the pounding didn't cease.

When I finally managed to grab the doorknob and twist, I was greeted by Brandon's flushed face.

"I can get you in to see Jesse."

I blinked, not fully taking in his words, until I rubbed the sleep from my eyes.

"What?"

He rubbed the back of his neck, mumbling to himself, "I guess I shouldn't have started off with that."

When I just stared at him, his face grew redder.

"It's dinner time. I can explain while we eat if you want?" His sheepish grin brought a smile to my face. He was so flustered and embarrassed. It was kind of cute.

As we walked to the cafeteria, his first words finally began to sink in. He could take me to Jae—or Jesse. First thing I needed to ask him was what to call him.

We sat at an empty table in the corner of the cafeteria with our food. Brandon got two sandwiches while I clung to fruit. My stomach still felt weak from earlier, so I didn't wanna push it.

He nervously glanced around as he chewed, knowing that I was waiting for him to start talking since he'd so gracefully woken me from my nap—which had started a massive headache that had no intention of dimming.

"Alright. I know you have a lot of questions," he began. "I don't know why they can't be answered by us and only Jesse. But I do know what it's like to not be told everything and get left in the dark."

I dropped my gaze to my sliced pineapple, chewing on the inside of my cheek. "It's worse when you don't have any memories."

"I bet." He sucked in a shaky breath, taking another bite of his sandwich. "Which is why I want to help."

"How are you going to do that exactly? Kenna and Damicén kinda seem set on the rules."

"They are. Which is why we have to be discreet."

"I'm listening."

He furrowed his brow, about to say something when Damicén slid into the chair beside him. Brandon shoved the rest of his sandwich in his mouth, grinning with his mouth full of food.

Damicén shot him a sideways smirk, glancing over at me. "Fruit again?"

I nodded, finally putting a whole piece in my mouth. "Still feel icky."

He frowned. "I'm sorry we threw it at you like that."

"No. It's okay. I wanted to know, and I'm thankful you actually told me instead of making me try to figure it out." I plopped another piece in my mouth, heart thrumming in my chest.

What did he hear? If Damicén had heard anything of Brandon's intentions, he didn't let on. I couldn't tell if that was a good thing or not.

"I think we're gonna show you the rest of the facility after dinner," Damicén stated, plucking something from his chin. "Unless you have something else planned."

Brandon cut his eyes toward me, silent, pleading in them. I wasn't going to tattle on him, not when he was going to help me. So I shook my head—maybe a little too aggressively.

"That's actually what we were just talking about," I added, hoping my shaky voice didn't give me away.

Damicén slightly narrowed his eyes before nodding. "Alright. I'll just chill here till you guys are done."

I gulped.

Trying to finish dinner was like eating chalk. My mind ran rampant with the thoughts of punishment I could receive. Scrub the cafeteria with a toothbrush? Push-ups? I wasn't part of their group. They could give me something worse. Especially since I'd been verbally told no one was allowed to see Jae.

Brandon would be in much worse trouble, though. He seemed close with Damicén and Kenna. How angry would they be at him for breaking the rules for me? I still didn't even understand how he'd get me there in the first place.

Damicén walked in front as he led us down the short hallway.

Taking a left through a door, we walked into a small workout gym. A couple people I didn't recognize were doing pull-ups while Rhydel and Sam ran the treadmill.

She flashed me a smile, sweat pouring down her face. Rhydel did a one-finger salute, panting.

Damicén stopped in front of them, arms crossed and smiling. "You look tired."

Rhydel bared his teeth as Damicén chuckled.

"This is what happens when you break the rules," he said, making a sweeping look at Brandon and me. Lingering his gaze on Brandon for half a heartbeat, he cocked his head to the side.

"If you ever want to work out or go for a run, you come here," he finally said. "You can't go above ground."

Brandon nodded, adding, "We're too open up above. No cover and nowhere to hide."

"Brilliant building this on a beach," Rhydel muttered in between breaths.

"I didn't build it," Damicén snapped.

"No, but you helped build the add-on rooms," Brandon countered, which warranted a glare from his friend.

"So did you."

"Yeah, but you did the hard labor."

Damicén threw his hands up and stalked away. "Whatever, let's keep going."

We went back into the hall and across the way through another door. We went in and out of several doors, seeing a library, a classroom, and a medical room.

"It's not much," Damicén said as we paused in front of another door. "But it's home for now."

"It's kept us safe for a long time," Brandon added, curls gleaming in the light.

"This door." Damicén gestured behind him. "Leads down into the holding cells." He stared at me at those last few words, daring me to ask the question.

"Where Jae is?"

"Yes."

Brandon's breath hitched in his throat. He ducked his head in defeat and sighed. Now what? Our punishment? Would I have to run laps on that treadmill?

Damicén's stoic face burst into a wide smile as he cackled, slapping a hand on Brandon's shoulder. "Why did you ever think you could slip it past me?"

Brandon shrugged off the hand, fisting his own at his side. "I didn't. I just thought you'd find out afterward."

"Next time you have a thought. Let it go." Smoldering ember eyes squinted with joy as Damicén continued to belly laugh. "I knew something was up when the only thing running through your mind was the lyrics to Carry On Wayward Son. Usually, there's some back chatter, but you completely tried to wipe your thoughts."

"Kansas is a great band."

"You only like it because it's basically the theme song to Supernatural."

I looked in confusion between them, still stuck on the fact Damicén basically said he heard Brandon's thoughts. "Wait, wait. What is he talking about, Brandon?"

He tilted his head toward me, still glaring at Damicén, and said, "He can read minds."

A chill ran down the length of my spine, ice cubes forming in between each nodule. "What did you say?"

Damicén stopped laughing just long enough to wipe the tears from his eyes and wag a dark eyebrow at me. "I can read minds."

My jaw almost hit the floor. Not at that revelation, so much so the fact that what I dreamed could be real. The fact he knew I'd hidden Vityul and the lake and that odd light in the cave. He actually knew about it. He knew about everything in my head. Even when I thought he looked like a God.

So did that mean I dreamed what could happen? Or what has already happened? Did he know about the dreams? Well, now that I'm thinking about it, he probably does.

I barely understood what went on inside my head. Now I have to deal with this onslaught of weirdness from my body? The light, the dreams. It was beginning to swamp me. I could feel it. I needed answers more than anything.

Damicén had stopped laughing entirely now and was gazing at me with a question in his eyes. He studied me like Grant had done the first night we'd met.

Was he in my head right now? Listening to me rant and ramble? Oh, God, this was embarrassing. Could he turn it off?

"I can't turn it off," he said, causing me to jump. He had been in my head.

"Why not?" Anger welled up in me, frustration, too. I didn't want anyone rummaging around in there when I was still trying to recover the pieces that remained.

He cleared his throat and leaned against the concrete wall. "It's like a radio. Each station is a different mind. If I focus, I can listen to an individual station. Most of the time, though, it's that station where a few overlap at once. It can't be turned off."

And just as suddenly, my anger came screeching to a halt. That sounded awful. The noise never stopped? If he was immortal, that meant he'd dealt with that for hundreds of years.

"Two thousand," he clarified, holding up two fingers. "I'm the oldest living Vampire."

My throat clogged with unspoken words. Unspoken apologies and questions. I felt guilty being angry he'd been in my head. He couldn't help it. How had he survived that long with the voices constantly in his head?

The corners of his mouth tugged upward in a sad smile. "I had help."

I don't think I will get used to him answering my thoughts out loud like that.

"I miss her too, pal," Brandon said softly, rubbing his arms for comfort.

They must've been talking about Talon. I would have to ask Brandon about her later, but now I took my chance and stared down Damicén. Which did me no good because when he stared right back, I couldn't hold his gaze.

"Well?" I folded my arms across my chest.

He didn't have to ask me what I was talking about. He knew because I'd asked the rest in my mind.

Glancing between Brandon and me with a soulful look, he clenched his jaw. I thought for sure he was going to say no. But something he saw in Brandon's eyes must've struck a chord.

He sighed heavily, holding up a hand. "You get five minutes. Kenna is hard-pressed about these rules, and I don't want to get in trouble along with you two."

Without thinking, I wrapped my arms around his neck in the biggest bear hug I could manage. He froze, even stopped breathing, for a few heartbeats. Then his arms slowly folded around me, one around my shoulders and the other at my waist.

His pine wood smell filled my nose, and the hardness of his muscles pressed into me.

As my cheeks heated, the more I thought about it, I gave him another squeeze for good measure and backed away. Now that I know he can read minds, I couldn't let mine run rampant on his…well, everything.

"Thank you," I said, hand to my heart in sincerity.

His gaze lingered on me for a moment before he quickly turned on his heels and opened the door.

I grew more worried when I realized I recognized the staircase from my dreams. It almost turned into a full-blown panic attack when we reached the bottom. It was the same room, the same door.

Steadying myself, I approached it under Damicén's watchful eyes. He took up space in the corner nearest the door, with Brandon beside him.

Jae was already at the window, face full of emotion and also clear of any previous wounds.

The closer I stepped, the more my heart pounded.

This was it. I could finally get the answers I so desperately craved. But as I stood there staring at him and his disheveled hair, I lost it.

Tears spilled over, and my throat closed with a sob. Memories flooded the forefront of my mind, and it took everything I had to not collapse on my knees. Every question I had evaporated from my mind.

As I stood there silently sobbing, Jae also began to cry.

"I'm sorry," he whispered, voice barely a breath. "I didn't have a choice."

Sharp anger shifted from the tears, and I snapped my head up to him. "You didn't have a choice?" I balled my fists at my side, stepping even closer to the glass. "No, I didn't have a choice, Jae. I didn't have my memories—I *still* don't have any memories—and I was at the mercy of all of you."

He looked down, shame ripe on his face. "You have to understand—"

"No, you have to understand!" I slammed a finger into my chest, bursting with rage. "I was manipulated, isolated, forced to watch Grant murder Jarred. Forced to live with that image. Forced to be at the mercy of his wishes and wants. Forced to rely on him for clothes every day. Left to wander and wonder. No one told me anything, and now I discover what I could find out he hid from me with that necklace."

Jae shut his eyes, bottom lip trembling. "I know. I'm sorry. I should've been there, should've done more."

"You have no obligation to me other than you should've told me the truth. That you knew me beforehand, knew who I was, and still allowed me to struggle. Watched me suffer and doubt."

"It killed me inside to witness that."

"Then why did you let it happen?" I was screaming now, so angry and hurt. So betrayed.

He ran his hands through his hair and paced around the cell. "He would've killed me if I'd told you. And I couldn't get you safely out if I was dead."

I paused, my hearing catching up to my anger. "You were gonna get me out?"

He stiffened, turning toward me. "When you told me about the shadow creature outside your window, I managed to connect the dots. I knew he'd be coming for you, and he could get you out better than I could."

"So the deceit grows. You also knew what the shadow was, who it was, and let me be afraid of it. Decided not to tell me."

"But you're not afraid of them anymore, Are you?"

"No."

"I did that. I made sure you wouldn't be afraid of them so you could get out."

I paused. "What do you mean?"

His jaw tensed with apprehension. He did not want to disclose this. "How much does she know?" The question was aimed at Damicén, who gave a resigned shrug in response.

"I'm right here," I snapped.

Jae scrubbed a hand down his face, clutching his jaw to the side as he stared me down. "I have an ability to glamor individuals. Hypnotize them, in a sense, to do and think what I want them to do. And they won't remember it."

The silence that settled between us was suffocating. My body began to feel as if quicksand were sucking me into its depths. Just to drown in my own fear on the way down. "You *warped* my mind?"

"I had to. You were too scared. You would've never gone willingly."

"So you manipulated me? How many times have you done that?"

He flinched, eyes pinned to the bottom of the door. "No."

I noticed his lack of answer on exactly how many times he'd done that to me. My instincts told me not to believe him, that I would be a fool to do so. But standing here, watching him breakdown with guilt, I couldn't help but cut him some slack. "You should've just told me."

"I couldn't. Grant had ears everywhere, you know that. That's why I had to get rid of Jarred. He would've been the reason you didn't escape."

Shock rippled through me, and I couldn't help it anymore. My knees buckled, and I hit the floor. Brandon was at my side instantly, checking me over. I ignored him, too hooked on the realization before me.

"You made sure he'd hear what we said to trigger him to do something that'd get him killed."

Remorse filled Jae's sunken face as he said, "Yes."

My heart cracked in two as I buried my face in Brandon's thick shoulder. My breathing came in quick gasps in between sobs, and black crept into my vision.

Jae destroyed me, made me witness that awful thing. On purpose. He had planned it all. Why would he do that to me?

"I never intended for you to see it, though." His words drew back my attention. Hesitantly, and through the space between Brandon's chin and shoulder, I looked.

"I thought Grant would just overhear it and kill him later. I swear I never meant for him to do it in front of you." The pleading in his voice made me think he was telling the truth. But after hearing how he'd lied to the others and now these lies to me, I was doubtful.

He must've seen it in my face because he doubled down. "I swear on my life I never wanted that to happen to you. When we found you by the lake, I was devastated. I didn't know what had happened. You were supposed to be with them." He jerked a thumb to Damicén.

"No more lies," I managed to croak out.

He shook his head. "No more. I promise. Anything you want to know, I will tell you."

I took a deep, reassuring breath and used Brandon's frame to stand back up. He offered me his arm to steady me, and I used it gratefully.

"Tell me everything you know about me." I surprised myself at the sturdy tone I used, considering my breakdown only moments ago.

Jae composed himself with a nod and a faint smile.

"Your name is Rosetta Cauldwell. You are twenty years old now and were adopted by Simone and Marina Cauldwell when you were five years old. Along with me. I'm your brother." He placed a hand on his chest, hiccupping a breath. "You love to draw, paint, and sketch whatever you can get your hands and eyes on. You don't like strawberry-flavored things but love strawberries. Your favorite place on earth is the Ferris wheel at the Santa Monica pier. You hate the cold and sleeping in complete darkness." He gulped, knuckling away his tears.

My own ran down my cheeks. Every word he said filled me with agony. I couldn't remember anything he said, couldn't verify it. And it hurt. He had all these memories, yet they'd been ripped away from me.

"Our adoptive parents died over a year ago in a car crash. We were the only survivors."

We stood in silence for a minute, maybe two, taking in each other's reactions and recovering from the information dump.

Once I'd regained some composure, he asked, "Anything else?"

I nodded. "Do you want to be called Jae or Jesse?"

He chuckled at that, the smile reaching his eyes for the first time. "Jesse."

When I didn't respond, he continued, changing the subject back. "I tried to protect you because I knew one day, they'd come for you. And they did."

"Why?" I croaked out, leaning into Brandon's firm grip. It comforted me to have a rock such as him backing me.

"You're special. You have something they want."

"The stone," I gasped, drawing Damicén's attention.

"You know about the stone?" He asked incredulously.

I nod, wiping away my own tears. "Yes. I'm not sure how, but I saw you down here talking about it with him. I don't know what it is, though."

"It's called the Resurrection Stone," a voice came from the other side of the room, from the shadows. Vityul stepped into the dim light, Jesse and Damicén bristling at his appearance. "It can bring back the dead."

Brandon jumped at the shadow man's entrance, muttering under his breath, "I wish he'd quit doing that."

I whirled on Jesse. "Is that why you said you can use it to bring back Talon? In the necklace, you showed me at the lake. Was she always in there?"

His face dropped. "How do you know about that?"

I shrugged. "Like I said before, I saw it."

"You can't use the stone to bring her back," Vityul bit out.

"Like I'm going to listen to what you have to say," Damicén spat. "You haven't been very forthcoming with the truth either."

Vityul didn't even spare a passing glance as he said, "You didn't need to know anything else about me."

"Bull!" Damicén stepped forward now, marching toward him with a newfound purpose. "I saw you were at the lake with her. And you left her there. You could've brought her here in the first place."

"No. I couldn't have," Vityul said numbly. "They were already too close to the lake. I would've been caught."

"Who are you?" Damicén barked. "Tell us, now."

Vityul lashed out, shoving Damicén back into the adjacent wall. The stone cracked under the impact, dust and rubble crumbling onto his head.

Damicén pounced, slamming his shoulder into Vityul's chest.

"Stop!" I cried out, reaching for both of them. "Stop fighting!"

Brandon grabbed me, hauling me away from the battling men. No matter how hard I kicked and fought to get away, he didn't let go. He was annoyingly strong.

"Let them figure it out," he grunted into my ear. "Neither of us can stop them."

Shadows flurried around the room, gathering near Vityul as he shoved back against Damicén's brute strength.

They wrestled each other to the ground, Damicén having Vityul in a headlock while Vityul struggled to free himself.

"Please," I begged, hearing the rip in my voice. "Stop fighting."

Damicén flicked his gaze to me, along with Vityul, both pausing their attack. Nobody moved. I thought Damicén was going to relent until a shadow reached out and wrapped around his leg, yanking him away. It dragged him across the room and was about to slam him into the wall once more when it halted in place, dangling him from the ground.

Vityul had his hand raised to it, calling it back with his fingers. It released Damicén, who crashed to the brick with a loud *thud* and slithered its way back across the floor to rest at Vityul's feet.

He sighed, shoulders hunching. Damicén brushed himself off, flicking Vityul the bird. But Vityul wasn't looking. He'd shut his eyes tight, going inside himself.

A struggle ensued as the shadows bounced and scattered around the room. He balled his fists at his side, knuckles going white, face straining with effort. A sharp jerk of his head to the left, and the shadows subsided, pulling back toward him. They melted into him, a deep breath pulling in his chest. After they settled, he still didn't move, recovering from whatever had just happened.

Damicén stood where he'd been dropped with a wary gaze. Brandon's hands didn't ease on me. In fact, I think I'd probably bruise later from the grip. Jesse stared through the door, eyes narrowed. It seemed like ages before he spoke again.

He opened his eyes, shadows dancing in the blazing purple. "You're right. My name isn't Vityul."

We waited with bated breath for him to continue, the silence swelling.

"My name is Raven Zamfira. And I am Talon's son."

Chapter Seventeen

The air stilled at his words. Damicén's eyes glazed over in shock, Brandon clapped a hand over his mouth, and Jesse stared with his mouth twisted to the side.

Raven made eye contact with every one of us, lingering on Jesse with a hard frown. *Are you happy?* He seemed to ask.

"That's…holy shit," Brandon mumbled behind me. "Talon had a kid?" He looked to Damicén, who still stood as fragile as cracked glass.

"The only child ever born into Vampirism," Damicén answered, finally coming back to life.

Raven nodded in acknowledgment. "So you know about me then."

"I know everything she knew."

Jesse slammed a fist against the door, surprising me. "Then how the fuck did you not know who he was?"

"I'd only ever seen him in her mind," Damicén said as he slid his eyes toward the window. "He looked a lot different there."

"He's a Vampire, immortal, never changing, and has shadow powers, for crying out loud! How did he look different?" Jesse cut off his rant, realization in his stormy eyes. "She didn't know."

Raven pushed his hair back and sighed. "I ran away when I was still a child—ten maybe—after my powers manifested. She never knew."

Brandon released me, taking a hesitant step forward. "That would make you seven thousand years old."

The wind kicked out of me. Seven thousand years on this planet. He's lived through every historic event and is older than most religions. It was so hard to believe this man, who looked no older than his early thirties, was actually thousands of years old. I already had trouble believing Damicén was as old as he was and he was five thousand years younger than him.

My brain swam the longer I thought about it. Two people, no, in fact, everyone in this room aside from Brandon and me, would've never met if time had continued as normal. Everyone separated by thousands of years now stood in the same room.

"Wait, Talon named you Raven?" Brandon's brow furrowed as he thought hard, seeming to stifle a giggle.

Raven shrugged. "She wasn't very creative back then."

"She didn't name you," Damicén interjected with a harsh bite to his words. "Your father did."

"I know."

"Why did you come? Why here?"

Raven said nothing, staring blankly at Damicén as his shadow quivered. I couldn't tell if he was debating his response or if he should even respond at all. But before he'd made a decision, Damicén's face shifted.

Not with emotion, but one of mental communication. One I'd seen him share with Kenna, which I now knew was him reading her mind.

He scowled, leveling a finger at Raven as he approached Jesse's door. "This isn't over, but we've got an emergency." Inputting a code to a keypad I hadn't noticed before, the door slid open.

Jesse stood stunned, hands raised.

"Now's the time to prove you're actually on our side." Damicén smirked with feral intent as he tilted his head toward the stairs. "Let's go."

Without hesitation, Jesse stepped from the cell and followed to the staircase. Brandon filed in behind them with Raven while I struggled to keep pace.

"Where are we going?" Raven asked when we reached the top.

Damicén whirled, fists clenched. "You are sitting here watching her." He pointed to me. "And you better get your story straight for when we get back."

I'd never seen a look of such icy disdain before now, and Raven wore it smoothly. They stared each other down, neither willing to back off. For Damicén, it seemed to be distrust, while for Raven, it seemed to be to prove a point.

After long enough Damicén must've decided it didn't outweigh the emergency, as he called out, "Brandon, make a portal to the Orlando coven."

Brandon had that deer in headlights look as he slowly turned away from us, purple mist winding up his arms. He made a series of odd hand motions, then squared his hands and pulled them apart. A swirling purple vortex appeared in the wall, wind whipping my hair in a frenzy.

Damicén took one final look over his shoulder at us before disappearing into the portal with Jesse and Brandon following behind him. It snapped closed when the last person crossed, leaving my hair piled in my eyelashes.

I fisted my hands on my hips, poking my lips out. "What just happened?"

But Raven wasn't listening. He'd already started walking down the hallway. I scrambled after him, calling for him to wait. He headed for the main entrance, determination in every step.

"Where are you going?" I asked.

He didn't look over as he responded, "I'm going somewhere you can't come."

Hearing those words floored me, boosting my stride until I was in front of him and blocking the door.

"I'm going."

A black eyebrow raised in amusement. "You don't even know where I'm going."

"You're going after them. It's obvious. And I want to go."

He reached a hand out and scooted me effortlessly aside, even when I tried to deadweight myself.

"You can't come."

The more he tried to tell me I wasn't allowed, the more I wanted to go. I was tired of being coddled. I handled the revelation that Supernatural beings existed and that Jesse was my brother. I could handle whatever else.

"You can't tell me what to do. You're not my father."

Raven whirled, eyes blazing. He opened his mouth to retort something before thinking better of it and continuing his march down the hall. "Stay here."

I followed him up the stairs at a full sprint. "Don't leave me behind again," I said the last word unintentionally—it just slipped out—but it caught his attention.

He halted, pivoting to face me at the final door. Something brewed behind his gaze, an idea. He took one calming breath before saying, "If it's what I think it is, it's more death."

Cold swept through me. Maybe there was one thing I couldn't handle. But something inside me whispered to go that I needed to see. So I braced myself, putting on my bravest face.

"Did I flinch?"

Raven searched my eyes for way longer than I was comfortable with. Then he relented, opening the door and pulling me outside with him.

I had no time to react before I was smashed against his chest, and we were moving. The world bent around us like a kaleidoscope, all colors ringed in black. My gut twisted and flipped with the molding world. I clenched my teeth to avoid anything coming up, and they groaned in protest.

It returned to normal a few moments later, where I now stood at the edge of a field in the shadows of pine trees. A lone brick house sat at the far corner, tucked behind a small orange tree orchard.

Birds sang their sweet melody in the branches above my head. The wind kissed my cheek. Life flourished around me, flirting with the bubble of death around the house.

It wasn't even a black mist that hung around the outskirts of the brick. It was a blanket. I could feel the tendrils creeping further into the light. Whatever happened in that house, the souls wouldn't move on by themselves.

I didn't see the others, and Raven kept me from walking into the field by holding my elbow. His touch vibrated a protective instinct through me, a fleeting emotion akin to a mother bear to her cubs.

"How did you do that?" I asked, head spinning.

He didn't answer, just narrowed his eyes at the house.

"Hello?" It was beginning to aggravate me how he'd sometimes refuse to answer things. He'd shut down and move on to another subject, or at least try to.

Purple shadows glanced down at me as he whispered, "Teleporting."

I blinked. "You can teleport?"

He shushed me, pulling me further back into the shadows. "Damicén can hear you from here if you get too loud."

Like I cared. He can teleport! "Why didn't you do that when we left Grant's?" We could've saved ourselves—and my feet—the trouble. "Is that how you managed to chase me around the house that one night?"

Raven rolled his eyes and predictably moved on to another subject. "I'm going to get us inside the house, in the walls. You're going to see some things you won't like, and I need you to try and keep your thoughts as quiet as possible."

He paused, cocking his head. "I know that's going to be difficult for you, but please try."

My face fell flat at the jab. "Very funny," I snipped.

"If you can't handle it, just give my arm a tap." The look he wore was deadly serious. So much so, in fact, it scared me. Flashes of Jarred popped into my mind, sending my heart rate scattering.

He raised an eyebrow as if he could hear it, and thinking about it, he probably could—being a Vampire and all. Could Damicén hear it, too?

I took a calming breath and nodded. "I'm ready." It shouldn't be too hard to keep my thoughts calm. "If you answer my question."

His jaw tensed. "Which one?"

I debated on the two I had, only to decide neither of them I really wanted an answer for right now. I'd thought of a new one. "Why'd you pick the name Vityul?"

If looks could vaporize, I might've been a pile of dust on the ground.

"It's the name of my shadow."

"What do you mean?"

But he was done talking. He pulled me close, and we teleported once more inside the home. I could still view the layout like the walls were see-through. Or at least the one we stood in. I couldn't see through to another room.

Currently, we stood at the back of a living room decorated with a loveseat, a rocking chair, and a small coffee table. A lit cigarette smoked in an ashtray next to a glass of dark liquid that still had ice in it.

The TV mounted to the wall played a cartoon of a mouse and cat, a baby cradle rocked empty underneath it. The tang of blood reached my nose.

Damicén and Brandon stood in the doorway to the other room, dark looks on their faces. I couldn't see Jesse but heard his voice in front of them.

"It's not him."

"Who then?" Damicén demanded as he crossed his arms. "Who else would do something like this?"

Brandon turned away from whatever they looked at and put his fingers to his eyes. "It's awful."

Jesse appeared in his stead, blood staining his first two fingertips. "It's not him, but it's definitely Hybrids."

Damicén's head snapped around to glare at him. "Hybrids? I thought you were the only one."

Jesse grimaced as he wiped his fingers on a nearby curtain. "I did, too, until about a week before Rosetta got out. Grant found around a hundred of them he'd previously stashed in hidden places."

"A hundred?" Brandon questioned with a gaping mouth. "How did he get a hundred when he only had four in the beginning? Of which three are dead."

"Two," Jesse clarified with a tired look in his eyes.

When the others said nothing, he continued. "That last night, he brought out Morgan and dedicated his service to Ketura. Along with making him commander of the hundred."

"Morgan?" Brandon slowly sat on the couch, rubbing his palms together in worry.

"The guys from Orlando," Damicén clarified. "The one you discovered for Talon. How did he bring him back?"

Jesse shook his head. "I don't know. There's no spell to bring back the dead, not like that." He shivered. "He looked exactly like he had when I knew him. Fresh as a ripe apple."

"Bad analogy," Brandon moaned, clutching his mouth.

I remembered Jesse paling at his entrance to the dining hall. His sharp words at him. It began to make sense.

"I saw it in Rosetta's head, so I'm not surprised. But I didn't expect there to be more, and I didn't expect him to be capable of *that*." Damicén jerked his thumb to the other room.

Jesse paled at some thought, wiping his brow with the back of his hand. "You didn't? All of us are his weapons, made for a single purpose."

Raven stiffened behind me, glancing at the doorway with narrowed eyes. He took me by the arm and dragged me through to the other side.

I stifled a gasp at the sight before me, stumbling into Raven's chest. He wrapped an arm protectively around my shoulders, covering my eyes with his hand. But it was too late. I'd already seen it.

The table had been overturned, scattering food and glass shards from the plates. Blood splattered the white cabinets neatly arranged around the three dead bodies on the kitchen floor.

Raven grunted something in a different language, hand tightening around me.

I reached up to pry his hand away, but it was like trying to move stone. I fidgeted and twisted in his grasp until he got annoyed enough to let go. Glaring at him, he only held a finger to his lips in a shushing motion.

Rolling my eyes, I turned my attention back to the horrific scene before me.

Near us, a man lay on his side, throat ripped out to the point of decapitation, with his hands limp near the wound. Beside the table, a woman lay with her pants around her knees and a silver spike in her back. Closest to the doorway was another man, face up and torso drenched in blood.

Two finger marks smeared the blood around his neck from someone checking for a pulse.

My heart galloped in my chest, tears brimming my eyes. These people had suffered. I could feel it in the air, see the black hanging over them. Their souls would rot here, unable to move on from the trauma.

Morgan had done this? Why? What had these people done to deserve this? I didn't feel well.

Moving to tap Raven on the arm, signaling I wanted to leave, something caught my eye. The faintest gleam of white broke through the black. I peered through it, searching for its owner, and my eyes came to rest on the man near the doorway.

A thin line of white light encapsulated his body. It pulsed with the thrum of a weak heartbeat, so weak in fact, I almost missed it, and Jesse did completely.

Instead of tapping Raven, I tugged at his shirt, pointing wildly at the man. Raven shook his head slightly, and my mouth fell agape. Was he just going to let this guy die?

I pressed my lips together and tugged harder, tipping my head toward the guy, mouthing, 'He's alive.' But Raven was having none of it.

'He's dead,' he mouthed right back.

I shook my head furiously. Could he not see it? Could he not hear it? If that guy was alive, we had to at least try and save him. I wasn't going to let this man die right in front of me without trying.

Frustrated, I turned back to the guy. I didn't know how Raven's shadow gifts worked, so I wasn't sure if I could step out of the wall to go to him. What would I even do if I could? I couldn't bring him back, and I didn't know CPR. Frankly, I couldn't even see his injuries to know if he was savable. There was only one option I could think of to get him help.

As loud as I could manage, I thought the words 'He's alive. He's alive. In the doorway. He's alive.'

The voices halted in the other room, and in the blink of an eye, Damicén loomed over the man pressing his fingers to the same spot Jesse had. He bent low, ear against the man's chest. He motioned for the others to join him and muttered, "He's got a pulse."

"What?" Jesse exclaimed. "I checked him."

"It's weak, but it's there. Let's get him back." He nodded to Brandon, who was already making a portal.

Jesse hesitated, lingering too long in the doorway.

"Jesse," Damicén snapped. "Get him." Then his eyes shot to the wall we hid in, making direct eye contact with me.

Raven hissed a curse and snatched me backward, teleporting us back to the edge of the field. He released me so quickly that I didn't have time to steady myself and fell flat on the grass.

"Are you an idiot?" he roared, fists clenched. "Or do you just like blatantly breaking rules?"

I propped myself up on my arms and scowled. "He needed help; he was still alive."

"He's dead."

"No, he's not. I saw—" I stopped abruptly, realizing I wasn't even sure what I really saw or how I knew it tied to his heartbeat.

Raven cocked a brow. "Saw what?"

But before I could respond, they descended upon us, springing through the swirling portal, faces blurred with differing emotions.

"Are you an idiot?" Damicén repeated the earlier jab but not at me. His ember eyes raged with fire as they bore into Raven's, who remained eerily silent.

"You could've gotten her killed," Jesse added, coming close enough to bump Raven's chest.

Raven put on a face of bored calmness as he said, "No."

Jesse scoffed, about to let loose a flurry of insults when Damicén stopped him. He pulled him back to stand beside Brandon with a warning look in his gaze.

When Damicén turned back, he was only able to utter a single word through his clenched teeth. "Why?"

Raven didn't respond, once again choosing silence.

Damicén rubbed his jaw, an irritated smirk on his lips. "First, you drop the bombshell that you're Talon's kid, and you lied to us the entire time. Then you go against direct orders for not only yourself but her." He pointed to me. The muscles in his bicep bunched and coiled like a cramp had overtaken them, but it didn't faze him.

"You bring her to see this death house, knowing the trauma she's already dealing with from living with Grant. Now you wanna bottle up and not speak again? No, that shit is over.

Either you tell us, or you can get the fuck out and never come back. I refuse to deal with this secret bullshit any longer." The more he spoke, the calmer he seemed to grow. A lethal resignation to any outcome.

As we waited for Raven to decide, Brandon approached and helped me up. I nodded my thanks, noticing how the freckles danced on his cheeks in the outside light, which glinted off his hay-colored curls.

"I thought she should see what Grant is capable of," Raven said finally, drawing our attention back to him. "It's not fair to keep things from her like this. She deserves to know." He left out the part where I begged him to go, which rang my curiosity bell.

"Like hell she does," Jesse spat. "She's just a kid."

That sparked Raven's own fire as he stiffened his shoulders and grew a couple inches in height. "She's twenty years old now and has already seen and experienced more than she should."

"That's exactly why she shouldn't—"

"You guys said Grant didn't do this," I interrupted, feeling immediate regret upon drawing their attention.

"No," Damicén agreed. "But his minions did under his command."

"I don't believe that." I didn't. I couldn't. I wouldn't. But I could. After seeing what happened with Jarred, I could believe he would be that cruel. That didn't mean I wanted to, though.

"That bonfire you witnessed at his rally?" Raven whirled on me. "That wasn't a bonfire."

"Raven," Jesse warned, a thunderous growl escaping his chest. My bones vibrated under the sound, the hair on my body standing stick straight.

"They take people—like the ones in there," he pointed back to the house, "—and burn them alive for sport."

My hand clamped over my mouth instinctively, my gut twisting in terror. "No."

"Yes."

Jesse grabbed me and hauled me backward. "This is exactly why she needs to stay away from this."

"This is why she *needs* to hear it. You can't keep hiding things from her until it's too late and then force it down her throat. Doing that is exactly how she ended up with Grant and how he's able to manipulate her." Raven narrowed on Jesse as he added, "Aside from the memory wipe."

Jesse pounced, fist aimed at Raven's jaw. He blocked it, stepping further into the field. Jesse followed, growing taller and sprouting fur.

I clutched my ears at the sounds of blows landing, closing my eyes tight as Jesse transformed before me. The old part of me not wanting to see whatever he turned into, the new side just begging for the fighting to stop regardless of who turned into what. I knew he was a Werewolf—they'd told me as much—and deep down, I didn't really care. I just wanted the fighting to stop for one day.

Brandon touched my shoulder apprehensively, and I jerked away from him. As my pulse roared, my breath coming faster and faster, I felt something building in me. Possibly a panic attack if my track record was correct.

I sank to my knees as blow after blow reached my covered ears, along with the inhuman hissing and snarling. Damicén shouted something unintelligible, startling me as he flew past and into a tree. Blood trickled down his forearm from a cut that knit itself back together in mere seconds.

Forcing my eyes closed once more, I began rocking back and forth, images of Jarred flashing before my eyes. Memories of the bonfire. My mind constructed an awful reality is someone burning there while everyone cheered, and I was none the wiser. I couldn't think of anything else, couldn't hear anything else but the fight.

"Make it stop. Make it stop. Stop. Stop. Stop," I whispered to myself, drawing in gasping breaths. Another touch to my shoulder, and I screamed, "Stop!"

Something burst from within, spreading through my body like lightning and exploding away from me.

The sounds ceased instantaneously, as did the turmoil inside me. My heart and breathing returned to normal, like the snap of a rubber band. I cautiously opened my eyes and was met with a sight I did not expect.

Everyone lay flat on their backs fifteen yards away from me, and every tree within those fifteen yards had been ripped from the root and shredded.

Jesse—returned to normal—sat up, rubbing the back of his head. "What the fuck?"

"Was that the stone?" Damicén asked, sitting up stiffly.

Brandon rolled over onto his hands and knees, eyes wide at me as he gasped for air. Like whatever had happened had knocked the wind out of him.

"No." Jesse shook his head with a wince. "That was—"

"Magic," Brandon interjected in a breathy whisper.

I looked between them, brows dipping down. "M-magic?"

Raven sat up last, cold and empty eyes piercing me. A sinking feeling settled in my gut at that look.

Brandon rushed over, hands outstretched but careful to not startle me like he approached a scared kitten. I took his hands and stood, glancing around the clearing.

The brick house had been leveled along with the trees. The ground was tilled where the trees had uprooted, and debris scattered where it didn't. It looked as if a twister had plopped itself down here and then vanished.

"What happened?" I asked, rubbing my eyes as a sudden wave of lightheadedness crashed down.

"You blasted us back," Damicén's voice echoed from my left. "We should be asking you what happened."

I turned to him, swaying slightly. I couldn't think clearly. My mind felt all jumbled, and my legs could barely support my weight. "I don't know." It was a different feeling from what happened in the cave with the spiders. Truth be told

I'm not even sure it actually happened. I could've been hallucinating. "I just wanted the fighting to stop."

Guilt swept over their faces. Jesse's even flushed with embarrassment.

"What do you mean magic?" As soon as the words left my mouth, my knees buckled, and I collapsed. The last thing I saw was Brandon diving to catch me as darkness swallowed me.

Chapter Eighteen

I dropped right in the middle of a conversation. Raven, Damicén, Jesse, and Kenna huddled around the table in their map room. Kenna and Damicén looked considerably angry, Jesse appeared maybe a tad annoyed, and Raven bored. As usual.

Now I knew for sure it wasn't a dream, that this was real. What I was going to do with this information, I had no clue, but I was definitely not going to pass on the opportunity to get info I may not get normally.

"You took an unprepared, unarmed child into a crime scene." Kenna glowered at the shadow man.

He snorted but remained silent.

"I'm so glad you find it funny." Damicén's face tightened, voice taut.

Raven picked a hair from his leather jacket and sighed. "She's fine. And clearly, it wasn't a bad idea since she was the one who noticed the guy wasn't actually dead." He sent that last sentence at Jesse, whose jaw worked overtime to keep his lips closed.

"I will say it was good she caught that," Kenna admitted as she lowered herself into a chair. Her black hair had been braided across her shoulder in a loose waterfall pattern, framing her high cheekbones and cat eyes. "But that's no excuse for purposefully exposing her to that kind of trauma."

Damicén nodded in agreement. "After what I saw in her head, she is in no position to continue seeing things like that. You saw her breakdown in the field. It leveled it."

"No, that was because of the fighting. She said so herself," Raven defended, propping himself on the table.

"I'm sure seeing the ripped-out throats and raped woman didn't help with that at all," Jesse mocked, eyes narrowing.

"The only reason I don't throw you back into the holding cell is that Damicén thinks your disloyalty is worth less than his." Kenna punctuated each word with a snarl. "And the only reason I don't throw *you* into a cell is that I know it can't contain you."

Raven sucked his teeth, purposefully not meeting her accusing gaze.

Kenna put her fingers to her temple, rubbing slow circles. "Alright, let's take this one bullet point at a time." She lowered her hands, face appearing relaxed but gaze steaming. "First. The man. Details."

Damicén plopped into an adjacent chair, crossing his legs. "Tom Caraway. Vampire. What little I could gather from his weakened mind showed they were attacked suddenly. The woman was watching TV next to the other man while Tom made dinner when they busted down the door."

"Morgan?" Jesse inquired, leaning closer to them.

"No." Damicén's eyes focused on the table corner as he remembered. "I didn't recognize them, but you were right. They were definitely hybrids. They killed the man and woman first. Tom only had enough time to react to try and grab the baby." He paused, taking a deep breath before continuing, "He didn't get very far, and they took the baby."

She then turned to Jesse and asked, "What do you know about this?"

Jesse fisted his hair. "I knew he was trying to find covens to slaughter or take as prisoners for his rallies. But the baby, I have no idea."

"My first thought would be more hybrids," Kenna pondered, thumb rubbing a pattern on her other hand.

"Possibly. We have no way of knowing."

"Why did you hesitate to help Damicén get him?"

His neck turned beet red. "I checked him. He was dead."

Narrowing her eyes, she moved on to Damicén. "Brandon is taking care of him?"

He nodded. "Guy was so close to death I'm surprised Brandon could do anything with him."

"What kind of injuries?"

"Gutted through the back."

She cringed, absentmindedly reaching around to touch her lower back. "Right. Keep me posted on his recovery. We might be able to pull some info from him if he makes it." She swiveled to Raven. "Next bit of business. Aside from the fact you've been lying to us about your identity—which I haven't forgotten—you took Rosetta. Disobeyed direct orders."

"You're not my boss."

"What if they had still been nearby? They would've killed her."

"And our only chance to bring Talon back," Jesse interjected.

"You can't use the Stone to bring her back."

Kenna raised her hand to silence them, sighing in annoyance. "Rosetta is more than the Stone, and I won't make her existence reliant on that. They could've killed her or taken her again."

Raven's jaw clenched, his eyes on the floor. "I had her. Not even Damicén knew she was there until she wanted him to. Not to mention the magic she surprised us with."

Kenna raised an eyebrow. "The magic she produced under high levels of immense stress. Magic that we don't know where it comes from."

"The Stone," Damicén countered. "That blast of power was nothing but pure energy."

"It's not the Stone!" Raven snapped. "And you can't use it."

Kenna sat back, crossing her legs with an interested look. "You keep saying that. Why?"

"That Stone is connected to her soul—her life force. If you use it while it's still in her, it'll kill her."

My eyes fluttered open, bringing me back to reality and the excruciating headache I had. Rolling over to shield myself from the bright lights, I almost rolled directly onto the floor. My arms shot out, flailing and grasping for a hold.

I managed to grab the metal edge of the cot before I fell too far and hoisted myself back up.

The room was too bright, too white. I was in the infirmary, that was certain, with an IV stuck in my arm. Turning my head, I saw Brandon hunched over the man from the house: Tom, they'd said. Purple light glowed, emanating around his midsection. Brandon made a few circles with his hands, like sewing something together in the air.

The light began to fade until it dissipated completely. Brandon rolled his shoulders, drying his hands on a towel in his lap. He turned to see me awake and smiled.

"Hey, sleepyhead. Feeling any better?" he asked as he pulled his chair next to me.

I groaned, laying an arm across my eyes. "I feel like I hit a brick wall going ninety miles an hour."

He chuckled, nodding his head like he understood. "Using magic for the first time drains you. First time I used it, I was drunk."

"What?" I lowered my arm so I could stare at him. He shrugged in a 'what can you do?' motion.

"Yeah...I got double the hangover, too. Here, drink this," he added, reaching under the cot and brandishing a juice box. "You need the sugar."

My arms shook as I propped myself on my elbows. He watched me struggle to stab the plastic straw in with a bemused look on his face before I gave up and extended it to him. With one flawless sweep of his hand, he poked the straw in and bent it to angle toward my face.

"Thanks," I whispered, cheeks heating. The juice was surprisingly sweet, almost verging on sour.

My body started to feel better the closer to the end I got—less stiff—but my headache never subsided. I handed the now-empty juice box back to him and rubbed my temples.

"When will this headache go away?"

Brandon pressed his lips into a thin line, pondering. "For me, it was a day. But you were so powerful I couldn't say the same."

Frustrated, I slumped back onto the cot. That's one more weird thing to add to the ever-growing list of things to get used to.

"What were you doing to him?" I asked, making a vague gesture toward the man behind him.

"Healing him."

I scoffed, the words slipping out before I could stop them, "Gutted through the back."

Brandon's demeanor flashed, blanching at my words. "How did you know that?"

"I just saw Damicén say it."

"How?" He looked up and down the cot, hinting with his expression that I'd been here the whole time.

"I don't know. I was just there, invisible, like the other two times. At first, I thought it was a dream until…it wasn't."

When he didn't respond, I sighed at seeing his utter confusion. "It only happens when I'm asleep."

Realization dawned in his eyes. He grabbed my wrist, ever so carefully removed the IV, and hurried us down the hall and to the main room. My legs buckled and caved the whole way, knees barking in pain.

Inside, Kenna, Damicén, Jesse, and Raven still remained in the same positions I'd seen them in.

They all turned wide-eyed at his intrusion, especially when they caught sight of me huffing and puffing behind him. I had no doubt my face was as red as I felt it was.

He dropped my wrist and exclaimed, "Astral projection!" Looking around, he expected them to be on the same page and was clearly disappointed when that wasn't the case. "That's how she's seen things she hasn't been around. She can astral project."

Kenna tilted her chin up, eyeing us. "How can you be sure that's what it is?"

"Tell them," he urged, "what you just told me."

My chest tightened at the sudden spotlight on me. "That I see things when I'm asleep?"

Brandon threw his arms out in a 'see?' motion, much to everyone's ever-growing confusion.

"What did you see this time?" Damicén asked, intrigue shaping his features. He'd already known I'd seen things, so it was no shock he was the first to ask. Though, I wasn't sure why since he could look into my mind.

"That you said Tom was gutted through the back. He was killed last after they took the baby. And you couldn't use the Resurrection Stone inside of me because it would kill me."

Kenna and Jesse's jaws hit the floor simultaneously while Damicén and Raven held cool looks of knowing.

"You heard all of that?" Kenna leaned toward me, crossing her arms on the table.

"And saw," I added. "I was standing—floating?—at the end of the table." Goosebumps pricked my skin as their eyes lingered on that spot.

"What other things have you seen?" She inquired.

I shrugged. "It always had to do with me, or at least a fragment of the conversation did, and it always happened when I was sleeping."

"Astral projection," Brandon stated once more as if he'd solved a great mystery.

Jesse frowned, nose wrinkling. "Can it be a trained skill?"

Brandon shrugged. "Possibly. It'll just take some time."

"Well, good thing you're already going to be helping her train her magic." Kenna grinned, crow's feet wrinkling around her eyes.

Brandon did a double take, index finger pointed to his chest. "I am?"

She gave him a beseeching look with a tilt of her head.

"Wait. Training?" My voice sounded hoarse and squeaky like someone chucked a dog toy down a staircase.

"Yes. You have powers, clearly, and you need to learn how to control them before you hurt someone."

Heat flushed my cheeks, running down my face into my neck. "I'm still coming to terms with the fact I have powers."

"Which is fine. You've had a lot thrown at you, and you've taken it all in stride. But you still must have some training, and Brandon can do that. I'll supervise," she added when Jesse groaned.

"Plus, we think your powers might be the key to unlocking your memories." Damicén pursed his lips as he eyed me.

"Really?" If there was a possibility I could regain my memories, I would do anything for that to happen. Even magic lessons.

"I do have one question for you, though, Rosetta." Kenna drew my attention back to her as she rose from the chair.

"What?"

"How did you know he was still alive? Our guest in the medic room."

My throat went dry, making me swallow hard before I could answer. "There was a light around him, really faint, and it pulsed like a heartbeat."

"A light?" She shifted her eyes to Damicén, who nodded that I spoke the truth.

"It was white."

"Aura," Damicén answered. "She saw his aura."

That struck a chord in me as I remembered Sebastian's words over breakfast that one day.

Kenna nodded thoughtfully, eyes searching mine. "We'll start training after you're rested. Which you should still be doing." She glowered at Brandon.

He ducked his head, curls bouncing. "Sorry. I just got excited. We could use that ability."

She shot him a look that sent him scuttling backward, dragging me with him. Before I was completely out of the room, I looked for Raven. Our eyes connected at the last moment, and I saw him shake his head before sinking into the shadows.

Brandon towed me all the way back to the medic room, where I planted my feet outside the door.

"What? You have to rest. You heard Kenna."

"I don't want to do it in there with the almost-dead guy."

By the shameful look on his face, I could tell he hadn't thought of that. He swiveled, hand gripping his chin. "I can put up the curtain between you two?"

At my cringe, he scowled. "I need to be able to check on you and make sure you don't have a concussion or anything."

"Can I just go to my room?" I wanted nothing more than to lay in bed. Which I felt somewhat bad about because I'd been doing that the whole time, but I really needed it now. My knees still wobbled, my head pounded, and I had a few things I needed to mull over.

He twisted his mouth to the side, glancing down the hallway. "Let me check your vitals again real quick. If they're good, you can go to your room and I'll come check on you every so often. Hopefully, without sounding and looking like a mega creep."

A giggle burst from me at the thought of Brandon sneaking around like a peeping Tom. "I promise I'll be clothed."

"And I promise I'll knock."

He held up his pinky finger, and when I enclosed my own around it, he flashed a heart-melting smile.

Leading me back into the room, he made sure to drag a curtain around Tom, blocking my view of the half-dead man.

Even if I couldn't see him, I still felt him; felt the pain on the outskirts of my own emotions.

I sat on a chair closest to the door, trying to avoid looking in the general direction of that man.

Brandon quickly took my vitals, staying silent to hopefully speed things along. As he held his index and middle finger to my wrist, my vision slowly tunneled to only see him. The way his blond curls shone in the dim light, like his own personal brand of sunshine. It was very befitting to his personality. I'd admired him so long that I didn't even notice he finished.

I blushed, hoping he hadn't noticed me watching for too long. "Well, will I live?"

His eyes lingered on me, drifting from my own down to my lips and back. He'd definitely noticed it. "Your blood pressure is a little low, but I think you'll survive. Something sweet will help it get back to normal."

My blush deepened, wishing I had the courage to say something mushy and cute like *'well it's a good thing I have you then'*.

"That's good," was all I managed to squeak out. *Coward.*

An awkward silence flourished between us, and I hated every second of it. I could tell he wanted to say something else, as his mouth opened and closed repeatedly. Finally, he sighed, turning to place the equipment back in their respective places.

"Go on." He relinquished with a tilt of his head. "I'll come by in a bit."

I rose, prepared to wobble as gracefully as I could, when he stopped me.

"Oh! Wait, wait, wait. I have something for you." He held up his hands as he scooted through the curtain. A moment later, he reappeared with a stuffed red binder and a flushed face.

He held it out to me with a less-than-steady hand, and upon taking it, I noticed the name stamped in the bottom right corner: Rosetta M Cauldwell.

"Is this...?" My throat swelled as I traced the letters.

"Yours." He finished for me, overcome with his own feelings. "It was yours before everything went down. It belongs to—with you."

I clutched the binder to my chest, eyes brimming with tears. "Thank you." I had something from my old life. Something tangible. Not just words spoken about memories I didn't have.

The walk back to my shared room was ripe with excitement and nervousness. The world defocused around me as I ran my fingers along the wrinkled and bent edges of the binder. Someone said hello, and I think I responded in kind.

Leaving the door unlocked for Brandon, I climbed cautiously up to my top bunk. My feet slipped a few times, along with my arms becoming jelly, but determination shot through me. After I hoisted myself up, I set the binder on my crossed legs and breathed deeply.

My heart pounded in tune with the headache as I shakily opened to the first page. It was a sketch of a stained-glass vase filled with an elaborate arrangement of flowers. Notes scribbled haphazardly in the corners about possible colors for the flowers and things of similar nature. This handwriting...I could guess was my own, but it looked only like a stranger's to me.

The next page was a charcoal drawing of space and then one of a brick staircase sitting in a forest.

Tears streamed down my face as I flipped again and again, coming to rest on a portrait near the end. Jesse and I stood with a middle-aged couple at a ski resort, all smiles and bundled to the neck in warm clothes. The differing signature in the corner and the fact that this was in plastic covering told me someone else had drawn this as a gift for me. Or for the old me.

I mourned for that girl. That old life where Supernatural beings were just movies and stories to be enjoyed. Magic stayed in my dreams, and I spent my life doing what I apparently loved so much. I mourned a stranger, for that's all she was to me now. And may always be.

When I slammed the binder shut, a piece of paper fluttered out, landing delicately beside me facedown. The edges were crinkled and slightly burnt, ink bleeding through the parchment.

My heart stilled at the faint outline, barely intelligible from the backside. But I knew what it was.

Taking two of my fingers, I gripped a corner and turned the page. My hand snatched away as if it'd been burned, and as I looked, I noticed a faint red line where the paper had touched my skin.

Blowing softly on it, my eyes traced the hundreds of the same small symbols scribbled deliberately all over the page. All circles and slashes, converging and centering one giant one that had been drawn with red paint. More like slopped on the paper, as there's no way a calm hand made this.

A perfect circle with a crescent moon and two slashes. Grant's symbol.

The hair on the nape of my neck stood on end as goosebumps pricked my skin.

I'd drawn this. I'd drawn this before I knew anything about this side of the world...or did I? I didn't have my memories to confirm what I knew back then and didn't. But if what they told me is true, there's no way I knew about all of this. No way. That means someone else did.

As I lay there, I thought about everything the new me had been through and how she'd responded. I couldn't help but feel angry.

She was scared, stubborn, lost. I'd been called a child one too many times by those around me. Called weak, unprepared, unstable. Sure, I still had nightmares involving Jarred. Sure, I would probably have nightmares involving the Orlando coven. But it's how I recover from these that will truly show who I am. And I could handle it. I would handle it. Or I will die trying.

Chapter Nineteen

The time came—a few nights later—for Brandon to finally give me a magic lesson. He said waiting for nighttime was the best, as we could see the magic easier and would be covered under the darkness. Even when I brought up that whatever would be after us would most likely have night vision, he waved it off. The others agreed with him, so I waited for dusk to arrive. Then walked with Kenna up the stairs and out into the courtyard.

Brandon sparred lightly with Damicén, who was kicking his butt. When they saw us, they parted, Damicén taking my place beside Kenna.

They gave us space and wandered around the vegetation pretending like they weren't watching us. I appreciated the effort to calm my nerves, but it was short-lived.

Brandon grinned at me. "You ready?"

"Not at all."

"Don't worry about it. It's as easy as breathing…once you get the hang of it."

"You're terrible at making people feel better," Damicén called, warranting a frown from Brandon.

"I will warn you, though, these first couple of sessions will bring the headache back," Brandon said as he stretched his shoulders.

"Great." I rolled my eyes.

"I made sure we stocked up on ibuprofen, so you should be good."

That eased my rampaging mind slightly. "Thank you for thinking of me."

He blushed, actually blushed, as he rubbed the back of his neck. "It's nothing, really. Alright, let's move over here, away from the wall," he added when I raised my eyebrows.

We moved as far away from the rock as possible while staying out of the shrubs and trees. There wasn't a lot of space out here, but it was better than being underground. Or at least that's what they told me yesterday.

"First things first. You need to learn what it is." He held up a finger, purple light sparkling from the tip like a mini firework.

"Isn't it just magic?"

He feigned offense. "Just magic? It's called the Flux. The process of flowing in and out, like the magic. Hold out your hand."

I did as he said, palm turned to the sky.

"Now, close your eyes."

"What does closing my eyes have to do with anything?"

"Close them."

Sighing, I did. His hand brushed my wrist, sending chills up my spine. It was a soft touch, just enough to keep me steady without gripping.

"Visualize your magic. How it feels, looks, behaves."

I peeked one eye open. "Behaves?"

With his free hand, he shut the open eye. "Yes. Magic is a part of you, but it is its own entity. Using magic is like a partnership. Now, how does it look? Tell me."

Digging deep inside myself, searching every corner, every crevice, for whatever had been there the other day, I came up empty.

"There's nothing."

"You're looking too hard. Relax." His hands moved to my shoulders, pushing them down from their heightened position. I'd unintentionally tightened every muscle in my body.

"Breathe in through the nose and out through the mouth. Like meditation."

I searched once more, feeling him press my shoulders down again in the middle of it. I groaned, slapping my hand down to my side in frustration. My arm hurt from the strain of keeping it out that long.

He chuckled when I glared at him, pressing my tongue to my cheek in annoyance.

"Is this how you learned?"

"For the most part, though, I learned from someone who couldn't do magic."

"That makes no sense."

He shrugged, moving his hands back to my shoulders. "Try again. Don't force the image."

"I'm not! I'm trying to find it. I've looked everywhere."

"Then don't *try* to find it. Let it come to you."

I closed my eyes once more, feeling Brandon's hand slide down my arm and raise it out in front of me. He held me more firmly this time, allowing my arm to rest on him.

"What color is it?"

I breathed in. Out. In. Out. For what seemed like several minutes, I breathed in silence, allowing myself to relax. Not letting any thought stick too long in my head.

Suddenly, I felt it creeping up to me from within a space in my mind I didn't see before. It curled around me, bringing warmth and protection.

"It's...like a yellow gold," I finally answered.

Brandon wasted no time in asking the next series of questions. "What shape is it? Where did it come from? How does it make you feel?" All I answered immediately.

Then he hit me with a demand I was not expecting. "Channel it down your arm and into your palm."

I almost opened my eyes in shock, which would've broken the connection. Sighing, I tried imagining it funneling down my outstretched arm and pooling in my palm. But the more I tried, the more it started to pull away from me.

I stopped when I realized what was happening, allowing it to come back out and around me again. It felt...scared. Not so much of me, but of everything else. I could feel it finding comfort around me but presenting itself outwardly in my palm seemed too daunting of a task.

Coaxing it gently, as one would a frightened animal, I cooed and spoke in soft tones. But when it still refused, I decided I wouldn't push it. Something told me if I did, I would be hard-pressed to get it back out again.

"It doesn't want to," I told Brandon, feeling the surprise at my words in his hands.

"Why?"

Calming the swirling gold around my mind, I opened my eyes to stare into his, feeling it begin to pull away back to my mind. "It's scared."

This stunned him. He took a step back and looked to Damicén for answers.

"Why don't you guys take a break?" He suggested. "You've been at this for over an hour."

Now it was my turn to be surprised. "An hour?"

We sat down near the others, Brandon wiping sweat from his forehead with a handkerchief.

"That's new," he said after a while.

Damicén plopped down beside him, swigging a bottle of water. "Very new," he agreed.

"So, you've never seen anything like that before either?"

Damicén shook his head. "No. It's usually the opposite. The people are more scared than the magic is."

"I'm not scared," I stated.

He grinned. "I know."

"Don't you uh…need to drink blood?" I asked as I watched him take another gulp of water. "Because you're a Vampire and all?" I added when he raised his eyebrows.

"Eventually, yes," he stated as he re-tied his brown hair at his neck. "But I'm old enough. I can get away with not having it for a lot longer."

"I honestly didn't even know you could have regular food."

"Of course. We also need it to survive."

"Both?" Maybe all the stories I'd heard about Vampires growing up weren't actually true.

Damicén chuckled, wrapping his arms around his knees. "It helps us heal, gives our body strength, and we do need it to survive. But it's just an additive. We still need water and food like you. What you're thinking of—the blood-sucking demon who drains their victims and burns in sunlight, hates garlic, etc.—is false, but rooted in truth."

I paled. Dracula is real?

At my thought, he burst out in laughter. "No. Dracula isn't real. But every time a Vampire is created, our first one hundred years of this new life are exactly like the legends. That's where they came from. We can't go into the sun. We can't be around garlic. And we can only drink blood."

"Why?"

He shrugged. "It has to do with whatever deal the original made to get his immortality in the first place. We all got the short end of the stick. Luckily, if we make it those one hundred years, we regain a lot of our humanity and can begin eating and drinking regular food. But not a lot. It takes a long time to be able to work up to the quantity I can consume."

I studied him, trying to imagine him as a blood-thirsty, ravenous monster. "What was the deal?"

Damicén hesitated, rolling the bottle around his hands. "That was thousands of years before my time, really. All you need to know is Eoghan wanted immortality. And he got it."

Brandon ran a hand through his hair, failure written across his face. He wasn't paying a lick of attention to our conversation, still wrapped up in the magic lesson.

I placed a hand on his shoulder, trying to give him some comfort. "It was working. You couldn't have anticipated I would have weird magic."

He gave me a lopsided smile and sighed. "I'm not that great of a teacher anyways. You would've been better off with mine."

"Yeah, who taught you? You said they couldn't do magic."

Both of their faces turned mournful, and I got my answer.

"Talon."

Brandon nodded. "She was an amazing teacher. I got it within my first couple of tries."

"He also got one of the Fairy Kings to show him some stuff," Damicén added.

"Oh, that was nothing," Brandon chided. "I was being held prisoner; I had nothing else to do."

I dropped the bottle of water Kenna passed to me. "I'm sorry, what? Held prisoner?"

"It's a long story," they said in unison.

Then Jesse strolled up, hands in his pockets. "And a nasty one," he added with a wink.

"I thought Talon was gonna kill you." Damicén slapped a hand on his thigh with laughter.

Jesse cringed and rubbed the back of his neck, clearly uncomfortable with that line of thinking.

I took a few sips of the water, letting the lesson sink in. "So, why couldn't she do magic?" I asked as I twisted the bottle cap back on.

The answer came from the shadows. "Because Vampires can't do magic." Raven stepped out into the moonlight, shrouded in darkness. "Because of a deal my father made with the Demon who created him. He gave up the light and power that came with magic for the dark and souls. Which in turn sealed the deal for the rest of us to come after him."

Damicén rolled his eyes and mumbled, "Edge lord over here."

"Souls?" I gulped. Every person killed by a Vampire would lose their soul?

Raven simply shrugged and picked a piece of lint from his leather jacket. "Vampires were originally reapers of souls. At least, that's what my father was created for. He decided to embark on a different path. And since he was the first of his kind, he could create more to help, but they wouldn't be as monstrous as him. We still retained shreds of our humanity. At least…" he cut his eyes to Damicén, "after the first hundred years."

Feeling hot, I took another swig of the water, letting it settle in my mouth before swallowing. "So, you're a direct descendant of the first-ever Vampire?"

"We all are," Damicén cut in with a growl, but Raven ignored him.

"The first ever Vampire and the first ever made Vampire. My mother was the first he made. He had an obsession with her."

Damicén glowered at the ground, receiving a light shoulder bump from Brandon, who jabbed his thumb toward Raven with a smirk.

"Why?" I leaned forward from my seated position, anticipation ripe within me.

"Because of her looks," Damicén answered.

My brows pinched together. "Her looks?" Come to think of it, I didn't know what she looked like.

"Seven thousand years ago, blonde hair and blue eyes were unheard of. Basically a mutation. For a woman to have it…my father became irrationally obsessed with her." Raven stalked around us, keeping a wide berth but still remaining in conversation. "He created an army to rule the world and suffered the consequences for it. But unfortunately, there's always someone craving power over others."

I sighed mournfully. "I wish I knew my family history like that." Hell, even knowing who my parents were was a start.

Ravens eyes glassed over, and his voice became unusually husky as he said, "Maybe one day you will."

I guess I deserved that pity for how I was acting.

"Why don't you get in on the lessons?" Jesse inquired with a stiff look.

Raven stopped in his tracks, turning a quizzical eye to the question. He didn't say anything, only waited for Jesse to further explain. Which Jesse had no problem doing, almost like he was rubbing it in his face.

"I've seen you struggle to control the shadows more than once."

"I'm fine," Raven hissed, any hint of that previous emotion gone.

"Seven thousand years, and you haven't learned to control them fully."

Kenna put out a warning hand to Jesse. "Don't start another fight."

Jesse reassured her with a smirk but turned back to Raven with a sneer. "You figured by now you'd have an ounce of control."

"If I didn't have an ounce of control, everyone here would already be dead." The silence after his words was deafening. "Seven thousand years I spent learning to keep them in. You can't command them."

"So you'll spend your time in fear?"

"Try being ten years old and waking up to your own shadow trying to kill your mother in her sleep. Or when your own shadow massacred a village in front of you. They can't be controlled or told what to do."

"But you did when you broke me out."

They all turned to look at me, heating my face under the weight of their gazes.

Raven turned away from us, rubbing his brow. "That was different."

"How?"

He said nothing more and disappeared into the shadows.

Jesse scoffed. "Of course. Always runs away."

Kenna folded her arms, giving him a disapproving look.

He spread his hands out and asked, "What? He said it himself. He can't control them. He needs to learn how."

"Maybe so, but he went through a lot of effort hiding who he was from us probably for that specific reason."

"Yeah, and that pisses me off," Damicén added, throwing a rock into the dirt. It lodged itself so deep in the earth I could've stuck my arm down the hole it created. It put into perspective how strong they really were.

"Well, with you two around to constantly hound him, I think I know why," she chastised as she pulled Jesse away from us by the crook of his elbow. Damicén reluctantly got up to join them, giving Brandon a reassuring pat on the back.

"Well." Brandon bit his lower lip, clearly dreading what was coming next. "Want to try again?"

We tried several more times to get my magic to manifest in my palm, but each time ended in failure. At the end of the session, Brandon seemed more defeated than I had ever seen him. I wanted to hug him. He really was a decent teacher; I just somehow got stuck with faulty magic.

I showered in water as hot as I could stand, hoping it would wash away my rising guilt. It didn't. And as Sam and Rhydel snored peacefully in their beds, I couldn't help but wonder what it was like to fit in. To know where you belonged and manage to stay there comfortably.

They both were content with their lives, from what I could tell. More so for Sam, who had Millie. I'd overheard them on the phone last night, and their tenderness for each other made me love-sick for someone I didn't have.

I toweled off my hair and stared at myself in the mirror. Red, stringy locks, wide golden eyes, and a willowy body left much room for improvement. My face had rounded out from the food I'd been eating, which was nice to see. It was better than the gaunt shell I'd become those last few days at Grant's.

Poking my hip dips, I sighed at the dream I'd never achieve of having a full figure.

Crawling into bed, I felt the headache Brandon warned come sneaking in. Realizing I'd forgotten to get the ibuprofen from him, I stuck to curling up under the covers. Maybe sleep would help.

But as my luck would have it, restful sleep wasn't in the cards for me. I lie awake with burning questions and spiraling thoughts.

Brandon had mentioned astral projection could be a learned skill. And if I couldn't get the regular magic down, maybe I could succeed in that department. I mean, I'd done it several times without meaning to.

What would happen if I meant to?

Chapter Twenty

Nothing happened. In fact, I ended up giving myself a version of sleep paralysis from trying. I woke myself up several times with twitches and shakes, each time more frustrated than the last. Eventually, I gave up, trying to sleep normally but had already caused the damage.

The rest of the day leading up to the training session was torture. I wasn't even sure I could do the training that night with how groggy and sleep-deprived I was. But when the time came, I pushed on.

Again I struggled to coax my magic to reveal itself, leaving me and Brandon drained.

We sat down once more with Damicén and Kenna, scratching our heads at what to do.

"It seems to only show itself in stressful situations." Damicén frowned. He'd left his hair down tonight, and I silently cursed him for being unable to sweat.

The damp ocean air was much clammier than I'd like to admit, only seeming to make me hotter with each passing breeze. Sweat poured down my face, stinging my eyes and dripping into my mouth. I couldn't even wipe it away with my arm, as it was just as wet.

"Immensely stressful situations," Kenna agreed. "Situations I don't want to replicate just for the sake of getting it to manifest. They do some damage in those scenarios."

"This is a different form of magic, one I'm not familiar with. It acts so unlike regular Flux."

"But Brandon said it was its own entity," I countered, patting my face dry with a towel.

Brandon cringed, pulling his knees to his chest. "Yes, but not to this extent. Yours seems actually sentient."

"Come take a walk with me." Damicén dragged Brandon from his seated position and walked him across the courtyard. I could see his hands working, trying to come up with an explanation.

Kenna took up residence in their place, wrapping an arm around my shoulder.

"Don't worry. It'll all play out how it's supposed to."

I fiddled with the straw of my juice box, shrugging. "Just seems my luck that I have a defective power."

This sent her into a giggle fit, only ending when she wheezed for air. "You're not defective, just different. If you were defective, you wouldn't have blown apart that field or saved Raven from those Cave Crawlers. Not everything is meant to be picture-perfect. Take me, for example."

Giving her a sideways look, I scoffed. "You're literally the most perfect person I've ever seen."

She smiled, squeezing my shoulders. "That's sweet, but no. I had my fair share of troubles growing up."

"Like what?"

She puffed her cheeks full of air as she raised her eyebrows. "Well, for one, I was the only person in my tribe to turn into a Wolf. And I only discovered it after I'd gotten into a fight with my brother. I almost took his head off by accident."

"Is it genetic? How were you the only one to get it?"

Kenna nodded, then tilted her head. "It is, and I don't know. Still don't to this day. We know now that it's mostly passed down through the male genes, but my father couldn't do it. And neither could his father."

I puckered my lips, crushing the juice box in my hand. "What about your brother?"

"No." She smiled at a memory. "He was the one who convinced me to stay. I was so terrified at first that I wanted to run away. He kept me from going, showed me a different path I could take. I protected my people. That's how I met Talon."

"What was she like?"

"We hated each other at first, our people not being the friendliest toward one another. I wouldn't call it enemies, but if we ever crossed paths, it was a fight." She absentmindedly touched the scar around her eye. The dull light from the half-filled moon cast a shadow through the jagged edges. "But when Grant...took out her family and the rest of the tribe, I decided we had a common enemy. After we teamed up against him, I discovered she wasn't that bad and was merely doing what I was doing. Protecting those she loved." Kenna knuckled a tear from the same eye. "She's smart, cunning, sarcastic, and loyal. So loyal. To a fault, unfortunately. She's family."

"I'm sorry." Talon's death had taken a toll on everyone, it seemed. And the more I thought about it, the more guilty I felt. I held the key to bringing her back, and I didn't know how to access it. Couldn't access it unless I wanted to die. That was another problem entirely. Did I want to die for a stranger? Did I even want to die in the first place? No. I didn't. And I didn't want to think about it anymore.

"What are Werewolves like? I mean...were you also created by a Demon?"

Noticing my shift in subject, she patted my arm and removed hers from around me. "A long time ago, a set of twins were born with this specific gene to turn into a Wolf. How they got it is unknown. One turned into an Armoni—what we are, down on four legs, the most closely resembling an actual Wolf. While the other turned into a Vixois—what Grant is, on two legs. They had their own children, who carried the gene, then they had children, and so on and so on. Today the Armoni is the largest group, with several thousand of us in the world. The Vixois, however, maybe only have a few hundred. That side was harder to pass down for some reason." She sighed wistfully. "So much is still unknown, and I want so badly to discover it all."

"You like science?"

"I love it. I did a lot back in the day before I got promoted to Faction leader. But then I was too busy." She turned her sorrowful eyes back to me. "That seems all for naught now. All that work just to be thrown back into the pits of war and lose the title."

Now it was I who wrapped an arm around her and squeezed. She reached a hand up to mine and held it. Not knowing how to continue on from that depressing point and still not fully understanding the war—but not wanting to ask—I changed the subject again.

"What do you want to do after this is all over?"

She pursed her lips in thought for a moment before smiling to herself. "Aside from discovering everything I can about the Werewolf gene, I really would like to just get away with my husband. I love my packmates. They are my family, truthfully. But I want to relax and see the world. We've been together so long, and we've barely been out of this country. If we make it out of this, that is."

"I think we'll make it."

She squeezed my hand, leaning her forehead against mine.

"How do you do it?" I asked.

"Hmm?"

"You always seem so calm and collected, like you've got everything under control and figured out. I feel like I've lost pieces of me, ones I can't get back. I don't know what to do."

Kenna frowned, staring at me as if I'd spoken another language. "I'm flattered you think that of me, Rosetta. But I'm quite the opposite." She turned back to the stars, lower lip quivering. "I've lost a huge piece of me I'll never get back."

I stayed quiet, waiting for her to continue. This was not a subject I could push for an answer.

"My name and, subsequently, my people."

"Your name isn't Kenna?"

She shook her head, tucking her black hair behind her ears. "That's the name the queen gave me after she came into power, as my real name was 'too difficult for her to pronounce.' She forced me to go by it and everyone else to refer to me as it under threat of punishment."

I couldn't contain my disgust and horror at that revelation. "Are you kidding?"

"I wish. Adaim is the only one to still use my real name, and even then, it's rare, so he doesn't get in trouble."

"But you're not under her anymore, right? Why not go by it now?"

Kenna rubbed my arm, giving me an all-knowing look. "When you've been going by one name for so long, it's hard to switch back. Almost everyone here knows me as Kenna. In fact, I've been going by that name longer than I had my real name. It's a hard transition that can't be done overnight."

My face fell at her words. I couldn't even begin to imagine how she felt, what she's lost. "Can I ask what it was?"

Her lower lip trembled. "I'm really not ready to say it yet."

Embarrassment was ripe within me. Of course she wasn't ready to discuss it. She'd had hundreds of years—most of her life—with her identity stripped. I understood her with that little portion, but her situation was so much worse. I'd lost my memories. She *could* remember her old life, her old self, and had to deal with the pain of losing it all this time.

"War makes everyone lose themselves, even innocent bystanders," she tilted her head to me with the last two words.

I bit my lower lip. "What if I'm not an innocent bystander?"

"You are," she assured me. "You are more than any of us."

Damicén and Brandon returned, still bickering about something, when they stopped in front of us.

"Training is over for tonight," Brandon said shamefully. "I need to do some research. We'll try again tomorrow."

There was no changing his mind.

Kenna helped me to my feet and walked me back to the room, trying in vain to comfort a sulking Brandon along the way.

I felt bad. It was my fault he acted that way. I was the weird one, the odd one out, that frustrated him. I couldn't help it and knew he didn't blame me. No one did. Except for me.

Dinner was quiet, everyone too wrapped up in their own problems to have any coherent conversation. It probably didn't help that the only people who actually joined me for food was my bunk mates.

What they were eerily quiet over I didn't know, didn't care to ask. Kenna's words flashed through my brain on repeat, making eating difficult.

I didn't know what to think. Everything, everyone, was pointing fingers at the other. I was a flag in the eye of a twister.

"How's training going?" Sam asked half heartedly, pushing her peas around her plate.

I shrugged. "I'm sure you've heard."

Rhydel thinned his lips, nodding solemnly. "I heard it was a shit show."

Grunting in agreement, I took a hesitant bite of toast. "You could say that. It's weird. Apparently, my powers are just a giant coward."

"Hell, you scare me as it is—," Rhydel's words cut off abruptly as he was elbowed in the ribs. Sam cut him a glare, stabbing her peas onto each individual fork prong.

He sighed, chewing a mouthful and swallowing. "Yeah. That is weird."

"How did you guys become a part of this?" The question popped out from my thoughts before I could stop it.

They stared at me, unblinking. Sam's fork slipped from her fingers and stabbed into the sliver of meatloaf.

"The pack," I clarified.

A shadow crossed their faces as they shared a knowing look.

I'd heard Kenna's story, and now curiosity was getting the better of me over theirs. I told them as much. I just wanted to know how and why they ended up on this side of events.

"I was born into it," Sam said simply. "When I came of age, I was assigned to Kenna's pack. I was the last to join, and they've treated me better than any of my blood family. Biggs was..." her throat bobbed. "He was my first love. Unfortunately neither of us was truly ready mentally for a relationship of that magnitude, and it ended rather poorly."

"She left him for Millie." Rhydel interrupted with a sly grin. Sam snarled in response.

"They like to spout that for the flare of the drama. But what really happened is far more detail than I'd like to discuss."

"I'm sorry." My heart squeezed in my chest.

Sam shrugged, picking up her fork and continuing eating. "We all have some kind of sob story. Rhydel's is worse."

His eyes guttered at that. "This isn't a competition, Sam."

I tried not to stare, feeling the anxiety begin to radiate from him.

Rhydel cleared his throat. "I was an orphan. I don't know who my parents are or what happened to them, if they're even still alive. I lived in the streets as long as I can remember. Until Adaim found me one evening when I stole a pot of his gumbo from the kitchen table."

My brows narrowed. "The whole pot?"

"I never said I was smart."

"That you're definitely not," Sam chuckled.

Rhydel ignored her and continued, "But he knew what I was instantly. Offered me a place with them. Biggs and Nia were already there."

"And those are the two who passed?"

"You can say that." Rhydel pushed his plate away, a disgusted look crossing his face.

"What happened to them?"

Both of them shuddered at some memory, the air suddenly turning cold around us.

"We don't talk about it."

The rest of the night, I spent tossing and turning, wondering how I'd managed to bring my powers up twice before without meaning to but couldn't now. I know they said it came in situations of high stress, but I *am* highly stressed, and it won't come out now.

Why did I have to get stuck with the magical equivalent of a scaredy cat? It can't be a reflection of myself because I'm not afraid of it. At least I didn't think I was.

No, they said it was sentient. Which means it's completely different from me.

I somehow managed to go to sleep at an undetermined time, brooding over my powers. Thinking about manifesting my powers. And then I dropped into a castle.

I looked around in confusion and with a hint of excitement. Had I managed to astral project again? But where did it take me this time?

Cobblestone walls climbed high to meet a like ceiling. Purple banners hung in between pillars adorned with a golden moon in a triangle.

Voices came from my left through a wooden door, voices I recognized.

I started to open the door when I remembered I was invisible. So I melted through the door.

It was a small room with a black altar at the center. A cauldron of similar color sat in front of it on a red mat.

Avalon stood at the cauldron, dropping in herbs and other items I wasn't familiar with. She whispered words as she did so, eyes glazed over.

Ketura stood to the side with Morgan, cradling a baby in her hands.

"Hurry up." Ketura pouted. "I'm tired."

Avalon snapped out of her glaze, frowning. "This spell takes time and complete concentration. Unless you'd rather find out where they are by yourself?"

Morgan put a steadying hand on Ketura's shoulder and motioned for Avalon to continue.

Ketura stared at him with wonder in her eyes, shaking her head in disbelief. "I can't believe you're all mine."

He bent down and planted a kiss on her forehead, fixing her crown where it tilted. "Along with the army."

Avalon groaned from where she lit four black candles around the space. "After Grant is finished."

Morgan bent his head in acknowledgment. "Of course. My first allegiance is to him for bringing me back."

"You brought yourself back," she hissed. "He designed you that way. Along with your brothers."

Morgan rolled his caramel eyes. "One of which is currently gallivanting around with the enemy."

"Jae made his bed, and he will lie in it."

Jesse is Morgan's brother? They look nothing alike. But that could explain the disdain Jesse showed for him that night at dinner.

Avalon walked back to the altar, cracking her knuckles and motioning to Ketura. "Give it to me."

For half a heartbeat, I was terrified they'd hand over the baby. It was a relief when Ketura bent down to a cage I'd missed before and extracted a chicken.

Its black feathers gleamed in the light, shifting hues of greens and blues. It clucked absentmindedly, flapping its wings as Avalon grabbed ahold of its feet.

My breath caught in my throat as she turned the chicken on its head and began chanting in another language. She walked around the altar to the cauldron, still chanting in a steady beat, and brandished a knife. The hilt was decorated with an array of red jewels and a carving of a wolf.

She dangled the bird over the pot, the animal now vehemently trying to get away, attempting to peck her fingers.

I watched in utter horror as she brought the knife up to its throat and sliced. Blood pooled into the cauldron as orange mist swirled in a vortex around us. She let the now twitching corpse plop into the pot, nose wrinkling in disgust.

An image sprang to life in the midst of a small courtyard filled with vegetation and surrounded by a rock wall.

"There!" she called out, pointing to a slight edge in the rock. A door was hidden in the stone so well one might not have seen it if they weren't looking.

My spine felt like ice as I watched Morgan break away from Ketura and approach the picture, orange mist ruffling his hair. He studied it with a feral grin before asking, "You're sure about this?"

Avalon threw him a sour look. "I just sacrificed a chicken to find this information."

He raised his hands in defense and backed away. "They'll be asleep right now," he said to Ketura as he planted another kiss on her forehead. "Perfect time to strike."

The orange vortex fizzled out, Avalon dusting her hands off on her shirt. "Don't kill them all. Grant wants some of them alive."

He waved her off. "Do you think I'm an idiot?"

"You don't want that answer."

He growled, "They'll be fine as long as I can get there before *he* wakes up," and led Ketura out of the room, leaving Avalon to clean up the mess.

I knew that courtyard. I'd spent the last two nights in it. Panic clawed through me. I needed to get out of this and warn everyone. But how do I get out? I'd never meant to before; it just happened.

I shut my eyes and focused, breathing in through my nose and out through my mouth. As difficult as that was after what I'd just witnessed. I knew I would vomit as soon as I came to, but the others needed to be warned. I willed my magic to come forward, feeling its warm tendrils seep into me.

Take me out. Take me out. Please.

I blinked, coming to stare at my ceiling in the dim light. My heart raced, and a thin film of sweat now coated my body.

I clambered over the side, missing the last few steps of the ladder and crashing to the floor. My stomach emptied its contents, burning my throat and drawing tears from my eyes. Sam and Rhydel bolted out of sleep, scanning the room for the sound.

Sam's eyes focused on me, and she shrieked, "Oh my God! Are you okay?"

"Where's Kenna?" I jumped to my feet, rubbing my sore butt from the landing.

"What?"

"Where's Kenna?" My voice barely croaked out loud enough for me to hear.

"Last door on the right," Rhydel answered with a yawn. "Why?"

Leaving my pile of puke to clean later, I shot out the door, slamming into the adjacent wall. My feet slipped on the concrete from the sweat, and it took everything in me not to faceplant.

Running down the hall, I bounced once more into the wall at the turn before banging wildly on the door Rhydel mentioned.

Within two seconds, Kenna opened it, wearing a fluffy black robe and rubbing the sleep from her eyes. "Rosetta?" When she saw the look on my face, she dropped her hands. "What's going on?"

"I was just somewhere in a castle, and I saw Morgan and Ketura and Avalon, and—oh my God, she sacrificed a chicken—then there was this orange mist, and then the image of the courtyard, and Morgan said we'd all be sleeping and Avalon said—" I rambled without pause or thought, only stopping when Kenna grabbed my shoulders forcefully.

"Breathe," she commanded. "Tell me slowly what you saw."

"There's going to be an attack on the base. Tonight."

She straightened, pulling her robe tighter. "You're sure about this?"

I nodded frantically, telling her about Morgan and the courtyard.

She stepped out into the hall before I finished and rapped on the door across from her. Damicén answered immediately, shirtless. Every single muscle on him was defined to its extreme like he was severely dehydrated. I found myself openly gawking at him.

Kenna opened her mouth to say something, but Damicén stopped her.

"I heard her coming," he mumbled as he pulled on a blue shirt.

We entered the map room, Kenna pressing a number sequence into a keypad on the wall as she asked Damicén, "Where's Brandon?"

"Doing his nightly check on Tom."

"Get him in here. We need to start the alarm." She hovered her finger over the metal numbers, looking impatient.

Damicén shook his head in exasperation. "You're not thinking of fighting them, are you?"

"We've no other choice," she countered.

"Evacuate."

"No. I won't run."

"Don't let stubbornness blind you." he chided, leaning against the frame of the door, blocking our view.

"You're one to talk." she argued, crossing her arms in defiance.

"We can't take on an army of hybrids in here. They will slaughter us."

She rubbed a hand across her face, staring at him through her fingers. "We can't run forever, either."

"Not forever, but we don't have the weapons necessary to take them down. Not here."

She continued to stare for what seemed like way too long before sighing and entering another number sequence. A fire alarm blared through the speakers.

"We'll go to Adaim." She started grabbing books and binders off the shelves and throwing them on the table. "Take everything we don't want them seeing."

Damicén joined her in pulling things down before moving to the maps. He ripped them from the walls and tossed them onto the pile.

Movement could be heard in the hallways as people poured from their rooms. I could only assume they'd trained for this and knew exactly what to do.

I helped shove things into a garbage bag, all but clearing the shelves entirely. Damicén slung the bag over his shoulder, telling us he'd be right back when the lights went red.

He froze with his hand on the door, raising a questioning brow to Kenna. She shook her head and put a finger to her lips.

Silence filled the halls now. Only the blaring alarm cut through. I held my breath, straining to listen. Everyone had to have evacuated by now unless they all went silent with us.

Morgan couldn't have gotten here this fast. It'd only been ten minutes at the most. There's no way he managed to get an army here in that amount of time. Unless they portaled in. Which was a very big possibility. Or maybe…

Kenna and Damicén held a mental conversation, scowling and grinding their teeth at whatever they were bickering about.

"Kenna," I whispered. "I forgot to tell you something."

She shushed me, not even passing a glance over her shoulder.

After a few more seconds of silence, Damicén cracked the door open. I could see over his shoulder that the hallway was empty. Everyone relaxed a little.

Then a hand touched my arm, and I jolted, turning to meet Raven's purple gaze.

"We've got to go," he pleaded.

Kenna made her way over to us, gliding silently across the floor. "What did you forget?" Her voice was as quiet as her steps had been.

"Morgan mentioned needing to get here before someone woke up."

She looked over her shoulder at Damicén, who stared back with an unreadable look. He stepped aside milliseconds before Brandon burst into the room.

His eyes were wild, and his breath came in ragged gasps. "We've gotta go."

"What's going on? Did you see Morgan?"

He looked surprised Kenna was here. "Morgan? No, it's—"

An unholy scream ripped through the air, silencing him. They all slowly turned in unison to the hallway. The hair on my arms stood on end, a cold shiver running down my spine.

"I told you he was dead," Raven warned as another wail pierced the silence, and the door to the medic room exploded open.

Chapter Twenty-One

"Close the door!" Kenna shouted as she rushed to help. "Get her out of here!"

Raven flashed over to them, pushing the door shut and holding it with his shoulder. "I can't. When you set the alarm off, the wards went in place; I can't teleport out of here. No one can."

She cursed and held the door firm alongside him. Thunderous banging sounded from the other side, along with more wailing.

"What is it?" I asked, fear winding in me.

"A trap," Raven answered. "I tried to tell you he was dead."

"I-I don't understand." I moved to help them hold the door, but they all shouted for me to stay in place.

"Tom turned into a Forsaken," Damicén clarified. "One of those creatures you saw at Grant's."

My stomach twisted, and I had to grab onto the table to keep from stumbling over. "What? How?"

Kenna dug her heels into the ground and the door bunched behind them. "They have a chemical gas that can turn anyone into one. They must've known we'd take any survivors."

"But why would they plan an attack knowing he would be turning?" Damicén asked, now leaning his whole body weight into the door. His heels dug literal holes into the concrete floor.

"I don't think they thought that far ahead," Raven answered. "Otherwise, they wouldn't risk killing all of us with this thing." He jabbed his thumb toward the door.

It buckled and moved against the weight of the creature pounding outside.

Kenna growled, "Brandon? Can you do anything?"

He shook his head, too breathless to utter a word.

"Shit. Shit. Shit…alright. I have a plan."

Damicén whipped his head to Kenna. "No. Bad idea."

"Do you have anything else?" She grunted as the door buckled further. "If not, then shut up."

Damicén groaned but said nothing more.

She turned to Raven next to her and nodded to me. "Get her and teleport out."

"What part of 'your magical wards are up, and I can't teleport outside anymore,' don't you understand?" he snapped.

"Not outside, down the hall. Just get her out of the firing line so we can fight this thing." When he didn't move for me her anger slipped the leash, and she yelled, "Now!"

He sighed and became a blur. I had no time to react before he grabbed me. We now stood in the hallway by my room, around the corner from the monster.

"Stay here," Raven demanded in a surprising fatherly tone.

I started to protest, but he was gone. Around the corner, I heard the door give in, and fighting ensued. Kenna barked orders to the others while faint flashes of Brandon's magic cut the red of the hall.

Steadying myself, I made to go around and help when a set of hands grabbed me from behind. I kicked and flailed, thinking Morgan had arrived. It was only when I landed a blow to the person's gut and heard his voice did I realize it was Jesse.

"I'm sorry," I gasped. "I thought you were someone else." I'd also been grabbed from behind way more than I wanted to be today.

"You're stronger than you look." He winced, clutching his stomach. Then his ears caught up to my words, and he blinked, making his way past me. "Who did you think I was? What's going on? Holy shit." He doubled back from the corner and lay flat against the wall. "Why is there a Forsaken in here?"

I tried to give him a short summary of events—which was hard to do with the ever-increasing sounds of fighting—him nodding along absentmindedly.

"Alright. First things first, let's get you out of here." He reached for my wrist, but I snatched it away.

"No. I want to help."

The right corner of his mouth twitched as he reached for me again. "There's nothing you can do. This thing is super deadly, and its vision is based on sight. Anything that moves it attacks. Anything it smells or hears it also attacked, so you've got to go."

Again I backed away from him. "I want to help."

Frustrated, he ran a hand through his wet hair and snatched me by the elbow so fast I couldn't even blink. He towed me toward the corner and forced me to look around it.

At the end of the hall stood the lumbering blue giant, leaking black fluid from every opening possible. Kenna and Damicén ducked and dove around it like a game of tag while Brandon flung magical spikes. The creature flailed wildly, catching Kenna in the ribs and knocking Damicén into the wall.

"There's nothing you can do," Jesse repeated.

"Why doesn't she shift?" Kenna could probably do a whole lot more damage if she shifted to her Werewolf form.

"There's no space," Jesse answered. "If any of us shifted, we'd be so cramped we couldn't fight."

"Why can it fight, though? It's so much bigger than you all."

"It's faster and nimbler than it looks."

"How?"

He growled in aggravation, "Magic. Let's go."

I knew the smartest and safest thing to do was exactly what they all wanted me to do. Leave. And a part of me wanted nothing more than to tuck tail and run. But watching their merry-go-round in the tight space gave me an idea.

I swiveled back to Jesse, but he was already shaking his head.

"I don't want to hear it."

"But—"

"No." He grabbed me by the shoulders and began to steer me toward the stairs leading up and outside.

"This will work!"

"I don't care."

I do. I would apologize to him later, but right now, I could save them. Quickly, I stepped to the side and elbowed him straight in the groin.

When he doubled over in pain, I snatched myself loose from his grasp and bolted down the hall.

If my memory served me correctly, there was a breaker panel in the back of the cafeteria. Something I'd only noticed in passing before, but if I could get to it, I could switch off all the lights in the base. Since the monster's vision is based on movement, it can't attack what it can't see. Even though it could still smell and hear, maybe the light vanishing would stun the creature enough they could get away. If they caught on to my plan and kept silent.

I narrowly avoided slamming my hips and legs into chairs and table corners as I sprinted through the room. The red glow made everything hazy, and I had trouble seeing exactly what it was until the last second.

At the very far right corner of the room, near the cooking equipment and built into the wall, was the rectangle box I was looking for.

Inside was a conglomerate of black switches, none labeled. Each one turns off something, right? So I started blindly flipping switches.

Jesse stumbled in, still half clutching his crotch. "What are you doing?"

When he reached me, the entire base fell into pitch black. In the hall, the sounds of the fighting ceased.

"That," I said proudly.

"How are we going to get out now?" he asked in a hushed, quipped tone.

"You can see in the dark, can't you?" I answered in the same voice.

He grumbled a response and dragged me back through the compound. I could hear the beast bellowing cluelessly down the hall and hoped the others grasped my plan to get out.

As Jesse reached what I assumed to be the first set of doors leading to the outside, a purple swirling vortex appeared beside us and sucked us in.

We tumbled through, landing hard on a patch of gravel. Damicén and Kenna's sour faces loomed above us.

"Are you okay?" Brandon bounded beside me, helping me up and dusting the rock off of me. Jesse mocked him as he did the same, but Brandon paid him no mind.

Damicén leaned in close to Jesse and said, "Pretty lady before you any day, right Jesse?" in a call back that obviously enraged, as he shoved Damicén.

"That was a genius move. You saved our asses." As Brandon spoke, I couldn't help but notice he had a busted lip and a bloodied shoulder.

"I should be asking if you're okay." I made to touch the lip, and he shied away, blushing.

"Ah, it's nothing. I can heal these with ease."

"I have to admit, it was a clever idea." Kenna relented, uncrossing her arms and giving me an appreciative touch. "Thank you."

"May have been clever, but it was still stupid. I must give you credit for catching him in the balls, though." Damicén chuckled as he motioned to Jesse, who snarled.

"Yeah...I'm sorry about that. But I didn't figure you'd let me go otherwise."

Jesse looked about as annoyed as a cat being woken from a nap. "You're right. But that was a cheap shot. Where are we?" He added when he finally noticed our surroundings.

It was dark, but I could faintly make out that the edge of a swamp sat to our left and a wide rolling river to our right. We stood at the beginning of a small pier with a boat dock at the end. A storm brewed just beyond a crop of tall pines with the wind in a frenzy. Thunder rumbled in the distance.

On the horizon, a three-story steamboat chugged into view, only distinguishable from the dark water by the many windows streaming light. Smoke billowed from the stacks, blocking what little stars could be seen from view.

A lone bellow of a horn sounded, and as the ship approached, I could faintly make out a figure waving to us at the head.

"We're exactly where we need to be," Kenna responded as she returned the wave.

The boat pulled as close to the dock as possible, which wasn't close at all because of its sheer size.

"Just portal in!" The man shouted when he realized he couldn't get close enough for us to board from the pier.

Brandon—now giddy with glee—obliged, not waiting for us before he stepped through.

We stepped out across from the man who'd spoken to us. He had long braided black hair with gold bands woven neatly into the strands, warm brown eyes, skin, and a beaming smile. His left arm was decorated with a sleeve of tattoos, non of which I could make out in the dark.

After he finished bear-hugging Brandon, he opened his arms to Kenna. Who wrapped her arms around his waist and planted a long kiss on his lips.

This man must be Kenna's husband: Adaim. If she was a queen, then he was her king, no doubt.

Brandon came to stand next to me, carefully reading my face and then snickering. "Yeah. Everyone in the Supernatural world is *extremely* good-looking." Then under his breath, "And insanely in shape." He patted his slightly distended belly.

Damicén clapped Adaim on the shoulder, then touched two fingers to his lips before circling them up to his forehead. Adaim mimicked the movement before they hugged.

He only nodded to Jesse, the faintest look of distrust in his gaze.

"It's good to see you all." His voice was deep with a distinct Cajun accent. "Come inside. Looks like rain is coming."

He motioned us to a metal hatchway door, and we followed him into the narrow hallway, where we walked down a flight of stairs and into a study.

A leather couch sat at the base of a bookshelf, across from a dark wood desk and rolling chair. The incoming storm flashed through the small peephole windows.

We took up residence on the couch as Kenna began to explain the night's events to her husband. Which meant I also had to explain what I saw during my astral projection. When I got to the chicken part, everyone gasped, and it was an effort to not hurl again—even if nothing would come up. Just another image to add to the ever-growing list of nightmare fuel.

"Black magic," Damicén declared when I finished.

"I knew she was ambitious, but that takes it to the extreme," Jesse affirmed, frown lines creasing his forehead.

Adaim asked, "Why would they attack when they left Tom to turn?"

Kenna—now perched in his lap—draped an arm around his shoulders. "That's the mystery. I would assume it was to wear us down before the army got there. Makes capturing us easier."

I shivered at the word capture. What would they do with us once they had us?

"Jesse, what do you think about Morgan resurrecting himself?" Damicén fiddled with a loose stitch on the couch arm, puckering his lips in thought.

Jesse stood, making his way over to lean against the window. "I guess when we found him in Orlando, that could've been the death that triggered his transformation. It makes more sense than his body being magically preserved for hundreds of years. I just always assumed when they first caught him, they killed him, but they could've kept him alive this whole time until they needed another hybrid."

"When you defected."

Jesse snapped his fingers before touching the tip of his nose. "I hadn't officially left them yet, but I definitely acted off when I checked in. They must've known something was up and let him turn just in case."

I couldn't hold my tongue any longer. I'd spared the details of Morgan's final few words past what was needed at the moment, but now I had to know. "Why did Morgan say you were his brother?"

Everyone paused in their small talk and swiveled to Jesse, who somehow managed to keep his face blank.

He sighed, running his thumb over the scar on his lip. "It's true. Morgan is my half-brother."

Damicén pinched the bridge of his nose. "And you were going to tell us this when?"

"Honestly, I was trying to avoid it. I didn't find out until after I thought he died the first time."

"What's the significance of this?" Kenna leaned forward, allowing Adaim to rub circles on her lower back.

Jesse tensed, working his jaw. He did not want to talk about this. That was clear. "No significance. I'll kill him either way."

His words settled in the silence that followed. Whether the others believed him or not, they didn't show it. Adaim regarded Jesse with newfound respect, even if the twitch of his mouth betrayed his true feelings.

"Where is Raven?" Kenna sat up, searching the room.

We'd been too preoccupied to notice he was missing. Had he even gone through the portal with us?

Kenna looked at me, but I just shook my head. "I haven't seen him since he teleported me to the corner."

"He's probably about to make some dramatic entrance," Damicén huffed.

"Well, *someone* had to stay behind and finish the beast off," a voice came from the corner of the room. Raven sauntered in from the shadows, hands in his jacket pockets. He stood coldly by the door, waiting for a response as if he expected us to ooh and ah.

Damicén lifted his hands with a smirk. "And there it is."

Raven cocked one eyebrow, studying him with feral intent.

But Damicén wasn't letting this go. "All you do is lurk and invade people's personal space. Can you not enter a room like a normal person?"

With a blink, Raven effectively ended any further contact with Damicén, instead focusing on Jesse. "I finished it for you."

"Those things are unkillable," he retorted.

A devious glint played in Raven's eyes when he responded, "Nothing is unkillable. You should know that after your encounter with one at the Cauldwell household."

My eyes flew wide as I tossed a look to Jesse. He wasn't looking at me, only staring knives at Raven.

He glanced at Kenna and continued, "I tried to warn them to leave Tom."

She tapped her nails on the desk, contemplating her next words carefully. "Why didn't you tell us exactly what it was? That would be warning us."

He rolled his eyes. "I shouldn't have to. Jesse knew, too."

How Kenna kept any of her composure during this was a feat of its own. She truly showed why she was the leader. "Jesse. Is this why you hesitated?"

Jesse slumped further down the wall, shoving his hands in his pockets to mimic Raven. "Grant knew you guys were taking the survivors. He mentioned potentially using them as Trojan Horses, but I didn't know if he was actually acting on it."

Raven scoffed, "Either way, they definitely meant to use Tom to keep us distracted. He could sneak in and snatch us up since the creature would listen to them. No doubt Grant gave the orders in the first place."

"Let's just kill him and be done with it." Adaim slammed his palm on the desk, agitated. "She and Jesse know where they are."

Kenna shot him a sideways glance before giving me a reassuring one.

"Cut off the head, and two more take its place," Raven warned. "Morgan would be first in line."

Jesse stiffened, rubbing his hands up and down his thighs. "He and Avalon would fight over it. She was in charge before bringing him back. But...that's not the main problem we have with that plan."

Adaim leaned forward with curiosity. "And what is?"

"We can't kill Grant."

"Sure we can." Raven clapped his hands together. At the exact same moment, the rain began to pour outside, beating pellets against the small windows.

"No. *We* can't." Jesse exchanged looks with Damicén before the former said, "We need to bring Talon back."

"You need to stop. She doesn't want to come back."

"And how would you know that?"

"Because I was around her for over two thousand years. She's done. Stop this madness of trying to bring her back. We can take Grant down without her. Let her rest." Damicén's voice cracked. He clenched his jaw, cleared his throat, and repeated, "We can take Grant down without her."

Jesse swallowed hard, pulling the necklace from his pocket. "No. We can't."

Raven narrowed his eyes, the wheels slowly turning behind them. His next words were more of a plea to be right. "Anyone can kill him."

"No," Jesse affirmed. "It has to be Talon."

"Why?"

"Because when he decided to start this war, he hired a Witch—"

"To hold his soul, yes, we know."

"Not only for that." Jesse held up a finger to silence anyone from further interrupting. "But to make sure only Talon would be able and able to kill him. If you were to take a silver bullet right now and shoot him, it'd bounce right off."

"But he did die. Or at least a little," Brandon added sheepishly. "With the trial and execution by fire."

Jesse shook his head in disbelief. "Again, they never burned his body. They just swapped it for a follower of his before collecting his soul to pretend like he was dead. They waited in the shadows until the right time to trade his soul for Talon's to ensure the only one able to kill him would be gone forever."

Chapter Twenty-Two

Everyone fell silent, the sound of rain the only reprieve. Thunder rumbled again, closer this time, and the boat began to rock as the river churned.

"He's playing the long game," Kenna shuddered.

"He's *always* playing the long game," Jesse affirmed. "If Ketura hadn't gotten sloppy and egotistical, it would've been over a lot sooner."

"Then why would you do what you did?" Damicén scrubbed his face. "If you knew she was the only way, why would you do it?"

Jesse glowered at the Spartan warrior. "Because that was the only way to ensure she'd be able to return. We've already had this discussion."

"Then let's re-hash it."

"Enough." Kenna raised a hand, voice booming louder than any of the men. "Jesse, are you sure about this?"

"I'm one of the only people who know."

She sighed, brows narrowing, pinching the bridge of her nose. "Then let's do this sooner rather than later."

"But how do we do that without killing her in the process?" Damicén argued, pointing to me.

I began to sink lower into the couch, face turning scarlet. "Can we stop talking about me like I'm not here? Just get it out of me."

"That's not as easy as you would think," Brandon cautioned in a hushed tone. "We don't know how it got in you, and that plays a big part in how we get it out."

Raven shoved his hands back in his pockets and turned from us, head down to look at the floor. "Where are the others? The ones in the base with us."

Kenna raised her head from her hands, face drained. "They're on their way to the pickup location. Sam and Rhydel have taken over for us to lead them there."

"Why not portal them in with you?"

"There's too many, and if we had been captured, they would've still been free and able to relay information to Adaim. Why do you ask?"

Raven nodded thoughtfully before blending back with the shadows and disappearing.

"I hate when he does that," Brandon chimed as he shook with a sudden chill. "Creepy."

"Let him brood, back to the matter at hand." Kenna snapped her fingers, drawing us back to her. "We need to figure out how to separate the Stone from Rosetta."

"I don't think there are any spells for that," Brandon half pleaded, hands grasped behind his neck. "I've never seen any, and I've done some slight research."

"Well, they got it into her with a spell, more than likely, so look harder."

"We still have that favor with the Fae," Damicén reminded. "I'm sure they would know what to do."

Jesse once again shook his head, beginning to pace around the room. "No to that as well. Mercury won, and the Fae realm has pretty much gone back to prehistoric times. No one has seen Tarragorn since the last of his troops fell."

An agonizing quiet befell the group as they stewed on his words.

"You played a part in that," Damicén growled.

Jesse slammed the side of his fist on the bookshelf. "Dammit, don't you think I know that? There's nothing I can do about it now."

"Why *did* you come back?" Adaim asked as he scooted his wife from his lap. He interlocked his arms behind his back and approached Jesse with an icy calm, who met his gaze with equal intensity.

"For my sister and Talon."

"You don't love her!" Damicén shouted, climbing to his feet and shooting across the room. "You said it yourself. You didn't."

"I said I didn't know. But I couldn't deny the connection."

"Oh, what a crock of shit. There's no connection!"

"I think we're mates."

This shocked Damicén, stumbling as if Jesse had hit him. "Those don't exist. They never have."

"That's the only thing I can come up with that makes sense."

"You read too many fantasy stories."

"Can we please?" Kenna raised her voice, clapping to draw their attention. "Let's not start arguing again. You can fight later, but right now, you have more important things to worry about."

Damicén scoffed and returned to the couch, leaving Adaim to size Jesse up. Adaim was much taller than him, but they were relatively the same size in build. I'd yet to see what either of them looked like in Wolf form—not counting my breakdown in the field, as I didn't really get to look at him—but I could only imagine it would be a tough fight.

"Rosetta?" Kenna's voice softened as she spoke to me. "I've yet to ask you what you want in this."

They all turned to me, causing me to slump further down into the couch. Brandon gave me a reassuring grin and nodded for me to speak.

I breathed deeply, straightening up to be taken more seriously. "I want to help. In any way I can. I thought that was obvious when I turned the lights off in the base."

She smiled and shared a knowing look with Adaim. He relaxed a little, making his way back to his wife, where he kissed the back of her hand.

"Let's think on it. It's still early in the morning, and sleep would do us some good." He motioned for us to follow him out. "I'll show everyone to their rooms. It's crowded, but we make it work."

I ended up receiving an empty room with three sets of bunk beds, given the reason I'd share with who we picked up tomorrow from the base.

An empty feeling began to settle over me. I'd gotten so used to the company Sam and Rhydel had given me, no matter how small of a feat that was. Just their presence alone gave me a level of comfort I didn't think I could replicate by myself anymore. I was alone again.

My mind spiraled with the events of the passing days. Everything happened so fast that I had no time to process anything. It's a surprise I didn't get whiplash from it all. How was I going to accomplish anything like this?

After a grueling amount of minutes passed, I decided Adaim was right: sleep would do me good. And this time, I think I would avoid trying to astral project.

Somehow I slept straight through the rest of the night into early morning, only waking when Brandon came to get me.

He held two Styrofoam cups in his hands, offering me one. "They actually have coffee here."

I took a sip and immediately spit it back into the cup. It was bitter and boiling hot; my tongue now pulsing and burning.

"Oh, I'm sorry," he hissed. "I forgot to tell you it's super hot."

I winced, touching my tongue with my fingertip. "Yeah, I figured that out. It also tastes disgusting."

He pushed his chest out and scowled. "It is not. Black coffee is what gets me through the day."

"Then take mine. I think I'll pass."

We walked down the halls of the boat, him showing me around and introducing me to everyone we met. About an hour in, my brain swam with all the rooms, people, and names. There'd be no way I could remember everything. It was nice getting to finally meet Millie. With her shining green eyes, coiled hair, and cheery disposition, she was the epitome of a ray of sunshine. I could see why Sam loved her so much. She oozed with enthusiasm I could only ever dream of having.

We finished the tour on the top deck, leaning over the railing and staring into the water.

"This is everyone we have," he said sadly. "Everyone who will fight with us."

It wasn't a lot. I didn't meet everyone, maybe a hundred—this ship could hold three at most—and it was mostly small covens or loners. They weren't soldiers like Grant had.

I wasn't sure what Grant's side looked like aside from the speech I went to. There were about as many people there as there were on this ship, and that was only one rally. Plus, he has the army of hybrids, who were apparently all trained super soldiers if Jesse was anything to go off of.

A crow swooped low near us, perching on the railing a few feet down. It pecked at the shiny rail and then turned an eye to me. It hopped closer, turning its head both ways to look at me out of each eye.

I reached a finger out, wondering if the events from my time at Grant's carried over. The crow wasted no time and bounded up to rest on my finger. It rubbed its beak against my other hand when I brought it over to pet it.

It cawed three times when I finished petting it and took flight, gliding on the winds above the river and drifting to the bank into a pine tree. My heart flew with it, drifting on the summer breeze. I wished I could be as free as that bird. Be able to fly wherever I wanted, whenever I wanted, and only had to worry about food.

Turning my attention back to Brandon, I raised my eyebrows when I noticed him wide-eyed beside me. His mouth hung slack, and he stared at me as if I'd been abducted by aliens in front of him.

"Did you just pet a wild crow?"

I shrugged. "I guess so."

He blinked several times, looking to the tree line, the railing, and back to me in rapid succession. "How did you do that?"

"I don't know. Ever since I woke up at Grant's, I've had this connection with animals. Well, not so much a connection, but I can walk up to them, and they come to me."

He furrowed his brows and chose to stare back out over the river instead of continuing the conversation.

The wind whipped my hair into my face, which then got stuck on the spraying water droplets from the churned river. There was no civilization in sight. Nothing but trees and swampland for miles. Under different circumstances, I might've actually liked to take a cruise like this.

The awkward silence began to gnaw at me. Was it something I said? Was it the bird? I was just as confused about it as he was.

Fidgeting with the bottom of my shirt, I asked, "Why does he want to kill you guys?"

Brandon sighed as if he knew this was coming and downed the last of my coffee cup before chucking it into the trash. "It's not so much *us* as it is just Vampires in general and anyone who associates with them."

"Why?" For every Vampire I'd met today, there were at least five Werewolves I met with them. Seemed to me like Vampires were a dying breed that posed no threat. In fact, they seemed to want nothing more than to be left alone.

Brandon retold the story Talon had told him last year, recounting her time with Grant. The longer he spoke, the more my heart shredded. So much hatred and anger…and jealousy. I'd seen that jealousy reveal itself with Jarred, and—even though Jesse meant for it to happen—it cost him his life.

"How many of them are left?" I asked when he finished.

"Less than a hundred," Damicén answered as he sauntered beside us wearing a pair of star-shaped sunglasses.

Brandon swiveled to stare at his friend, eyebrows furrowed. "Where did you get those?"

"A kid gave them to me. You think I'm gonna say no to them?"

"There are kids on here?" I asked incredulously.

They nodded in unison, looking confused as to why I'd even ask that. "There's whole families on here, Rosetta. Those trying to get away from Grant and his persecution. You saw what happened to the blended family in Orlando."

My stomach twisted as I remembered the bodies and that poor baby. I still couldn't wrap my head around the fact that this was all Grant's doing. Even with his jealous streak, I never saw that evil side of him.

Damicén frowned at my thoughts. "He is what he is. And he'll never stop until he gets what he wants."

I gulped. "And he wants Talon."

"He wants our extinction. Doesn't matter if she took him back or not. It's too late for that."

"He's doing all of this because Talon broke up with him? I just don't believe it."

"I didn't either," Brandon mumbled, but his words were barely audible over what was said next.

"Well, believe it. Believe what you saw," Damicén snapped, stripping the glasses from his face. "I've dealt with this man for hundreds of years. What you saw, the aftermath of his command, is what you get with him. He would kill every child on this earth if they had even held the door open for

Vampires. I'm sorry," he added when he saw my face drop. "I don't mean to get loud, but you better start seeing what's right in front of you. Or you'll wind up in a grave with the rest of us."

"On a lighter note," Brandon said thickly, eyeing Damicén. "I think I know how to help you manifest your magic."

This perked me up, especially as it completely washed away any thoughts of Grant. I waited with bated breath for his fix to my problem. Only his answer faded my smile and sent Damicén into a fit of laughter.

"Hypnosis?" he cackled. "I never thought this day could get any better, but you've proved me wrong."

Brandon was less than amused and crossed his arms begrudgingly. "It's an actual thing. We could hypnotize her magic into coming out."

"That's not going to work," Raven called as he stepped into the light.

"Oh, great. He's back," Damicén muttered. "Come to say some cryptic words of wisdom and then vanish into the night?"

Raven smirked, rubbing a thumb across his lower lip. "Coming to save your asses yet again." He motioned with two fingers for us to follow him back inside the ship.

"He's more infuriating than Jesse ever was," Damicén snarled.

Brandon thinned his lips and said, "For once, I actually agree with you."

We walked back down the halls to the study, where it seemed Raven had already gathered the others.

Everyone stood idly, refusing to sit when he asked. The room buzzed with anticipation.

He paced methodically in front of us, nodding and shaking his head to his inner monologue.

Kenna appeared to have reached the end of her patience with him, and no amount of soothing from Adaim would settle her. "What's this all about?"

"I've given it some thought," he said finally, not stopping his walk. "And I know how to get the Stone out of her."

"Oh, you've given it some thought, have you? How kind of you to tell us."

"I could've kept it to myself and let you run around like chickens with your head cut off."

Kenna raised her eyebrows at the threat, then narrowed her gaze. "Being condescending is only going to get you a swift kick off this boat."

"Go ahead. You'll never find out what I know and will be stuck under Grant's thumb."

Jesse stepped forward, arms crossed defensively across his chest. "Who says we can't? I knew who you were before they did. I can find anything out."

Raven paused his steps for a moment to throw Jesse a sneer. "Because none of you even know they exist."

"Who?" Damicén strode up next to Jesse, forming a formidable wall of muscle between Raven and me.

He began pacing once more, hands behind his back. "The reason her magic seems different is that it *is* different. More different than any of you could ever know."

"Genius," Damicén scoffed. "You came up with that yourself?"

"Damicén," Kenna chided. "Just let him get it out."

I squeezed my way through the two men, his words lighting a fire in me. "What do you know, Raven?"

"I know how to get the Stone out of you, so we can bring back Talon and finish this."

Kenna groaned, pinching the bridge of her nose. "You wear my patience thin. Out with it."

Brandon placed a hand on my arm, trying to pull me away, but I planted. No one could drag me from this.

"We're going to go to the person who put it in her in the first place and get them to take it back out."

My heart leaped into my throat, which tightened around my words. "You know who did that?"

He stopped walking once more and looked at me as he whispered, "Yes."

"Who?" Jesse uncrossed his arms, clearly stunned at this revelation. "I've known her since she was a small child, and she had the Stone in her even back then. Who could've put it in her that young?"

A look I could only describe as disappointment flashed across Raven's face. He took a deep breath, shoved his hands in his coat pockets, and said, "Her mother. The Queen of Angels."

Chapter Twenty-Three

My knees buckled, and I collapsed into Brandon's arms.

My mother. He knew my mother. He'd known the entire time who my mother was, my birth mother. And that she was an Angel. Did those even exist? Hell, Vampires came from a Demon; what's stopping Angels from also existing? There in-lies another question: if Vampires were from Demons, what were Angels from? Angels were the opposite to Demons, and nothing topped it that I knew of…unless it was a God who did it.

But the Queen of Angels, my mother? Where had she been all these years? Why did she give me up?

Brandon gently guided me over to the couch to sit us down as chaos broke out. I folded into his arms, feeling as numb as I had those last few days at Grant's.

Kenna stood between Damicén and Raven, who seemed to be screaming at each other. I couldn't actually tell because the world had been muted in favor of a high-pitched whine.

Jesse got beside Damicén, trying to push his way past Kenna's outstretched arm. He flailed a fist and a pointed finger.

Adaim walked up behind Damicén, wrapped Jesse in his arms, and lifted him away from the argument.

Shadows flurried behind Raven, all clawing to be released from their holds. And it seemed Raven struggled to contain them.

Brandon's mouth moved, speaking wordless things. I blinked, wide-eyed. His brow furrowed, and he pulled me in tighter, burying my face in his shoulder.

The world slowly faded back to my ears, and it was filled with loud voices. I winced, squeezing my eyes closed.

My pulse pounded in perfect sync with the flipping of my stomach. Realizing the madness around me wouldn't stop on its own, I tried to take a calming breath. It felt like ice down my throat, in my lungs, and it did nothing to calm me down.

Pushing myself away from Brandon, I stalked toward them. They all quieted at my approach, staring at me with equal apprehension.

"How do you know my mother?" My voice came surprisingly steady and commanding.

Raven clenched his jaw, cheeks heating. "We're friends."

Anger flashed through me, blazing off my skin. "You're friends with my mother—knew she was my mother this whole time—and didn't tell me?"

He took a cautionary step back, hands raised. "I wasn't sure you were hers until that day in the field."

"That was days ago!"

Everyone stepped two feet back from us, but I paid it no heed.

"You watched Brandon struggle to teach me, watched *me* struggle to bring out my magic, knowing it would never work. Why?"

"Rosetta. You've got to calm down." Kenna's liquid gold voice yanked me back into my body, rinsing the hatred from within me.

I noticed everyone, including Raven, standing several defensive feet away from me. And I was glowing. Power radiated off me, my magic whipping around like a cat's tail.

"I-I'm sorry." I shook my head, the power thrumming through me so hard, so fast it made me light-headed. Shutting my eyes and letting it dim, it slowly melted off my body and retreated back to my mind.

When I opened my eyes again, the magic was gone, but no one had moved. They all stood as if I'd still been rampaging.

"Tell me everything," I demanded.

"I met her not long after I left on my own. I stumbled across the Angel's existence while fleeing from my shadows' rage. She was a child like me." Raven laughed dryly at some memory. "We became fast friends, both heirs to something we didn't ask for. I lost contact with her about three hundred years ago…right after she found out she was pregnant."

My eyes stung with tears I refused to let fall. They might bring the anger with them. And I was angry. Over and over again, I've had to beg to be told things involving me and my past: important things. I was done with that.

"I didn't know you were hers until that day in Orlando when you leveled the field. I'd seen the same type of power in her once. And after I thought about it, I saw her in you. In your features and mannerisms. Plus, the incident with the crow earlier."

"The crow? What does the crow have to do with anything?"

"Angels have an affinity with animals…it's best I let her explain this to you."

Jesse pushed past me, finger raised in opposition. "Whoa, now. You're telling us that woman gave her up—and she's actually three hundred years old on top of that—and we're just going to waltz right back to her? You said you lost contact years ago. How do you even know she put the Stone in her?"

Raven stood rigid by the desk, eyes narrowing. "Context clues. The Resurrection Stone was last in her family's possession, conveniently after she found out she was pregnant and is now in Rosetta."

"Damicén, I thought the council hid the stone away with a Witch after our first war with Grant?" Kenna asked as she slid around us to the bookshelf at the rear. She pulled an old leather-bound book out and flipped through its pages.

"They did," he answered, rubbing his chin in thought.

"To the Angels," Raven said matter-of-factly.

"So, now you expect us to believe the Council always knew about the existence of Angels?"

"Believe what you want. But that's the truth, and it's the only way we can get the Stone out of her."

"How did you even know they gave the Stone to them?"

Raven smirked, adjusting his jacket collar. "I gave them the idea. I was the only person who knew of their existence back then, so it was the safest option. It was after they got the Stone that I lost contact; I'm not sure what happened."

Jesse spared a sideways glance at me, a question in his eyes. "Rosetta? What do you think?"

I chewed on my cheek, studying Raven. "This is the only way?"

He nodded, face innocent and needy. "I can't say why she gave you up or why she hasn't contacted you…or me. We won't know unless we go and find out for ourselves."

Turning my attention back to Jesse, I dipped my chin. "We'll go, then."

"You don't have to if you don't want to," he prefaced with a soft tone. "No one would blame you or resent you for it. Not even me. We can always find another way."

I shook my head, wrapping my arms around me for comfort. "No. It's okay. We could also use this as a way to find out how to control my magic. When do we leave?"

Raven leaned an arm on the desk, eyeing Kenna at the back of the room. "The Angels live in a different realm of existence than us. Much like the Fae, they have their own world. Unfortunately, doorways to that world only open on the solstices."

"The summer solstice is tomorrow," Kenna announced as she slammed the book closed. "And the history log mentions nothing about Angels. Only the Witch who be-spelled the Stone into hiding."

"Well, sure. Why would the Council want you all knowing about the existence of Angels?"

"Are they biblical?" Brandon spoke suddenly, drawing everyone's eyes to him.

Raven considered the question with a tilt of his head. "Yes and no. They do not follow the Christian God, if that's what you're asking. At least not when I knew them."

Kenna fisted her hands on her hips, firmly planting several feet in front of Raven. "I assume there's a ritual involved in opening the doorway?"

He nodded. "I know what you'll need."

"Good. Then you can go get them. How much longer till we reach the pickup location for the others?" She asked as she turned to her husband.

He lifted a silver etched watch up, considering its face. "Another day's travel, for sure."

She nodded, lifting her chin to Damicén. "Will you stay with the ship when we go tomorrow?"

He raised his eyebrows, clearly taken aback by this request. "Kenna, I think I'd be more help going—"

"Jesse and Brandon will go. You're needed here in case an attack occurs. You can find out faster than any of us about impending danger."

"*If* I can," he muttered under his breath. "Can't read anyone's minds on that side."

She threw him a beseeching look, one so pitiful even I felt obliged to agree on his behalf.

He held his hands up in defeat, slapping them on his thighs when she walked away. Turning to Brandon, he leveled a finger. "Don't do anything stupid."

"We're leaving that with you," he retorted with a cocky smile and a pat on the shoulder. "It'll be alright. Jesse is the universal killing machine, after all."

At the drop of my jaw, they cringed.

"Don't ask." Damicén flicked his wrist, "It's a long story. And what's with *you* not knowing this information?" He turned his suspicions on Jesse. "Since you claim to know everything. How'd you not know she was an Angel?"

Jesse's neck turned red. "I had no clue they existed. Same as you. They keep their existence very well hidden."

Damicén scoffed, waking after Kenna. "Some universal killing machine tracker you are."

My eyebrows shot up as I turned incredulously to my brother. "I'm sorry—what did he just call you?"

He avoided my gaze as I searched his face for an answer. "It's a hybrid thing," was all he could muster up.

Brandon approached me, brown eyes soft and hands outstretched. "What a day. Find out your mother is alive, and you're part Angel."

"It's a lot at once," I agreed. "But I'm getting used to the fast-paced learning environment here. Universal killing machine?"

Jesse smiled sadly, blatantly avoiding the jump back to the previous question. "I'm proud of you for going, and I'll be with you every step of the way. When you meet your mother—"

"Wait," I interrupted, feeling that rage trickle up in me again. "Does this mean you know my father, too?" I whirled to where Raven stood, or where he once stood because he was gone now. I tsked my tongue and fisted my hands on my hips. "I hate when he does that."

"Join the club," Jesse snorted as he gave me a final squeeze and pulled Adaim out into the hall, mumbling choice words about the trip tomorrow, leaving Brandon and me alone.

Without thinking, I reached out and hugged him tightly. "Thank you for holding me. I was freaking out."

He hesitated a moment before wrapping his arms around me and leaning his cheek on the top of my head. "You're welcome."

When my stomach began to flip, I pulled away, puffing air through my cheeks. "I think I want that coffee now."

He full belly laughed and hooked his arm through mine, leading me down the hall. "I think we can manage that."

The coffee was still too bitter for me to stand, but after adding a few packets of cream and sugar, it was tolerable. I felt an instant boost of energy and an immediate relief from the stress.

"I bet you want to go back to your room and lay down for a bit," Brandon mused as he bit into a biscuit.

I chuckled warily, munching on my own slice of toast. "Actually, I think I'd rather do anything else than sit with my thoughts right now."

He perked up, a mischievous grin forming on his lips.

I quirked a brow, a similar smile playing on mine. "What idea did you just get?"

Grabbing my arm, he towed me through the halls of the boat. We giggled and hid from anyone who might pass us, making our way down several flights of stairs, ending up in a large empty room with a pool in the center.

The water was clear, allowing me to see the sea turtle mural painted on the bottom. It was maybe ten feet at the deepest, but it still made my heart race. The feeling of drowning washed over me again, and I absentmindedly clutched my throat.

Brandon winced as he began pulling his shoes off. "I know you probably don't want to swim after what you've been through. But dipping our feet in is just as good and relaxing."

"Are we even allowed down here?"

"Not at all. So don't go blabbing my secret hideout."

"Secret hideout?" I slipped off my tennis shoes and followed his lead in sinking my feet into the water up to my ankles. Rolling up my pants leg, I sunk them in further, swishing around in the lukewarm liquid. I felt the sigh kick out of me without even meaning to. As long as I didn't think about the vast depth of this pool and the fear of drowning again, I could handle this. I could imagine it was a small bathtub, especially with how warm the water was.

Brandon watched me coyly, running his hands along the water's surface. "Before I left here to join you guys at the base, this was my favorite place to be. The water's always warm. I could relax, get away from all the noise and my thoughts."

"Thank you for showing me. I promise not to give it away." How he was the only person who knew about a giant pool in this boat was beyond me, but after my time here, I've learned to just go with the flow. Sometimes questions only add more to ask.

"Good. I'd have to cast you overboard if you did. Mutiny and all."

"What's Damicén like?" I asked suddenly, curiosity finally getting the better of me. I'd been around him for the better part of a week and a half now, and with everything coming to a head, I didn't have time to really get to know him.

Brandon got a look on his face I could only describe as mournful guilt. He then proceeded to tell me a story all about Damicén's favorite thing in the whole world. His car. He told me about the adventure they'd been on in it to save me and how, after I disappeared, Damicén had to lock it away in a storage facility. How it crushed him but was necessary to avoid being found.

"There's really not much else to him other than his sarcasm. He's just sarcasm and cars. I feel bad he had to give it up, though. At least I still get my computers."

"Yeah, of which you looked up hypnotism?"

He chortled, flicking drops of water at me. "I was working off low information. I thought it was normal magic."

Our smiles slowly faded as we both reconsidered our nearly hopeless situation.

"No one's really been the same since we lost Talon. We all had to take on different roles and lost a lot of morale."

"It's gotta be difficult. She saved your lives."

"It's more than that." His eyes turned red with unreleased tears he tried furiously to blink away. "She's family. The only family I have left."

"You're Human, right? Like m—" I stopped myself before I could finish. I'd almost said 'like me,' but I'm not Human. I'm a Supernatural creature.

Brandon graciously ignored my slip-up. "The only person left from my birth family is my mother, and when you're best friends with two of the oldest beings alive, you have to make some hard decisions on who you keep around."

So, he gave up his birth mother to be with Talon and Damicén. He gave up the only person blood-related to him for two beings of the night.

I rolled on my side to face him, pulling one leg in from the water. "I wish I had a family like yours."

"You do. And not just Jesse," he added when I went to object. "You're a part of our family now. Me, Damicén, Kenna, and even Adaim will protect you to our deaths if necessary."

"I hope it's not." I shifted uncomfortably.

"I hope it doesn't come to that, either." He reached a hand out and interlocked his fingers with mine. The stark resilience in his eyes gave me a spark of hope. Maybe we could do this after all. If he could go through everything he'd told me, I could find the strength to continue.

We stayed there for a few minutes, enjoying the comfort of each other's company. The sounds of the ship and our feet kicking the water became our entirety for the span of ten wonderful minutes.

In that time, I began to notice even more things about him. The two freckles on each point of his upper lip, the yellow ring in his chocolate eyes, and even the small wrinkle under his nose when he smiled.

"This isn't all I brought you down here for. The water is just a bonus, but I have something better that will take your mind off everything." He pulled his feet back, stretching his arms and standing.

My eyebrows raised, along with the corners of my lips. "Oh?"

He reached down and helped me up with a sheepish grin. Then he cupped his hands together, brought them close to his lips, and whispered something. A moment later, he opened them, and a purple butterfly made of magic floated from his palms. It danced around my head, fluttered across the tip of my nose, and faded in the air.

I beamed. "That was so cool."

"You think?" He did the motion again, adding a small spin of his body, and released a dozen magic butterflies. They swirled around us, creating a small vortex of light and wing beats.

My heart leaped from my chest, feeling so full of emotion that I reached out and touched his cupped hands, letting my power flow into him. The next batch of butterflies glowed gold and pulsed with life, wings so great in size they dwarfed the others.

He watched in awe as they took to landing on his shoulders and head. Gently scooping one from his hair, he tipped it toward me. His smile radiated a joy so deep I couldn't bear to look at it anymore.

I leaned in, pushing his hands aside, and kissed him. He froze. Immediately I pulled away, shame flooding my face. I stumbled for an apology or an explanation, but he only grabbed my face and kissed me harder.

Butterflies exploded from us—purple and gold mixed together, dancing together. So many flew in the air that it kicked up a wind, swirling our hair as our lips tangled together.

When he pulled away, my entire body buzzed. He was breathless, looking at me like I was his only reason for breathing.

We lay on the tile together, my arms around his shoulders, his around my waist. Our feet dangled in the water again, kicking splashes to each other.

A loud beeping sounded near our heads, snatching us from our fantasy. He swore and pressed a button on his watch, ending the sound.

"Dinner time."

I raised an eyebrow. "You have an alarm set on your watch for dinner?"

"Yes. It's spaghetti night."

I giggled, tracing a finger around the watch's edge, jerking it away just as fast when it started to shift. It went from matte black to a shining gold. He sat up, inspecting the new change, looking back and forth from me to the watch with bewilderment on his features.

"Did you do that?"

I shrugged, sitting up with worry drilling in my gut. "I don't know. Not intentionally."

"It's solid gold," he observed, glancing over his wrist at me. He tucked that hand behind my ear, smiling softly at me. "We'll figure that out later. Let's go eat."

Chapter Twenty-Four

Raven showed up an hour before dusk, a black bag slung over his shoulder. Everyone was thoroughly annoyed at his late arrival, me more so at his constant avoidance of any interaction.

I would have to pin him down soon and muster up the courage to confront him about it. I needed to stop skirting the issue and finally ask him why he was at the lake and why he was hiding it from everyone else. Even if Damicén and Jesse already know, which makes it even more confusing, he isn't saying anything. He has to know they know, so why continue to lie? Well, you can't lie if you always avoid it, I guess.

Of course, he paid no attention to anyone's feelings and emptied the contents of the bag on the deck floor. He'd said we had to do it on top of the ship in the open air, and no one felt like arguing with him anymore. It wouldn't accomplish anything anyway. He knew things we didn't, and no one could argue that we needed his help.

The bag contained a few crystals—colored pink, purple, orange, and clear—an owl feather, two white candles, and salt. When asked what he planned to do with all of these items, he chose silence, setting it up while we watched.

He started by creating a ring of salt, large enough for the five of us to stand in, with the candles on either side. The crystals he laid out in four corners inside the salt and kept the owl feather on his person. He asked Brandon to light the candles, and with a flick of his wrist, they flamed to life.

Raven then escorted us inside the salt circle, taking the owl feather and holding it over the smoke of the candles. He swirled it around our heads and down our bodies. Jesse fixed him a look of pure disgust when it was his turn but kept his mouth shut.

As soon as the sun hit the horizon over the river, he began chanting in another language I didn't understand. And by the look on everyone else's faces, neither did they.

He repeated a singular phrase over and over again, spinning the feather rapidly in his hands. He did this until the sun had almost completely set, leaving my back aching from standing for so long and my ears ringing from his chant.

Then the deck began to wobble and tilt, making all of us feel like we would slide right off.

"What's happening?" I called. "Is the boat sinking?"

Kenna shook her head, pointing to the deck chairs nearby that never swayed. "Whatever is happening is happening only inside here."

"I think I'm gonna be sick." Jesse leaned over, almost tumbling right out of the circle before Kenna grabbed ahold of his shirt collar.

A portal opened above our heads, swirling bright white, and sucked us from the ground.

"I'm being beamed up!" Brandon shrieked, grasping for anything to hold on to, settling for my arm.

We were violently yanked through the portal, feeling like fitting a thread through a needle during the process. The light blinded me, dulling every one of my senses; the only thing keeping me tied to reality being Brandon's hold on me.

After ping-ponging us around, it spat us out on a dirt road. I somehow managed to fall on top of Brandon, smacking our foreheads together.

Kenna and Jesse collapsed beside us, groaning and rubbing their heads. Raven landed on his feet, brushing some nonexistent dirt from his jacket.

I don't know why he insisted on wearing that thing twenty-four-seven. It was hot enough in short sleeves. Not to mention the more I looked at it the more I noticed it didn't fit him quite right. The sleeves were just a few inches shy of his wrists, and the shoulders looked taut across him. Why would he continue

Climbing to my feet, I noticed we landed on a crossroad in the middle of a dense forest akin to the one we'd driven through on the way to Grant's rally—minus the snow.

"Oh, great," Jesse mumbled, coming to the same realization I had. "I never want to see these trees ever again."

Raven bent down and pinched some dirt between his fingers, letting the wind carry it from his hand. His jaw tensed, and when he straightened, I could see the wheels spinning behind his eyes.

"What's wrong?"

"This dirt hasn't seen any footwork in years."

"You can tell that by just picking it up in your hand?" Jesse asked incredulously, letting Kenna use his arm to haul herself up.

She wore that same look of disdain the others did when interacting with him. "Where are we, Raven?"

He turned over his shoulder, not meeting her eyes as he scanned the trees. "The realm of the Seraphim."

"Yes," she sighed. "But *where* are we in there?"

"This crossroad is where everyone who portals lands. It's about a mile from the town. You're supposed to go through the guards stationed here, like a border crossing of sorts."

"Well, maybe things have changed in the last three hundred years."

Raven didn't respond; his silence said everything for him.

We trekked down the path, Raven leading and Jesse taking up the rear. As we walked, I noted the forest was quiet. Too quiet. It took me back to the woods surrounding Grant's. That eerie silence, where not even the bugs chirped, that set your skin crawling.

Kenna stepped on a particularly loud branch, making Brandon jump straight in the air. She winced and held up her hand in apology.

Raven never said a word the entire walk but was quick to stare daggers at any of us that made a sound, which was rare. We felt the pulse of something very wrong here.

The town was completely abandoned. The few shops all had their windows busted, and doors boarded up. One building even looked to have been set ablaze, only smoldering black boards holding it up.

"Something's wrong," Jesse noted as Raven took a look inside what he claimed to have been an inn for travelers. "This place looks like a war zone."

"Maybe it was," Kenna responded, crossing her arms in a wary stance.

"One thing bothers me, though."

"What?"

"Why is it so quiet?"

Raven stepped out of the broken window and dusted off the debris. "Because the forest knows when there's a predator in it."

I gulped. "We're not the predators, are we?"

Goosebumps prickled my arms, and I rubbed them away. What predator had been in Grant's woods?

Everyone turned to face me, apparently I'd unintentionally spoken that question aloud. Raven giving me a reproachful look, giving the slightest shake of his head as if to say 'not now'. Jesse pursed his lips and gave me a reassuring touch to the shoulder, refusing to answer as well as we continued on.

Great. That's fine. Totally fine.

Another few miles and we had to stop. The blisters on my feet from our journey through the caves were beginning to reform, and I needed a break. Unfortunately, we stopped right next to a cemetery. Even more unfortunate, whatever had happened in the town had made its way here.

Thousands of headstones littered the ground, some so old the words had been erased by weather and some so fresh they still shined.

There were more broken ones than whole, and the ground had been dug up so much that no grass grew. Craters the size of a small car scattered amongst the hillside.

At the back of the cemetery, right next to the bottom of the hill, stood a lone Mausoleum with a giant marble slab at its front gate. The words written on it were so few, yet so bold I could read them from here.

'There are too many to be buried or named. God has abandoned us.'

In the distance, the faintest sounds of chains could be heard dragging through the trees. At first, I thought I imagined them until I caught the others staring in the direction of the sound.

Brandon peered hard into the thicket, a bead of sweat dripping down his brow. "We're not alone."

"Let's get moving," Raven ordered, much to our delight. No one wanted to sit idly by that ruined graveyard with the distant sound of chains to fill our ears—I'd rather my feet bleed.

As we continued, everyone stayed on high alert. The feeling of being watched now crept up the nape of our necks, forcing us to keep a constant awareness of our surroundings.

Eventually, we reached what appeared to be a village.

Wooden and brick houses lined the small road, huddled together by connecting fences and surrounded by forest. They were small in stature and resembled any normal house you'd see back in our realm. In fact, this place looked so similar to ours. I might not have even noticed it was different if not for the blinding vortex we got sucked through.

The more I looked, though, the more I saw things were different than what I'd originally glanced over. Doors and windows were shuttered closed, chimneys barricaded with cages, and gates swung loose in the stiff breeze. Though, no fire seemed to have touched this place like the town. I wasn't sure if that was a good thing or not.

The silence stirred fear in me. Even in the quiet of my rooms, there'd still been background sounds or animals. It was complete dead noise here.

Raven turned a full circle, taking in every house before saying, "That's not good."

He sped off down the road, leaving us to scramble after him. He moved so lightning fast that only Kenna and Jesse could keep up, causing Brandon and me to ride on them piggyback style.

Through the blur of the world, I noticed every house lay the same: dark, empty, boarded up. Abandoned children's toys lay dirty and broken in one front yard, the swings still squeaking in the absence of the wind.

It was a ghost town.

We came to rest at the entrance of a two-story, brown brick house. The gate was latched with a padlock, which Raven broke easily.

Despite our pleas and begs for him to explain what was going on and 'don't do that, that's trespassing,' he pushed on, ignoring us.

Jesse growled under me, "I'm about ready to take his head off. Is this how I was before?"

"Yes," Brandon and Kenna answered in unison.

"I'm so sorry."

"Relax," Kenna bit out.

"Relax? We're in a completely different realm, with no answers or information to *anything,* and he's breaking and entering!"

Reluctantly, we followed Raven up the gravel path, stopping just short of the front door.

He turned over his shoulder and announced, "This was her house."

My heart thudded in my ears as a wave of nausea crashed through me. My mother's house, empty and silent on a bed of wildflowers.

Raven held an ear to the door, listening for any kind of movement before it was yanked away from him and a sword pressed to his throat.

He froze, tilting his eyes up to the perpetrator. A smile crept on his lips as he breathed, "Anahel?"

The sword quivered at his neck, pressing ever so lightly into him and nicking the skin. Blood trailed down his neck for a split second before the wound knitted itself back together.

The door opened wider, and a tall man with cropped red hair, golden eyes, and freckles stepped into view. "Raven Zamfira."

The smile on Raven's face dropped as a look that rang of confusion took its place at the sight before him. "You?"

The man lowered his sword, sheathing it at his waist. Which looked more than out of place as he only wore sweatpants and a stained tank top.

Raven went sheet white, leaning against the porch railing to keep him upright.

Golden eyes glanced at me, realization flickering in them. "You finally brought her."

I blanched the same shade Raven had, feeling clammy.

"Who are you?" Kenna demanded.

He placed a hand to his heart and said, "I'm Khamael. Anahel's son. Come," he beckoned. "It's not safe out here anymore."

We exchanged looks of concern, then followed the man inside.

The interior of the house lay as bare as the exterior, with only a kitchen table and a rocking chair to take up the space. No pictures hung on the walls, nor paintings—only weapons and reinforced steel.

"She told me you'd come back and that you'd bring my sister." He leaned against the kitchen counter, eyes boring directly into mine.

Every time he looked at me, my blood ran cold. Something sparked in the back of my mind, near where my magic stayed—like it recognized him. His eyes connected with mine once more, and I realized his magic felt mine as well.

Wait.

Did he just call me his sister? I had a brother? A blood brother? My head swam, a sinking feeling settling in my gut. This wasn't like discovering Jesse was my adoptive brother. This was an out of body experience, also not like my astral projecting. Now I felt like I was stuck in the mud—quicksand actually. Every breath sunk me lower and lower in the earth as she pulled me beneath the surface. It didn't feel real.

The more I studied him, the more I noticed he looked so scarily similar to me that it was almost like staring into a mirror. The doe eyes that watched my every move, the full lips that pursed and frowned, the blood-red hair. But he had no wings, no halo, no indication he was an Angel.

I reached my powers out, attempting to get a feel for his intentions. Without touching him, I couldn't be too sure, but I could've sworn I felt a tinge of regret melding with longing. There weren't any vengeful, rage-filled emotions. It all just felt so…depressing.

He locked eyes with me, and my magic recoiled, feeling the instant recognition between us. A faint blue/gray aura came into view, surrounding his bulky frame.

"Who told you?" Raven questioned, looking around the space like he'd been kicked in the gut.

"My mother. Drinks?" He added as he pulled open the black fridge, showing it to be empty aside from a mason jar of dark liquid and a case of water.

We all declined, just trying to find a place to stand comfortably. Though, I imagined the others were looking for an escape route should things go horribly wrong. I would've been doing that had I not been so stunned at the man before us and the fact he was my brother.

"Where is Anahel?" Raven snapped, banging his fist on the table.

Khamael simply raised his straight eyebrows and smiled. "Sit." He gestured at the empty table.

"There's nothing to sit on," Kenna retorted, hackles raised.

Khamael snapped his fingers, and five chairs materialized in the air, thudding to the ground around the table. "Sit," he repeated.

We awkwardly obliged, me being forced in the middle and the furthest from him.

He took a deep breath, watching all of us carefully. "I never thought this day would come. I should know better than to not listen to her words, as they often come true."

Jesse glanced at me nervously, shifting his body to block most of mine with his shoulders. "You knew we'd come?"

Khamael nodded, grabbing a glass from his sink and filling it with the dark liquid from the fridge. "Anahel prophesied it."

"Where is she?" Raven repeated more sternly this time.

A muscle feathered in Khamael's jaw as he said, "She died. About a hundred years ago."

Dead. A hundred years dead. Now both of my mothers are dead, both I had no memories of.

Raven's shoulders sagged. "I don't believe you."

Khamael snapped his fingers and brought in his own chair, straddling it. "Why would I lie about that?"

"Okay, okay, hold up. What the hell is going on?" Jesse interrupted, hands balling into fists before him. "Who is

Anahel? Where are we, where is everyone, and why does it look like a war zone out there?"

Raven scooted back from the table, retreating upstairs with a heavy step. Khamael watched him go, taking another swig of the liquid with a defeated look in his eyes. "They're gone. And you're in the realm of the Seraphim, abomination."

Now it was Jesse who paled, storm clouds rolling in his eyes. "What do you know about that?"

"I know everything about you."

Everyone else shifted uncomfortably.

Khamael flicked his attention to Kenna, thumbing the rim of his glass. "Why do you let him join you? You know what he is."

Jesse bristled at the words, knuckles white, tongue in cheek.

"It doesn't matter what he is," Kenna replied coolly. "He helps us."

Khamael chuckled dryly, half rolling his eyes. "You may use a spear as a walking stick, but that does not change its intended purpose." He brought the glass to his lips once more before muttering, "You would be wise to remember that."

A bulging silence filled the space across the table. I could hear Raven rummaging around above us—the sound of his footsteps the only distraction. Finally, I couldn't take it anymore.

"You're my brother?" My voice carried barely more than a whisper.

Khamael put the glass down, folded his arms across the back of the chair, and nodded. "Yes."

A lump formed in my throat, catching the shallow breath in my chest. "I don't understand."

Raven returned, flashing to the table and slamming a picture frame on the wood, pushing it in my direction. The glass had already been shattered, leaving the picture exposed to the elements. Dust and dirt had claimed their territory upon the photograph, staining and marring the image.

A woman with fiery red hair, the same golden eyes, and a sweet smile stood next to a very young Khamael, carrying a swaddled baby in her arms. She looked exactly like me, an older version of me, but me. Or rather, I guess I looked like her—a near exact replica.

On the back of the frame, three sets of names were written in cursive: Anahel, Khamael, Aurelian.

"Your mother is Anahel. She named you Aurelian," Raven said quietly. "This realm is called Illfall."

"Was," Khamael corrected bitterly.

Raven slowly lowered himself back into the chair, taking the frame from me and pulling the photo out. He stared at the picture for a long time before handing it to me. "You should keep this."

"You can't just grab things from someone's house," Kenna started but stopped when Khamael shook his head.

"Let her have it. I have plenty, plus my own memories of her."

I gingerly took the picture, tracing my mother's face with my finger. Brandon shifted next to me, taking a look over my shoulder. I handed it to him and said, "Will you put it somewhere safe for now? I don't have pockets."

His eyes mirrored my own—tinged red and downturned—as he plucked it from my fingertips and put it into his pack.

Khamael drew our attention back with the clearing of his throat. "After we got the Resurrection Stone, those with greedy hearts tried to take it for their own and caused a civil war. What you saw on your way in is the aftermath. Majority killed themselves off when my mother sent her away." He motioned to me. "Only a very small few of us survived, and they fled to your realm for safety. Now only creatures of the dark exist in their place."

"But aren't Angels supposed to be holy and non-wanting?" Brandon flicked a brow up, disbelief in his features.

"You put too much truth into the bible," Khamael answered as he began sipping from the glass again. "We are not those creatures. Real biblical Angels are quite terrifying to look at, so they used us to represent them instead. We have similar powers, anyway."

"So…what are you then? If you're not the biblical Angels?"

"Does it really matter? You're here to find out about Anahel, how to control her powers, and get the Stone out."

Jesse rolled his eyes, dragging a hand down his face. "So tell us then."

Khamael tumped the glass, chugging the last of it as he stared at Jesse over the rim. "I will do so only because you cannot stay here too long. You will draw the attention of the Ener, and I do not wish to fight them today."

I furrowed my brow, looking around the room for anyone else to share in my confusion. But they just watched on with calm intrigue.

"Our mother ruled as Queen. And as such, she had the ability to foretell the future at will. She knew what would come of your war and knew the Stone would be brought to us for safekeeping. She also knew that a war of our own would break out over it. So, she did the only thing she could think of to protect us." He pointed to me. "Raven brought the Stone right before you were born, and before the initial fights broke out, she replaced it with a fake, putting the real into you. To prevent your discovery, she then sent you to their realm, where you would be hidden." Khamael rose, dumping his glass in the sink and staring out the window. "Our father didn't like this idea. Mother never told me the full story—and I was too young at the time to ask any good questions—but he went and got himself killed off." He cut his eyes to Raven momentarily, then looked back out. It was so fast that I wondered if anyone else noticed. They made no signs they did.

"You were the only one, Aurelian, who could bear the weight of the Stone. Anyone else, and it would've vaporized them."

I gulped. "Why me?"

Khamael turned back and shrugged. "I do not know. Our mother said you were our only chance."

Something twisted in my gut, a sweeping feeling of despair settling there. Brandon's hand found its way to mine, and he rubbed soothing circles.

"Your powers are young, immature. She hid them from you until the right time. But even now, it's too early. I'm not sure what triggered their appearance."

Raven scoffed, drawing Khamael's attention—and his annoyance. But when Raven brandished a silver necklace with dark blue stones, Khamael snatched it from his fingers.

He traced the ocean-colored jewels, inspecting them with a scientist's hands. "Iolite. Where did you get these?"

Raven leveled a finger at me. "It was given to her. Blocked her from seeing Supernatural creatures."

"It did more than that." Khamael tossed it back to him.

"I always had my suspicions."

"Wait," Brandon interrupted, pushing his glasses up his nose. "Are you telling me that Iolite necklace is actually responsible for bringing her powers out?"

"That's exactly what I'm telling you."

"How do you know that?"

Khamael gave a wolf grin as he said, "It's part of our abilities to be able to tell when and what magic has been used. In time she'll be able to do it as well."

That meant Grant knew the whole time I had powers and was secretly trying to bring them forth. But to what end? What would be the goal of doing that to me when I didn't know my left from my right?

Truth be told, I'd never paid much attention to my magic manifesting. With everything else going on, I didn't even know what I was experiencing was different. But thinking back on it now, I did start seeing auras not long after I got the jewels.

"But she must learn to control it, or it will control her." Khamael jerked the top of his tank down, revealing a massive scar across his chest. "It could end badly for everyone, including yourself."

Fear settled in my gut, remembering my breakdown in the field and how I'd destroyed it. That must only be a fraction of what my magic is capable of. And what fraction did I need to be able to do what he did to himself?

"But how do I control it? We've tried, and nothing works."

He pursed his lips with a studying glance over me. "Every time your powers have manifested, what was happening?"

"I was stressed."

"Your emotions were heightened," he corrected, flashing a set of chipped teeth. "Our powers come from our emotions. Which is why we can be so powerful, yet so dangerous at the same time."

I sank lower in my chair, pulling my hand from Brandon's. This seemed too high a task. I still spiraled over the missing information in my life and the death I'd witnessed. How will I ever learn to control it?

"How do we even know you're actually what you say you are?" Jesse rubbed a spot on his chin, sending daggers through his eyes. The deep mistrust of this entire situation was written all over him.

"I agree," Kenna added. "How do we know you're actually a Seraphim?"

Khamael straightened, double-taking a worried glance out of the window. When he turned back, the lights dimmed and flickered rapidly as two wings of energy spread from him.

They were the same golden color as my magic and so big they tucked in at the cabinets.

Sparks of power danced along the wingspan, mimicking the appearance of feathers.

My mouth fell agape at the sight, and upon glancing at my companions, I noticed they, too, were stunned into silence.

He folded them back into place, the lights returning to normal as he leaned against the sink. "Good enough?" His voice betrayed how drained he was. Exposing his wings had taken a lot out of him.

He had wings. That meant I had wings.

"Those also come with time and practice. A lot of practice."

My excitement over being able to fly was instantly crushed. I wasn't sure why I thought I'd be able to go back and instantly take flight, but that's exactly what I'd planned to do. Until he said that. Who knows how long it would take me to reach the point to manifest them? And we didn't have very much time at all.

He strolled back to the table and crossed his arms. "What can you do?"

Uh oh. There it was. My deer in headlights moment. My mind went completely blank. I couldn't think of a single thing I was able to do. Not one thing.

"She can astral project and has a thing for wild animals," Brandon answered for me, drawing a sigh of relief from my chest. I'd almost said something embarrassing like 'cry and sleep.' Though, I noticed he didn't mention the field incident…or me turning his watch gold.

Khamael narrowed his eyes as if he knew there was more we weren't saying, but he let it slide. "That's a start. More will come: like being able to control material objects." He waved a finger, and a cabinet over the fridge opened, where he withdrew a red bag tied at the top with white ribbon. "As for the last request, here is everything you will need." He dropped the bag on the table before us.

"Why did you stay behind?" Jesse questioned with a hesitant flare to his voice. "You said the others fled. Why didn't you?"

With obvious disdain for him, Khamael snapped, "Anahel knew you'd come back and prepared everything. Someone had to stay to give it to you when the time came."

Kenna was skeptical. "Everything we need? To remove the Stone? Just that easy?"

"You're used to things being difficult—deadly even—to get where you need to be. Take the reprieve for once and be thankful."

She scowled and snatched the bag, clipping it to her belt loop. "Great. Are we done?"

Khamael nodded, turning his downtrodden eyes to me. "It was nice to see our mother's face one last time."

Heat flooded my cheeks as I turned my eyes to the ground. Why did that sentence fill me with dread? Why was it so final? I still had so many questions.

"But wait! How old am I? When was I actually born? What was my mother like?"

Khamael started, like the question caught him by surprise. " It's hard to say. Time works differently here."

"How different?" Brandon asked with a newfound interest gleaming in his eyes.

He sighed, glancing out the window once more. "How old are you in your realm?"

"Twenty."

"Then that is the age you are."

"That makes no sense," I argued, feeling my temper flare.

"Our mother died not long after she sent you away."

"But you said—"

"A hundred years ago, yes. In *our* realm."

Cold swept over me, my knees going weak. Jesse steadied me, giving me a reassuring nod.

Brandon's mouth twisted, eyes frantically searching for a reasonable explanation for this. "So a hundred years here is only a quarter of the time in our realm?"

Khamael nodded, chest catching at the sound of the wind picking up outside. "It's time for you to return now."

"Hold on, I'm not done yet. Is there a way for me to get my lost memories back?"

Khamael shifted back and forth nervously, still looking out the window. "I cannot tell you."

"What? Why? Just tell me."

"You all must leave."

I stamped my foot and snarled, "We just got here. I'm not leaving until I get some answers!"

He froze, eyes focusing on me as if he was truly seeing me for the first time. I was just as shocked about my outburst as him. Before I could apologize, he'd taken an authoritative step toward me, using his extra foot and a half to loom over me.

"It's time for you to leave. Mind the darkness in you in the future."

Jesse growled behind me, that deep thunderous rumbling he somehow made from his chest. He stepped between us, backed by Brandon.

Khamael never wavered, unblinking against the challenge before him. Whatever he was nervous about from outside vastly outweighed anything—or anyone—in here.

Kenna slapped Jesse on the back of the shoulder. "Let's go."

He begrudgingly stepped away, tongue in cheek. "Whatever."

We started to make our way to the door when the wind outside roared with such ferocity it caused the house to creak and groan. The lights flickered, and water spewed from the sink pipe as it burst.

Khamael flashed forward, slamming a steel rod across the front door. "Get back, all of you." He demanded, "To the bunker, now!"

"What? Why?"

The house continued to groan, the walls seeming to shrink in on us. The sound of chains could be heard just outside the door, accompanied by ghostly screams mimicking the sound of a child crying. Very badly.

"It's too late." Khamael resigned himself, pulling his sword from its sheath. "They're here."

Chapter Twenty-Five

Magic roared to life up Brandon's arms as the screeching outside persisted, growing closer. The walls squeaked and hissed as the creatures searched for a way in. The door jiggled a few times, the steel rod holding it in place.

We backed toward the stairs, eyes trained at the front door. The windows burst, spilling glass up to our feet. The metal across the door started to bend.

"What is it?" Kenna asked in a hushed tone.

"The Ener," Khamael answered. "Ghostly revenants of the Seraphim."

"They're Angels?"

"Not anymore. It's what happens when we aren't laid to rest properly. The war caused mass graves and improper burials. They hunt the living for retribution."

Jesse began to roll up his sleeves. "What can kill them?"

Khamael hesitated.

Something smashed against the door. I shrieked at the sound, tripping on a lip in the floor.

Jesse grabbed my elbow, keeping me from face-planting the shards of glass. "Dammit, what kills these fucking things?"

"Nothing."

Kenna and Brandon gaped at Raven. He closed his eyes in defeat as he repeated, "Nothing kills them. You can only hide."

"I'll kill them," Jesse huffed, hauling me back onto my feet.

When I was righted, I noticed it wasn't a lip at all: it was the edge to a trap door.

"Is this the bunker?" I bent down to open the lid, just managing to pry it open, when the front door violently ripped from its hinges.

With a blast of wind, the doorway was suddenly blocked by three titanic entities. Six empty eyes stared at me with harrowing excitement, and another child-like shriek echoed from one of their open mouths.

A plume of shadow escaped the creature's crooked nostrils, set within a skeletal nose.

Chains were melted within its flesh—perhaps the remnants of an encounter in a different world—with runes covering the metal.

Three sets of skeletal wings extended themselves fully. Cracked bones and incorporeal membranes stretched upward side by side.

Still, the creatures looked at me, and as a paralyzing fear swept through me, I realized I couldn't look away either.

The awful mimic of the crying children sounded garbled close up. Like the creature simultaneously drowned as it tried to screech.

I had a horrifying feeling they used this sound to lure people to their deaths, thinking a child needed rescuing. I could only imagine how they felt when they realized it was death calling.

Khamael swung his sword, colliding with the Ener's chains as they used them like whips.

Kenna and Jesse shifted to Wolf form, finally allowing me to see what they looked like. Jesse, tall on two legs and black as night. Kenna, a fawn color on all fours. They were ethereal and absolutely breathtaking. But I couldn't dwell on it.

Someone shoved me into the hole, and I tumbled before crashing down onto the concrete below. The wind kicked out of me, followed by a round of fiery coughs. The trap door slammed closed, but I was too busy struggling to breathe to scramble up to it.

Spine-tingling screeches pierced the dark, my hands clamping over my ears. For a moment, I thought they might've come from down here, but when I heard something heavy slam into the floorboards above, I knew it was up there.

Finally regaining some oxygen, I stumbled around the darkness, looking for a light switch. Instead, I found the cool metal rungs to the step ladder that lead down here.

Gripping them so hard my palms screamed, I carefully made my way up to the trap door. Nudging it with my shoulder, I came to a halting realization it wasn't going to open. Whether I'd been locked down here intentionally or it was stuck didn't matter. It wasn't opening for me, and I didn't think I was strong enough to force it.

What sounded like a lightning strike exploded not far from the trap door, and Brandon's agonizing yelp tore through the darkness.

Fear ripped through me, and like a cornered cat, I clawed at the door and pounded. In my panicked state, I somehow managed to literally burst through the wood and pull myself out.

Power radiated off me in a white pulsing glow, sucking in every ounce of light in the room.

The house was in ruins. Giant holes reminiscent of those at the graveyard lay in the walls and roof. Smoldering pieces of floor scattered about, mingling with glass.

Before me, Jesse—in Human form with his back shredded—lay draped over Brandon's limp body, taking hits from the chains while Kenna defended the pair against the last two Ener. She was bleeding badly, red staining her tan fur. One tooth at the front of her open maw hung by a partial root.

Khamael was several feet to my left—crumbled and unconscious next to the body of an Ener—his sword in pieces at his side. A thin trail of golden ichor leaked from his ears and nostrils.

Raven squatted in a corner, arms over his head and shadows whirling in tornadic fashion around him.

I looked once more at the creatures, now wrapping their chains around Kenna's rib cage. She howled in pain, claws digging into the floor to keep from being dragged. The wood splintered as she was yanked anyway.

Khamael's previous words flashed through my mind as I slowly raised my hands toward the creatures.

They turned their dead eyes to me, a ravenous excitement building. A horrifying grimace spread on their chapped bc half-missing lips as they tossed Kenna aside. She yelped as she hit the wall near Raven, him recoiling from her.

The Ener took two hobbling steps toward me, chains scraping the floor. I closed my eyes, focusing on my rage and fear. Nothing else flooded my mind aside from the sound of their closing steps.

Rotting breath and garbled screams reached me at the same time I heard their chains swinging in the air.

I squeezed my eyes tighter, chest heavy with panic. Nothing was happening. Something *had* to happen. Unless I misunderstood him earlier, but I didn't. I know I didn't.

The creature squealing in pain had me opening my eyes, jolting back when I saw the shadows gathered on the Ener like ants to an enemy.

In the corner where Raven once cowered, he stood, eyes flaming and fists clenched. His face read pain. However, he showed no signs of letting go. But something was different. Unlike at Grant's, where everyone passed directly through the shadows, the Ener could touch them.

They ripped them off, shredding their forms with their nails. The shadows would instantly reform and attack, but every time they were torn apart, Raven flinched.

Kenna was back to her Human form, and she clutched a wound in her side. Jesse reached a hand out to her, blood pooling from his back where the chains had landed—still shielding Brandon's body.

Enough was enough. I could stop this. I know it.

The shadows were nothing but mere annoyances to the Ener now, and they set their sights on the others.

Now I didn't focus. I just let it be. Light as golden as rays of the sun erupted from my fingertips, dousing the creatures.

They shrieked and flailed, backing toward the outside. But that wasn't good enough. I didn't want them to go back out into this world—my home world. I wanted them destroyed.

On instinct, I slid to my brother's body and placed my free hand on his arm. Siphoning his power into mine, I used it. Now the light came from my entire palm, pulsing with heat and intensity, and wherever the light touched the creatures, it burned.

Their skin—their bones—fizzled at the runes and spread like wildfire. They screamed, still batting the shadows.

"Rosetta, stop!" Kenna's voice came to me muddled through a fog. "You're killing him!"

Of course, I'm killing them. These creatures would do the same to us and others if allowed. I pushed harder, expelling every ounce of power I could muster.

Suddenly, Raven appeared, grabbing me with both arms and squeezing tight. "I've got you," he whispered. "It's okay, I've got you. I've got you. You can stop. You have to stop now, Rosetta. Stop."

The last of the Ener struggled, still wailing before they crumbled into dust. The fading sounds of their chains were the only thing proving they were there at all.

Blood Return

I released my hold on Khamael, the sudden weight of the power too much and the emptiness from giving it up exhausting. Collapsing in Raven's arms, I sucked in ragged breaths.

One hand reached up to cup the back of my head, the other pulling me even tighter into him. My arms hung weakly at my sides, my body gasping for energy I no longer had.

Turning my head, I saw Kenna had collapsed to her knees. Jesse had pulled Brandon up to a sitting position, leaning his body on his shoulder. A fresh trail of blood stained his jaw.

I looked back beside me to Khamael and screamed. Scrambling up, I clawed at Raven to get away. He held fast, fingers digging into my skin as he kept me from running away.

His mouth opened and closed with words I was unable to hear. For the corpse in front of me swallowed my senses.

The skin had shriveled and shrunk to the bones, eyes sunken, and hair straggly gray. No colored mist hung over him, no heartbeat. A skeleton. Suddenly Kenna's words echoed in my head. *You're killing him!* She wasn't talking about the Ener.

Oh. God. Oh God, oh God, oh God, I killed him. I killed my brother.

I started to crawl back to his skeletal frame when strong hands gripped me under the arms and towed me backward.

I kicked and screamed, hot tears burning down my face. "I didn't mean to. I didn't know."

Raven's face came into view, eyes bloodshot, his own tears leaving track marks down his cheeks. "We have to go. More are coming."

Through my sobs, I could faintly make out the clanking of chains in the distance. The chaos here must've drawn their attention.

I didn't resist when he threw me over his shoulder, and we began running. Jesse followed carrying Brandon, while Kenna limped behind us. The haunting wails of the creatures followed us the entire path. I paid no mind to them, though. The only thing I thought about was him and how we didn't bury him. And how now I had inadvertently caused him to become one of those creatures.

I'd killed him, and I didn't even take a second look.

We somehow portaled back to the boat, all landing in a big pile of tears and anguish. It was daylight now, the sun high over our heads.

Adaim appeared, confusion written upon his features. "It's been three days, what—" He paused as he took in our appearances.

Rushing to us, he lifted his injured wife into his hands. Blood still stained her clothes, but the wound had healed a considerable amount. It was no longer a gaping hole but rather a lengthy gash.

If I wasn't too grief-stricken, I would've still been shocked at their healing abilities. But sorrow was all I felt.

Jesse staggered to his feet—his back also healing—dragging a half-conscious Brandon down the bow of the boat. "He needs medical attention."

With an encouraging nod from Kenna, Adaim kissed her forehead and jogged over to pick up Brandon's feet, disappearing through a door.

In between sobs I could hear more people beginning to gather when Millie and Damicén came into view.

Millie bent beside her leader, analyzing the still-healing wound with delicate touches. Her shortly-cropped brown hair was still wet from a fresh shower.

Damicén looked between us and exclaimed, "What the hell happened?"

"I killed him," I whispered.

His face softened. He didn't ask who, and by the warm feeling washing over my head, I knew he'd seen it. I think it was supposed to be a comforting feeling, but it made me feel all that much worse. "I killed him," I repeated.

Raven reached out to touch my shoulder, but I jerked away from his touch. "Don't."

"Rosetta, it's okay," Kenna croaked.

I shook my head, my red hair getting stuck to my wet cheeks. Another reminder of the blood I'd shed. "I killed him. I didn't know. I just knew I could use his powers. I didn't know it would kill him."

"We know." Damicén crouched down beside me, eyes as wounded as I felt.

"How could you possibly know? I didn't even know." The image of his corpse burned behind my eyelids every time I shut them. This was so much worse than Jarred.

"Nobody *touch* me!" I screamed as I rolled away from Damicén's outstretched hand. What if I did the same to them? What if I drained them? I didn't know how to control my powers. I didn't know. I didn't know.

It didn't help I'd gotten them all hurt and possibly killed Brandon on top of it because I couldn't let my stupid questions go. Khamael knew they were coming and tried to get us away, but I wouldn't budge. I should've just left. None of this would've happened if I hadn't stayed.

Water encased me, dragging me back to that lake. I was drowning again. I could feel the burn of the liquid entering my lungs, the pain. My breaths were ragged, wrenching themselves from chest as my throat closed. My vision tunneled, blackening with each wheezing gasp. Vomit began to rise, threatening to escape from me.

I'd killed him. I killed my biological brother.

Vaguely, I heard someone crying—or screaming. Subconsciously, I knew it was screaming, and that it was me doing it.

Then purple eyes came into view, pulling me from the darkness the same way they'd pulled me from the water. He was reaching for me again, and I snapped at him. Magic poured through me, pushing everyone to the railing of the ship.

I leaped to my feet, backing away from them. Everyone trained their eyes on me, gasping, whispering, and glaring at me. I could imagine their thoughts.

Psycho.

Crazy.

Murderer.

Kenna clutched at her wound, now reopened from the impact of hitting the rail. Damicén and Raven had landed on their feet, the former checking on her.

Again, I spiraled at the realization I'd done this. All because I couldn't control myself. Kenna, Brandon…Khamael.

When it was too much to bear, I turned and bolted down the hallway of the ship. Tripping, stumbling, and crying until I reached my room, where I bundled myself under the covers. Wishing I could die alongside him.

I couldn't escape it, though. The dark was crawling with faces and truths I was desperate to flee from. But as I lie there, curled up on myself, I couldn't stop the crushing thought that I'd liked it. Deep down, some small part of me liked how it felt to use my powers like that.

Chapter Twenty-Six

It was after midnight when I finally crawled out of bed, head aching and eyes puffy. I'd cried myself into numbness but couldn't fall asleep. Not when I saw Khamael in the dark. Not when he stood side by side with Jarred behind my shut lids.

Again, I'd been haunted by the dead into restlessness. I was completely alone, and in the silence of the ship, I was thrust back to that room at Grant's. The same overwhelming sensations crashed down on me, except this time, I couldn't lock myself in a room to get away from the murderer. I was the murderer now.

No one had come after me, knocked, or entered. Whether that was a relief for me or not, I wasn't sure.

Vaguely, I remembered they should be here by now—Sam, Rhydel, and the others from the base. But the boat felt empty. Where was everybody? More importantly, was Brandon okay? I'd been so wrapped up in my own problems I didn't even spare a thought to him.

He seemed badly injured when they carried him off. Or at least I think he did. My memory was hazy and unfocused. The only thing I could see perfectly clearly was Khamael.

Stepping out into the dimly lit hallway, I padded to where I remembered the medic room was. Before I got there, I passed the cafeteria, where a few people sat silently at a round table. No food or drink lay in front of them, and they all held hands.

A sinking feeling settled in the pit of my gut as I approached the medic room. I felt slightly better when I heard voices and recognized one of them to be Brandon's.

Stopping just short of the door, I decided to eavesdrop before actually going in.

Anxiety picked a pace in my heart, and I worried they would be mad at me for what I'd done. I know what Kenna and Damicén had said up on deck, but I didn't believe them. Maybe it's because I didn't believe myself.

Regardless, I wasn't ready to tackle that yet, so if I overheard them talking bad about me, I could run away and avoid it.

"When, exactly?" That was Kenna's voice, deep and melodic as a flowing river.

"In the tunnels," Jesse answered. "Right after we pulled her out."

"So that's what you were whispering into her ear." she concluded, a silence falling upon the room.

"What do we do?" Brandon asked, a hitch in his voice.

There was a pause as whoever was in the room with him decided what to say next.

"I think we should give her some time," Kenna finally said.

Adaim was quick to respond against that. "We don't have time, love. Every moment we wait is a closer death sentence."

"She just lost her brother."

"And we're losing our pack."

Jesse's deep tone cut through the voices. "Let her read the note, and then she can decide. We can't force her, and we shouldn't. That's how we ended up here in the first place."

"No, we ended up here because of you," Kenna snapped.

"No, it's Raven's fault. How was I supposed to predict anything that followed the coliseum?"

"Stop," Damicén hushed them. "We have a visitor."

The room fell silent, and before I could react, Damicén rounded the doorway. Brow furrowed in frustration, he grabbed me by the elbow and towed me into the room.

I stood wide-eyed at the cluster of people in this tiny space, basically piled on top of each other, with Brandon lying on a table. A thick bandage was wrapped around his midsection, with a smaller one stuck across the bridge of his nose. His glasses now had a huge fracture across one lens and sat at a crooked angle on his face.

Kenna was in fresh clothes with no sign of being injured, right alongside Jesse.

Crossing my arms, I tried desperately to keep down the flush that crept up my neck. Swallowing felt raw. I knew my face still betrayed that I'd been crying for hours, and that made the embarrassment worse.

"Are you okay?" Brandon asked after another languishing moment of silence.

I met his eyes, so full of warmth and safety. And then I looked at his injuries and couldn't stop the flow of tears from escaping once more.

I should've asked him if he was okay first. He was the one injured, yet I stood there mortified until he felt the need to ask me. Nothing was even wrong with me aside from the fact I'd killed someone. "Why aren't you healing?"

He patted his bandages with a wince. "Whatever powers the Ener had is causing my healing magic to not work correctly. We got most of the nasty part, but it's going to have to finish the natural way."

"I'm sorry," was all I could muster. It's all my fault. If I hadn't gone digging into my past and just accepted that I'd never get my memories back, we wouldn't be here.

'You've got to stop blaming yourself.' Damicén's voice echoed in my head, causing me to flinch at the sudden invasion of my mind. *'No one blames you. You saved their lives.'*

'By taking someone else's. One that didn't deserve it.'

"No one ever really deserves it," he said aloud, drawing cumulative nods of approval from the others. I guess they could assume what he was referring to.

If that was supposed to make me feel better—make me feel as if it wasn't my fault—it didn't.

But now, every time I thought of Khamael, saw him, the image was replaced in my mind with beautiful scenery. A waterfall, a mountain face, a snowy cabin, flowers on a river bed.

My brows pinched together, and upon glancing at the others, Damicén gave me a wink.

'Are you doing that?' I thought.

He nodded.

A small smile lit my face as I wiped the tears away, thankful for that small reprieve from torture.

Kenna took a hesitant step toward me, hands outstretched. I placed mine in hers, feeling her warmth spread through me.

Kindness radiated up my arms, flooding my anxiety-riddled brain. The light around her shifted between yellow and pink. The sheepish 'cat that ate the canary' look told me exactly what she was about to ask me.

"I know it's still fresh, but I need to ask you some questions about what happened."

A deep sigh escaped me, catching a few times on hiccups that developed from my crying. "Okay," I said meekly.

She frowned. "I don't mean to be intrusive or cause you more trauma. We're just on a much tighter time crunch than expected. And we need to help you figure everything out as quickly as possible."

"Just get it over with."

"Before we left, when you destroyed those creatures and...well, how did you do it?"

I clenched my teeth involuntarily at the memory, trying hard not to be dragged back there. "I don't know. It was instinct. I just *knew* I could draw power from him and that my power could kill them...the Ener, that is."

She glanced at Adaim and shook her head at whatever he'd said mentally. It somewhat annoyed me that half of the people in this room could communicate telepathically with each other. I wanted to know what was being said. I wanted to be in the loop from the beginning for once.

Turning back to me, Kenna squeezed my hands. "We think that your powers are being hijacked by the Stone."

"Hijacked?"

Adaim cleared his throat, coming to stand beside his wife. "Its power is messing with yours, making them unstable."

"It's boosting them," Damicén added. "To the point they're almost uncontrollable.

"What do I do?" I whispered, lower lip quivering, half on the verge of another breakdown.

Kenna dropped my hands. "No one can tell you what to do aside from yourself."

"But I don't even know."

"That's a mental block you're going to have to figure out on your own." She reached down to the red bag still clipped to her belt, withdrew a white envelope from inside it, and handed it to me. "This is for you. Maybe you can find some clarity in it."

On the paper, in the same handwriting from the photo, was the name Aurelian in neat cursive.

My throat tightened with my chest at the sight.

"Take your time," Kenna urged. "Let us know what you want to do."

I half nodded—harshly aware I really *couldn't* take my time. They'd mentioned their pack being lost, which must include Sam and Rhydel. They were lost, and time was of the essence.

As I turned and exited the room, it took everything in me to not tear through the halls and find the darkest corner possible to lie in. Instead, I walked, knees shaking with every step, down several flights of stairs and into the pool room.

How I was able to even remember how to get back here, I have no idea. My mind fogged up, and I was running on pure autopilot at this point. Lucky for me, it was the middle of the night, so I didn't have to worry about anyone following me down here.

Sitting at the edge of the pool, I let my feet dangle into the warm water. At the back of my mind, I wondered how they managed to keep it so warm all the time, but that question didn't have any weight in the grand scheme of it all. I had plenty of other things to ponder.

My fingers trembled, heart raced, and mouth ran dry as I carefully pried open the envelope. Tucked neatly inside was a cream paper with torn edges.

At first, my eyes wouldn't focus, and everything was blurry, but slowly I began to see the words written on it.

Aurelian,
If you are reading this, that means my son, your brother, is dead. Do not worry yourself over it, even though I know you will, as he knew this would happen. I am so sorry for everything that has happened and will come to happen and for the fact I cannot be there for you. Letting you go was the single hardest decision I have ever had to make in my long life, and not a day goes by that I don't miss you more than ever. You are so loved, not only by me, your father, and your brother but by the other family you will come to know. I know why you are reading this letter, so I feel the need to also warn you that if you should choose to remove the Resurrection Stone, it will be the most painful thing you will ever experience in your lifetime. You are a weapon of war, regardless of my wishes for your

future, and you must keep that in mind when making decisions. You are more powerful than you could ever imagine. I love you with all my heart and know in the end, you will make the decision that is best for you and you alone.
 Always with you, Anahel.

After staring at the words for God knows how long, I laid the letter down, hot tears falling onto my lap—but I didn't weep.

Her message bounced off the walls of my mind in a chaotic whirlwind. I couldn't make sense of any of it. The Stone makes me a weapon of war, and taking it out will be…

I didn't even want to think about it. My brain needed a break, or I was going to implode. That letter helped me none, aside from making me more confused and scared.

Leaning back on the tile, I wrapped my arms over my head.

The door squeaked open, and I sprang up from the floor, expecting to get in trouble for being there. But Jesse strolled in, a plate between his teeth, a bowl of food in one hand, and two Styrofoam cups carefully grasped between his fingers in the other.

I shifted, unsure what to make of this.

As he approached, he tried to give me a smile, but it appeared as if he bared his teeth with the plate in his mouth.

He handed me the cups, took the plate out, and sighed. "Brandon told me you'd probably be here. You've been gone for hours. It's breakfast time now, and I thought you might want some food."

My mouth watered as I stared at the bowl filled to the brim with fruit, bread, and jam packets. But my stomach turned just as quickly. The words from the letter filling my mind once more.

We pulled some chairs out from under sheets at the wall and made a makeshift table with one of them.

I picked at the strawberries and watermelon while Jesse slathered grape-flavored spread on a slice of toast. He watched me the entire time, nodding to the cup beside me.

"Do you not like coffee?"

A flush crept up my cheeks as I barely shook my head. I felt bad he'd taken the time to bring it to me, and I didn't even like it. But he just smiled and said, "Good thing it's not coffee, then."

I frowned as I lifted the lid to smell the contents of the cup, and a wash of relief came over me when I realized it was tea. Taking a small sip, I let the warmth spread down me, savoring the slight apple taste.

"Chamomile," Jesse said between his chews. "We don't have the stuff to make blackberry, so I had to make do."

"It's just as good. Thank you." The soothing, delicate feel that coated my insides made my appetite come back. And I scarfed down the rest of the fruit, even stealing a piece of Jesse's toast. Once we finished, we sat in silence, staring at the still water.

He stood abruptly, walking over to where I'd sat the note, and gingerly plucked it from its position. Water droplets—or was it tears?—had smeared some of the writing, and he took great care not to touch those parts. When he held it out to me, I instead looked down at my hands.

He crouched in front of me, hands on my knees and eyes despondent. "I'm guessing it didn't have good things to say."

I shook my head, blinking away more tears that tried to escape. "It wasn't too bad, just confusing."

"Those that can tell the future normally are." His thumb rose to wipe a stray tear, and he twisted his mouth to the side in thought. "There's no pressure on you to do anything, Rosetta. And if your mother cared anything about you, she wouldn't force you either."

"She didn't." I shot to my feet, hands in my hair, and paced around the pool. "She basically said I could make whatever choice I wanted to."

He heard the hesitation in my voice and asked, "But?"

"But I want someone to tell me what to do because I don't know. I don't know what will end up being the right choice or who I might get killed in the process, and I am just tired of that." Plopping down onto the tile, I stuck my feet into the water once more—barely registering its warmth now.

Jesse wrapped an arm around my shoulders, pulling me in tight. He said nothing in response to my rant, only letting me cry into his shoulder.

"Apparently, Khamael knew he would die," I croaked between sobs. "That's what he meant before we left. That it was nice to see our mother's face one last time. He knew he was going to die and that I would cause it. That's why he was so antsy to get us to leave, he was trying to avoid it, and I just furthered his death by refusing to go. I got so angry over nothing. How can I live with that?"

Jesse took a long pause before answering, and I could almost hear the gears grinding away in his head. "Killing someone, accidental or intentional, is never easy. But it's not the act that defines us. It's how we recover afterward. What we do and how we feel in those moments after is what truly makes us."

"What does that make me?"

He pushed my face back and cupped my cheeks. "Someone who has the weight of the world on her shoulders." Planting a firm kiss on my forehead, he tucked me back into him and slowly began rocking me.

Through the buttons of his shirt, I could make out the necklace from before around his neck, the golden spiral catching in the small part of light that could reach it. Talon was in there, or so he said.

"You knew I had the Stone in me the entire time, didn't you?"

His voice was barely a whisper as he said, "Yes."

"I want to know everything."

He was silent for so long that I thought he didn't hear me. Just as I was about to repeat myself, he sighed deeply. "You just have to remember that I was a different person back then. I'd been fed stories and propaganda my entire life."

I nodded, encouraging him to continue, burying myself into his chest and listening to his strong heartbeat. Now more than ever, I needed to know everything. It was time everyone stopped pretending I couldn't know for whatever reason they conjured up to excuse it.

Tipping his face to the ceiling, he drew in a shaky breath. "Your mother may have sent you here to avoid evil in her world, but she sent you straight into the hands of evil in this one. Avalon found you first and sent me to keep watch over you until you were of proper age to be used. I glamoured our parents into adopting both of us. They were wealthy and secluded, so I knew you could be hidden there. But the longer I spent with you, the more I grew attached. I couldn't let Grant have you. So I broke off contact with them, and it went well until Talon and Damicén showed up. I thought they were with Avalon, so I contacted her, and then they took you. That's when I learned who they really were, and I knew I could trade her for you…" He trailed off, tilting his face back down to me with a knowing look.

"But you got attached to her as well."

"They were so different from what I'd been told my whole life. Everything had been turned on its head; I couldn't let them kill her, knowing it was all a lie. But I couldn't lose you either."

"That's what you meant when you told Damicén you had to choose."

He nodded, smirking ironically. "There was a prophecy I never understood until those last few days, and there's still a part of it I don't understand."

"What is it?"

"Angel blood fell, and the soul was tinted gold. You must lose the one you love to gain control."

My heart fell into my gut. "Sebastian."

His stone-gray eyes peered at me through lowered lids. "How did you know?"

"He said something similar to me over breakfast one day. He gave the prophecy?"

"Yes. It's the only one he's had for a couple hundred years."

My jaw dropped open. "He's *that* old?" I'm not sure why this amazed me, as I now know significantly older people. Maybe it was the fact he never gave off the vibe of someone incredibly old like the others, whatever that vibe was.

Jesse nodded. "His spirit is. The body he's in is only thirty-something. He switches bodies whenever the current one gets too old to contain him any longer." Something clicked behind his eyes, and he slapped his forehead in disbelief. "Of course. You're the final bit of the prophecy. I thought it was all Talon and couldn't make sense of it, but it was about both of you. It was always both of you."

Angel blood fell, and the soul was tinted gold. That part was definitely me, but that means the last half...

"I love her," he whispered, staring into the rippling water as if under a trance. "This means I do love her." The hair on his arms stood on end as goosebumps littered his skin. Then he muttered a single word, "Eternally," so low I almost didn't catch it. Some part of me warned that he hadn't meant for me to hear, so I changed subjects.

"How do I look like her?"

"What?" My question brought him back to reality and away from his clearly wandering thoughts.

"People keep saying I look like her. How do I look like Talon when I look just like my mother? Do they look the same?"

Jesse frowned, the scar on his lip stretching thin. "No, I don't suppose they do. But it's quite common to look like someone else. Take me, for example. I got most of my features from my mother: the black hair, the eye shape, other stuff too. But I also..." he trailed off, giving me a pointed look.

"You also look like Grant," I finished.

"Lots of people look like others. It's said everyone has at least one doppelgänger out in the world. Maybe Talon is yours."

He rocked me for another few minutes in silence, gently stroking my head. I stared at the necklace under his collar, completely entranced with the ever-shifting golden spiral.

"What would you guys do if you couldn't bring Talon back?"

I'd once again managed to catch him off guard, and as he drew in a shaky breath, I heard his heart skitter.

"We would find another way. He was defeated before without killing him; it can be done again."

"I still don't fully understand why he has to be defeated at all."

"You saw it, Rosetta. You saw it but don't remember. Anything he touches or creates is evil."

"Is that why you don't go by your real name?" I'd struck a nerve. I knew it. He went still around me, back straightening.

I pulled away, watching his eyes turn a dark stormy gray.

"Yes," he confessed. "That name belongs to someone under his control, someone he manipulated and made into a monster. That is not me anymore."

I scoffed, picking at a loose thread from my jeans. "I don't even know who Aurelian was, who I could've been. I don't even know where she came up with that kind of name."

After a moment's hesitation, he whispered. "It's a lily."

"What?"

"Aurelian is a type of lily—a trumpet lily. They have huge blossoms."

My heart slammed against my chest, my stomach flipping circles. "Like the ones Grant grows?"

Jesse almost seemed reluctant to nod. "Almost all of the lilies he grows are Aurelian, yes."

Standing once more, I grabbed the letter from its position on the chair and folded it into my back pocket. Determination was ripe through me, amongst many other whirl-winding emotions.

He gave me a puzzled yet hopeful look as I tucked the envelope beside the letter.

There was only one more question I needed to be sure of the answer to before I continued with my haphazard plan. "What's going on with Sam and the others from the base?"

"They're missing. They weren't at the pickup location, and no one has been able to get in touch with them since. Not even telepathically."

I nodded, packing up the remnants of our breakfast in a flurry of motion. When I tossed it to him, he caught it with one hand.

"What are you doing?"

"I'm going to go find them." I beelined for the door, stopping only when he placed himself in the way.

"And how are you going to do that?" He raised a brow.

"Whatever it takes."

S. D. Sampley

Chapter Twenty-Seven

    Jesse followed me up to the room, asking me questions a mile a minute. I didn't have time to answer them, though, not in the way he inevitably needed me to answer them. To be honest, I wasn't even sure I knew how to answer them that way. I only knew the basics, like he did.
    My idea might not even work; it didn't when I tried before, and I gave up. But now I didn't have that liberty. It needed to work. It *would* work.
    Almost slamming the door in Jesse's face, he caught it with the toe of his shoe. "Give me some kind of answer!"
    I smiled confidently, feeling none of it. "Give me ten minutes. Wait out here if you want."
    He relented, letting the door shut, and I bolted the latch. I wasn't sure exactly what would happen, and I didn't need him breaking my concentration by barging in.
    Leaving the room in the same darkness I'd entered it in, I lay in the nearest bed, ensuring none of my limbs touched my body. Then I closed my eyes and waited.
    Emotion. I needed to use my emotions. All I had currently was nervousness and confusion, and I didn't know how to use those. So I dug deeper and deeper and deeper until I found something else.

Blood Return

Next to my magic, at the corner of my consciousness, was a spark. Not one that would ravage and grow on its own, but one that could be tended to and kindled.

Pushing my nerves aside, I cupped the spark in my hands and felt the surge of emotion I needed. Courage.

Instantly, I was sucked through my body and dropped in the middle of the dining room at Grant's house. The walls and paintings were so familiar yet so foreign to me.

I was alone, but that didn't mean entirely. If my past experience was anything to believe, what I needed to see or hear was close by.

Turning on my heels, I saw the doors to his study were slightly ajar. A small flickering light the only indication someone was in there.

Phasing through the door, I saw the room lay in chaos. Bookshelves were turned on their sides, the books themselves gutted, and the desk broken in two. It looked as if a bomb had gone off in here.

Sitting in front of the shattered wood was a man, hunched over, with a lantern at his feet. Hay-colored hair hung over the person's face, obscuring my view. But I knew who it was. The broad shoulders and tensed arm muscles told me as much.

Floating over to him, he straightened suddenly. His head cocked to the side as if he listened intently.

"I knew you'd come back. I've missed you," he whispered as he turned and stared directly at me.

I froze, feeling like a bucket of ice had been poured down my spine. He couldn't see me, could he? I was invisible. I'd always been invisible. But his eyes pinned me to the spot.

He smirked as he looked me up and down. "Judging by your corporal form, you haven't come back for good. But for information."

He could see me. He could definitely see me.

My pulse roared in my ears, and I floated a few steps back automatically. This gesture seemed to hurt him, and it was then I noticed his appearance.

His hair was matted and greasy, hanging like pieces of wet straw over sunken eyes. Dark bags settled under his green eyes, which looked more of a moss color than his usual emerald. He was dull all around—a zombie.

"You've come for information on those from the underground base," he stated, facial expression that of boredom.

It took everything in me to nod slowly and keep my mouth shut. What I would've said if I'd opened it, I wasn't sure. Maybe nothing. Maybe every curse under the sun I could come up with. Best to stay silent. But this did confirm my suspicions that they'd taken them, and that's why they didn't show up at the pickup spot.

He sighed, turning back to his desk. "Why are you doing their dirty work?"

"Why are you kidnapping people?"

I jolted when he slammed his fist against the crippled wood, springing to his feet. "They stole you from me!"

"I am not yours to be stolen."

"They killed my people to take you, and you let them. I understand you're upset with me over Jarred, and I've apologized countless times. Everything I have done has been to protect you from *them*."

"They're good people—" I silenced myself at his venomous glare, gulping.

"Good people?" He repeated, speaking the words like they tasted bad. "They're liars and killers."

"Like you lied about knowing who I was? What my name was? Like you and Avalon aren't murdering animals for your sick rituals?"

"She what?"

"Oh, stop pretending. That's how you guys found the base in the first place."

"I had no idea she was doing that—"

"Enough lies!" I screamed, power flashing through the room. In the corner of my eye, something flitted in the shadows, but when I looked, nothing was there.

Grant cleaned the rim of his reading glasses, taking the time to think of his response. "I knew who you were, yes. But you were still struggling immensely with your memories. If I'd told you you were a Seraphim and every monster you could ever dream up actually existed in the world, you wouldn't have been able to handle it."

"How dare you tell me what I can and can't handle—"

"You know I'm right, Rosetta! You needed to discover it for yourself to not make it as jarring."

"So lying to me was the solution? Then it's worse knowing everyone knew and didn't tell me because they thought I was weak."

"I don't think you're weak." He took a hesitant step toward me, eyes brimming with emotions I couldn't place. "I think you're stronger than you could ever imagine. Stronger than anyone could ever imagine."

"Then you should have trusted me from the beginning."

We stood in silence for a few heartbeats, both stunned at my outburst, before I managed to squeak out, "Where are they?"

Realization dawned on his face, and he nodded to himself, steepling his fingers together. He took a few more moments to consider my question, going back and forth with himself before saying, "Tell Kenna that they are at the base, and I will hand over the group in exchange for you."

I recoiled, hand flying to my heart. "What if I don't want to be with you?"

"You will. Once you realize who they really are."

"*They* actually believed I could handle it. *They've* told me the truth."

"Have they? There's not one sliver of doubt in you that they could be hiding something?"

I opened my mouth to retort back, but no sound came out.

He smirked, placing his glasses back on his face. "They're only using you for the Stone. When that's out of you, you'll be cast aside. Those dirty bloods only care about saving their own skins and will take down anyone who opposes them. You will see." He turned back to the chair, sitting with no lack of effort, glancing at me once more with eyes bloodshot and glassy. "Tell her that every day that goes by, I will take one of their lives as recompense."

With a wave of his hand, I was slingshotted back to my body. I screamed, sitting up in a panic and nearly taking myself out on the bottom of the bunk above me. My gut swirled and cramped as I sucked in air. Getting thrown back involuntarily felt like being pulled through a dough sheeter.

Pounding sounded at the door, followed by the continuous jiggle of the doorknob.

"Rosetta? What's going on?" Jesse sounded just as panicked as me.

Rolling from the bed and half crawling to the door, I unlatched it and collapsed as he swung it open. Drenched in sweat and panting, I told him what I'd just witnessed. His face grew darker with each passing word, and by the end, I could hear his teeth grinding.

He gathered me in his arms and carried me back to the medic room. Conveniently everyone was still there, piled on top of each other with plates of food scattered about.

They all jumped at our sudden entrance, Kenna leaping over to me.

"What happened?" She snapped as I fell to my knees once more, placing the back of her hand to my forehead. "You're burning up."

"I know where they are," I gasped. "Grant has them at the base."

She reeled back, looking at Adaim. He climbed to his feet, rolling up his sleeves, and gave her a small nod.

"Wait!" I screamed, grabbing his pant leg as he scooted past. "There's more." I divulged the rest of the story once more, watching everyone's faces turn the same shade of red Jesse's had.

When I was done, Kenna sat back on her heels, puffing air through her cheeks. "That *is* a dilemma."

Brandon grunted as he shifted off the table, clutching his wraps. "Don't worry. We won't let him take you."

"We have to do the trade," I demanded, not willing to let anyone else die because of me.

"Rosetta, there are other ways we can go about this," Damicén insisted, looking at me with pleading eyes. He'd been in my head, knew what I was thinking—where I was headed with this.

"He's right," Kenna agreed. "We can't let Grant have you. He just wants you for the Stone."

Ironic. He'd said the same things about them. Doubt began to swell at the back of my mind. Who it was aimed at had yet to be determined, but I would make a mental note of this.

"Then take it out." I clenched my fists and rose to my feet. "Take out the Stone, and then we can figure out a plan. That way—just in case—he won't have it."

"You're not going to willingly give yourself over to him, are you?" Brandon's face flushed with anger as his brown eyes bored into me.

"If it saves even one life from being senselessly slaughtered, then yes, I will."

Kenna stepped between us, sensing the rising tension. "But maybe it doesn't have to be that way."

"We won't know until you get this thing out of me."

Jesse put a hand on my shoulder, pulling my focus to him. "You do know what you're saying, right?"

I swallowed thickly. "Yes." But that was a lie.

The room fell eerily quiet as they all exchanged looks with one another. I didn't have time for them to think on this. *They* didn't have time.

"We're getting it out of me, tonight. You can think of a plan before and after, but tomorrow we're going to the base. Whether we have a strategy or not doesn't matter to me; no one else is going to die. No one," I repeated when Brandon opened his mouth to say something combative.

He didn't like this idea, and to be honest, neither did I. But there weren't any alternative options.

Kenna frowned, chewing on her lower lip before conceding and forcing Brandon to agree to do the ritual.

"Fine," he huffed. "But I can't read the stupid language it's in."

"Raven will be able to." I wasn't sure what made me so confident in that fact, but deep down, I knew he could read it.

"Alright. We'll make port around sundown," Adaim explained as he fiddled with his watch, a stark contrast to the dark ink of his tattoos. "There's an abandoned marina I know will have enough space to do the ritual."

"We aren't doing it on the boat?" I questioned.

He shook his head with a slight chuckle. "I have no idea what this will be like, and I'm not risking sinking our last lifeline."

Of course. Getting the Stone out of me might end up being a bigger mess than I'd anticipated.

He stepped past me, giving me a reassuring pat on the shoulder. If I didn't have my arms tightly crossed around my body, he would've felt me shaking.

"Where's Raven?" Kenna asked as she turned to exit after her husband.

Damicén snorted. "Probably off in a dark crevice."

"Nobody's seen him since we got back," she said, looking to me for a response.

I shrugged. I hadn't seen him, not here.

"Let him be." Damicén waved a hand. "He'll pop back in right when he's needed, as usual."

"Jesse, go find him. And you," she leveled a finger at Brandon, "teach her something."

"What?"

"Now that she's been told how to control her powers, teach her something."

"Doesn't really matter if her powers are being hijacked."

"I just want her working until we make port. Keep her mind off everything."

"Oh yeah, let's drain her of energy before we suck the life out of her. Great idea, Kenna."

She snarled, "Do it." And disappeared into the bowels of the ship.

"Just because I know how doesn't mean I can," I murmured, heat rising to my cheeks.

Brandon pinched the bridge of his nose, wincing as he repositioned himself on the table.

I crossed my arms, noticing his refusal to respond to me and the aggravation radiating off of him. "Are you really going to be upset with me over this?"

"Hell yes I am. Rosetta, you are just willingly waltzing back into the place we worked so hard to get you out of. To protect you."

My arms fell to my side, contempt replacing my determination. "As I recall, you guys didn't do anything. Raven had to go behind your backs to get me."

"Yeah, ahead of *our* original plan. His put ours in jeopardy if he failed to retrieve you."

I rolled my eyes. "It doesn't matter now. I'm different than I was then. I can protect myself."

"Can you? If it really came down to it, could you kill someone *intentionally*?"

Thinning my lips, I took a step back, and a half-cocked grin spread on his face.

Damicén had stayed relatively still this entire time—looking like he'd rather be counting the rivets on the ship—but when Brandon asked for help up, he was by his side in seconds.

"You're coming with us to the top deck," Brandon demanded as he limped beside his friend.

Damicén rolled his eyes. "Clearly, since I'm the only thing holding you up right now."

My pride and irritation kept me from openly chuckling when Brandon thumped Damicén behind the ear.

I followed them up, always remaining a few paces behind the pair. I didn't want to get in Damicén's way or incur Brandon's harsh words.

Storms lurked on the edge of the horizon, a fierce wind carrying their dark shapes toward us. Lightning spiderwebbed across the sky, reaching higher into the clouds. In my mind, I imagined it to be my anger penetrating the Angel realm and destroying it. Along with all of the nasty creatures it harbored.

Damicén propped Brandon on a deck chair and took the piece of paper he'd somehow snuck out of the infirmary.

"Take this target and stand across the way for her to aim at," Brandon pointed to the railing.

Damicén blinked at his friend. "I would literally rather touch a slug."

Brandon ground his teeth together and tried to shove him. "Just do it. Rosetta, come stand beside me."

We traded places, Damicén holding the paper as far from his body as possible.

"Why do I have to hold it? Why can't we just set it up on a table?"

Brandon gave him a withering glare. "Because we're on a moving boat with wind, and she needs a steady target."

"You know what else is on a moving boat with wind? Me!"

I raised an eyebrow as Brandon began instructing me and ignoring Damicén's complaints.

"All you have to do is turn that piece of paper into an origami goose."

I gave him the same look Damicén had. "A what?"

"An origami goose."

"I don't even know what that looks like."

"It doesn't matter. You're just turning paper into a paper goose."

Biting the inside of my cheek, I looked at my hands. They clenched and unclenched with nervousness. "How do I do that?"

"I'm so glad you asked. Intent."

I clenched my mouth shut to keep from popping off a smart-assed response. I knew he was angry with me for my decision, but I didn't deserve the attitude; I was doing this to help people. People we cared about.

"When you push your power out, especially when making spells, you have to have the right intent. Otherwise, you're going to overshoot or undershoot it." He added under his breath, "But for you, I'm more worried about the overshooting aspect."

"So for this 'spell,' don't I need to say magic words?"

"No. Just intent. In your mind."

"And my intent is to turn paper into a paper goose."

"Yes."

"What does this accomplish exactly? Why is this the lesson I'm learning?"

"To learn intent with something nondeadly. Since your powers are kind of like a rampaging wildebeest, we have to start with something mundane."

I sucked in a deep breath and turned my focus to Damicén, who was now fuming that we'd been ignoring him. But when he noticed my attention, his eyes went wide with regret.

"Just not the face," he pleaded as he turned away from his outstretched hand.

I raised my own, mind racing a million miles a minute. I couldn't quiet it down. Grant, Jarred, Khamael, my mother. Their faces and words flashed through my head at back-breaking speed, not allowing me to concentrate.

So when I brought forth my magic and shot it at the paper, I missed.

Scowling, I tried again and still missed. Damicén yelped the second time, wheezing out, "I felt that one slide past my arm hair."

"Just hold still," I said through clenched teeth as I aimed again. This time I tried to shove thoughts to the forefront to overpower the rest.

Turn paper into goose. Turn paper into goose. Turn into goose. Turn into goose.

I had it this time. I knew it. I'd calculated my previous errors and adjusted accordingly. I would hit the paper this time. But when I shot my magic forward, I was off by a few inches in the opposite direction, instead hitting Damicén in the forearm.

A golden plume of smoke obstructed our view of him momentarily, allowing Brandon to chastise me. When the air cleared, we were met with Damicén as he was…but wasn't. He now had his arms crooked at his sides and neck elongated as far as it could stretch.

Brandon and I exchanged a glance before he called out, "You okay?"

Damicén honked in response, twisting his head from side to side to look at us out of each eye.

"Uh oh." I ducked my head. "I think I overshot it—"

"You definitely overshot it." He pinched the bridge of his nose under his glasses. "Instead of turning the paper into a goose, you turned *him* into a goose."

Goose Damicén squawked and flapped his elbows.

"I can turn him back!"

"No!" Brandon caught my hands and pushed them down. "Let me do it, just in case you overshoot it again and actually turn him into a real goose."

Damicén leaned down—neck first—hissed and waddled toward us in anger.

"Dude, you peck me, and I'm leaving you this way."

Brandon sat up, clutching his side. When he raised his free hand, he flinched, sucking in a breath. Purple mist swirled up his arm, zipping across to the toddling Vampire.

He jerked upright as it shot through his chest and out the other side. For half a heartbeat, I thought Brandon had killed him until he flipped us the middle finger.

"You assholes!" He shook his head and rolled his shoulders, popping his neck. "I'm done being the test dummy for everyone's magic." He stormed past us, spewing what I assumed to be every Greek curse under the sun.

"I'm sorry!" Brandon yelled after him, frowning when he got the door slamming as a response. He peered up at me, eyes as chilled as the wind like he was silently blaming me for his friend's actions.

My temper flared. "Look, Brandon, I know you're upset with me, but I don't deserve this."

"You're going to get yourself killed."

My magic began to stir, whipping itself into a frenzy inside of me. If I'd let it, it would've swallowed him. "So? If it's to save the others, I'd do it. You suddenly don't want to support me because it's not something you approve of?"

"Because you're making the same mistake Talon did, and I can't watch another person I care about destroy themselves. You're not ready to take this on."

"I'm not Talon."

He shook his head. "No. She was smarter than you."

His accusation sent a flutter through me, making my magic even hungrier. But I wasn't going to retreat from my decision. "Just get the Stone out of me, please. Then we can decide what I'm capable of after." Pivoting, I stomped down the deck, needing to get away from his scrutiny.

I couldn't handle it from him, not right now. He'd been behind me this entire time, and when I needed it most, he flipped the switch.

I *needed* the reassurance, the comforting touch. I was about to go through the worst pain of my life, and I'd just turned Damicén into a goose, for Christ's sake.

"Rosetta, we're not finished here."

"Oh, yes, we are," I snapped as I made my way into the ship. He could sit out in the oncoming storm for all I cared. There was someone else I knew could give me comfort and confidence. He'd done it before I'd even known he existed.

I didn't know where he was currently, but I could find him. I'd seen him briefly before. He was in that flicker of movement that'd caught my eye at Grant's house, a shadow.

Chapter Twenty-Eight

I did manage to find him before sunset, hiding in a broom closet of sorts. I chose not to ask him about his appearance in my astral projection and instead sat beside him against the wall.

He was leaning against a water pipe, knees up and arms resting on their tops, not so much as glancing at me when I entered. Even with his face obstructed, I could still tell he'd been crying. Between his clenched hands, I could see small pieces of paper crumpled there.

"I guess she left you a letter, too, then?" I asked as I mimicked his pose.

He tilted his head back, staring at the lightbulb dangling from its chord above us. "Yeah."

"We're taking the Stone out of me in a couple hours."

This piqued his interest, and he side-eyed me. "Are they now?"

I nodded, sweat forming on my palms. I rubbed them absentmindedly on my pants, hoping this nervousness would fade before time. But I had a sinking feeling I'd only grow worse as it neared.

If what my mother said was true, then I was about to experience a whole new world of pain, and internally I debated whether it was worth it or not.

A strong part of me knew it was. I'd save all those lives in the process, and that was worth the pain. But another equally strong part of me was terrified beyond belief and wanted to tuck tail and run.

"It's going to hurt," he muttered.

"I know. That's why I'm here."

He arched his brow but said nothing, choosing to leave me marinating in my own nerves.

Continuing to rub away the wetness of my palms, I shrugged. "Kenna and them are looking for you."

He let out a quick burst of laughter with no hint of amusement. "I'm sure they are."

"But," I continued, "I came to see if you would, um…comfort me during it."

Now he raised both brows, my request taking him by surprise. "You want *me* to comfort you?"

"I remember what you did for me after the cave incident when I was having a panic attack, and I know that was you at Grant's."

"Me?"

"Yeah. The shadow that kept me company during my spiral into madness not long before you came to get me?"

Raven carefully observed me, gaze filled with newfound recognizable respect. Why that made him respect me more, I had no idea, but I continued anyway. "I was wondering if you could comfort me for this."

"I can try."

We shared a smile, one he broke away from suddenly when tears flowed down his face. I wasn't sure what had happened for him to cry like this, and I wasn't sure if words could comfort him the way they did me, so I just rested my hand on his back.

He seemed to flinch from the touch instinctively like he expected it to be violent instead of soft.

Blood Return

The horn of the ship sounded, letting me know we were about to pull into the port. My heart thrummed in my ears as a slight panic began to settle in my gut.

"I have to tell you something." His voice cracked at the end as he recoiled from my hand.

"What?" This was not the right time to drop a bombshell on me. My nerves were stripped as they were, and I needed whatever I had left to get through tonight.

"Your father didn't kill himself when your mom sent you away..." his throat bobbed. "I killed him."

My breath hitched in my chest, burning the same way it had when I was drowning, and my eyes flooded involuntarily with tears. I couldn't stop the shuddering breath I took that filled the silence.

No words came out, lodging themselves deep in my throat. What could I have even said to such a confession? He killed my father, and lied about it.

I began to pull away, hand shaking with a building emotion I'd yet to identify.

"It was an accident. I didn't really mean to. I was only defending myself." He grappled for me, eyes pleading.

My voice was raspy as I asked, "What do you mean?"

Raven wiped his eyes with the back of his hand. "He was a jealous person, especially of your mother and I's friendship. When she learned I was going to fight Grant in the first war, she came to visit me before I left and tried to convince me to stay. Your father found out about it, and when I returned with the Stone, he confronted me. One thing led to another, and I...Vityul ended up killing him."

My chest weighed with sorrow, cracking in two at his words. "Your shadow."

He dipped his chin, a ragged half held in sob escaping his lips. His voice took on a desperate edge as he said, "I'm so sorry. If I could've controlled it better, you might not have been sent away. Your parents together might've been able to protect you. But I forced your mother's hand, and bless her, she covered for me so I could flee. I never saw her again. Never got to apologize."

Swallowing became painful, my own weeping trying desperately to surface. "She knows you're sorry."

"The last thing she said to me was that she never wanted to see my dastardly face ever again." Shadows fell across him, a strand reaching out to wipe a tear.

I reached for him once more, but instead of laying my hand on him, I grabbed his own. I squeezed gently, letting him know that I was not inherently angry with him. Devastated at the true death of my father, yes, but angry at him for it? No. I watched him struggle with his shadow powers, watched him deal with the aftermath of it. I now understood the few instances he'd been able to use them—rescuing me, distracting the Ener—were exceptions, not the rule.

He was afraid of his powers, and after all they'd done, I couldn't blame him. That's why he lived in a cave, and that's why he was too ashamed to actually say it out loud. I understood that, too. Because saying it out loud makes it real. And the things we want to ignore or shove down can't be real. They just can't.

What was another person dead I'd never known? How could I mourn someone I never knew? Especially when I'd been told before that he was dead, now I just knew the truth of his death.

Another horn bellow and I knew the ship had come to a stop at port.

"I don't blame you for not being able to control your powers. I can't control mine, either. I just turned Damicén into a goose."

Worry lines creased his forehead. "A goose?"

"He's back to normal now, don't worry. Brandon fixed it."

"I would've paid good money to see that."

I chuckled, not feeling any of the humor. On top of the heartbreaking revelation Raven had just given me, I was panic-stricken at what was about to happen when I stepped off this ship. No matter what brave face I put on for Brandon, I was scared.

Raven returned my hand squeeze. "So, you need me to comfort you? Is that all?"

"Well…it's also because Brandon can't read the words of the spell. It's in the Angel's language, and I assume you're the only one who knows how to read it."

"Rosetta." Suddenly, he gripped my hand harder. "There's something else you need to know."

"What?" If possible, my heart hammered faster. Something was wrong, I could see it behind his eyes.

Was it about why he'd saved me? Was I finally going to know? Then why was I filled with so much dread? Whatever he was about to tell me filled me with more fear than I'd ever felt, and he hadn't even opened his mouth yet.

"What is it, Raven?" I repeated, breath turning shallow.

He hesitated, a shadow curling around his chin.

Tell me. *Tell me.* Please. Why did you save me? Why did you hide it?

The horn bellowed again, longer, more demanding. *'Now!'* it seemed to say.

But Raven was still faltering. His mouth opened and closed with a series of unspoken words caught in his throat. A war raged behind those indigo eyes, shadows battling each other in the dim light of the room.

I decided to let my obsession with him saving me go, under the pretense that if it was really that important, he would tell me. He's currently telling me he killed my father, and I have faith that if it was as big as that, he would also tell me. And the fact that I would make him tell me afterward, if I survived.

"How about this," I offered, "you come support me in the ritual. And afterward you can tell me any and everything you want. I promise not to get upset or ask more than you're willing to offer, either."

He considered me a moment too long to be comfortable before he heaved a heavy sigh and climbed to his feet. "Let's go."

We walked in silence to the top deck, meeting the others along the way. Nobody said a word as we deboarded the boat and made our way to the empty building of the marina.

It used to be a restaurant, as posters of different fish dishes littered the walls and ground. A broken menu clung to its last leg on the wall above a counter, where I assumed the registers once sat.

We cleared the space of any remaining chairs and miscellaneous objects as best we could before I laid down flat on the cold tile. I was instructed to starfish and quite literally hold on to the floor.

My fingertips burned from their death grip on the grout, and I knew if I really needed to hold on, this wouldn't do anything to help with that. But the pain took my mind off of my ever-increasing nausea.

The more items Kenna took from the bag and placed around me, the more I began to regret this decision. But there was no going back now.

After showing Brandon the pronunciations and running him through the instructions, Raven took up a spot near my head, giving me a reassuring smile that didn't reach his eyes. Great. That totally made me feel better.

Brandon appeared on the opposite side, a thin plank of wood between his fingers. He looked hesitantly at my mouth and back up at my eyes. "I'm sorry for getting upset with you."

"It's fine."

"It's not. I shouldn't have said what I said. I have unresolved trauma from Talon dying, and I took that out on you. I'm sorry. I just care about you and don't want you getting hurt anymore."

"Before or after, you make me experience the worst pain in my life?" I meant it to come off a bit humorous, but when he cringed, I knew he hadn't picked up on it.

Blood Return

"Bite down on this. It might help," he said softly as he handed me the wood. Before I could respond, he got to his feet and walked to where Kenna and Damicén stood.

After saying a few words I couldn't hear, Kenna nodded and turned her two-toned gaze to me. "Are you ready?"

"Not at all," I mumbled as I put the plank between my teeth, just praying I wouldn't break them off.

"Just try to relax and...think of something else," she offered with a pained smile. "The rest of us have to stand at these specific points and chant, so we won't be able to help you."

That's what Raven's for, I thought, but I actually said, "I thought Vampires couldn't do magic?"

"We can't," Damicén huffed. "I'm just a conduit, again."

They all took up their places around me in the four directions: North, South, East, and West. Brandon being at South, with Kenna at East, Damicén on West, leaving Jesse at North. Raven sat between the two men, reading over his crumpled note once more.

Brandon began the chant, purple tendrils swirling from his arm to wrap around my limbs. It tingled like they'd all fallen asleep, but nothing hurt yet. The others gradually picked up the same words in a circle around me until they reached Brandon once more. He picked up a vile of powder, spread it between his hands, then grabbed my ankles. And I burned.

I bit down reactively to the pain, thankful the wood was there. It spread like wildfire up my body as sweat began to pool. Molten lava filled my fingertips, and I tried to wiggle them to ease the pain but couldn't.

Frantic, I tried wiggling any part of my body to no avail. I was frozen. Paralyzed. Burning.

A scream welled up in my throat, followed by my erratic heartbeat. It only calmed when Raven grabbed my wrist, pulling my attention to him.

His eyes burned with me, carrying an intensity I had never seen before. "Look at me."

I looked the best I could without being able to turn my head. I knew I looked as panicked as I felt.

"What's your favorite color?"

My favorite color? Had this man lost his mind? I was burning internally. I couldn't think of anything else, much less my favorite color. Plus, I had this plank in my mouth.

Another wave of fire and my teeth groaned as they bit harder into the wood.

"What's your favorite color?" He repeated.

"Yellow," I said through the wood.

"Good. What color is the tile?"

I should've never asked him to comfort me if all he was gonna do was ask me stupid questions the entire time while I writhed in pain.

"What. Color. Is the tile?"

I couldn't turn my head to see the tile, but I remembered it was a dingy green—covered in dust and dirt.

"Ugly Green."

He chuckled. "It is an ugly shade, isn't it?"

Jesse watched us like he was taking notes, chanting along robotically. When he met my eyes, he winked.

My heart wasn't as erratic, and I felt like I could actually breathe through the pain. I didn't even notice Brandon was no longer holding me. Instead, he now held a small tube of liquid.

He carefully made his way around the circle, chants going silent as he approached each individual. His magic still coiled around me like a snake in waiting.

'I'm sorry,' he mouthed as he removed the wood from my lips and downed the tube in my throat. I choked at first, not prepared for the liquid. Coughing and sputtering, he put the plank back between my teeth and started a new chant phrase as he walked back.

Raven's grip on me tightened. "Hold on."

I went to side-eye him—as I was currently paralyzed and couldn't hold on to anything—when it hit me like a freight train.

Scalding, drilling, crushing, stinging, agonizing, you name it, and I was feeling it. All at once throughout my entire body, my entire being. The pain swallowed my mind, and I didn't even bother holding the wood. It clattered to the ground as I screamed.

My body lifted into the air, the magic twisting around me violently. It dug its way under my fingernails, and I could feel it coursing underneath my skin.

My throat hurt from the never-ending screaming, but I couldn't stop. I would scream until I ripped my vocal cords apart.

Even with my eyes squeezed tightly shut, I could tell my vision wavered. Black spots danced behind my eyelids, intercut with sharp splatters of red.

The pain became all I knew. No longer did I hear the voices of those surrounding me, nor the touch of the friend comforting me. It was only pain. I never thought it would end.

At some point, I started to beg for an end to my suffering. Whether they stopped the spell or snapped my neck, I didn't care. I wanted it to end. But an end never came.

Something hot and wet coursed its way down my face, and in the back of my mind, I recognized them to be tears. I was crying, screaming, begging for it to all be over.

Just when I thought I couldn't take it any longer, that I would burst at the seams, something erupted nearby.

Debris scattered about the room as a cloud of dust mushroomed inside. Three figures appeared through the cloud, and Raven shot to his feet in defense.

A blue blast of energy beelined toward him like a bullet. He ducked just in time, the ball narrowly missing Jesse as it whizzed by.

Trinity stepped forward into the light, staff in her hand and knives at her waist. Raven immediately launched an attack, pulling her focus from us and moving the blast range.

Grant followed next, with Avalon trailing behind him, holding up a shield of her orange magic in front of them both.

The four people surrounding me exchanged looks of alarm, but none moved from their position.

"Hurry up!" Kenna called to Brandon, who grunted in response. "Raven, keep her busy."

"What do you think I'm doing?" He shouted back, slamming Trinity against the counter. She got right back up and smacked the staff across his jaw. Blood splattered the wall across from him. "Don't let him stop the ritual!"

Grant didn't seem interested in stopping the ritual, though, as he never approached any closer to us. He stood smugly at the opening he'd created in the side of the building.

"It was so easy to find your location after your visit with me," he scolded, tsking his tongue. "Once we discovered you could astral project, Avalon made a very lovely tracking spell we attached to your spirit."

"You're not getting the Stone," Damicén bit out.

Grant's eyes flashed, now back to their normal emerald shine. "I don't want the Stone."

"What do you want?"

"Her."

Kenna growled, "You already made the agreement to hand her over in exchange for my people."

"True. However, I think she deserves to know the whole truth before she makes that decision."

"What are you talking about?"

"You wanted the lies to stop, right?" He asked me, ignoring the others' presence. "Let's put everything on the table. Then you can decide who you want to be with."

"She'll never go with you," Jesse spat. "And you'll never have her. You're the only liar here."

He raised a blond brow. "Oh, am I now? Rosetta, did you ever find out how you lost your memory?"

Another wave of pain crashed through me, arching my back and catching my breath. Did he really think I'd be able to communicate at all with him right now? I couldn't think straight through the pain.

At my lack of an answer, he nodded his head with a smile. "Of course not. Would you like to know how you lost your memory?"

"Do you really think this is the right time for this?" Jesse retorted, struggling with his hold of the magic at the top of my head.

"Someone do something," Damicén hissed.

"Brandon can't stop the spell. We have to finish it," Kenna reminded, staring despondently at Grant.

"You know, the first day we met, and I said my son did a good job when you couldn't remember anything but your name?" An evil glee spread across Grant's face as he watched me think back.

I did remember. At the time, I'd been told not to worry about it.

"That's because he *did* take your memory. All of it. Completely wiped. On purpose."

Splitting pressure in my skull wrenched another shriek from me, but it didn't dull the sudden pang in my heart.

Jesse had wiped my memory? He'd acted so concerned and confused, just like the others. They'd feigned confusion and sorrow, pretending they didn't know what happened to my memories either. I couldn't believe it.

I shook my head, trying to clear the thoughts of distrust. I could trust Kenna, Damicén, Brandon...even Jesse. I could. They'd taken care of me, helped me with my magic, forgiven me for killing my brother. They wouldn't hide something that important from me.

"You're lying," I managed to croak out between the pain.

"Ask him. Ask any of them. They all knew."

"Stop it!" Jesse snarled but refused to meet my gaze. They all did. Every person around me avoided my eyes when they landed on them. Guilt wrote a poem on every one of their faces.

Tears streamed down my own once more, but not from the pain of the spell.

"Is it true?" I gasped.

Jesse swallowed hard, finally sliding his eyes to me. They were red as he gave the smallest nod of his head.

The magic began to pool in my chest, stretching my rib cage and sending me into another screaming fit.

"Make it stop," I pleaded.

"He's not the only liar either." Grant's voice deepened as he pointed to Raven, who still fought with Trinity. Both were bleeding, with bruises already welling up on their exposed skin.

Shadows frenzied around him, his face tight with the effort to keep them contained.

"While you've been away, I discovered there's a reason he was the one who pulled you from the water. I'm guessing he didn't share that with you, either?"

I didn't want the answer this time. I didn't want to know. But I did. All those burning questions, unanswered and avoided. I had to know. He'd told me there was nothing else to tell me. Was it a lie?

Grant took another cautious step toward me, expression grim. "He pulled you out because he's the one who drowned you in the first place."

Magic exploded from within me, golden light mixed with Brandon's purple, and I collapsed to the cold tile below. I didn't stop screaming even as the pain subsided.

A glowing stone the size of my fist hovered in the air where I'd once been. Brandon's magic curled back into him as he dropped from the exertion.

"Raven?" My voice no longer sounded like mine.

He cursed under his breath as he dodged another energy blast. His lack of answers told me everything I needed to know. He didn't answer because he was busy fighting, either. He didn't answer because Grant was right.

"Did you know, too?" I demanded of the others, furious tears making their own river down my chin.

Damicén, who'd grabbed Brandon before he hit the floor, nodded. Brandon, half-conscious and weeping his own silent feelings, also nodded.

Jesse moved to touch me, to grab me, and I erupted.

"Don't touch me!"

Everyone aside from Grant and Avalon was propelled into the walls as my powers whiped a vicious vortex around me. Despair and betrayal filled my gut, my heart splitting in two. "I trusted you all."

Grant pushed forward toward me, Avalon's magic wavering against the force of my own. Her painted lips scrunched with effort.

"Tell her why you tried to kill her. She deserves to know after you've pretended to be her friend and savior."

Raven clung to the countertop, still struggling to contain his shadows. He bared his teeth at Grant in response, fangs protruding.

"Release your shadows!" Kenna called to him from the floor. "Do something!"

"I can't." He gritted his teeth against the ever-bearing weight of my powers.

"Tell her," Grant repeated, inching ever closer to me.

Raven didn't meet my eyes as he said, "Because I knew how dangerous you could be."

I sat up on my knees, wrapping my arms tightly around my midsection as I wept. My mother's words from the note flashed through my mind. *You are a weapon of war. You are more powerful than you could ever imagine.* He'd known, too. Had known all along how deep my powers went. He didn't just discover me in the field; he couldn't have if my power was the reason he tried to kill me.

Louder this time, he spat at Grant. "Because I knew you could destroy the world if you wanted to. You could wipe everyone from the face of the earth. I didn't want to take the chance of it happening, but…"

"But you couldn't follow through with it. Tell her why." Grant pried the words from him like poison from a wound.

Through my sobs, through my white light, I connected my eyes with his. The indigo in his now appeared more maroon as his own tears flooded them. He shook his head, pressing his lips together in a thin line and refusing to say anything further.

"Tell her!" Grant pointed an angry finger at him, jaw tight. "You tried to kill her. Now tell her *why* you couldn't!"

"Raven, don't," Damicén pleaded, coming to a realization I'd yet to.

Raven gulped, his own face begging for this to end.

"Tell me. Please," I whispered. I had to know. Had to know why he would ever do that. Why would he drown me, then save me, then pretend to save me from Grant? Why? I thought he was my friend.

Raven closed his eyes for a brief second before uttering a sentence that would ruin me eternally. "Because I couldn't kill my own daughter."

I wailed, a gut-wrenching howl of the betrayal and heartbreak I felt. The pain from this revelation went unmatched by the pain I'd been experiencing only moments ago. My magic unleashed itself upon them, slamming them into the walls and ripping the tile from the floor. Bits and pieces of whatever I'd broken swam around the tornado I'd inevitably created with my sorrow.

Glowing wings of silver energy burst from me, cocooning me inside this havoc.

"That's right," Grant gleamed. "He knew you'd be too powerful for them to control because not only are you of royal Seraphim blood, but you are a direct descendant of the first-ever Vampire. A combination, unlike anything this world has ever seen."

Raven had lied about almost every single thing imaginable. Is what he even told me about my supposed father true? Was it an accident, or did he murder him for my mother? And they all knew about the lies. Knew I'd been desperate for the truth and had promised me they'd given it to me.

Looking at their faces, I knew it was true. All of it. They knew and kept it from me. They'd lied to me over and over again. They'd watched me struggle and suffer for their personal gain. They were just like Grant had warned me about.

"Rosetta." Grant's voice was close now, and I saw he knelt just outside my vortex of anguish. "I may have done some rash things, but I have never lied to you."

"Don't listen to him!" Damicén shouted as he clutched an unconscious Jesse. "We didn't know that part, I swear."

"Why should I believe you?" My voice was nothing but a whisper in the storm. Raw, unyielding, silent, but dangerously powerful. "You've done nothing but lie to me. Why?"

No one answered. All too afraid.

"I trusted you all!" I shouted, another ripple of power slamming into them.

"Grant." Avalon struggled against the might of my strength, heels digging into the freshly exposed dirt.

"They have lied about everything important to you, only used you to get this Stone and resurrect their leader. That's all they care about. They don't value you. They don't think you can handle yourself. They are afraid of you," Grant whispered in rapid succession, his voice somehow reaching me through the chaos of my magic. "My only mistake was thinking you couldn't handle it. I won't make it again." He reached a hand out, parting the twisting mass around me. "Come with me, and I will ensure you flourish."

Through my sobs, I glanced at the others, all shame ridden and holding on for dear life against me. Brandon gave the faintest shake of his head, clutching his ribs.

I grabbed Grant's hand, and through the vortex, I could see his sly smile as we teleported away.

Landing on the floor of his study, he pulled me into his arms as I cried. I wept for what felt like hours while he stroked my hair.

Avalon and Trinity left us alone, not even reentering when light crested through the windows the next morning.

I'd cried myself into a stupor by that point, feeling every raw edge of emotion I had remaining. Grant never left my side.

Silently, I vowed that this would never happen again. I would never be lied to again. Never be beaten, or threatened, or made to feel meek. I also made a vow that they would pay for this betrayal. They would pay for my tears and misery. They would know my wrath. I'll show them; I'll show them what they should really be afraid of in me.

I will destroy them all.

Epilogue

The lights were too bright. Pins and needles filled my eyes, and as I raised a hand to cover them, voices slowly came into range.

"Is she awake yet?"

"No. You've got to give her time to adjust."

They were male voices, oddly familiar, even though I couldn't place where I knew them.

The light faded enough for me to remove my hand shield, and I blinked rapidly. Everything was blurry. It hurt to look, but I could tell I was in some kind of medic room.

"I stand corrected," a voice came from the doorway.

Whipping my head—and tweaking my neck in the process—I narrowed my eyes on the out-of-focus individual.

"Who are you? Where am I?" I asked as I sat upright. The abrupt gesture sent a jolt up my back, and I pressed a hand there with a small gasp.

He came closer, sitting down next to me. As my eyes adjusted, the first thing I noticed were his. They swirled like a dying fire, glowing embers stared directly back at me. His long brown hair had been braided out of his face, which was sculpted after a Greek God.

"Damicén," I breathed, latching on to the back of his neck. The smell of pine trees filled my nose, drawing stinging tears to my eyes. It waned the discomfort of using them only slightly.

"Talon." His arms wrapped around my waist, pulling me into his lap and holding me tight. His body shook with silent sobs as we lay in each other's embrace.

The door opened, and another voice cheered, "She's awake!"

A cluster of people filed into the room, all still very out of focus until they got up close. Kenna, Adaim, Rhydel, Sam, and Millie all cooing and crying, excited to see me.

"Don't crowd her," Rhydel boomed as he ushered people out of my personal space.

"Where am I?" I asked Damicén once more, still having trouble placing my whereabouts.

He shied at the question, choosing instead to ask me, "Wanna go to the cafeteria?"

I nodded, going to stand but immediately falling as my legs gave out from under me.

Shock rang out as I realized my legs were complete and utter jelly. There wasn't an ounce of strength left in them.

"What's going on?" I turned my face up to Damicén, who'd luckily caught me before I could do any serious damage.

His thick brows deepened as his lips thinned. "I'll explain when we get there."

He hoisted me in his arms, stepping around the small crowd of people and walking down the hall. Every so often, we'd shift weight unintentionally, like being rocked back and forth. When he crouched through an oval-shaped metal doorway, I knew where we were.

"Are we on a boat?" I exclaimed, looking at the pipes above us with newfound interest. Things were starting to clear up in my vision, but it still ached to even use them.

With a big sigh, Damicén nodded. "Adaim's steamboat."

My eyebrows shot up. "Adaim owns a steamboat?"

"He does now."

That may have pulled a chuckle from me at another point in time, but now felt too strange. I still had trouble believing I was even alive again.

We took a sharp left turn into a small cafeteria, buzzing with activity. Small children ran around with their toys while others chatted over plates of food. They all hushed at my entrance, staring at me with reverberated awe.

Damicén sat me in a black chair at a round table, immediately following this by wrapping a blanket around my shoulders.

I didn't realize I'd been shaking until I felt the warmth of the wool encase me. I pulled it close, feeling the icy cold touch of my fingers slip across my jaw.

He sat beside me, with Kenna and Adaim sitting across. They all watched me observantly, like a science project.

"Are you going to tell me what's going on?" I snapped impatiently. The last thing I remembered was being shot in the head. Now I'm in a boat surrounded by people I'd last seen escaping through a crematory chimney.

Damicén cleared his throat. "Do you want the long answer or just the basic hit points? It's a lot." When I cast him a look of pure confusion, he clarified, "It's been almost a year since you died."

My head suddenly felt light, and I grabbed the edge of the table to steady myself, even though my fingers slipped weakly off it.

A year? Had it been that long? It felt as if only a moment had passed—a blink. Though, when I put together my odd aches and pains throughout my body, it made a little sense. I definitely felt stiff enough to have been gone a year.

"We brought you back with the Stone and had to recreate your body entirely. What's the last thing you remember?" Damicén began but silenced himself when my attention was drawn behind him.

A figure lurked in the doorway, hands in pockets. A tingling sensation wrapped up my spine at the same time, the feeling of a rubber band snapped around me.

Gray eyes below hooded lids watched me like a predator. Gel-slicked black hair shined in the dull ship lights, and a scar on his lower lip—smaller than the top lip—jumped out at me. He met my gaze and gulped.

My mouth fell open but snapped shut just as fast. Sharp venom flowed through me at the sight of him, filling me so full I wanted to run over and strangle him with my bare hands.

Damicén followed my gaze, placing a hand over mine as he turned back. "Yeah. That's part of the long story."

"Better be one hell of a story."

"It is," he promised. "Just promise you won't get mad at me."

"It sounds like I need a drink for this." I chuckled dryly, finally allowing my burning throat to come to the forefront of my mind.

Anything involving that monster, that…abomination required a stiff drink. A dull pang ached in my heart, and I hated myself for feeling it. He deserved no sympathy, not one ounce of emotion from me. But damned it be I felt sorrow at the events that had transpired.

Kenna leaped from the table with vigor and disappeared into the kitchen. A moment later, she returned, brandishing a blood bag.

Instantly forgetting my want for liquor, I greedily snatched it from her fingers and began taking giant mouthfuls of the substance. Only to spit it out all over the table, coughing and gagging at the taste.

Metal. I tasted metal, like a penny; absolutely disgusting.

Everyone at the table exchanged worried looks as I dropped the bag at my feet.

"Are you trying to poison me?" I rasped.

Damicén stuck the tip of a finger into the spilled blood and cautiously held it to his tongue. His face paled when he tasted it.

"There's nothing wrong with it," he declared with a wild look in his eyes.

"Nothing wrong with it? It tastes like metal. It's disgust..." I trailed off as another shadowy figure caught my eye.

In the corner of the room stood a flickering shadow with purple eyes that watched our every move.

Completely forgetting I couldn't walk, I jumped up from my chair and fell face-first onto the floor. Not even my arms had the strength to break my fall. He was at my side in the blink of an eye, pulling me up as I sucked in air. Now in his true form, I placed my wavering hand on his cheek. Feeling the warmth and genuine realness of his skin, I couldn't help but begin to cry.

"Raven. My boy."

He was wary of me, but I could see the longing in his gaze. "You knew it was me?"

"Of course I did. I will always know it's you, even in shadow form."

He blinked in astonishment, clearly not expecting me to know about his shadow powers. What he doesn't know is I was awake the night his shadow attempted to take my life. But before I could talk to him about it and try to help him work through it, he disappeared. It destroyed me.

Damicén appeared next to me, the bag of blood still in his hands, and the dots started connecting in my head. "You brought me back and had to give me a new body with the Stone?"

They all nodded, Damicén being the only one in the same thought pattern as me.

I looked at him wide-eyed as I tried to push my fangs out, but none came. My fingers danced hesitantly across my teeth, all perfectly straight and square. Not one sharp edge to them.

"What's wrong?" Kenna's worry-stricken face popped over Damicén's shoulder. "Is everything okay?"

Damicén and I shook our heads in unison, sharing a panicked moment together.

The blood wasn't bad. And it wasn't being dead that made me so weak and stiff.

I was completely and utterly Human.

Made in the USA
Columbia, SC
26 May 2023